Literary Landscapes

Literary Landscapes

From Modernism to Postcolonialism

Edited by

Attie de Lange, Gail Fincham, Jeremy Hawthorn and
Jakob Lothe

palgrave
macmillan

Excerpts from THE DIARY OF VIRGINIA WOOLF, Volume IV: 1931–1935, copyright © 1982 by Quentin Bell and Angelica Garnett, reprinted by permission of Harcourt, Inc.

Excerpts from THE DIARY OF VIRGINIA WOOLF, Volume V: 1936–1941, copyright © 1984 by Quentin Bell and Angelica Garnett, reprinted by permission of Harcourt, Inc.

Excerpt from THREE GUINEAS by Virginia Woolf, copyright © 1938 by Harcourt, Inc., and renewed 1966 by Leonard Woolf, reprinted by permission of the publisher.

Excerpts from THE YEARS by Virginia Woolf, copyright © 1937 by Harcourt, Inc., and renewed 1965 by Leonard Woolf, reprinted by permission of the publisher.

Excerpts from THE CAPTAIN'S DEATH BED AND OTHER ESSAYS by Virginia Woolf, copyright © 1950 and renewed 1978 by Harcourt, Inc., reprinted by permission of the publisher.

First published 2008 by
PALGRAVE MACMILLAN
Houndmills, Basingstoke, Hampshire RG21 6XS and
175 Fifth Avenue, New York, N.Y. 10010
Companies and representatives throughout the world

PALGRAVE MACMILLAN is the global academic imprint of the Palgrave Macmillan division of St. Martin's Press, LLC and of Palgrave Macmillan Ltd. Macmillan® is a registered trademark in the United States, United Kingdom and other countries. Palgrave is a registered trademark in the European Union and other countries.

ISBN-13: 978–0–230–55316–3 hardback
ISBN-10: 0–230–55316–8 hardback

This book is printed on paper suitable for recycling and made from fully managed and sustained forest sources. Logging, pulping and manufacturing processes are expected to conform to the environmental regulations of the country of origin.

A catalogue record for this book is available from the British Library.

Library of Congress Cataloging-in-Publication Data
Literary landscapes : from modernism to postcolonialism / edited by
   Attie de Lange, Gail Fincham, Jeremy Hawthorn and Jakob Lothe.
      p. cm.
   Includes bibliographical references and index.
   ISBN-13: 978–0–230–55316–3 (alk. paper)
   ISBN-10: 0–230–55316–8 (alk. paper)
   1. Place (Philosophy) in literature.   2. English fiction—20th century—History and criticism.   3. South African fiction (English)—History and criticism.   4. Commonwealth fiction (English)—History and criticism.   5. Space in literature.   6. Space and time in literature.   7. Identity (Psychology) in literature.   8. Postcolonialism in literature.   9. Modernism (Literature)—English-speaking countries.   10. Postmodernism (Literature)—English-speaking countries.   I. De Lange, Attie.   II. Fincham, Gail.   III. Hawthorn, Jeremy.   IV. Lothe, Jakob.
   PR888.P525L57 2008
   820.9'358—dc22   2008015862

10   9   8   7   6   5   4   3   2   1
17   16   15   14   13   12   11   10   09   08

Printed and bound in Great Britain by
CPI Antony Rowe, Chippenham and Eastbourne

Contents

Notes on the Contributors

Carrol Clarkson did her DPhil in English at the University of York in the UK, and now teaches at the University of Cape Town in South Africa. Her main research interests and publications are in philosophy of language and in post-apartheid South African literature and art. She has also published articles on post-apartheid jurisprudence and is currently editing a collection of essays and writing a monograph on J. M. Coetzee.

Attie de Lange is Professor of English and was Director of the Research Unit 'Languages and Literature in the South African Context' at the Potchefstroom Campus of the North-West University in South Africa from 2001 to 2007. He collaborated with Gail Fincham as editor and co-editor of *Conrad in Africa: New Essays on 'Heart of Darkness'* (2002) and *Conrad at the Millennium: Modernism, Postmodernism, Postcolonialism* (2001) respectively.

Gail Fincham is Head of the Department of English at the University of Cape Town. She has edited, co-edited and contributed to three collections of essays on Conrad: *Under Postcolonial Eyes: Joseph Conrad After Empire* (1996), *Conrad at the Millennium: Modernism, Postmodernism, Postcolonialism* (2002) and *Conrad in Africa* (2003). She has chapters in three forthcoming books: *Joseph Conrad: Voice, Sequence, History, Genre* (ed. Lothe, Hawthorn, and Phelan); *Zakes Mda: Ways of Writing* (ed. Bell and Jakobs); and *J. M. Coetzee and the Aesthetics of Place* (ed. Clarkson). Co-editor of *The English Academy Review*, she has written articles for South African and international journals.

Harry Garuba is Associate Professor at the Centre for African Studies, University of Cape Town, with a joint appointment in the English Department. His recent publications include 'Explorations in Animist Materialism: Notes on Reading/Writing African Literature, Culture, and Society' (*Public Culture*, Spring 2003); 'The Unbearable Lightness of Being: Re-Figuring Trends in Recent Nigerian Poetry' (*English in Africa*, May 2005); and 'A Second Life: Museums, Mimesis, and the Narratives of the Tour Guides of Robben Island' in *Desire Lines: Space, Memory and Identity in the Post-Apartheid City* (2007).

Johan Geertsema is Assistant Professor in the University Scholars Programme, National University of Singapore. Among his research interests are Romanticism, particularly theories of irony and of the sublime as these intersect with colonialism; the politics of space, empire, and the rule of law; and the theory and practice of translation. His recent essays have appeared, or are forthcoming, in *Emergencies and the Limits of Legality* (ed. Victor V. Ramraj); *Translation and the Classic* (ed. Alexandra Lianeri and Vanda Zajko); *Journal of Postcolonial Writing*; and *Journal of Commonwealth Literature*.

Ina Gräbe is Emeritus Professor of Theory of Literature at the University of South Africa (UNISA), Pretoria. Her most important publications include a book-length study on poetic language and stylistics, a monograph on the interpretation of poetic metaphor, a monograph entitled *Landscape as a Troubled Space* (1997), as well as a number of articles on narratology and South African narrative focusing on the novelistic practice of J. M. Coetzee, Zakes Mda and others. She is the general editor of the six-volume proceedings of the 16th triennial congress of the International Comparative Literature Association (ICLA), held at UNISA, Pretoria, in August 2000 (2004–2007).

Jeremy Hawthorn is Professor of Modern British Literature at the Norwegian University of Science and Technology, Trondheim. His third monograph on Joseph Conrad, *Sexuality and the Erotic in the Fiction of Joseph Conrad*, was published in 2007. He has edited two of Conrad's novels for Oxford World's Classics and has published many articles on Conrad's fiction. The fourth edition of his *A Glossary of Contemporary Literary Theory* was published in 2000, and the fifth edition of his *Studying the Novel* in 2005, both by Arnold.

Jakob Lothe is Professor of English Literature at the University of Oslo. His books include *Conrad's Narrative Method* (1989) and *Narrative in Fiction and Film* (2000). The author of numerous articles, he has edited or co-edited several volumes including *European and Nordic Modernisms* (2004), *The Art of Brevity* (2004), and *Joseph Conrad: Voice, Sequence, History, Genre* (2008). In 2005–2006 he was the leader of the research project 'Narrative theory and analysis' at the Centre for Advanced Study, Oslo.

Merry M. Pawlowski teaches at California State University, Bakersfield. She is the author of *Virginia Woolf and Fascism: Resisting the Dictators'*

Seduction (Palgrave Macmillan, 2001). Her article 'Virginia Woolf's Veil: The Feminist Intellectual and the Organization of Public Space' is forthcoming in *Modern Fiction Studies* 53(4). Her work has also appeared in several volumes of *Woolf Studies Annual*, including the recent 'Exposing Masculine Spectacle: Virginia Woolf's Newspaper Clippings for *Three Guineas* as Contemporary Cultural History', *Woolf Studies Annual* 9 (2003), pp. 116–140.

Frederik Tygstrup is Director of the Copenhagen Doctoral School in Cultural Studies, and Associate Professor of Comparative Literature at the University of Copenhagen. His primary specialization is in the history and theory of the European novel, documented in the two monographs *Fictions of Experience: The European Novel 1615–1857* (1992) and *In Search of the Real: Essays on the 20th Century Novel* (2000), both in Danish. His present research interests focus on the intersections of artistic and other social practices, including urban aesthetics, the history of representations and experiences of space, literature and medicine, literature and geography, and literature and politics.

Marita Wenzel is Associate Professor of English at North-West University, Potchefstroom (South Africa). Her particular fields of interest are Feminist Studies, Comparative Literature (South African, postcolonial and Latin American novels) and Translation Studies. Apart from regular international conference attendance, she has also published several articles on South African and Latin American writers. She is a member of the English Academy of Southern Africa, the International Comparative Literature Association, the European Association for Commonwealth Literature and Language Studies and a former member of the University of South Africa Centre for Latin American Studies. She is also an accredited translator and examiner for the South African Translators' Institute (Afrikaans, Spanish and German into English).

Merle A. Williams is Personal Professor of English at the University of the Witwatersrand, Johannesburg, and Assistant Dean for Graduate Studies in the Faculty of Humanities. She is the author of *Henry James and the Philosophical Novel: Being and Seeing* (1993), and is currently completing a monograph entitled *The Challenge of Prometheus: A Reassessment of Shelley's Thought*. She has written articles and book chapters on aspects of Romantic poetry, as well as on Henry James in relation to Modernism and the interplay between literary texts and contemporary Continental Philosophy.

Acknowledgements

This collection of essays stems from an international research project that originated in South Africa. This project was supported by the National Research Foundation (NRF) of South Africa under GUN 2053707: 'Space in Modernist/Postcolonial Fiction', and the editors gratefully acknowledge this invaluable contribution. The opinions, findings and conclusions expressed in this volume are those of the authors and should not be attributed to the NRF.

Gail Fincham, Jeremy Hawthorn and Jakob Lothe would also like to thank Attie de Lange for initiating this project, and the Research Unit 'Languages and Literature in the South African Context' of the North-West University (Potchefstroom Campus), for hosting the Colloquium at which many of the chapters in this book were born.

The editors would also like to thank the Centre for Advanced Study and its leader Professor Willy Østreng for very kindly acting as host to a meeting between the editors in 2006 and for offering two of the editors the most ideal conditions imaginable for research and writing during the academic year 2005–2006.

The editors and publisher thank The Society of Authors as the Literary Representative of the Estate of Virginia Woolf for permission to include short extracts from *The Years*, *Three Guineas*, *The Diaries*, and 'Mr Bennett and Mrs Brown'.

See also the copyright page at the front of this volume.

Introduction

The anywhere space of modernism

Anti-modernist though he may have been, the dismal conclusion reached by Philip Larkin in his bitter 1954 poem 'I Remember, I Remember' that nothing, like something, happens anywhere, could well stand for the popular view of the importance of place to the modernist movement in general. Franz Kafka's universalized fictional places – the town, the Castle – serve, like the near-empty stage-settings of Samuel Beckett, as tokens of the modernist view of space for many readers. After all, if your characters are deeply alienated both from other people and from the places where they find themselves, then all places share the quality of 'not home' for you. Indeed, a strong sense of place, a belief that the individual is linked to a particular area and community by mutually defining bonds, is enough to inspire the suspicion that a writer is not really a card-carrying member of the modernist party. Hugh Stevens opens a recent essay on the fiction of D. H. Lawrence with a challenging question: 'Can fiction be modernist when it aims to help us to recapture a premodern, or even "primitive", relationship with nature and with our own bodies, and dissolve boundaries between the self and the world?' (Stevens 2007, p. 137). Those boundaries between the self and the world, boundaries that reduce *all* spaces to 'not us' and thus homogenize them, have often served as one of our litmus tests of modernism. It is, for this reason, perhaps easier for us to perceive the later Lawrence with his restless wandering from unsatisfactory place to unsatisfactory place as a modernist writer, than it is to recognize the modernist impulse in those early short stories that seem almost to be the short-story equivalent of the regional novel. Much the same might be said of the fiction of Thomas Hardy, a writer who does not merit a separate chapter in the recently published *The Cambridge Companion to the Modernist Novel* – in spite of the fact that, as Peter Brooker points out in an essay in this collection, Hardy's character Tess, 'in a much-quoted phrase, "feels the ache of modernism"' (Brooker 2007, p. 33).

If we confront this family of often unspoken attitudes head-on we must quickly recognize that it constitutes at best a set of half-truths. Were we to ban from the modernist pantheon all novelists whose characters feel a strong and defining sense of belonging to a place and its people, then we would have to decide that James Joyce, Knut Hamsun, Virginia Woolf, William Faulkner, Elizabeth Bowen and many other familiar figures must be denied entry. This is not to argue that these figures present us with characters fully and happily integrated into organic communities rooted in an ancient relationship with a particular geographical location. But it is to suggest that typically modernist experiences of alienation, ennui, the *unheimlich* and the sense of being an outsider do not preclude subtle and probing investigations into the complex interrelationships between particular individuals and particular spaces and places.

Once we recognize this double element of belonging to a place while simultaneously feeling alienated both from it and from the people who live in it, we can start to recognize that writers who at first sight belong on different sides of the realism–modernism divide have much in common. Conrad's Marlow returning to a Europe to which he no longer feels he fully belongs has perhaps more in common with Hardy's returning native than we have hitherto conceded.

So much for one divide. But what about the divide between modernism and postcolonialism? With postcolonialism the unspoken prejudices go in a quite different direction. How can you have a colony without a particular space on which your settlers settle? If colonialism is to be superseded, as our 'post' implies, then this must surely involve a change of political power as it is exercised in a specific place. Even a novel such as J. M. Coetzee's *Waiting for the Barbarians*, set in a universalized colony with its 'natives' and its oppressors, is read not so much as Kafkaesque modernism (although its debts to Kafka are surely undeniable), but as a postcolonial allegory that draws the reader's attention in the very specific direction of the context of South Africa during the apartheid period in and about which its author wrote.

The present volume does not wish to polemicise against our general use of large literary categories such as realism, modernism, and postcolonialism. But it does seek to remind its readers that writers who belong or are assigned to such movements supersede their predecessors in part by adopting aspects of their predecessors' vision. What then becomes important is to fine-tune our sense of both continuities and innovations. If landscapes and cityscapes are important to the 'classical realist' novelists of the nineteenth century they are also important to modernist novelists such as Joseph Conrad and Virginia Woolf, and to postcolonial writers such as J. M. Coetzee and Zakes Mda. But this importance is often of a different order, and it needs to be explored by investigating the textual details of individual works.

Older readers may recall a joke in the BBC series *The Goon Show* where a character when asked 'What are you doing there?' replies, 'Everybody's got to be somewhere'. Being is not, however, belonging. The novelist cannot portray characters who are not somewhere. But *how* they are where they are relates to matters cultural and political that it is also the task of the writer of fiction to investigate. In this volume our contributors attempt to investigate these investigations. We believe that this is a timely project, coming as it does when the success of attempts to isolate the particularity of the postcolonialist impulse needs to be qualified by a sense of the substantial links and overlaps between modernism and the postcolonial. The title of an influential book by Terry Eagleton reminded readers how often modernist writers were either 'exiles or émigres'. It hardly needs pointing out that the same is true of postcolonialist writers – and of their characters.

Narrative, place and space

Place is an element of space. Moreover, very often, and certainly when used about the fictional texts discussed in this volume, the concepts of both place and space are possessed of a narrative dimension. In a narrative text, the plot, that is the dynamic development of the action and the interplay of the characters contributing to this action, will usually occur in one or more defined places. As several of the fictional texts discussed in the following chapters show, this spatial segment is often, for a variety of reasons, particularly important for the characters who inhabit it. Place is linked to identity, and not only to identity-formation but also, under given circumstances, to a sense of threatened identity.

The linkage between place, character, and identity is variously explored in the chapters following. These chapters are essentially essays in practical criticism, that is close readings of one or more texts. In spite of being text-oriented, however, the chapters also focus attention on to issues of context and history. In our view, text and context are by no means mutually exclusive, and close reading is a critically necessary strategy if one is to engage adequately with both of these fundamental dimensions of literature. Moreover, the variants of contextualized close reading presented here repeatedly, and in one sense paradoxically, serve to highlight the texts' historical dimensions in thought-provoking ways.

Two conceptual problems related to thinking about place must be mentioned here. The first problem is inseparable from the interdependence of place and space. Like time, space is notoriously difficult to define philosophically – because as in the case of time, what we understand as space is both an aspect of physical reality and also the varying ways in which human beings experience and conceptualize this reality. The difficulty is also related to the fact that – again as is the case with time – our conception of space constitutes one of the instruments that we use in order to think, write, and read. As Kant observes in *Kritik der reinen Vernunft* (Critique of Pure Reason) (1781), 'one can never represent that there is no space, although one can very well think that there are no objects to be encountered in it' (Kant 1998, p. 158). One of the authors discussed here, Virginia Woolf, gives a brilliant fictional illustration of Kant's insight in her novel *To the Lighthouse* (1927), although her philosophical sources were probably English rather than German.

Second, given the problems of accurately defining place and space, we choose in this volume to link our understanding of both terms to the way in which place and space are *presented* in the literary texts under consideration. Seen thus, place, while still possessed of a distinctly spatial quality, becomes imbued with a temporal dimension. (In *To the Lighthouse*, we may recall, Virginia Woolf reconfigures time as radically as she does space.) For a narrative presentation of place is inevitably – as several of the following essays demonstrate – subject to temporal instability, change, and progression. An illustrative example is provided by Joseph Conrad's *Heart of Darkness* (1899), a key modernist text which has also become a major point of reference in postcolonial studies. The dominant space presented in this novella is the immense African continent. But since the narrative structure assumes the form of a journey – or more precisely, the narrative representation of that journey – which the narrator Marlow makes from Europe to Africa and back, a 'European space' is also continually present, thus underlying, and giving narrative shape to, the novella's forceful critique of European imperialism. Moreover, since parts of the journey take place at sea and on the Congo river, we can see ocean/water/river as a third, relatively neutral and mediating space, positioned between Europe (powerful, dominant, 'civilized') and Congo (suppressed, exploited, 'primitive'). Marlow's journey repeatedly and insistently actualizes the temporal dimension of his experience of space, and of the places he visits along the way.

'Space contains compressed time', notes Gaston Bachelard, 'that is what space is for' (Bachelard 1994, p. 8). In common with many theorists, Bachelard stresses the link between place and identity-formation. For Bachelard, this quality of place is affiliated with the question of when, and how, an empirical person (or a fictional character or narrator) is situated in a given place, and how this place is related to the larger space of which it forms a constituent element. Distinguishing between different variants of space (both in a literal, physical sense and a metaphorical one), Bachelard places strong emphasis on the house – and particularly on the house's significance for us as children. Since this kind of significance typically becomes clearer, and greater, with hindsight, Bachelard links the house closely to the intricate mechanisms of human memory. Yet although the house (as one instance of place) can contribute to the formation of human identity, it does not follow that place, or places, cannot complicate and disturb our sense of identity as well. The house marks a boundary, a transition from something controllable and safe to something larger, something attractive but potentially dangerous. This kind of transition actualizes Mikhail M. Bakhtin's concept of the chronotopic motif: a place or limited zone in which the dimensions of time and space are peculiarly compressed. Out of the chronotopic motifs identified by Bakhtin, the most important in novels discussed in this volume include the *road* and the *threshold* (Bakhtin 1982, p. 248).

At this point we would like to expand our discussion of a term that, as we have already remarked, is central to postmodernist and postcolonialist literature: *exile*.

What we want to stress in this Introduction is the connection – obvious but often ignored – between exile and place. Exile is a difficult yet crucial topic to discuss because it is not just a critical term but also a concept which purports to illuminate, in one sense even represent, a particular kind of human experience. As Edward W. Said puts it in *Reflections on Exile*, 'exile is strangely compelling to think about but terrible to experience' (Said 2000, p. 173). The French author Christine Brooke-Rose has suggestively distinguished between '*involuntary exile*, usually political or punitive' and '*voluntary exile*, usually called expatriation', undertaken for more personal reasons (Brooke-Rose 1996, p. 291, original emphasis). There are, too, those (many) borderline cases involving those who choose to leave their homeland for economic reasons: do we call this voluntary or involuntary?

Whether involuntary or voluntary, however, exile means removal from the place where the author or fictional character used to live, and where, in many cases at least, his or her identity and sense of belonging was formed. And yet, as many modernist and postcolonial novels demonstrate, this kind of complex distance from the author's or character's place of origin can serve as a basis for, and significantly contribute to, the artistic formation of narrative fiction of the highest order.

There is a sense in which 'landscape', a key word in the title of the present book, negotiates the difference between the relatively fixed term 'place' and the more indeterminate 'space'. A landscape typically consists of several places, and yet it is linked to an area, a region, in a way space is not. The texts discussed in this volume present a variety of such landscapes, each of which has its particular history, its particular involvement in human lives.

Landscape and (post)colonialism

As Denis Cosgrove has demonstrated, the concept of landscape developed during an identifiable period in the evolution of European societies. Communicating 'a way of seeing – a way in which some Europeans have represented ... the world about them and their relationships with it' (Cosgrove 1988, p. 1), the European concept of landscape also implies 'an attempt to sustain the moral order [of] ... pre-capitalist conceptions of human relations with the land and nature against the economic order of industrial capitalism' (Cosgrove 1988, p. 252). By the end of the nineteenth century, this concept of landscape, squeezed out by economic and technological forces, could no longer be sustained.

Space and place have arguably been less satisfactorily addressed in narrative theory than has that other crucial co-ordinate of human life – time. But cultural geographers remind us that space and place remain central to our experience:

> If places are no longer the clear supports of our identity, they nonetheless play a potentially important part in the symbolic and psychical dimension of our identifications. It is not spaces which ground identifications, but places.
>
> *How then does space become place? By being named: as the flows of power and negotiations of social relations are rendered in the concrete form of architecture; and also, of course, by embodying the symbolic and imaginary investments of a population.* Place is space to which meaning has been ascribed. (Carter *et al.* 1993, p. xii; our italics)

The reconfigurations of modernist and postcolonial writers which challenge and offer alternatives to the Western notion of landscape are frequently metafictional because, as Carrol Clarkson remarks in this volume, writing about place becomes an interrogation about the place of writing (Carrol Clarkson, this volume, p. 126). So Henry James looks back in his American fiction at his homeland in terms which suggest 'the artifice of their constructed spatiality and chosen fictional conventions', (Merle Williams, this volume, p. 21) while Joseph Conrad's engagement with place in *Lord Jim* escapes simple geographical delimitation as significantly as does J. M. Coetzee's engagement with place in *Foe*. Both novels invoke heterotopic spaces and symbolic borderlands to create a 'new space'. E. M. Forster finds this new space away from England in his Italian novels, and in an India that has much in common with the fiction of later magic-realist writers, while Jean Rhys insists that 'where you are' cannot be defined separately from 'who you are'.

We have argued that modernist and postcolonial texts frequently dramatize unexpected links between time and space. This is evident in Virginia Woolf's *The Years* and in Thomas Hardy's experimental and space-focused fiction, which is associated with a character's identity-formation and sense of belonging. These examples prefigure the presentation of space in Franz Kafka's *The Castle* and J. M. Coetzee's *Waiting for the Barbarians*, while Salman Rushdie's novels dramatize the changing spatio-temporal perspectives associated with migrancy and globalization: 'The histories of [characters'] lives take place in spaces undergoing processes of radical change, just as their lives are changing the spaces in which they unfold' (Frederik Tygstrup, this volume, p. 198).

Since *Literary Landscapes* grew out of a South African funded research project, and seven of its twelve contributors work in South Africa, it is not surprising that several of its chapters investigate different writers' depictions of Africa. Questions they ask include 'What is distinctive about African as opposed to European constructions of the rural (as the home of tradition) and the urban (as the locus of modernity)?' and 'how can the negative spaces of apartheid and post-apartheid South Africa be imaginatively transformed?' Drawing on Gaston Bachelard's phenomenology of space and M. Crang's cultural geography so as to connect traditional with postcolonial explorations of rationality, the unconscious, and the links between memory and storytelling, one contributor links recent South African with South American fiction. Another interrogates postcolonial critics' interpretation of Pauline Smith's Karoo landscape as furthering 'a justificatory myth of the Afrikaner people' (Johan Geertsema, this volume, p. 106) by demonstrating the ambiguities of her ideological position. Links between the fiction of J. M. Coetzee and the contemporary graphic art of William Kentridge are investigated by a contributor who remarks that '[Like Kentridge], Coetzee is also preoccupied with a stroboscopic vision of landscape: temporally different, yet spatially coincident images of the past and of the present are superimposed, throwing the landscape into historical relief' (Carrol Clarkson, this volume, p. 137). This fusion of

geographical with historical elements complicates the reader's perception of both space and time, as it merges synchronic ('in the present')
elements with diachronic ('through time: past present and future')
elements.

* * *

'Bush Pieces' – the painting reproduced on our cover – is by the !Xun
Khwe artist Flai Shipipa and serves to present some of the issues concerning time, space, culture, and identity engaged with in different ways
by our contributors. The !Xun artists, displaced by ethnic violence from
their native Angola and Namibia, now live in Platfontein, South Africa.
Pre-literate, their art is integrally related to the birds, animals, and plants
of the desert environment on which they previously depended as hunter-
gatherers. Their world-view may therefore be connected with what Denis
Cosgrove sees as pre-capitalist conceptions of land and nature that were
destroyed by industrial capitalism. But in order to survive their trans-
plantation into a post-industrial world, the !Xun are involved in complex
cultural renegotiations such as the translation of the bow and arrow
into a symbol linking past, present, and future. Recently celebrated in
European art galleries displaying postmodern paintings, !Xun artworks,
neither entirely representational nor entirely abstract, transmit values
rooted in their creators' mythology, religion, and culture. These values
create a dynamic relationship to a past which would otherwise have
been lost in their experience of cultural fragmentation and loss of linguistic community. !Xun paintings juxtapose interior domestic objects
with the shapes, colours, and textures of the physical environment. Of
'Bush Pieces' Flai Shipipa remarks: 'it is the pattern of a hut. This is
inside the hut [dark blue] and this is outside [red]. The bushpieces are
very soft and you cut them to put them on the floor. It is also the pattern of a hide women used to wear'. As Nigel Crawhall notes, '!Xun
and Khwe artists are both preserving and inventing "tradition" as it is
constantly changing and adapting to a world in flux, with modernity,
Christianity, tourism, the art market, first-nation politics, and so many
other factors shaping !Xun and Khwe art and society. Similarly, their art
stands at the crossroads between the interests of national and indigenous
politics on the one hand, and a multicultural art market on the other'
(H. Rabbethke-Schiller 2006, p. 23).

Just as the !Xun artists challenge their viewers to reconceive identity
in relation to place and time, so the modernist and postcolonial writers
investigated in this volume involve their readers in new ways of seeing.
Exactly how they do so varies from writer to writer, and work to work.

Our contributors have set themselves the task of exploring these varied investigations.

* * *

In the opening chapter of the volume, 'Space, Time, Narrative: From Thomas Hardy to Franz Kafka and J. M. Coetzee', Jakob Lothe argues that the narrative presentations of space in the novels under consideration are interestingly related to each other, thus indicating significant points of connection between early modernist and postcolonial literature. Inspired by Gaston Bachelard's theory of space and Mikhail M. Bakhtin's concept of the chronotope, the chapter provides a close reading of the opening of Hardy's novel *The Return of the Native* (1878). It then proceeds to relate this experimental and space-focused beginning to two passages from Hardy's *Tess of the d'Urbervilles* (1891), which also point in the direction of modernist fiction. A main point argued in the chapter is that in Hardy's fiction the landscape of Wessex assumes the form of an extended house (as Bachelard defines the house), an element of space associated with the character's identity-formation and sense of belonging. The concluding part of the chapter compares Hardy's literary landscape with the presentations of space in one fully-fledged modernist and one distinctly postcolonial novel, Franz Kafka's *The Castle* (1926) and J. M. Coetzee's *Waiting for the Barbarians* (1980).

Merle A. Williams traces Henry James's thinking on spatiality – as represented principally by the spaces of consciousness, social interaction, and historical change – from *The Europeans* (published in 1878, the same year as Hardy's *The Return of the Native*) through *The Bostonians* (1886) to *The American Scene* (1907), a more autobiographical record prompted by a visit to America after an absence of nearly 20 years. As she shows, all of these texts are deeply concerned with spatial configurations, at once physical and metaphorical. Williams begins by considering the early James of *The Europeans* as a traditional realist writer who in some ways is teasingly modernist, and she ends by exploring the justifications for reading the two other works as modernist texts that point in the direction of later trends such as postmodernism and postcolonialism. One concluding point made by Williams is that *The Bostonians* ultimately refuses the imposition of boundaries, while the self-authoring of the novel's characters opens up uncharted literary terrain. Overall, she considers James's American spaces to be unusually rich and ambiguous, since prevailing cultural patterns are frequently in sharp conflict with an individual consciousness which, by the stage of *The American Scene*, seems capable of swallowing an entire continent.

Gail Fincham's chapter on space and place in E. M. Forster's fiction argues that in *Howards End* and *A Passage to India* the novelist abandons a belief in the possibility of that 'free space' celebrated by his earlier novels. In Forster's last two novels, Fincham claims, the forces of capitalism and imperialism crowd out the possibilities of the liberal humanist world-view and of its belief in a place to which the individual can retreat. Thus while in the early novels movement from one geographical setting to another – from England to Italy, for example – can represent a movement from rigid class stratification and compartmentalization to social mixing, in *Howards End* the combined effects of capitalist commodification and imperialist exploitation rule out the possibility of such liberating forms of social escape. In *A Passage to India*, too, attempts both to retreat to a purely personal, private space (Mrs Moore's 'cave of my own') or to create a space of genuine equality and reciprocity (the polo field, Fielding's bungalow) are doomed to be, at best, short-lived.

As Jeremy Hawthorn insists in his chapter, the geographical, social, cultural, and historical markers that define a space out of a neutral territory are always inflected by gender. If Virginia Woolf reminded her readers that a room of one's own meant different things depending upon whether the 'one' in question was male or female, for Jean Rhys a room occupied by a penniless woman constitutes a different space from a room occupied by one lucky enough to be in possession of the £500 a year that Woolf famously inherited. Woolf's room of her own can easily become a tomb of one's own for the penniless, deracinated, single woman. As a number of recent commentators cited by Hawthorn have indicated, the 'space' of Bohemia, a space that is both metaphorical and geographical, is by no means an identical territory for men and women or for rich and poor. When Rhys's character Sasha Jansen (from *Good Morning, Midnight*) declares that 'All rooms are the same' she means that they are all the same for her, not that they are all the same regardless of who lives in them.

Turning to one of the most original and influential modernist authors, and responding to the question 'Where am I?', Merry M. Pawlowski discusses variants of feminine space and time as presented in Virginia Woolf's *The Years*. Pawlowski shows how, working against what Julia Kristeva has called 'Father's time' or linear time, Woolf poses a non-sequential arrangement of years as faultlines. She thus leaves the reader to wonder why these years were chosen and others left out. In *The Years*, Pawlowski argues, history and individual existence unfold as a series of repeating patterns suggestive of a feminine, cyclical (time folding back on itself), and circulating (space folding back on itself) conception of space and time which has little to do with linear time but much to do with what Kristeva has labelled 'imaginary space'. Appropriating Kristeva's notion, Pawlowski also links her argument to Henri Bergson's more gender-neutral but controversial conception of duration, familiar to Woolf and her Bloomsbury contemporaries. Finding that Woolf resists the unfolding of history as a patriarchal chronicle of external events, Pawlowski argues that she simultaneously explores two worlds – that of global events and that of life as experienced by individuals in their daily lives.

Johan Geertsema's chapter on the South African writer Pauline Smith's short story 'Desolation' (1930) builds on the fact that a landscape is not 'sublime' in itself but rather has its sublimity bestowed upon it through a process of perception in which not just the location but also the identity of the perceiver is crucial. This, he argues, has important implications for the narrative representation of both landscape and the sublimity that it evokes. These implications have, moreover, ideological implications in the politically charged atmosphere of South Africa both at the time that Pauline Smith is writing, and also during the apartheid era when her work becomes the focus of arguments about 'white identity' in the country. That familiar (one might almost say founding) distinction donated by Gérard Genette to the study of narrative that is indicated by the questions 'Who sees?' and 'Who speaks?' turns out to have an inescapably political and ideological significance in Smith's story and in the history of South Africa. As Geertsema points out, the position one takes (where position = stance or opinion) is dependent upon social position, and social position is in turn related to physical position.

For Attie de Lange, Joseph Conrad's *Lord Jim* and J. M. Coetzee's *Foe* share a number of narrative and thematic traits which offer the reader mutually-enriching representations of modernist and postcolonial conceptions of space. In both novels, argues de Lange, geographical space intersects with and is affected by issues of gender and race. Moreover in both novels the authors isolate many of their characters in 'heterotopic spaces' – symbolic borderlands, or liminal spaces which can be read as sites of struggle between oppositional groups or forces. De Lange points out that, for Conrad, there is a dialectic between space as an entity and space as part of an interpretative process. As for so many of the writers considered in this volume, there is no such thing as space-for-itself in Conrad; Jim and Jewel may inhabit the same geographical space but it is a space that is marked by the interpretative mappings of gender and race. Similarly in Coetzee's novel *Foe*, the space of the island on which Cruso and Susan are isolated is not a common or shared one: different parts of the island represent spaces that are gendered in different ways.

Carrol Clarkson's chapter imbricates the geographical or topographical with the typographical. She shows how in the fiction of J. M. Coetzee concepts of geography and history, landscape and community become fused in the imprints of language. The focus of her chapter recalls the poetry of the contemporary South African poet Jeremy Cronin. In his poem 'To Learn How to Speak' Cronin exhorts his readers to learn words in South Africa's many languages by remembering history while trying to understand landscape. Relationships between history, geography, culture, and language are central to this volume; so also is the idea of *positionality* which Clarkson explores. Her work, like David Attwell's, draws attention to the tensions between Coetzee's metropolitan intellectual affiliations and the pressures to which his writing responds, which are local and national. A concern to explore the concept of *positionality* links authors, contributors, and readers in the essays in this collection, and this exploration has an important role to play when connections between modernist and postcolonial fiction are investigated. Clarkson foregrounds these connections by juxtaposing Coetzee's texts with Beckett's, discussing his 'postcolonial countersignature to a modernist text'. Writing about metafiction, Clarkson draws our attention to Coetzee's naming of a recognizable world as well as to those references to fictional discourse of his, which raise central questions about metafiction's connections with history and politics. Finally, Clarkson's remarks about naming and the named in relation to issues of cultural domination, control, and power connect directly with J. M. Coetzee's non-fictional writing.

Drawing on Bachelard's phenomenology of space, which is also discussed by Jakob Lothe in the first essay in the volume, Marita Wenzel shows how houses can be associated with the social and psychological dimensions of fictional protagonists' worlds, histories, and memories. Noting that the symbolic function of houses can be traced in a wide variety of nineteenth-century novels such as those of Charles Dickens and Emily Brontë, Wenzel shifts her investigation to three contemporary postcolonial novels from Latin America and South Africa, by José Donoso, Rosario Ferré, and André Brink. These novels dramatize the importance of the past as a foundation for the future. The menacing implications of flawed or precarious foundations are figured in cellars and caves, in relation to which houses acquire labyrinthine dimensions, contain brooding silences, and store deep and dangerous secrets that emerge as haunting spirits from the past. Subterranean regions are depicted both literally and metaphorically, as the texts expose the decadence and corruption of the power relations that are the legacies of colonization, gender discrimination, and racism. These legacies are explored on two levels in the respective 'fictional houses': in the superficial or overt lives of the depicted families and in the symbolic repressed regions of houses or psyches that contain proverbial skeletons rattling in the closed cupboards of history. Donoso's novel illustrates the tensions of master–servant relationships and power structures, while both Ferré and Brink focus on power relations dominated by the male–female binary.

Zakes Mda is among South Africa's most distinguished contemporary novelists. In his novels the socio-political spaces of apartheid and post-apartheid South Africa are transformed into newly imagined places which conspicuously lack the Afro-pessimism of Coetzee's *oeuvre*. Ina Gräbe investigates these vibrant transformations. Discussing *Ways of Dying* (1995), whose grim subject-matter is the turbulent years preceding the first democratic South African elections in 1994, Gräbe describes the constant presence of death in the violence-infested space of black townships and squatter camps, and the narrative devices of *telling* and *acting* which Mda creates for Toloki, the professional mourner who is the novel's chief protagonist. She shows how through imagination and resourcefulness Toloki creates meaningful and even beautiful spaces amid the horrors of his surroundings. In *The Madonna of Excelsior* (2002) Mda continues his strategy of rewriting history by suffusing his narrative with visual representations of the landscape and its people. In the three texts under discussion, Gräbe demonstrates Mda's remarkable capacity to orchestrate a postcolonial subjectivity free of the stereotypes present in colonial writing about Africa.

Harry Garuba begins his chapter by describing the novel of the cultural nationalist period of modern African literature. This depicts the rural as a 'pure' space where characters lived in harmony with nature and achieved social integration before the disruptive and alienating advent of colonialism. With the advent of colonialism, links between the African self, the social order, and the natural world were severed. This notion of alienation was spatialized: the city was seen as the space of its location in a version of alienation not very different from Western reactions to the mechanization and bureaucratization of life in modern post-industrial European society. But Garuba distinguishes between postcolonial alienation in African literature and colonial alienation in the West and he argues that African postcolonial alienation results from the wholesale transference of rural norms into the space of the city. Garuba shows how *Links*, whose Somalian author Nuruddin Farah has always been concerned with issues of space and subjectivity, collective representation, and individual identity, reconfigures concepts of public and private space by undermining binary oppositions between 'clan' and 'civil society', 'blood' and 'ideology'. The specifically African alienation which Farah's novel dramatizes is different from the alienation born of urban bureaucratization and mechanization experienced by Kafka's characters or T. S. Eliot's hollow men because it is grounded on the epistemological division between the values of the city and those of the village.

Frederik Tygstrup's essay starts from the premise that the changing spaces of our contemporary world demand mapping techniques that can supplement, and in part supplant, the basic processes of registration and plotting with a more sophisticated reading-practice that engages with these complex spatial configurations and spells out the relational mechanisms on which they rest. Literature, he argues, plays a key role as a medium capable of grasping the multifarious and richly stratified structures issuing from late twentieth- and early twenty-first-century life forms. Modernist fiction's propensity for spatial arrangements – as observable in the radical experiments serving to establish new patterns of spatial perception and representation in the fiction of Proust, Kafka, Musil, Woolf, and Joyce – develops a rich repertoire of techniques for the rendering of space. This repertoire of techniques is adopted and further developed in contemporary fiction. Observing that Salman Rushdie is among those novelists who have most relentlessly and innovatively explored our present spaces, Tygstrup argues that Rushdie's fiction often defies our sense of normality and reality by insisting on accepting the consequences of the way in which spaces are changing around us. Aided by theoretical notions expounded by Heidegger, and Deleuze and Guattari, Tygstrup's discussion centres on Rushdie's latest novel, *Shalimar the Clown* (2005), and he reads this text as an illustrative example of the author's mapping of the 'visible but unseen' spaces of contemporary reality.

This volume, thus, aims to present the reader with a variety of approaches to the different ways in which space is presented in modernist and postcolonial fiction. As the essays following demonstrate, there are a number of significant connections between the literary landscapes of modernist and postcolonial works. For both modernist and postmodernist writers the intersections of the axes of time and space are crucial: if there is rarely, if ever, a sense of place-in-itself in any of their pages, one reason for this is that the identities human beings bestow on (and are given by) geographical areas are negotiated in response to issues of class, gender – and history.

But our contributors show, too, that for all that postcolonial writers borrow themes, techniques, and assumptions from their predecessors, they bring something different to the fictional creation and presentation of space. There is a greater political specificity and urgency – more indeed of a call to action – in their representations of the geographical locations that define and are defined by human beings. Where space is contested, these contestations are likely to be more socially, culturally, and politically specific in postcolonial fiction – even, paradoxically, when these specificities are part of the homogenizing process that we know as globalization.

James, in the closing pages of Virginia Woolf's *To the Lighthouse*, corrects his initial reaction that 'So that was the Lighthouse, was it?' with the immediate afterthought 'No, the other was also the Lighthouse'. One vision does not replace the other. In like manner the space of postcolonialism does not replace the space of modernism, but each enriches our understanding of the other.

Works cited

Bachelard, G., *The Poetics of Space* [1958]. Trans. M. Jolas (Boston: Beacon Press, 1994).

Bakhtin, M. M., 'Forms of Time and Chronotope in the Novel', in *The Dialogic Imagination: Four Essays*. Ed. M. Holquist (Austin: University of Texas Press, 1982), pp. 243–250.

Brooker, P., 'Early Modernism', in *The Cambridge Companion to the Modernist Novel*. Ed. M. Shiach (Cambridge: Cambridge University Press, 2007), pp. 32–47.

Brooke-Rose, C., 'Exsul', *Poetics Today*, 17: 3 (Fall 1996) 289–303.

Cosgrove, D. E., *Social Formation and Symbolic Landscape* (New Jersey, Tototwa: Barnes and Noble Books, 1988).

Carter, E. Donald, J. and Squires, J., *Space and Place: Theories of Identity and Location* (London: Lawrence and Wishart, 1993).

Kant, I., *Critique of Pure Reason* [1781]. Ed. and trans. P. Guyer and A. W. Wood (Cambridge: Cambridge University Press, 1998).

Rabbethke-Schiller, H., *Memory and Magic: Contemporary Art of the !Xun and Khwe*, (Johannesburg: Jacana Books, 2006).

Said, E. W., *Reflections on Exile and Other Literary and Cultural Essays* (London: Granta Books, 2000).

Stevens, H., 'D. H. Lawrence: Organicism and the Modernist Novel', in *The Cambridge Companion to the Modernist Novel*. Ed. M. Shiach (Cambridge: Cambridge University Press, 2007), pp. 137–150.

1
Space, Time, Narrative: From Thomas Hardy to Franz Kafka and J. M. Coetzee

Jakob Lothe

It is part of the singularity of literature to dramatize fictional narrators' and characters' attempts to understand, accommodate, and finally perhaps resign themselves to the complexities of space and time. The ways in which they do so actualize an accompanying dimension of literature's singularity: its ability to change the perspective, to defamiliarize, to represent a different and yet recognizable otherness (see Attridge, 2004, p. 19; cf. Miller, 2000, pp. 18–19). As readers, we tend to sympathize with the attempts of narrators and characters to come to terms with these problems, because they echo our own. Although the relationship between narrators and characters on the one hand, and space and time on the other, can assume a variety of forms, this essay will argue that the narrative presentations of space in the novels under consideration are interestingly related to each other, thus indicating significant points of connection between early modernist and postcolonial literature. Adopting a tripartite structure, I will first make some theoretical comments on space – particularly narrative space. Aided by these theoretical notions, I will then proceed to discuss the presentation of space in Thomas Hardy's fiction. Hardy's novels arguably provide a particularly interesting example of how space (including the narrator's and characters' experience of space) is both accentuated and problematized in British fiction of the late nineteenth century. Although it would be a gross exaggeration to claim that Hardy's works reject the established paradigm of spatial representation in realist fiction, they modify and to some extent question that paradigm. This is one reason why – in common with the fiction of authors such as Henry James, Joseph Conrad and the early Knut Hamsun – Hardy's novels are distinguished by a distinctly transitional quality: as most literary historians agree, late

1

nineteenth-century fiction marks the beginning of European modernism. This transitional aspect of Hardy's works, exploiting and combining constituent elements of realist as well as modernist fiction, is particularly noticeable in the passages I will discuss from *The Return of the Native* (1878) and *Tess of the d'Urbervilles* (1891). In the third part of the essay, I will link my observations on Hardy to the beginnings of one fully fledged modernist and one distinctly postcolonial novel: Franz Kafka's *The Castle* (1926) and J. M. Coetzee's *Waiting for the Barbarians* (1980). Throughout my discussion, I relate space to the presentation of narrative.

If, as noted in the Introduction to this volume, place is an element of space, narrative space can be defined as the fictional universe presented by the narrative discourse. As Sabine Buchholz and Manfred Jahn observe, this narrative space – in which the events of the story occur and in which the story-internal characters move about – is characterized by a complex of parameters: '(1) by the boundaries that separate it from coordinate, superordinate, and subordinate spaces, (2) by the objects which it contains, (3) by the living conditions which it provides, and (4) by the temporal dimension to which it is bound' (Buchholz and Jahn, 2005, p. 552). The constituent elements of all four parameters contribute to the formation of the narrative space; moreover, complicating the critic's task, they do so simultaneously. The difficulty of separating the characteristics and effects of the different parameters from one another does not reduce the critical value of Buchholz's and Jahn's observation, however.

In order to elaborate on the parameters which characterize narrative space, and also on the ways in which they are linked, we may helpfully remind ourselves of the distinction between 'story space' and 'discourse space'. As Seymour Chatman notes, this distinction parallels that between 'story time' (the time period covered by the narrative) and 'discourse time' (the time of narration) (Chatman, 1978, pp. 96–97). 'Story space' refers to the immediate spatial environment in which an event or episode occurs; this environment is constituted by existents (i.e. entities that perform or are affected by an event). 'Discourse space' denotes the narrator's environment. If the author uses a first-person narrator (who typically combines the functions of narrator and character), this narrator's current environment is often more easily identifiable than that of a third-person narrator – who essentially serves as the author's narrative and evaluative instrument (see Lothe, 2000, pp. 21–22). As we shall see, however, the ways in which third-person narrators are positioned in, and related to, space vary very considerably.

While the distinction between 'story time' and 'discourse time' has enabled narrative theory to coin and employ terms such as analepsis, prolepsis, perspective and repetition, that between 'story space' and 'discourse space' has not resulted in a corresponding proliferation of critical concepts. That relatively few narrative terms are subsumed under the broad category of space can partly account for the relative neglect of this important dimension of narrative. Yet, such an explanation is inadequate, for our tendency to concentrate on time rather than space can be traced all the way back to Aristotle. In his *Poetics*, Aristotle is primarily interested in literary composition, which he studies as temporal *succession* rather than spatial *situation* (Aristotle, 1995, p. 57 and *passim*). A poet and critic who has furthered the same tendency is Gotthold Ephraim Lessing, whose influential study *Laokoon* (1766) describes narrative literature as a 'temporal' art, as opposed to 'spatial' arts such as painting and sculpture.

The resurgence of interest in space over the past decades is prompted partly by an improved understanding of the significance of narrative's spatial dimension (cf. Friedman, 2005, pp. 192–197) and partly by a new, or perhaps rather renewed, recognition of the crucially important function which space has for the formation of human identity – including the representation of human identity in and through narrative. Some of the most important impulses for this spatial turn have come from phenomenological studies such as Gaston Bachelard's *The Poetics of Space* (1994 [1958]). Particularly significant is the notion of 'lived space' (*espace vécu*). Constituting 'the humanely embodied counterpart of the three-dimensional, empty, and basically unoriented spaces of physics and geometry... Lived space is deictically oriented space as perceived and talked about in everyday life' (Buchholz and Jahn, 2005, p. 553). Such an understanding of space presupposes a subject – a man or woman (or, in narrative fiction, a male or female character) who experiences space through his or her existential living conditions. Moreover, this phenomenological understanding of space links the term not only to place but also to time. For Bachelard, our experience of space is associated with identity and identity formation, and this quality of space is closely related to *when* and *how* we inhabit a given place.

As an element of space, place is less abstract in that it is located. As Tim Cresswell puts it, places 'have fixed co-ordinates on the Earth's surface' (Cresswell, 2004, p. 7); they also have fixed co-ordinates within the fictional universe of a novel. In many works of fiction, and certainly in the novels under consideration here, the borderline between a place (or a literary landscape constituted by different yet related places) and the space outside it proves particularly significant for the narrator and the characters alike. The boundary or border, along with the possibilities of transition associated with it, actualizes Mikhail M. Bakhtin's critically useful concept of the chronotope or the chronotopic motif: a place or limited area where dimensions of time and space are curiously compressed in a way that can generate not only work and playing activities but also tension, conflict and pain. Typical chronotopic motifs include the road (in travel literature), the castle (in the Gothic novel), the saloon (in novels by Stendahl, Balzac and Proust), and the threshold. Bakhtin considers the chronotope of the threshold as particularly important (Bakhtin, 1982, p. 248). It can be a corridor, a hall, a window, a door or a veranda – marking a zone of neutrality, but also one of transition, hesitation, reflection and memory. To take an example from Bakhtin's favourite author Dostoevsky, in *Crime and Punishment* (1866) it is in a corridor that Raumikhin realizes that Raskolnikov is the murderer. The chronotopic motif is in a specific place, while at the same time marking a border between coordinate, superordinate and subordinate spaces. Constituting and yet also complicating the characters' sense of identity, the chronotopic motif provides a helpful supplement to Bachelard's notion of space.

Turning to Hardy, I reiterate that I regard him as a transitional writer whose work, though rooted in and contributing to European realism, is possessed of distinctly modernist features. As Michael Levenson has suggested, it is helpful to talk of 'diverse *modernizing* works and movements' rather than Modernism as one well-defined and easily identifiable period (Levenson, 2001, p. 3, original emphasis). For example, while Scandinavian authors such as the Swedish poet Tomas Tranströmer and the Norwegian novelist Tarjei Vesaas produced modernist literature after the Second World War, the Norwegian authors Henrik Ibsen and Knut Hamsun, employing and experimenting with the genres of drama and the novel respectively, made significant contributions to the formation of European modernism in the 1880s and 1890s.[1]

Hardy's novel *The Return of the Native* begins in a manner that, departing radically from the realist paradigm, points in the direction of what we have later come to think of as modernist fiction. And it does so primarily in its description of, and sustained focus on, fictional space:

A Saturday afternoon in November was approaching the time of twilight, and the vast tract of unenclosed wild known as Egdon Heath embrowned itself moment by moment. Overhead the hollow stretch of whitish cloud shutting out the sky was as a tent which had the whole heath for its floor. (Hardy, 1969, p. 2)

In the genre of the novel, it is highly unusual to devote a first chapter exclusively to a description of place. In the Hardy canon too this is exceptional; as regards the narrator's positioning of the character in the landscape, the novel's *second* chapter resembles the beginnings of texts such as *The Mayor of Casterbridge* and *Tess of the d'Urbervilles*. The first sentence of chapter 2 reads thus: 'Along the road walked an old man' (p. 5). In the first chapter, no human character is mentioned. Instead, Hardy makes the third-person narrator focus on the landscape – on Egdon Heath as a place, as one particular element of space. If we look at the map called 'Thomas Hardy's Wessex',[2] we spot Egdon Heath just below the W in 'South Wessex'. Like William Faulkner's Yoknapatawpha County, Wessex, including Egdon Heath, is a literary landscape within a fictional universe. And yet, as the information in the upper left corner of the map interestingly indicates, Wessex contains not just fictitious but also real names. If Faulkner's Yoknapatawpha is inseparable from the American South, Hardy's Wessex is an imaginary space whose characteristic features are derived in large part from the topography, history and ways of living in this part of Britain in the mid-nineteenth century.

I want to make two comments on this striking first chapter. In an essay on variants of genre in Hardy, I have suggested that the description of the heath's form as 'Titanic' (p. 3) supports a reading of the first chapter not only as a prologue to the action but also as a prolepsis of tragedy (Lothe, 1999, pp. 112–129). In the context of my argument here, I stress the great significance attached to the heath's 'face' (p. 2). This noun, which we commonly associate with human beings, is a key word in the title of chapter 1: 'A Face on Which Time Makes But Little Impression' (p. 2). But here it refers to the heath, not to a male or female character. Employing an anthropomorphic figure of speech, Hardy personifies the heath while at the same time emphasizing its essential difference from human individuals. Thus the spatial dimension of 'face' is accentuated. Yet although the word serves to stress the heath's capacity for withstanding the workings of time, it also, because we unavoidably link it to human beings, paradoxically accentuates the spatial dimension of human existence. There is a strong sense in which human characters are irrelevant to the description of the heath, whose 'ancient permanence' (p. 5) will outlast all the characters. Suggesting its immense power, the heath's titanic form contrasts with the frailty and vulnerability of human 'form'. Hardy's description of the heath resembles, indeed adumbrates, Virginia Woolf's presentation of human absence in Part II of *To the Lighthouse* (1927). This modernist novel too has significant features of loss and isolation, and just as Woolf, in the absence of characters, personifies the wind and the waves, so Hardy's heath is endowed with distinctly anthropomorphic qualities. The opening chapter of *The Return of the Native* illustrates how physical objects are placed or positioned in space, and how they seem to be subordinated to the space which precedes them. As the Czech philosopher Jan Patočka has noted, this kind of positioning and distribution of objects within one space – a space considered as an independent yet empty entity – is linked to a modern perspective (Patočka, 1991, p. 65). And yet the relative stability of the place Hardy presents us with (in spite of the process of subordination) is different from the changing and disturbingly ungraspable modernist spaces observable in Woolf or Kafka.

This last comment brings me to my second point about Hardy's presentation of space in chapter 1 of *The Return of the Native*. While in the narratives of Kafka and Woolf the third-person narrator's presentation of space is repeatedly – in various ways, and more or less strongly or obviously – both linked to and influenced by the characters' experience of time, in Hardy, and certainly in this chapter, the way in which space is focused and highlighted is inseparable from, and depends on, the dominant and relatively stable voice, perspective and experience of the third-person narrator. It is significant that the narrator is not just a voice but also a perspective – a vantage point from which the space of the heath is perceived and portrayed. We have noted how the chapter (and the novel) begins. The narrator perceives and describes the heath in and through time. Significantly, the time of his spatial description is twilight, 'this transitional point of its nightly roll into darkness' (p. 2).

I would argue that, as experienced and presented by the narrator, 'the time of twilight' bears an interesting relation to Bakhtin's chronotopic motif. The dimensions of time and space are compressed and closely related here: 'The distant rims of the world and of the firmament seemed to be a division in time no less than a division in matter' (p. 2). Although the motif is linked to or situated in front of the heath, its exact position is not specified. It cannot be, for it is closely associated with the unidentified narrator, whose perspective enables him to 'understand the heath' at the time of twilight: 'It could best be felt when it could not be clearly seen' (p. 2).

The narrative situation established here is similar to those of key modernist novels such as Conrad's *Lord Jim* (1900) and Faulkner's *Absalom, Absalom!* (1936). When day blends into night, Marlow, addressing his narratees on a veranda in an unidentified place, shows himself 'willing to remember Jim...to remember him at length, in detail and audibly' (Conrad, 1996, p. 24). Similarly, in the narrative discourse of *Absalom, Absalom!*, the verb *muse* (defined by the *OED* as 'To be absorbed in thought; to meditate in silence; to ponder') indicates how, in this complex novel so strongly inspired by *Lord Jim*, the narrative about Sutpen assumes the form of a sustained act of memory furthered, indeed necessitated, by the troubled history of the American South.

In *The Return of the Native*, the heath, which metonymically represents Wessex, is 'a spot which returned upon the memory of those who loved it with an aspect of peculiar and kindly congruity' (p. 3). As an element of nature, the heath is 'Titanic' – that is both powerful and beautiful; and yet like the ship named *Titanic* (which inspired Hardy to write his masterly poem 'The Convergence of the Twain'), it is also fragile and vulnerable.[3] The ecological dimension of this poem is observable in this first chapter too: 'Indeed it is a question if the exclusive reign of this orthodox beauty is not approaching its last quarter' (p. 3).

Hardy's presentation of space, then, is linked to, indeed dependent on, two temporal vantage points which coexist in a peculiarly alogical yet thematically productive manner. On the one hand, the narrator senses and presents Egdon Heath at the time of twilight; thus there is a sense in which he seems to be there, blended with the place at (and because of) a transitional point in time. On the other hand, the momentary identification with this element of space seems to occur in memory only. Even though it is difficult to determine exactly what the place of Egdon Heath means, devoting the novel's first chapter to it signals that this landscape is crucially important. The heath's varied functions are comparable to those Bachelard attributes to the house.[4] This connection is suggested by, or at least implied in, the overall description of the landscape; it is also indicated more specifically through the use of metaphors such as the tent: 'Overhead the hollow stretch of whitish cloud shutting out the sky was a tent which had the whole heath for its floor' (p. 2).

To the chronotopic motif of twilight is added, in the first chapter's last paragraph, that of the road. For Bakhtin, the road is a classic chronotopic motif; and it is a significant one in Hardy's fiction too. We note the way in which Hardy makes his narrator relate the road, as an element of space, to the Romans who built it nearly two thousand years ago. As in Conrad's *Heart of Darkness*, the reference to the Romans serves to widen temporal perspective. Or more precisely, while in *Heart of Darkness* Marlow's reference to the Romans both extends and problematizes the frame narrator's point of reference (and of orientation), here the vast temporal extension of the heath's space is corroborated by the linking of the road built by the Romans to the same road used by the character introduced in the first sentence of chapter 2. The Roman name of the road, Via Iceniana, provides a further intertextual link to *Heart of Darkness*. Via Iceniana means 'The road of the Iceni'; Iceni was the name of one of the native tribes defeated by the Romans around year 50AD. Thus the issues of power and influence are activated in the narrative discourse, and they are both linked to the relationship between man and nature.

Moving on to *Tess of the d'Urbervilles*, another major Hardy novel published 13 years later, we note how carefully – in both novels – Hardy situates his characters in the fictional universe. In *Tess of the d'Urbervilles* too, Hardy uses a third-person narrator: he, or perhaps rather it, is located on the extradiegetic level of narration and not, as, for instance, in Coetzee's *Waiting for the Barbarians*, on the diegetic level of action. And yet *Tess of the d'Urbervilles* illustrates a further point, which that just made may tend to obscure: although apparently a reporter and commentator rather than an active agent in the plot, Hardy's third-person narrator is still paradoxically and problematically involved in the lives of the characters he presents. Uneasily combining different narrative inclinations – distance and sympathy, knowledge and a pervasive sense of helplessness – this involvement has a notable existential dimension which partly explains, and even justifies, the various inconsistencies pertaining to the narrator's position and function. In Hardy's fiction, what can be problematically inconsistent on the level of narration can still be rhetorically effective and thematically productive. The presentation of nature (as a dimension of space) is a case in point. Although in one sense the narrator's attitude to nature is problematically variable and undetermined, it is also rewardingly ambiguous: illustrating that the relationship between man and nature is intrinsically difficult, it furthers a range of possible responses and interpretations. In Hardy's fiction, man's ambiguous relationship with nature constitutes an area of narrative and thematic exploration closely associated with the narrative presentation of how the characters interact.

A revealing example of this kind of interplay – that is, the relationship between character and nature on the one hand, and character and character on the other – is provided by the opening of chapter 47:

It is the threshing of the last wheat-rick at Flintcomb-Ash Farm. The dawn of the March morning is singularly inexpressive, and there is nothing to show where the eastern horizon lies. Against the twilight rises the trapezoidal top of the stack, which has stood forlornly here through the washing and bleaching of the wintry weather. (Hardy, 1975, p. 309)

This is a descriptive, strikingly visual, first paragraph; and although it is much shorter than the chapter we have just been considering, it interestingly resembles the beginning of *The Return of the Native*. It is true that, in contrast to the passage from the earlier novel, this chapter of *Tess of the d'Urbervilles* is concerned with the human activity of threshing. Yet the focus of this first paragraph is on the landscape in which the farm is situated, and of which it forms an integral part. The haze and inexpressiveness of the sky and the eastern horizon call strikingly to mind an impressionist painting such as Claude Monet's 'Sunrise'. Narrative approximates to description here, and this descriptive effect is enhanced by Hardy's use of the present tense. A further highlight of the passage is the linking of the words 'dawn' and 'twilight'. As we recall, twilight is a key word in the first chapter of *The Return of the Native*. Even though in this chapter of *Tess of the d'Urbervilles* it refers to the coming of day rather than the approaching night, here too twilight indicates a brief, transitional point when space is seen in a special, possibly clearer, way because it assumes a different form – because it is perceived differently by the narrator.

There is a strong suggestion in this passage that the narrator's impression of the 'singularly inexpressive' March morning is shared by Tess, and by implication by the reader too. However, as Tess and her companion arrive in this beautiful setting, the kind of work awaiting them is not of the traditional, manual sort, but instead work conditioned by the newly introduced 'red tyrant that the women had come to serve – a timber-framed construction, with straps and wheels appertaining – the threshing-machine which, whilst it was going, kept up a despotic demand upon the endurance of their muscles and nerves' (p. 309). The metaphor 'red tyrant' and the adjective 'despotic' leave the reader in little doubt as regards the narrator's attitudinal distance from the machine. Both the metaphor and the adjective adumbrate the characterization of the engineer in the fourth paragraph:

What he looked he felt. He was in the agricultural world, but not of it. He served fire and smoke, these denizens of the fields served vegetable, weather, frost and sun. He travelled with his engine from farm to farm, from county to county, for as yet the steam threshing machine was itinerant in this part of Wessex. (p. 309)

If, as I have suggested, Egdon Heath metonymically represents the part of Wessex not yet controlled or mastered by man, Wessex as portrayed here metonymically represents nature. The threshing machine and the engineer are incongruous in this setting. That they also pose a threat to nature is signalled by the negative effect they have on Tess. Thus, if Egdon Heath metonymically represents nature in the first chapter of *The Return of the Native*, the tension noticeable in Tess's adverse relation to the threshing machine has a comparable function: she is presented as integral to nature in the sense that she is not in a position to change or damage it; she also respects it and enjoys it. One indication of this kind of stable relationship is that both Tess and her father are pedestrians: their actions and decisions are associated with the chronotopic motif of the road. There is an interesting connection between this passage – the presentation of the threshing machine and the engineer – and the narrator's observation in the opening chapter of *The Return of the Native* that 'it is a question if the exclusive reign of this orthodox beauty is not approaching its last quarter' (p. 3). In both instances, the narrator's presentation of one element of space is coloured by his sense of nature's fragility and a distorted ecological balance created by the mechanics of modern society.

Even though, overall, Hardy is a nineteenth-century novelist on the threshold of modernism, significant aspects of his narrative are more modernist than they appear to be at first sight. One illustrative example is provided by the two different endings of Hardy's last novel, *The Well-Beloved*; another instance is, as I have tried to show, the first chapter of *The Return of the Native*. In this novel as in *Tess of the d'Urbervilles*, Hardy effectively employs and yet starts to question the paradigm of realist narration – thus, like Dostoevsky in *Crime and Punishment* or George Eliot in *Middlemarch* (1871–1872)[5] – providing part of the basis for the modernist fiction of James, Conrad, Proust, Kafka, Woolf and Faulkner. I now proceed to comment on the beginnings of two novels which, though they may be closer to each other than to Hardy, both present fictional space in ways that invite comparison with the two Hardy novels just considered.

I have linked Patočka's point about the modern conception of space as an independent entity in which objects are situated to the way in which Hardy carefully situates his characters in the region of narrative space which he names Wessex. Yet as we also have seen, the characters of Hardy's universe are not only positioned and defined by means of a space which envelops and precedes them. They are also defined spatially through their relationships with Wessex and through their relations to other characters who inhabit, or enter, this literary landscape. According to Patočka, this kind of threatened and unstable space tends to predominate in the twentieth century, and at this point there is a significant connection between Hardy and Kafka.

This is how Kafka's novel *Das Schloss* begins:

> Es war spät abend als K. ankam. Das Dorf lag in tiefem Schnee. Vom Schlossberg war nichts zu sehn, Nebel und Finsternis umgaben ihn, auch nicht der schwächste Lichtschein deutete das grosse Schloss an. Lange stand K. auf der Holzbrücke die von der Landstrasse zum Dorf führt und blickte in die scheinbare Leere empor. (Kafka, 1982, p. 7)

> It was late evening when K. arrived. The village lay deep in snow. There was nothing to be seen of the castle mount, mist and darkness surrounded it, not even the faintest glimmer of light suggested the great castle. K. stood long on the wooden bridge which leads from the highway to the village and looked up into the seeming emptiness.[6]

The beginnings of Kafka's novels are very complex, not least when it comes to the presentation of space. We first note how, in this opening of *The Castle*, space is accentuated and yet peculiarly obscured. We are told about a village deep in snow, and we understand there is a castle in, or rising above, that village. Moreover, we glean from 'ankam', the past tense of the verb 'ankommen' (arrive), that K. has reached his destination. He hesitates before entering the village, however. As time and space are compressed in this beginning, the chronotopic motif of the threshold is activated. It becomes conspicuous when, as if picking up strength before being able to proceed, K. stands for a long while on the bridge. Although Hardy provides much more detailed information about space than does Kafka, one of the most accurate comments one can make on the presentation of space in the opening of *Das Schloss* is actually given by the narrator in the first paragraph of *The Return of the Native*: 'It could best be felt when it could not clearly be seen . . . ' (p. 2). If Hardy's third-person narrator feels the heath is coming nearer as it disappears from sight, Kafka makes his character K. feel strangely close to, even threatened by, the enormous castle hidden somewhere in the darkness.[7] He cannot see the castle, but he knows it is there. It is as though the castle is given: the castle, not the village, is the goal of K.'s journey. '[D]as grosse

Schloss' seems to be linked to an impression or idea (formed earlier and elsewhere) on the part of K., perhaps motivating him to embark on the journey in the first place. Thus placement is generating progression in this narrative beginning.[8]

Second, although (here as in *The Trial*) Kafka uses a third-person narrator, this narrator is far less knowledgeable than the Hardy narrators in *The Return of the Native* and *Tess of the d'Urbervilles*. Even though the voice here is clearly the narrator's, narrative perspective approximates to that of K. to the extent of limiting the narrator's view of space to the protagonist's. Paradoxically, the anthropomorphic qualities of natural space so noticeable in Hardy are less apparent here. This is, I suggest, partly due to the approximation of the narrator's perspective to that of K.

This last point blends into a third comment: while in Hardy the relationship between the character and the landscape in which he or she is situated is crucially important, in this Kafka passage the predominant relationship is that of K. and the castle. Although the castle is a man-made element of space – or perhaps, rather a vague, indiscernible form – it appears wholly to dominate the physical space surrounding K. Thus the castle, which, we gather from the novel's title, is what K. is searching for, is invested with a measure of power which colours the relationship between this object (a special variant of the house) and the character hesitantly approaching it. Hence there is a sense in which, in this novel, anthropomorphic qualities are attributed to one particular spatial object. Yet although the castle is man-made, the way in which it is presented (by the narrator) and perceived (by K. and the narrator) calls the third-person narrator's description of Egdon Heath strikingly to mind: like the heath, the castle represents a kind of permanence and mighty power; in both novels, the observer (narrator) is filled with awe and wonder. Thus, both the heath and the castle are invested with qualities of the sublime.

As in chapter one of *The Return of the Native*, narrative progression is slowed down here. To use a phrase from Michel Foucault, K. is placed in a spatial order, rather than in a narrative sequence involving progression and closure. Kafka was unable to finish *The Castle*, and the novel, which is actually a long fragment, ends in mid-sentence without a closing full stop. What invest this spatial order with both tension and suspense are the discordant qualities of the castle, including the allure of power associated with it. Appropriating Foucault, we could say that power here is related both to a particular spatial region and to a social construct representing unspecified forms of discipline, control and possible punishment (Foucault, 1980, pp. 68–69; cf. Foucault, 1994, pp. 349–364).

There is an interesting connection between the relationship of K. and the castle and that of the two characters we encounter in the opening sentences of J. M. Coetzee's *Waiting for the Barbarians*:

> I have never seen anything like it: two discs of glass suspended in front of his eyes in loops of wire. Is he blind? I could understand it if he wanted to hide his eyes. But he is not blind. The disks are dark, they look opaque from the outside, but he can see through them. He tells me they are a new invention. 'They protect one's eyes against the glare of the sun,' he says. 'You would find them useful out here in the desert. They save one's eyes from squinting all the time. One has fewer headaches. Look.' He touches the corners of his eyes lightly. 'No wrinkles.' He replaces the glasses. It is true. He has the skin of a younger man. 'At home everyone wears them.' (Coetzee, 1997, p. 1)

Here, as in *The Castle*, we sense a tension between the two agents: the first-person narrator (who is also the novel's protagonist, the Magistrate of a frontier settlement) and the character he is looking at. I am by no means suggesting that this character, who turns out to be Colonel Joll, can be equated with the castle. But it is significant that, like K. in Kafka's novel, the narrator finds it difficult to see the other; and the latter's hiding behind dark glasses creates a feeling of unease, uncertainty and unidentifiable power.[9] In this beginning, as in those of *The Castle* and *The Return of the Native*, what is not seen is strongly felt.

The sense of looming or approaching confrontation noticeable at the beginning of *The Castle*, and in some ways also in *The Return of the Native*, is intensified through Coetzee's effective use of the present tense. This form of verbal representation, unusual in the genre of the novel, here generates a form of urgency and immediacy not commonly achieved by narratives written in the past tense. In this particular passage, the present tense stresses the here-and-now of the meeting, while at the same time endowing it with a peculiarly timeless quality. This double dimension of time is closely linked to, and partly dependent on, the extreme and potentially dangerous location of the desert – far from the 'home' to which Colonel Joll refers. Moreover, the present tense decreases the interval and thus complicates 'the relations between the time of narration (the moving now of the narrator's utterance) and the time of the narrative (referential time)' (Coetzee, 1981, p. 557). Linking Coetzee's description of 'time, tense and aspect' in Kafka's short story 'Der Bau' (The Burrow) to *The Castle* and to the beginning of *Waiting for the Barbarians*, I concur with David Attwell's observation that Coetzee shares

'Kafka's concern with the relation between narrative and the experience of time' (Attwell, 1993, p. 101). And yet in *Waiting for the Barbarians*, as in *The Castle*, the complications of temporal relations are blended with the threatening destabilization of spatial ones.

If both Hardy's Egdon Heath and Kafka's castle are possessed of characteristic features which are disconcertingly discordant, rather than comfortably reassuring, the desert in *Waiting for the Barbarians* is similarly endowed with diverse qualities: it is unspecified, yet it borders on the places surrounding it; it is arid, yet the 'barbarians' have managed to survive in it for centuries. Various facets of the landscape of the desert are registered, and highlighted, by different observers with dissimilar perspectives; and the settlement functions as a threshold in Bakhtin's sense of the word. Already in this opening paragraph we sense the irony (though it is more apparent on a second reading) in the presentation of Colonel Joll's glasses. Enabling him to see better in the sun, they actually prevent him from seeing what he is unable to or does not want to see: Joll's modern sunglasses (which is what they probably are) are emblematic of the Empire's darkened vision of everything and everybody outside its borders. Attwell finds that, for the first time in the Coetzee canon, in *Waiting for the Barbarians* history is 'an object in itself – that is, a discursive field' (Attwell, 1993, p. 71). This important point links the novel's narrative trajectory to its political and historical ones. More obliquely yet equally importantly, it also highlights the thematic significance of the opposition between two spatial fields, desert and Empire, of which the former will outlast the latter.

These observations form the basis for three concluding points. First, we have seen that in Hardy's fiction the landscape of Wessex, as represented by Egdon Heath in the first chapter of *The Return of the Native*, assumes the form of an extended house – an element of space associated with the character's identity formation and sense of belonging. Yet we have also seen that this sense of belonging in one stable place is jeopardized by the unstoppable advance of modernity, reaching (in the mid-nineteenth century) the rural area of Wessex. Hinted at in the narrator's comments in chapter 1 of *The Return of the Native* and metonymically represented by the threshing machine in *Tess of the d'Urbervilles*, this temporal process significantly changes the characters' relation with the landscapes in which they live. It is also indicative of the extent to which, in the literary universes of these novels, geographical space is blended with individual, cultural and national variants of space. Hardy's fictional exploration of the intricate ways in which the different dimensions of space further the characters' identity formation is an important connection between his work and texts by other modernist and postcolonial writers.[10] To make this point is of course not to suggest that Hardy's presentation of space is more original than that of Kafka or Coetzee. In all the novels discussed here, the narrative presentation of space is an integral part of the work's literary identity. And literary identity involves 'both repetition of what is recognized as "the same" and openness to new contexts and hence to change' (Attridge, 2004, p. 75).

Second, we have found that in all these beginnings both the narrators' and the characters' sense of place – its immediate presence, its enticing force and power, its seeming permanence and endurance – is just as strong as their sensation of time. It is sometimes suggested that film is the only art form in which the dimensions of time and space are wholly coordinate. The fictional openings considered here would seem to counter that suggestion by demonstrating that, in these very different beginnings, the narrator's sensation of, or perhaps rather exposure to, place is so strong, overwhelming and irreversible as to initiate the process of narration. A possible, partial explanation of this exposure – approximating, albeit in different ways, to a confrontation – is suggested by the anthropomorphic qualities of place. While these, as we have noted, are associated with the heath in *The Return of the Native*, in *The Castle* they are inextricable from that element of space which serves as the novel's title. For K., however, the castle appears nonhuman or superhuman; it is like a sublime mountain inspiring both awe and wonder. In *Waiting for the Barbarians*, the anthropomorphic aspect of the desert is not easily identifiable in the novel's first paragraph. On a second reading, however, we can appreciate the contrast between Joll's limited vision of the desert and the narrator's much deeper understanding of it: an amateur archaeologist, he has conducted excavations in the desert, thus uncovering different temporal layers in the same place. There is a sense in which, in this strangely parabolic novel, the desert is represented not just by its vast geographical space and the nomads who inhabit it, but also by the dead bodies uncovered by the narrator as, digging in the earth, he reflects that he might have been one of them.

Finally, in all these beginnings the significance of space is paradoxically strengthened by the narrators' and characters' failure to separate their experience of space from that of time. Variants of this paradox are operative in all the textual passages considered here. As a spatial location, the desert is more open and unspecified than the castle, and far less accurately delineated than Egdon Heath. And yet all these spaces are presented in ways that highlight the characters' dependency on nature, thus actualizing their vulnerability and the brevity of their lives. In all three beginnings, there is a striking limitation, and intensification, of human experience of space to the present time, to the here and now. For the German philosopher Leibniz, *spatium est ordo coexistendi* (space is the order of coexistence). This definition is associated with that given by Kant, who considers space as a constellation of observable elements. To stress the observation of space, however, is, as all our texts demonstrate, to draw attention to the time when the space was perceived.[11] A particularly illustrative example of how a keen experience of being arrested in space is at once heightened, extended and problematized by an equally strong perception of being in time is the first stanza of Hardy's poem 'Wessex Heights' (1896):

> There are some heights in Wessex, shaped as if by a kindly hand
> For thinking, dreaming, dying on, and at crises when I stand,
> Say, on Ingpen Beacon eastward, or on Wylls-Neck westwardly,
> I seem where I was before my birth, and after death may be.
> (Hardy, 2001, p. 319)

Notes

1. See Moi 2006 and Humpál 1998. For a discussion of the opening of Hamsun's *Hunger* (1890) see Lothe 2002, pp. 88–95.
2. This map is reprinted in many editions of Hardy's work, including Macmillan's New Wessex Edition.
3. 'The Convergence of the Twain' was published in 1912. For a fine analysis of the poem see Hawthorn 1996.
4. Cf. Introduction, p. xv above.
5. One remarkably modernist aspect of *Crime and Punishment* is the protagonist's tendency to improperly distinguish between his experience of outer reality and his equally strong (if not stronger) sensation of inner states of mind. Modernist features of *Middlemarch* are identified and discussed by several contributors to Chase 2006.
6. *Ad hoc* translation by Speirs and Sandberg 1997, p. 104.
7. The German word 'scheinbar' indicates (more accurately than does the English equivalent 'seeming') that the emptiness actually contains a physical object, which K. cannot see. The problem of ascertaining what you are actually looking at – what is in front of you, and what your best course of action is – looms large throughout the novel.
8. I thank James Phelan for drawing my attention to this significant feature of the novel's opening. For a helpful discussion of narrative progression see Phelan 2005.
9. In her contribution to this volume Carrol Clarkson discusses the significance of names and naming in Coetzee's fiction.

10. On this point, there is an important connection between the two Hardy novels considered here and the novel discussed by Gail Fincham in her contribution to this volume, E.M. Forster's *A Passage to India* (1924). See especially pp. 45–54 below.
11. In the second edition of *Narratology*, Mieke Bal stresses that narrative perspective also involves perception. See Bal 1997, p. 143.

Works cited

Aristotle, *Poetics*. Trans. S. Halliwell (Cambridge, MA: Harvard University Press, 1995).

Attridge, D., *The Singularity of Literature* (London: Routledge, 2004).

Attwell, D., *J. M. Coetzee: South Africa and the Politics of Writing* (Cape Town: David Philip, 1993).

Bachelard, G., *The Poetics of Space* [1958]. Trans. M. Jolas (Boston: Beacon Press, 1994).

Bakhtin, M. M., 'Forms of Time and Chronotope in the Novel', *The Dialogic Imagination: Four Essays*. Ed. M. Holquist (Austin: University of Texas Press, 1982), pp. 243–250.

Bal, M., *Narratology: Introduction to the Theory of Narrative* (Toronto: University of Toronto Press, 1997).

Buchholz, S. and M. Jahn, 'Space in Narrative', *Routledge Encyclopedia of Narrative Theory*. Ed. D. Herman, M. Jahn and M.-L. Ryan (London: Routledge, 2005), pp. 551–555.

Chase, K. (ed.), *Middlemarch in the Twenty-First Century* (New York: Oxford University Press, 2006).

Chatman, S., *Story and Discourse: Narrative Structure in Fiction and Film* (Ithaca: Cornell University Press, 1978).

Coetzee, J. M., *Waiting for the Barbarians* [1980] (London: Minerva, 1997).

———, 'Time, Tense and Aspect in Kafka's "the Burrow"', *Modern Language Notes*, 96: 3 (April 1981) 556–579.

Conrad, J., *Lord Jim: A Tale*. Ed. T. Moser (New York: Norton, 1996).

Cresswell, T., *Place: A Short Introduction* (Oxford: Blackwell, 2004).

Foucault, M., *Power/Knowledge: Selected Interviews and Other Writings 1972–1977*. Ed. C. Gordon (Brighton: Harvester, 1980).

———, *Power*. Ed. J. D. Faubion (New York: The New Press, 1994).

Friedman, S. S., 'Spatial Poetics and Arundhati Roy's *The God of Small Things*', *A Companion to Narrative Theory*. Ed. J. Phelan and P. J. Rabinowitz (Oxford: Blackwell, 2005), pp. 192–205.

Hardy, T., *The Return of the Native* (New York: Norton, 1969).

———, *Tess of the d'Urbervilles* (London: Macmillan, 1975).

———, *The Complete Poems*. Ed. J. Gibson (London: Palgrave, 2001).

Hawthorn, J., 'Ideology, Myth, History: The Literature of the *Titanic* Disaster', *Cunning Passages: New Historicism, Cultural Materialism and Marxism in the Contemporary Literary Debate* (London: Arnold, 1996), pp. 109–125.

Humpál, M., *The Roots of Modernist Narrative: Knut Hamsun's Novels* (Oslo: Solum, 1998).

Kafka, F., *Das Schloss*. Ed. M. Pasley (Frankfurt a.M.: Fischer, 1982).

Kant, I., *Critique of Pure Reason* [1781]. Ed. and trans. P. Guyer and A. W. Wood (Cambridge: Cambridge University Press, 1998).

Levenson, M. (ed.) *The Cambridge Companion to Modernism* (Cambridge: Cambridge University Press, 2001).

Lothe, J., 'Variants on Genre: *The Return of the Native, The Mayor of Casterbridge, The Hand of Ethelberta*', *The Cambridge Companion to Thomas Hardy*. Ed. D. Karmer (Cambridge: Cambridge University Press, 1999), pp. 112–129.

———, *Narrative in Fiction and Film: An Introduction* (Oxford: Oxford University Press, 2000).

———, 'Openings: Thomas Hardy's *Tess of the d'Urbervilles* and Knut Hamsun's *Hunger*', *English and Nordic Modernisms*. Ed. B. Tysdahl, M. Jansson, J. Lothe and H. Riikonen (Norwich: Norvik Press, 2002), pp. 77–101.

Miller, J. H., *On Literature* (London: Routledge, 2000).

Moi T., *Henrik Ibsen and the Birth of Modernism: Art, Theater, Philosophy* (New York: Oxford University Press, 2006).

Patočka, J., 'Der Raum und seine Problematik', *Die Bewegung der menschlichen Existenz: Phänomenologische Schriften II*. Ed. K. Nellen, J. Nemec, and I. Strubar (Stuttgart: Klett-Cotta, 1991), pp. 63–131.

Phelan, J., *Living to Tell about It: A Rhetoric and Ethics of Character Narration* (Ithaca: Cornell University Press, 2005).

Speirs, R. and B. Sandberg. *Franz Kafka* (London: Macmillan, 1997).

2
The American Spaces of Henry James

Merle A. Williams

Exergue

Jacques Derrida adopts the notion of an *exergue* – that which stands outside of the work – in place of a preface or an introduction. Literally, the *exergue* is the space on a coin or medal which accommodates the inscription, as well as the French term for an epigraph. Yet the words of the *exergue* disseminate themselves throughout the text that follows, tracing fruitful patterns of potential meaning (Derrida, 1982b, p. 209). How is this formulation to be understood with respect to the treatment of space in selected novels by Henry James?

James can legitimately be regarded as displaying strong affinities with modernism in that his highly crafted fiction adopts a 'spatial form' in its foregrounding of intricate linguistic inter-relations and textual structures (see Waugh, 1984, p. 23). He equally shows a qualified fascination with entering the space of 'self-conscious reflexiveness', with probing the 'uncertainty' of human experiences, which are neither neatly given nor readily interpretable (see Childs, 2000, p. 18). However, James is also implicitly beyond modernism and already postmodernist in many of his literary practices. Borrowing from Linda Hutcheon's astute synopsis of the interplay between modernist and postmodernist orientations or strategies, it is not difficult to argue that James's writing is intensely alive to 'the absence within presence'. It highlights 'the *process* of making the *product*', while creating vivid tensions between centring and dispersal, immanence and transcendence (Hutcheon, 1988, p. 49). But such abstract statements are far too loose and general; they need to be disseminated through the unfolding of a sustained philosophical commentary which is closely engaged with the concrete complexities of James's texts.

This takes the shape of a triple interaction between Mikhail Bakhtin, Jacques Derrida and Henry James.

I

'It's a bad country to be stupid in – none on the whole so bad. If one doesn't know *how* to look and to see, one should keep out of it altogether', James admonishes himself as he approaches Richmond, Virginia in the course of collecting material for The *American Scene* (James, 1968, p. 368). In fact, more than 20 years have passed since he last set foot in the country of his birth, so his nervousness about re-engagement with such unfamiliar geographical and cultural terrain is not without sound reason. Only four of James's completed, full-length texts are set in the United States (clearly setting aside his short stories, autobiographical and critical writing), while three of these were written within a decade. *The Europeans* (1878) captures the angular Puritan freshness of old New England in its vivid and contradictory self-sufficiency, while the drama of *Washington Square* (1880) emerges within the claustrophobic domestic setting of a burgeoning New York which has long since been superseded. *The Bostonians* (1878) in its turn sets out to plot the exuberant and often bizarre transformation of identities, values and beliefs after the Civil War, as Americans reinvent themselves and their relations to their environment, not to mention their unstable ideas of nationhood. Against this background, *The American Scene* (1907) follows in its own belatedness and with its own purpose of restoring contact, challenging vision, releasing the adventurous novelist turned travel writer into a dauntingly foreign landscape of shifting social conditions.

This preliminary outline of the selected American works serves to sketch in advance the extent to which place is significantly inhabited and social for James. The world conceived as dialogue and exchange, as the delightfully bewildering panoply of human interaction, is the hallmark of his endeavour. Deep as his fascination with the unrestricted play of individual consciousness may be, his writing also shows an intense awareness of Mikhail Bakhtin's stricture that 'a single person, remaining alone with himself, cannot make ends meet even in the most intimate sphere of his own spiritual life, he cannot manage without another consciousness. One person can never find fullness in himself alone' (Bakhtin, 1984, p. 177). James's creative perception depends on the influences of consciousnesses shaping and reconfiguring one another, as he recognizes from a congruent point of view in his preface to the New York edition of *Roderick Hudson*: 'Really, universally, relations stop nowhere, and the exquisite problem of the artist is eternally but to draw, by a geometry of his own, the circle within which they happily appear to do so. He is in the perpetual predicament that the continuity of things is the whole matter...of comedy and tragedy' (James, 1962, p. 5).

This fictional disposition strikes intriguing resonances with Bakhtin's account of the inevitably dialogical aspect of all relations. In his lucid exposition of the Russian's thought, Michael Holquist points to the inherent quality of existence as project and collaboration, the simultaneous event of co-being. According to Bakhtin, each individual is launched on the ineluctable task of self-authorship, stitching the inchoateness of the isolated 'I' (a pronoun without a fixed referent) to the communal space of objects, occurrences and other human beings (Holquist, 1990, pp. 23–25). In this view, language itself is understood not in formal linguistic or grammatical terms, but as utterance; this acknowledges the addressivity or necessary responsiveness of others as human beings, even before any discussion is opened (Danow, 1991, p. 16). Moreover, the existential maps analogically onto the aesthetic, not least because Bakhtin imagines all relations as architectonically proportioned between non-absolute centres (see Holquist, 1990, pp. 150–151). The discourse of a novel offers itself within the framework of the chronotope or a physically and culturally shaped space–time, for utterances invoke successive temporal contexts, while their spatial dimension is expressed both through human interaction and through reference to specific persons or objects (see Bakhtin, 1981, pp. 284–292, helpfully summarized in Danow, 1991, pp. 38–39). James's comments on the artistic imperative to curtail relations can thus be refracted through Bakhtin's treatment of the chronotope to delineate a space which is both lived and explored through utterance, rich in its own specificities but correlated with the unrestricted possibilities of other possible spaces.

Attractive as this approach to reading James through the Bakhtinian lens of 'authoring' may be, it misses the crucially self-reflexive aspects of his American texts. Although the concern with the space of dialogue and interacting consciousnesses remains central, these works – even as early as *The Europeans* – equally highlight the artifice of their constructed spatiality and chosen fictional conventions. Here an appropriate theoretical resource is supplied by the Derridean notion of iterability or the differential play of signifiers within a conventional system, constantly deferring the inherently unattainable prospect of a plenitude of settled meanings (see Derrida, 1982a, pp. 309–330). Clearly, a literary text cannot take on the status of an achieved performative, that of language (or even the utterance) realizing itself as a wholly accomplished creative act, precisely because 'there is no literature without a *suspended* relation to meaning and reference. *Suspended* means *suspense*, but also *dependence*, condition, conditionality. In its suspended condition, literature can only exceed itself' (Derrida, 1992, p. 48). This excess paradoxically comes to define each of the American texts in its singularity, for the appreciation of such generative uniqueness concomitantly requires participation in an aesthetically accepted genre or some generalizable code. 'Singularity is never one-off...closed like a point or a fist.... [It] differs from itself, it is deferred...so as to be what it is and to be repeated in its very singularity' (Derrida, 1992, p. 68). In this respect, James's writing follows the movement of the Derridean mark, at once reinscribing familiar linguistic modalities and advancing into virgin space whose very newness depends on its infusion by the traditional.

Such theoretical contentions can readily be fleshed out through an examination of *The Europeans*. At first sight, the novel offers its readers a reassuring sequence of settings in accordance with prevailing nineteenth-century realist practice. The narrative opens at a Boston inn overlooking a gloomy graveyard, with the 'ineffectual refreshment of a dull, moist snowfall' to add colour to the perversely unseasonable spring weather (James, 1984a, p. 33). The modest hospitality of the Wentworths' home, trustingly open to all comers, is juxtaposed to Robert Acton's house with its scrupulously tended collection of glimmering Oriental artefacts, while Eugenia's draping of her cottage to introduce a sophisticated European ambience counterbalances both local styles. There is also a generous supply of gorgeous sunsets, from the display of molten gold which tempts the Baroness to seek her fortune in the New World to the crimson conflagration in the Celestial City that enchants Felix's visual sensibility (James, 1984a, pp. 43 and 159). Nonetheless, Kenneth Graham shrewdly notes the stage-managed quality of the novel's pictorial effects; this technique at once draws on the available scenic capital, yet slyly exposes it as calculated contrivance. Perhaps the most striking instance, as Graham indicates, is the episode when Felix takes Gertrude boating on the Wentworths' pond (Graham, 1988, pp. 26–28):

> She went with him to the edge of the lake, where a couple of boats were always moored; they got into one of them, and Felix with gentle strokes propelled it to the opposite shore. The day was the perfection of summer weather; the little lake was the colour of sunshine; the plash of the oars was the only sound, and they found themselves

listening to it. They disembarked, and by a winding path ascended the pine-crested mound which overlooked the water, whose white expanse glittered between the trees. (James, 1984a, pp. 119–120)

The perfection of the summer idyll is deftly composed, as the young lovers float on liquid sunshine to their private spot in gentle, syn-aesthetic fulfilment. The scene anticipates the light-saturated delicacy of an Impressionist painting, but this is not Eden – nor is the stead-ily developing relationship entirely innocent.[1] As the narrative voice astutely reminds the reader, the 'golden age' has already passed and been duly replaced by 'New England's silvery prime' (James, 1984a, p. 51). Gertrude still carries the constraining burden of her assumed commit-ment to Mr Brand, Charlotte must keep secret her yearning for the young minister's regard, and Felix wonders whether he has abused his uncle's hospitality by acting upon his attraction to Gertrude. The joy that Felix seeks to bring becomes entangled with the informing decen-cies and transparent simplicity of a Puritan lifestyle. The literary text exceeds itself through the cultivated tension between desired plenitude and inevitable disillusionment, the longing for happiness and assured beauty which is compelling only because it is infused by their persistent opposites.

In effect, the Wentworths' estate is turned into the site of an encounter with European manners and modes of living which promises both to undermine and to enrich an already fragile 'silvery prime'. The dialogue between Felix and Gertrude, despite her uneasy doubts and his polished evasions, confers on each the opportunity for continuing authorship of the self. At first, it appears that the benefit will fall principally to Gertrude, as internalized restraint and a reluctant denial of pleasure are thawed by Felix's sunny attention. He assures Charlotte during the patently theatrical proposal scene, which hovers wittily between the far-cical and the moving, that her sister is 'a folded flower. Let me pluck her from the parent tree and you will see her expand.' Yet Felix too finds an opportunity for growth through the unusual effects of Ger-trude's addressivity. Despite his agitation at having to claim his bride from her uncomprehending protectors, he is able to affirm that Ger-trude 'affects me strongly – for she *is* so strong. I don't believe you know her; it's a beautiful nature' (James, 1984a, p. 176). So the altered New England chronotope liberates the pair into a more congenial and pro-ductive space–time, both literally and figuratively. In keeping with the unstated sub-text of the novel, their regenerative power comes to be felt almost more strongly when they are absent in Europe than during their residence, for the staid Wentworths begin to cherish the spectral sound of remembered and expected laughter.

The dialogue between the Baroness and Robert Acton constitutes a different and darker case.[2] While each is eager to engage with the other, the space of the encounter becomes one of potential manipulation for Eugenia and initially cautious probing for Acton. Both participants rapidly resort to the *microdialogue* of the 'double-voiced word', a unit of utterance which is already permeated with the inflections, intentions and value judgements of a range of previous speakers (see Bakhtin, 1984, pp. 74–75 and Danow, 1991, pp. 28–29); the conversation can thus be construed as both discretely private and thoroughly over-determined by competing cultural assumptions. As the scale of the rural setting changes, from a view of distant hills to a road with a 'wide, grassy margin, on the farther side of which there flowed a deep, clear brook', to a sharp focus on the Baroness's stooping to pick a daisy, so the course of the exchange moves from a consideration of the Baroness's unfortunate history to its tantalizing culmination, the possible renunciation of her dubious marriage to the Prince of Silberstadt-Schreckenstein (James, 1984a, pp. 103–106). The landscape is not unlike Schreckenstein, but it is drawn into unsavoury relation with the European atmosphere of salacious court gossip and hypocrisy. Once the scene becomes shadowed by its other, the dialogue starts to twist and turn as consciousness neatly parries consciousness, before the exchange peters out in irresolution and implicit dissatisfaction.

The final round of this dialogical sparring is set as slick drawing room comedy on the piazza in front of Mr Wentworth's house. By this time, however, the Baroness's exploitable resources have failed her, while Acton experiments relentlessly with the bait of deceptive half-revelations. Eugenia defensively denies any further reciprocity – and the scene fades out into her imminent departure (James, 1984a, pp. 190–192). Yet the deployment of spatial figuration exceeds this withdrawal into isolated consciousness with the same adaptability as it reincorporates the ghostly laughter of Gertrude's children.

> [Eugenia] found her chief happiness in the sense of exerting a certain power and making a certain impression; and now she felt the annoyance of a rather wearied swimmer who, on nearing shore, to land, finds a smooth straight wall of rock when he had counted upon a clean firm beach. Her power, in the American air, seemed to have lost its prehensile attributes; the smooth wall of rock was insurmountable. (James, 1984a, p. 152)

If this passage carries the suggestion of drowning and oblivion, an impression reinforced by Eugenia's view of the graveyard at the beginning of the narrative, it also refers specifically to the American air as inhospitable and American manners as presenting a blank wall to European talent.[3] But the Baroness is a strong swimmer, only 'rather wearied', and she is 'annoyed' – not alarmed – at the obstacles which face her. The return to Europe may represent extinction from the New England perspective, but it nonetheless offers a more accommodating milieu, albeit on compromised terms. Moreover, the negative discrimination implicitly points in both directions. The rigidity of natural barriers (which perhaps corresponds to the intractability typical of the New England temperament) is clearly resistant to all reasonable human endeavour. So the text of *The Europeans* plays out its own complexities, qualifying and endorsing the Baroness's humiliated suffering, denying dialogue and implicitly relocating its possibilities, opening and foreclosing literal or metaphorical spaces. The narrative's symmetrical comic poise is deceptive, because it subtly masks the centrifugal energy of latent semiotic forces.

II

Whereas *The Europeans* offers both a joyous and a painfully sentient transgression of boundaries within the poised flexibility of its well-made design, the plot of *Washington Square* steadily contracts into the narrow confines of Catherine's consciousness. This movement is searchingly examined in James Gargano's (now dated) discussion of the novel as a 'study in the growth of an inner self' (Gargano, 1976, pp. 355–362), although this frequently penetrating interpretation requires some careful critical reassessment. On the face of it, *Washington Square* includes the usual descriptive gestures of a realist work: Dr Sloper's first house and the custom-built, scientifically designed residence in Washington Square are evoked in all their solid respectability. By contrast, Mrs Almond's family home, full of boisterous activity, is located in a remoter uptown region 'where poplars grew beside the pavement (when there was one), and mingled their shade with the steep roofs of desultory Dutch houses, and where pigs and chickens disported themselves in the gutter' (James, 1984b, p. 40). The rapid commercial growth of the city, as well as its exuberant geographical expansion, is suggestively sketched; the dominant trends towards modernization and social reorientation are effectively brushed in too. Conversely, a backward looking corrective is briefly offered in the form of James's nostalgic reminiscence of his childhood visits to Washington Square, his first nursery school run by its quaintly tea-drinking teacher, and the sensory appeal of his grandmother's home (James, 1984b, pp. 39–40). This autobiographical intrusion, which bypasses the functional role of the narrative voice, initiates the process of overlay, appropriation and rewriting which is to shape and repeatedly displace the text.

Mrs Penniman, with her penchant for sentimental fantasy and her disturbing lack of insight into the ethical risks of self-indulgent fabrication, turns New York into the theatre of a melodrama as soon as Morris Townsend shows signs of interest in Catherine:

> Mrs Penniman delighted of all things in a drama, and she flattered herself that a drama would now be enacted. Combining as she did the zeal of the prompter with the impatience of the spectator, she had long since done her utmost to pull up the curtain. She too expected to figure in the performance – to be the confidante, the Chorus, to speak the epilogue. (James, 1984b, pp. 78–79)

She imports the appurtenances of stylized Gothic fiction into the brashly pragmatic context of a New York intent on transacting profitable business; she is thus imaginatively nonplussed when she discovers that 'her niece preferred, unromantically, an interview in a chintz-covered parlor to a sentimental tryst beside a fountain sheeted with dead leaves' (James, 1984b, p. 77). Yet Mrs Penniman's walking of the city in her various assignations with Morris superimposes her perceptions and expectations until, however shakily, New York comes to figure as the locus of romantic transformation. The dialogue with Morris is scripted in clichés and anachronisms, a stage affair which seems to evacuate the utterance of any inter-personal significance and to reduce language to merely citational signification. Nonetheless, a perverse authoring of selves does take place as Mrs Penniman seeks to mould the unpromisingly expedient material of Morris into romantic elevation or to reconstitute Catherine as a stock heroine. In the moment that the text is deconstructed through its comic exorbitance, it is also reanchored in an understated sense of existence as an event of co-being which enforces participation.

The doctor also promotes the processes of textual overlay and appropriation. His outlook is avowedly objective and scientific, although his ruthless interrogation of Morris's sister (Mrs Montgomery) exposes the hollowness of his pretensions through his willingness to trade on spurious paternal devotion. Nonetheless, Dr Sloper's irony and fondness for epigram are perhaps even more effective than Mrs Penniman's melodramatic impulse in reconfiguring the space of the text, since each of its encounters is reformed by a sequence of sharp, self-sufficient semantic reversals. When Mrs Almond raises the possibility of the doctor's accommodating himself to Catherine's proposed marriage to Morris, Sloper responds with smooth assurance: 'Shall a geometrical proposition relent? I am not so superficial', before reminding his favourite sister that geometry treats surfaces profoundly (James, 1984b, p. 137). In abstract terms, the latter claim is apt and convincing, yet the doctor's conduct gives it the lie in the particular instance. His controlling ironic formulations translate the situation of the novel into a rhetorical square, with each of the main characters positioned at one of its corners. Millicent Bell is perceptive in explaining that '*Washington Square* is all about language', although she then proposes that words such as 'clever', 'natural' or 'sincere' are the leading players (Bell, 1991, p. 70). However, the fictional examination is as much concerned with the expression of will through discourse as it is with semantic ambiguity and the imaginative rewriting of the cityscape. Dr Sloper in his ironic mode, Mrs Penniman in her melodramatic effusion, Morris with his chameleonic capacity for urbane persuasion and pastiche, and finally Catherine in her simple linguistic reserve – these four engage in dialogue and contestation along the sides and across the diagonals of the rhetorical square.[4] Each aims at creating his or her preferred system of static equilibrium, but the forces of interaction are dynamic. The square distorts and wavers, realigning its structural co-ordinates, until it is at last absorbed into the recessive privacy of Catherine's consciousness.

The driving motive of the doctor's rhetorical effort is to turn dialogue into monologue, imposing his view irresistibly upon Catherine's psyche. Yet, as in *The Europeans*, the dialogic principle proves too strong, reinstating interchange under the assault of overbearing homogenization. So Dr Sloper contrives an alternative, pseudo-fictional script for reconstituting Catherine in terms of his insistent expectations. He tries to reform her (in both operative senses of the word) through his *transgredience*, or his capacity for seeing her whole existence from the outside in ways which both register and exceed her knowledge of his observation (see Holquist, 1990, pp. 32–33). Nonetheless, Bakhtin sets out two clear and different stages in an author's planning towards creating a character distinct from himself: first identification and empathy, and then a reverse movement of *exotopy* or a return to his own subjective position (see Todorov, 1984, p. 99). Because the doctor proves incapable of identification, despite his frequent demonstration of surgically sharp insight, his undertaking fails. He is not in the end a novelist, projecting a fictional universe which, as Derrida highlights, must depend on

the suspension of reference and even meaning as transcendently understood. Within the frame of *Washington Square* Sloper is a parent and a
medical expert, whose skill in healing is perversely effective only outside of his own family. Moreover, he becomes an unwitting victim of
the ludic self-referentiality of the text when he asserts that he is 'not a
father in an old-fashioned novel' (James, 1984b, p. 93). He is and he is
not. The results of his behaviour are as negative for Catherine as though
he had been a conventional nineteenth-century patriarch. By contrast,
his decisions are subtly more malicious and damning than those taken
by fathers in the familiar melodramatic line, while *Washington Square* is
a more elusive fictional construct than initially appears.

If Dr Sloper's determination to exploit his *transgredience* in relation
to Catherine is stillborn, frustrated by its implicitly monological inclinations, Catherine too becomes aware of the possibilities of her own
transgredient faculty, particularly with regard to her seemingly Olympian
father. Her dialogical interactions are modest and restrained, yet this
should not devalue them (see Gargano, 1976, pp. 356–357). As early as
the party at her cousin's house, she quietly deflects enquiries about her
reaction to Morris, first from Marion and then from the doctor. When
Sloper asks with cultivated irony whether Morris has proposed yet, Catherine plays him at his own game of wittily opaque engagement, first
suggesting that 'perhaps [Morris] will do it the next time', then trumping
her own ace in private with the sparkling rejoinder that Townsend had
indeed proposed and she had refused him (James, 1984b, p. 58). Later
in the conflict, Catherine demonstrates her ethical lucidity by reasoning that her unwillingness to obey her father should deprive her of his
kindness and protection (James, 1984b, p. 146). Here Catherine seeks
to develop an open discussion on an equal footing, effectively obliging
the doctor to terminate it with ironic dismissiveness. However, the pro-
foundest illustration of Catherine's unselfish dialogical aptitude occurs
when she not only pleads the cause of her father's widowed deprivation to Morris, but also makes the anguished disclosure that Sloper
despises her (James, 1984b, pp. 166–167). As Bakhtin contends, it is not
feasible to live the life of a single person in willed isolation from the
contributions of others. Yet Catherine converts the outcome of dialogical co-existence into a painfully unfolded, self-consonant inwardness,
which is nevertheless striated with the attitudes and emotions of her
closest companions.

When Catherine settles down with her fragment of fancywork at the
end of the novel, this does not necessarily suggest that the range of
her consciousness and experience has shrunk in proportion. Nor has

she been accorded a tragic transcendence, which is underwritten by the integrity of her suffering (see Gargano, 1976, p. 362). The rhetorical square has now vanished, partly in consequence of the disappearance of the two male protagonists from the scene. However, the text has also exceeded itself by consuming itself, turning dialogue inside out through refiguring it as the exchanges which have incrementally shaped a particular consciousness. Silence becomes dominant, not as denial or withdrawal, but as an aporetic enactment of *transgredience*, knowledge of the self not only through the other but as the other, the locus of a spectrally reduced conversation.

III

While the narrative of *Washington Square* is consummated in silence, *The Bostonians* is full of the noise of stridently competing voices which break out in the novel's multiple locations. In fact, setting and voice, dialogue and its framing scene, are locked into a productive interplay throughout the novel. So Boston, with its narrow domestic interiors and equally narrow cultural outlook, gives way to New York, the site both of popular egalitarianism and Mrs Burrage's elite assertion of accumulated wealth in the service of cultivated aestheticism. The peaceful shabbiness of Marmion offers a pastoral interlude, only to be replaced (again in both the literal and figurative senses) by the overflowing, vulgar vitality of the Boston Music Hall in the grip of a feminist assembly. Each of these scenes is rich in geographical and cultural specificity, an American space in its own inalienable right. But the spaces are equally filtered and formatted through the ideological debates which they at once host and inflect in their turn. Bakhtin's remark about Dostoevsky's fictional practice seems closely applicable to the James of *The Bostonians*: he thinks 'not in thoughts but in points of view, consciousnesses, voices' (Bakhtin, 1984, p. 93). In this way, the places and the contentious social or political issues are humanized and individualized, once more brought into intricate patterns of dialogical relationship.

Nonetheless, this order of explanation scarcely accounts for the phenomenon of James's adventurously capacious novel. Whereas the neatly defining structure of *The Europeans* is infused with tensions and half-articulated ambiguities, which entice the reader into playful variations on its alternative possibilities for textualization, *The Bostonians* for all its amplitude bursts its seams in sheer exuberance, overflowing the containment of any informing design. This may constitute the formal dimension of Sara Blair's argument that the broadest concerns of *The Bostonians* entail the challenge of building a viable 'national culture' (Blair, 1998, 152). David Howard's approach takes the angle of 'union', the Union of North and South and the union of man and woman (or perhaps two women?) being the most obvious examples. Yet Howard records that James's attempt at writing 'a very American tale' had led him to recognize his production of a very 'curious' one (Howard, 1972, pp. 60–61 and 80). In short, *The Bostonians* resists even the most attractive invitations to thematic, cultural and formal unity – or even the semantically related notion of union. Instead, scenes and discourses are juxtaposed to one another, each shadowing and commenting on the others while retaining its individuality. Ultimately, though, the parts exceed the whole in keeping with the kind of Derridean literary singularity, which both confirms and overrules generic criteria.

One way of exploring these features of the novel is to concentrate on a specific illustration, the episode at Marmion when Olive fears that Verena has either absconded or been drowned in her boating expedition with Ransom. The first phase of her search is drenched in the pure light of the northern coastline.

> She went very far, keeping in the lonely places, unveiling her face to the splendid light, which seemed to make a mock of the darkness and bitterness of her spirit. There were little sandy coves, where the rocks were clean, where she made long stations, sinking down in them as if she hoped she should never rise again. (James, 1966, p. 353)

This is Olive's journey to her Calvary. Although the description is shot through with the spotless illumination of the summer seascape, Olive is in soundless dialogue with past and future events; she has certainly gone very far. A vast moral and metaphysical emptiness yawns in relation to the safe confinement of her parlour in Boston, the setting for her most fulfilling closeness to Verena and the protected nerve-centre of her feminist planning. The passage clearly elicits a metaphorical reading too, since the dazzling light in which Olive cannot see is translated into the darkness of vision at her holiday house. Here she finds Verena, just as she has realized the utter desolation of losing her through death rather than an abandonment of the feminist cause. The two women engage in a wordless dialogue of erotic touch as night gathers, a dialogue which simultaneously restores and attenuates their bond under the aspect of an engulfing shame. That notion is repeated three times, relentlessly, poetically and ambiguously (James, 1966, pp. 356–357).[5] It is Verena's shame for being so intensely drawn to Ransom's assertive male attract-iveness, for beginning to accept that she may be just that 'inflated little figure (very remarkable in its way too), whom [she has] invented and set on its feet, pulling strings, behind it, to make it move and speak, while [she tries] to efface [herself] there' (James, 1966, p. 293). This citation automatically haunts the holiday cottage with the disturbingly delight-ful encounter in New York's Central Park and all those other encounters with Ransom in the woods and on the beaches at Marmion. The dark-ness is full of Verena's ghosts. But the shame belongs to Olive too for her intransigent possessiveness and her purchase of Verena in slave fashion from her family.

The idea of 'shame' becomes a useful tool for prizing out some of the complex interconnections within the novel. Although the word immediately suggests a loss of honour or disgrace in the eyes of oth-ers, it also carries the implication of guilt or self-condemnation for one's own failings. Presumably, Verena is ashamed of her near-desertion of the feminist project, just as she acknowledges her incipient and closely intertwined betrayal of Olive. So 'shame' is positioned on the cusp between the public and the private, a distinction which comes to carry considerable weight in *The Bostonians*. While Ransom admits to shame regarding his inability to earn a satisfactory income, he is also dogged by a veiled shame at the conclusive defeat of the South. Conversely, there are figures who are ostentatiously shameless: Mat-thias Pardon in his function as gossip columnist and Selah Tarrant with his mania for publicity.[6] The awareness of shame plays itself out in the narrative organization of the text too. If Olive and Verena stand arm in arm, watching the stars come out on a wintry Boston night, the curtains are drawn when they turn back at tea-time to pursue the history of women's oppression. The implication of pos-sible lesbian desire is left unelaborated (Shaheen, 2005, p. 293). In reviewing these diverse tensions between the public and the private in post-Civil War society, Ian Bell emphasizes the corruption of pos-itive usage until 'the public' comes to be synonymous with publicity (rather than action in the service of the community) and 'the private' with self-interested advancement (rather than personal integrity) (Bell, 1991, pp. 131–144). The drama of the novel goes forward under the impetus of these prevailing ambiguities. An encounter of excoriating intimacy between Olive and Verena takes its unique shape because the ambivalence of the public has blended with the private, usurp-ing psychic space and striking Verena as dumb as Ransom might have wished, although for the opposite reason. Binaries are dissolved into distorted communication; debate is often mere babble, while the generative capacity of silent affirmation is transmuted into an admission of defeat.

The Music Hall scene in Boston should deliver the logical fulfilment of events at Marmion, leading private effort to its implied realization as public performance; yet deep suffering explodes into farce, scattering already unstable conceptual and spatial categories. The wordless dialogue between Olive and Verena degenerates into a parody of futile entreaty, while the hastily contrived monologues of substitute speakers are offered to placate the inarticulate disgruntlement of the audience. Spatial valences are reversed too. Whereas Basil's exclusion was previously the measure of his frustration, he is now the vindicated outsider, carrying Verena off in triumphant assurance. Conversely, Olive is thrust on stage, probably to be 'hissed and hooted and insulted' (James, 1966, p. 389) in apparent poetic justice for her coercion of Verena. But even as chaos seems imminent, the text bursts open fresh spatial and dialogical possibilities. Whether Verena and Ransom are headed for New York or the Southern plantation, her tears suggest a different kind of dialogue which will challenge Basil's claims, transforming liberation into a sad constraint not unlike her mother's failed marriage. Olive, on the other hand, meets a public silence, which may signal either impending humiliation or a new kind of political dialogue as compensation for the loss of Verena. James has honoured the contract of creative *exotopy* to the extent that his characters are on the verge of authoring themselves in a proliferation of textual singularities.

IV

The writing of *The American Scene* began 24 years after the publication of *The Bostonians*. The tone of this commentary is far from exuberant, but initially tentative, self-doubting and circumspect. Yet the concerns which James examines and the techniques that he deploys serve as an instructive reflection on his engagement with both American space and textual spaces. As he approaches New York after his extended absence, James muses that treating such an unfamiliar milieu will be 'a matter of prodigious difficulty and selection – in consequence of which there might be a certain recklessness in the largest surrender to impressions' (James, 1968, p. 3). This cautious optimism is qualified when he reaches Baltimore in the less accessible South and conceives himself as a 'lone visionary, betrayed and arrested in the very act of vision'. One of his solutions is to let his perception establish itself 'by a wild logic of its own', thus relying on his writerly sensibility even at the risk of sub-mitting himself to self-serving pseudo-dialogical relations (James, 1968, pp. 306–308). And James frequently struggles. Commercial transactions have accelerated beyond his wildest expectations, skyscrapers tower over cities, rapid rail travel has become the norm and European immigration is in full swing. New York becomes a test of both his tolerance and his sensitivity, as he tries to fathom the cultural difference of the Jewish quarter on the East Side, or finds himself an alien in the Bowery Theatre, where he misses the boisterously good-natured Irish audiences of his adolescence. When imaginative engagement fails, though, James quite frequently resorts to a process of fictionalization to forge links with his current context. In Newport as one of the holiday haunts of his youth, for example, he addresses the genteel streets as timid little old ladies, while in New Jersey he commiserates with the rapidly built, ostentatious villas on their embarrassing awareness of temporariness and inadequacy (James, 1968, pp. 215 and 11).[7] When there is a story to be told, James is in his element; he finds the appropriate intellectual purchase, probing his circumstances with a restored, yet subtle, confidence.

The visit to Charleston in South Carolina encapsulates the complex-ity of James's finely modulated responsiveness, once he has fashioned a chain of malleable interactive modalities with his environment. He has never before been this far south, so he contemplates with something of a thrill 'the Battery of the long, curved sea-front, of the waterside public garden furnished with sad old historic guns, with live oaks draped in trail-ing moss . . .'. Moreover, the scene contracts telescopically as he recalls the famous siege of Fort Sumter near the mouth of the bay during the Civil War. Predictably, a virtual dialogue is launched and a story unfolds as James deftly tests and interprets the judgement of a Northern friend: 'Filled as I am, in general, while there . . . with the sadness and sorrow of the South, I never, at Charleston, look out to the betrayed Forts without feeling my heart harden again to steel.' Compassion is interfused with venerable hostilities in this revealing *microdialogue*, which distils a multi-plicity of opposing regional values and prejudices. Even as he is haunted by the romance of this unusually evocative chronotope, though, James embraces the pastness of the conflict, which has interfused and condi-tioned the present: 'the smitten face, however flushed and scarred, was out of sight . . .'. Then comes the movement of reconciliation and rein-tegration: 'The Forts, faintly blue on the twinkling sea, looked like vague marine flowers; innocentness, pleasantness ruled the prospect; it was as if the compromised slate, sponged clean of all the wicked words and hung up on the wall for better use, dangled there so vacantly as almost to look foolish'(James, 1968, pp. 412–414). The conclusion is vitiated by a hint of glibness, by too easy a return to the comfort of nature, by a tired metaphor and an incipiently facile moral reduction of convoluted human motivations to 'wickedness'. Yet James as 'restless analyst' (a term which recurs throughout the Charleston chapter) is alive to the rich complexity of relations which invites and eludes his grasp, making discrimination a potentially arbitrary affair and implicitly exposing any reading to repeated reformulations.

Later in the day, James enjoys hot chocolate, sandwiches and 'Lady Baltimore' cake at the quaintly named Exchange, while reviewing the strange 'feminization' of a South which still seems devoid of men decades after the severe losses of the Civil War. In spite of his receptiveness to the 'tea-house' as a theatre that 'really contained . . . the elements of history, tragedy, comedy, irony', James is unsentimental in his estimation of the unrelieved devastation of these states. He traces it clear-sightedly to a 'mono-maniacal' attitude that insisted on conquest and the shrunken system of human rights which permitted slavery; he laments the ossification of searching social thought which has left W. E. B. du Bois's *The Souls of Black Folk* as the only significant book produced in years (see James, 1968, pp. 416–419). Although Ross Posnock over-estimates James's political acumen, especially with regard to racial policy (see Posnock, 1998, pp. 237–244), there can be little question that his return to the continent of his birth has put him in touch with the fluid ambivalences of a radically transformed United States, a country which is still coming into being and exploring a range of futures, just as it must negotiate both the accomplishments and the daunting failures of its past.

On his journey to Charleston, James is briefly stranded at an isolated railway station in the darkness of the small hours. As he waits for his train, he speculates on the implications of his having begun to 'wander', and out of obscurity a vision of 'the Margin' emerges.

> The sense of the size of the Margin, that was the name of it – the Margin by which the total of American life, huge as it already appears, is still so surrounded as to represent, for the mind's eye on a general view, but a scant central flotilla huddled as for very fear of the fathomless deep water, the too formidable future, on the so much vaster lake of the materially possible. . . . The fact that, with so many things present, so few of them are not on the way to become quite other, and possibly altogether different, things, conduces to the peculiar interest and, one often feels tempted to add, to the peculiar irritation of the country. (James, 1968, pp. 401–402)

Wandering and wondering, a margin as spatial in both the geographical and textual senses, but also carrying suggestive temporal connotations.... This extract is written very much in James's late manner, with its constant pauses, qualifications and self-reflexive turns. It is a meditation on the bewilderment, mystery and apparently limitless opportunity of the American future. It also reaches for the materiality of 'things', the local, cultural and personal specificities which are too richly numerous to encompass. Yet the piece aptly captures the themes of this essay, guided as it has been by notions of dialogue, fictionalization and textuality. For James the local acquires its fullest resonance only when it has been refracted through consciousness – in fact, multiple consciousnesses in converse with one another – and subjected to the pressure of textual exploration. And the text becomes a new and almost infinitely accommodating space, at once marking its conventional limits and exceeding restraint in an exorbitance of literary singularity.

From a stylistic perspective, *The American Scene* engagingly marks James's growing affinity with postmodern experimentation, preoccupied as the commentary is with the making, unmaking and remaking of textual and physical spaces. The narrative repeatedly shifts or blurs the boundaries between intellectual or emotional states and concretely identified places. As questioning meta-enquiries emerge, the everyday world is felt to be increasingly dependent on linguistic conventions and structures – in the extreme for James, perhaps no more than a spectral linguistic construct. Absences encroach and hollow out presences which would otherwise resist interrogation, as in the unfolding of the Charleston episode. In this climate of uncertainty, the landscape of the text sometimes implicitly, sometimes wilfully, exposes its ripeness for reinterpretation through the continuing dissemination of vulnerable significations. In this last of his American spaces, James at once affirms and renews his modern-postmodern literary endeavour, while opening out still further prospects for the future.

Notes

1. Robert Emmet Long offers a useful elaboration of this theme in *The Great Succession: Henry James and the Legacy of Hawthorne* (1979, pp. 57–58).
2. David K. Danow reviews the work of several scholars who question the assumption that dialogue will by its very occurrence deliver positive and healing results for the participants. There is an opportunity for dialogical exchange between a torturer and his victim too (see Danow, 1991, pp. 132–136).
3. In an often ingenious article on 'staging whiteness and postcolonial ambivalence' in *The Europeans*, Chamika Kalupahana argues that Eugenia cannot

succeed in New England because her exoticism and questionable whiteness compromise her in relation to prevailing American norms and colonial ambitions. However, the evidence advanced for doubting Eugenia's 'whiteness' seems superficial (Kalupahana, 2003, pp. 119–135).
4. This account of the linguistic patterning of *Washington Square* comes closer to an earlier reading by Millicent Bell published in the *Sewanee Review* (see M. Bell, 1975, pp. 19–38).
5. Kenneth Graham gives a nuanced interpretation of this scene in terms of Olive's *Liebestod* (see Graham, 1988, pp. 50–52).
6. David Kramer provides insight into the pervasive rhetoric of 'newspaper making', as well as the masculine rivalries that are enacted in the novel (Kramer, 1998, pp. 139–147).
7. John Carlos Rowe has noted James's effective use of prosopopeia, while Gert Buelens comments shrewdly on his capacity for stimulating awareness by attributing human characteristics to the inanimate (see Rowe, 1985, pp. 214–215 and Buelens, 2000, pp. 210–214).

Works cited

Bakhtin, M. M., *The Dialogic Imagination*. Ed. M. Holquist (Austin: University of Texas Press, 1981).
——, *Problems of Dostoevsky's Poetics*. Ed. C. Emerson (Manchester: Manchester University Press, 1984).
Bell, I. F. A., *Henry James and the Past: Readings into Time* (London: Macmillan, 1991).
Bell, M., 'Style as Subject: *Washington Square*', *Sewanee Review*, 83 (1975) 19–38.
——, *Meaning in Henry James* (Cambridge, MA: Harvard University Press, 1991).
Blair, S., 'Realism, Culture, and the Place of the Literary: Henry James and *The Bostonians*', in *The Cambridge Companion to Henry James*. Ed. J. Freedman (Cambridge: Cambridge University Press, 1998), pp. 151–168.
Buelens, G., 'Pleasurable "Presences": Sites, Buildings and "Aliens" in James's *American Scene*', *Texas Studies in Literature and Language*, 42.4 (2000) 408–430.
Childs, P., *Modernism* (London and New York: Routledge, 2000).
Danow, D. K., *The Thought of Mikhail Bakhtin: From Word to Culture* (London: Macmillan, 1991).
Derrida, J., 'Signature Event Context', in *Margins of Philosophy*. Trans. A. Bass (Brighton: Harvester Press, 1982[a]), pp. 307–330.
——, 'White Mythology: Metaphor in the Text of Philosophy', in *Margins of Philosophy*. Trans. A. Bass (Brighton: Harvester Press, 1982[b]), pp. 207–271.
——, '"This Strange Institution Called Literature": Interview with Derek Attridge', in *Acts of Literature*. Ed. D. Attridge (London: Routledge, 1992), pp. 33–75.
Gargano, J. W., '*Washington Square*: A Study in the Growth of an Inner Self', *Studies in Short Fiction*, 13.3 (1976) 355–362.
Graham, K., *Indirections of the Novel: James, Conrad, and Forster* (Cambridge: Cambridge University Press, 1988).
Holquist, M., *Dialogism: Bakhtin and His World* (London: Routledge, 1990).

Howard, D., '*The Bostonians*', in *The Air of Reality: New Essays on Henry James*. Ed. J. Goode (London: Methuen, 1972), pp. 60–80.

Hutcheon, L., *A Poetics of Postmodernism: History, Theory, Fiction* (New York and London: Routledge, 1988).

James, H., 'Preface to *Roderick Hudson*', in *The Art of the Novel*. Ed. R. P. Blackmur (New York: Charles Scribner's Sons, 1962), pp. 3–19.

———, *The American Scene*. Ed. L. Edel (London: Rupert Hart-Davis, 1968) [first published: 1907].

———, *The Bostonians* (Harmondsworth, Middlesex: Penguin, 1966) [first published: 1886].

———, *The Europeans*. Ed. T. Tanner (Harmondswoth, Middlesex: Penguin, 1984[a]) [first published: 1878].

———, *Washington Square*. Ed. B. Lee (Harmondsworth, Middlesex: Penguin, 1984[b]) [first published: 1880].

Kalupahana, C., ' "*Les beaux jours sont* passés": Staging Whiteness and Postcolonial Ambivalence in *The Europeans* by Henry James', *Canadian Review of American Studies*, 33.2 (2003) 119–138.

Kramer, D., 'Masculine Rivalry in *The Bostonians*: Henry James and the Rhetoric of "Newspaper Making" ', *Henry James Review*, 19.2 (1998) 139–147.

Long, R. E., *The Great Succession: Henry James and the Legacy of Hawthorne* (Pittsburgh, PA: University of Pittsburgh Press, 1979).

Posnock, R., 'Affirming the Alien: The Pragmatist Pluralism of *The American Scene*', in *The Cambridge Companion to Henry James*. Ed. J. Freedman (Cambridge: Cambridge University Press, 1998), pp. 151–168.

Rowe, J. C., *The Theoretical Dimensions of Henry James* (London: Methuen, 1985).

Shaheen, A., ' "The Social Dusk of That Mysterious Democracy": Race, Sexology, and the New Woman in Henry James's *The Bostonians*', *American Transcendentalist Quarterly*, 19.4 (2005) 281–298.

Todorov, T., *Mikhail Bakhtin: The Dialogical Principle*. Ed. W. Godzich (Minneapolis: University of Minnesota Press, 1984).

Waugh, P., *Metafiction: The Theory and Practice of Self-Conscious Fiction* (London and New York: Routledge, 1984).

3
Space and Place in the Novels of E. M. Forster

Gail Fincham

Introduction

> Space, understood in its most primitive sense (a distance to be crossed, an openness between points, one of which is occupied by a perceiving subject, filled by something, sunlight, moonlight, hot dust, cold mud or emptiness) seems omnipresent in literature, but rather hard to place. There doesn't seem to be a vocabulary sufficiently capacious to discuss space. You may talk about deictics, copresence, coordination, distances, surfaces, exteriors, interiors, volume and plasticity, but the units of measurement are lacking: literary space, in being conceptual, cannot be measured, but it can be experienced. It is this experience that leads us to claim that space is invariably present in fiction though never precisely so. (Wilson, 1995, p. 215)

For E.M. Forster, individuals' experience of space, in the places in which his novels are set, is simultaneously geographical, cultural and psychological. Eudora Welty insists: '[Forster] must surely have strengthened my recognition of place as a prime source of enlightenment in fiction. He gave me help, help not abstract, but directly useful towards identifying in place my own most trustworthy teacher' (Welty, in Herz and Martin, 1982, p. 199). For Forster, place can enable growth and imaginative transformation. Though his fictional and non-fictional outputs span disparate genres,[1] I believe that there is more to connect than divide his writing. One way to illustrate this is to demonstrate a pattern of constriction and expansion – containerised space versus free space – which is striking in all the novels until *Howards End* and *A Passage to India,* and may also be found in the short stories and essays.[2] I return to the opening quotation

38

of this chapter, 'literary space, in being conceptual, cannot be measured, but it can be experienced'. I will argue that protagonists' experience of space in Forster's novels is always significant. But, whereas in the novels preceding *Howards End* and *A Passage to India* free spaces or places exist, in these last two works the experience of space becomes increasingly fraught for both the author and the fictional protagonists. Culturally and ideologically, Forster's imagination can no longer envisage the free spaces which his earlier novels celebrate. In his last two novels, the forces of capitalism and imperialism crowd out the possibilities of the liberal humanist world-view.

Constriction versus expansion in the novels up to *Howards End*

Before *Howards End* and *A Passage to India*, a pattern of free space versus constricted space strikingly recurs in Forster's short stories and novels. This free space allows both Forster and his fictional protagonists to escape the constraints of suburbia. I begin with *The Longest Journey*, frequently claimed as the most autobiographical of Forster's fictions. The novel is built around a tripartite structure ('Cambridge', 'Sawston' and 'Wiltshire') that anticipates *A Passage's* 'Mosque', 'Caves' and 'Temple'. It opens in Cambridge, with Ansell's philosophical challenge about the cow, which either *is* there or *is not* there. For Ansell, the brilliant son of a working-class father, Cambridge is arguably a place of imaginative expansion. He gets a first in the Moral Science Tripos and is elected to a Fellowship. But Rickie (like his author) gets only a 'creditable second' in the classical Tripos. Cambridge, which had 'taken and soothed him, and warmed him, and . . . laughed at him a little, saying that he must not be so tragic yet awhile, for his boyhood had been but a dusty corridor that led to the spacious halls of youth' (Forster, 1907, p. 10), can only be an interlude. Its significance for him is in any case ambiguous. For Rickie (as for Forster himself) Cambridge represents both psychic growth and psychic constriction. Stoll's psychoanalytic reading notes: '[For Rickie] Cambridge prolongs adolescence and fosters dependency even as, to use Lacan's term, it provides him with a renewed sense of himself in admitting him to the "symbolic" order of masculine society . . . In his rooms at Cambridge, which he loves "better than any person", Rickie feels "almost as safe as he felt once when his mother killed a ghost in the passage by carrying him through it in her arms"' (Stoll, 1995, p. 36). So his rooms at Cambridge are a place of retreat where Rickie can enact the struggles with identity which result from his unresolved relation to his parents.

There are however two spaces or places where Rickie can achieve imaginative transcendence. Both demonstrate that the self is constituted in and through language. There is The Dell, outside Madingley, a magical site of creativity for Rickie, and the Cadbury Rings. Both are connected with speech and self-identity. The Dell, which Rickie discovers in his second term at Cambridge, becomes for him 'a kind of church – a church where indeed you could do anything you liked, but where everything you did would be transfigured' (Forster, 1907, p. 25). By no coincidence, it is in the Dell that he tells his life-story to his undergraduate friends. Another place of escape and imaginative growth is the Cadbury Rings in Wiltshire, sanctified by its connection with the dead. Based on the Figsbury Rings, an Iron Age earthworks about which Forster wrote in his diary and which are associated with the rare Chalk Blue Butterflies, the Rings in Wiltshire are connected with the rustic past,[3] for they are 'the resting place of common soldiers and farmers, who died in defending their homes' (Stoll, 1995, p. 32). It is at the Rings that Rickie first learns that Stephen Wonham is his brother and at the railway level crossing close to the Rings that he rescues, at the cost of his own life, his drunken brother from the rails. And although Rickie's escapes first to the Dell and then to the Rings are short-lived (because he dies) his memory is celebrated at the end of the novel in the 'ingenious pastoral coda' (Colmer, 1982, p. 119) in which Stephen Wonham can escape marital entrapment in his wife's bed by going out into the woods with his little daughter, to sleep under the stars. To his daughter, he has given the name of both his and Stephen's mother.

In the Italian novels, the reader moves from the authorial anxieties foregrounded in Stoll's analysis to the authorial imperatives implicit in satire. Here Forster the essayist, the creator of 'What I Believe' (Forster, 1951) is anticipated. He can laugh at his countrymen and women, they of the 'undeveloped heart', because he wants them to shed their parochialism and join that 'aristocracy of the sensitive, the considerate and the plucky [whose] members are to be found in all nations and classes' (Forster, 1951, p. 82). Though in the Italian novels his travellers' attempts to transform themselves through tourism are generally doomed, Forster continues to yearn for the imaginative awakening made possible by exposure to other countries, other cultures. This dream of cultural, social and sexual liberation is reflected in his own guide-book on Alexandria, home of the poet Cavafy and site of Forster's liberation as a homosexual. Italy provides a particular challenge to timid English protagonists, for, as Ian Littlewood remarks,

For Forster, as for a long line of tourists from Goethe onwards, the meaning of the Italian journey lay in its seductive invitation to recognise aspects of himself that had been suppressed at home...The sensual tones of Italy – its landscape, its climate, its sexual tolerance – expressed a world of possibilities that stood in direct opposition to the deadly proprieties of suburban England (pp. 87–88)....When the sunlight and sensuality of the Mediterranean countries go to work, it is a whole class-bound English culture of grey skies and lace curtains that they undermine. (Littlewood, 2001, p. 105)

The Mediterranean setting becomes, for Forster's protagonists, what Bohemia is for Rhys's heroines. But the important difference is that Forster's travellers are comfortably middle class, able to afford rooms with views.

In the Italian novels, Forster's satire is directed at his characters' imbrication in the culture of the Baedeker guidebook. Baedeker's *Italy from the Alps to Naples* of 1904 – on which Forster probably drew for *Where Angels Fear to Tread* (Forster, 1905) and *A Room with a View* (Forster, 1908) – makes entertaining reading. The train compartment in *Where Angels Fear to Tread*, in which the suffering Harriet (who insists on leaning out of windows and so continually gets smuts in her eyes) travels to Central Italy, must surely have been first class, for Baedeker states that 'the first class is more used than in most other countries, especially when ladies are of the party'. But it is when we approach the arena of culture that Forster's mockery of Baedeker becomes most insistent. In Section VI of the Introduction, dedicated to 'Churches, Museums, Theatres, Shops', the Baedeker guidebook informs the traveller interested in attending an Italian opera performance that 'the pit (*platéa*) to which the *biglietto d'ingresso* admits, has standing-room only. For the reserved seats and stalls (*poltrone, posti distinti*) additional tickets must be taken at the door. A box (*pálco,* where evening dress is usual), which should be secured in advance, is the best place for ladies or for a party.' When Philip Herriton takes Harriet and Caroline to a performance of *Lucia Di Lammermoor*, in the little town of Monteriano where they have come to 'rescue' the baby Lilia has produced by the Italian Gino Carelli, they have no evening clothes, and the opera performance is an amateurish local production. Nevertheless the evening is inspired. Philip ends up, after enthusiastic greetings from Gino, being pulled into his box from the stalls where he has been sitting with his party:

Philip had whispered introductions to the pleasant people who had pulled him in – tradesmen's sons perhaps they were, or medical students, or solicitors' clerks, or sons of other dentists. There is no knowing who is who in Italy. The guest of the evening was a private soldier. He shared the honour now with Philip. The two had to stand side by side in the front, and exchange compliments, whilst Gino presided, courteous, but delightfully familiar. Philip would have a spasm of horror at the muddle he had made. But the spasm would pass, and again he would be enchanted by the kind, cheerful voices, the laughter that was never vapid, and the light caress of the arm across his back. (Forster, 1905, p. 107)

Such mixing would surely have dismayed Baedeker, concerned as he is to protect the English from the predations of the Italian working class:

Drivers, gondoliers, porters and their congeners are all more importunate than in northern countries, and noisily besiege the traveller who approaches their stations. Having chosen a carriage or a boat, he should name his destination (e.g. *Duomo, all-Isola Bella*, etc., *quanta volete?*) and ask for the tariff (*la tariffa*). The fewest words are best, and signs are even better understood, while tact and good temper go a long way. (Baedeker, 1904, p. xxi)[4]

Baedeker does not forbid social mingling with Italians, of course, but his conscientious shepherding of the English abroad continually reasserts their class separation from what they are observing. What Philip experiences at the opera in Monteriano is, by contrast, a breaking down of class barriers amongst people who are both ignorant of and indifferent to the values which constitute identity in suburban Sawston. No wonder that in *A Room with a View* the only escapee from English middle-class mediocrity – Lucy Honeychurch, who ends up marrying the unconventional George Emerson – is parted from her guidebook, in a chapter ominously entitled 'In Santa Croce with no Baedeker'.

A Room with a View, whose very title illustrates the pattern of constriction and escape, has an unambiguous moral schema. As John Beer remarks:

the main theme is familiar and presents no difficulties to the commentator. We have simply to see George [Emerson] as protagonist of Life, Cecil [Vyse] of Art, and Miss Bartlett of Anti-Life, for the main struggle of the novel to be evident. Lucy thinks that she loves Cecil, being ashamed of her franker love for George. Cecil, who thinks that he loves Lucy, really loves her as a work of art, not as a person. (Beer, 1968, p. 55)

The contrast between Cecil and George is brought out in two key passages (also quoted by Beer). The first is a conversation between Lucy and her fiancé Cecil occurring in a chapter subtitled 'Lucy as a Work of Art':

'I had got an idea – I dare say wrongly – that you feel more at home with me in a room.'

'A room?' she echoed, hopelessly bewildered.

'Yes. Or, at the most, in a garden or on a road. Never in the real country like this.'

. . .

She reflected a moment, and then said laughing:

'. . . When I think of you it's always as in a room. How funny!'

To her surprise, he seemed annoyed.

'A drawing-room, pray? With no view?'

'Yes, with no view, I fancy. Why not?'

'I'd rather,' he said reproachfully, 'that you connected me with the open air.' (Forster, 1910, p. 114)

A contrasting passage is the joyous epiphany in a chapter subtitled 'The Reverend Arthur Beebe, the Reverend Cuthbert Eager, Mr. Emerson, Mr. George Emerson, Miss Eleanor Lavish, Miss Charlotte Bartlett, and Miss Lucy Honeychurch, Drive out in Carriages to see a View. Italians Drive Them.' Lucy, who has lost Mr Beebe and Mr Eager and anxiously enquires of the driver *'Dove buoni homini?'*, misses her footing and falls into a field of violets:

Light and beauty enveloped her. She had fallen onto a little open terrace, which was covered with violets from end to end.

'Courage!' cried her companion, now standing some six feet above. 'Courage and love.'

She did not answer. From her feet the ground sloped sharply into the view, and violets ran down in rivulets and streams and cataracts, irrigating the hill-side with blue, eddying round the tree stems, collecting into pools in the hollows, covering the grass with spots of azure foam. But never again were they in such profusion; this terrace was the wellhead, the primal source whence beauty gushed out to water the earth.

Standing at its brink, like a swimmer who prepares, was the good man. But he was not the good man that she had expected, and he was alone.

George had turned at the sound of her arrival. For a moment he contemplated her, as one who had fallen out of heaven. He saw radiant joy in her face, he saw the flowers beat against her dress in blue waves. The bushes above them closed. He stepped quickly forward and kissed her. (Forster, 1910, p. 75)

The contrast between the passages, and the symbolism of constricting space versus edenic freedom, requires no commentary.

Howards End begins and ends with the Greenwood England of the wych-elm and the hay, the poppies and vine-leaves of the house called 'Howards End'. Connected with the past, with rural tranquillity, and with Forster's own rural past at Rook's Nest, Stevenage, the house is, for both old Mrs Wilcox and later for Helen Schlegel, a 'spirit rather than a place' (HE, p. 94). This vision of a pastoral England recalls that described by Forster in 'The Abinger Pageant':

Houses and bungalows, hotels, restaurants and flats, arterial roads, bypasses, petrol pumps and pylons – are these going to be England? Are these man's final triumph? Or is there another England, Green and eternal, which will outlast them? I cannot tell you, I am only the Woodman, but this land is yours, and you can make it what you will. (quoted by Delany, 1995, p. 72)

That this pastoral vision is contrasted with the 'red rust' of London – the sprawling city which consumes and commodifies and instrumentalises – is clear. But the pattern of enclosure and escape traced in the earlier novels has now become complex and ambiguous. The novel's narrative perspectives are complicated by a split between authorial omniscience and figural focalisation, which prefigures the subversion of authorial omniscience so striking in *A Passage*.[5] Malcolm Bradbury, in a still influential reading, sees *Howards End* as 'about the circumstances in which the moral life, which is also the full life of the imagination, can be led in society, about the compromises which it must effect with itself if it is to do so, and about the moral and imaginative value of making certain compromises' (Bradbury, 1966, p. 130). The question the novel asks, according to Bradbury, is: who shall inherit England? But even in Bradbury's positive reading, Margaret Schlegel's famous sermon 'Only Connect' remains a desideratum rather than an achieved fact: 'Forster has realized throughout the action that his central character – and his own voice as commentator – can be criticised both from the point of view of the vast reaches of the infinite and by the impersonal process of history. Both are belittled by the future; both are ironically placed' (Bradbury, 1966, p. 142). David Medalie takes a more materialist view of the historical processes enacted in the novel:

> For all the concern in *Howards End* with ephemerality, depletion and sad alteration, here is the frank recognition that among the most intransigent of social phenomena is the fact that those who have money tend to cling to it and that conditions of privilege tend to renew themselves. Capitalism, according to Margaret's diagnosis, is made up of exploitation and envy; it requires, too, the brutal premise that only a small section of the population will ever be able to find a place on terra firma. (Medalie, 2002, p. 11)

Jeremy Tambling similarly sees the novel as linking capitalist commodification with imperial exploitation: 'The rentier class represented by the Wilcoxes is involved with imperialist projects abroad (e.g. Paul Wilcox works in Nigeria and the novel refers to India and South Africa); its capital goes overseas ... A consequence of capital going overseas [is] the increase of working-class poverty' (Tambling, 1995, p. 78). In Medalie's and Tambling's views, then, *Howards End* already registers the political and cultural impasse – the lack of spaces into which protagonists can escape – that I argue is central to Forster's depiction of the Anglo-Indians in *A Passage to India*.[6]

Constriction in *A Passage to India*

In *A Passage to India* (1924), the leitmotifs of containment and enclosure I have sketched as evident in the earlier novels become insistent, recurring on almost every page. The novel's narrative structure graphically dramatises Wilson's remarks quoted at the opening of this chapter on space as 'a distance to be crossed, an openness between points, one of which is occupied by a perceiving subject, filled by something, sunlight, moonlight, hot dust, cold mud or emptiness'. Both the title of *A Passage to India* and Adela's project of seeing 'the real India' draw the reader's attention to distances to be crossed, as well as to the gaps or spaces between geographical locations. The contrast between free space and regulated space is insistently foregrounded from the first sentence of the first chapter, which moves from the city of Chandrapore to the far-off, tantalising Caves: 'Except for the Marabar Caves – and they are twenty miles off – the city of Chandrapore presents nothing extraordinary.' Dominating the novel physically and symbolically, the Caves are, from the start, mysteriously distant and disturbing. Wilson's 'sunlight, moonlight, hot dust, cold mud or emptiness' also finds echoes in this novel. The pivotal scene between Aziz and Mrs Moore plays out in moonlight, whereas blinding sunshine and hot dust characterise the climactic season in which Aziz is brought to trial. Wilson maintains that 'literary space, in being conceptual, cannot be measured, but it can be experienced.' *A Passage* graphically dramatises the unease of the colonial situation, where for coloniser and colonised alike interaction in the politically and culturally compromised space of the Raj produces intense emotional trauma.

From the opening chapter Forster juxtaposes culture and nature in ways which undermine the Anglo-Indians' desire to control. The Indian city of Chandrapore resists human aspiration and interpretation: 'Houses do fall, people are drowned and left rotting, but the general outline of the town persists, swelling here, shrinking there, like some low but indestructible form of life' (Forster, 1924, p. 9). Contained within the amorphous Chandrapore is the neatly constructed Anglo-Indian Civil Station: 'sensibly planned, with a red-brick club on its brow, and farther back a grocer's and a cemetery'. Its bungalows are built along roads intersecting at right angles, and its appearance is acceptable if uninspiring: 'It has nothing hideous in it, and only the view is beautiful; it shares nothing with the city except the overarching sky' (p. 10). In this carefully contained space, English culture determinedly harnesses Indian nature: 'viewed hence Chandrapore appears to be a totally different place. It is a city of gardens. It is no city, but a forest sparsely scattered with huts. It is a tropical pleasaunce washed by a noble river' (Forster, 1924, p. 9). In the spaces of the Club, the bungalows of the Turtons and the Burtons and the court-room where Aziz is brought to trial, the xenophobia and racial hatred of the Raj are played out. Here surely the moral and physical constriction of Sawston in the English novels is writ large. As Kuchta remarks:

Like [Leonard] Woolf, whose autobiography records his gradual dis-illusionment with imperialism, Forster, Waugh and Orwell distance themselves from Britain's *mission civilatrice* by deriding colonial soci-ety as unforgivably suburban. Cataloguing the clichés of villadom with particular venom, their portrayals of imperial civil stations and clubs reflect suburbia's longstanding association with the pretensious and second-rate. (Kuchta, 2003, p. 307)

'Mosque' opens with the Indian protagonists discussing, over their hookahs, whether it is possible to be friends with an Englishman (or woman). Summoned to the Club only to have his tonga seized by Mrs Callendar and Mrs Lesley, Aziz turns for consolation into a mosque at the edge of the Civil Station. Here he meets Mrs Moore, recently escaped from a performance of 'Cousin Kate' at the Club, which she has found stifling. Talking together in the moonlight, Aziz delightedly exclaims, on discovering that he and Mrs Moore have both lost their life partners, 'Is not this the same box with a vengeance?' (Forster, 1924, p. 23). But despite the promise of this large-spirited encounter in the radiance of moonlight, Aziz and Mrs Moore are hardly 'in the same box', since she cannot ask him back to a Club which debars Indians. Subsequent encoun-ters between the English and Anglo-India – like the 'Bridge Party' (which the Collector explains is intended to bridge the gulf between East and West) – are unsuccessful. The Indians are entertained in the Club's gar-dens – 'Hullo! There he goes – smash into our hollyhocks. Pulled the left rein when he meant the right. All as usual' (Forster, 1924, p. 41) – where Adela discovers that although the ladies can speak English ('Eastbourne, Piccadilly, Hyde Park Corner') she cannot engage them in conversation. The narrator, slyly prefiguring the Marabar catastrophe, remarks that Adela 'strove in vain against the echoing walls of their civility' (For-ster, 1924, p. 43). Juxtaposed against this constricted and constricting space of Anglo-India are, once again, the Marabar Hills. Fielding finds Adela in the middle of the Bridge Party 'looking through a nick in the cactus hedge at the distant Marabar Hills, which had crept near, as was their custom at sunset; if the sunset had lasted long enough, they would have reached the town, but it was swift, being tropical' (Forster, 1924, p. 45).

Just as the Marabar Hills remain inaccessible, so does Adela's project of 'seeing the real India' continue to elude her. Surrounded at the Club by parochial, complacent Anglo-Indians, she is determined not to become like them in their insensitivity to India and Indians. But in her mind's eye she has a bleak vision of her future with Ronny Heaslop:

'Yes, Ronny is always hard-worked', she replied, contemplating the hills. How lovely they suddenly were! But she couldn't touch them. In front, like a shutter, fell a vision of her married life. She and Ronny would look into the club like this every evening, then drive home to dress; they would see the Lesleys and the Callendars and the Turtons and the Burtons, and invite them and be invited by them, while the true India slid by unnoticed. Colour would remain – the pageant of birds in the early morning, brown bodies, white turbans, idols whose flesh was scarlet and blue – and movement would remain as long as there were crowds in the bazaar and bathers in the tanks. Perched up on the seat of a dogcart, she would see them. But the force that lies behind colour and movement would escape her even more effectually than it did now. She would see India always as a frieze, never as a spirit, and she assumed that it was a spirit of which Mrs. Moore had had a glimpse.[7] (Forster, 1924, pp. 46–47)

Against this negative epiphany is balanced the endless vistas of Mrs Moore's initial focalisation of India, a vision of horizons that continue to open out: 'Outside the arch there seemed always an arch, beyond the remotest echo a silence' (Forster, 1924, pp. 51–52). But this celebratory vision is directly contradicted post-Marabar, when Mrs Moore, radically demoralised and refusing to participate in Aziz's trial, announces flatly: 'I'll retire to a cave of my own' (Forster, 1924, p. 195) and bitterly denounces 'all this rubbish about love, love in a church, love in a cave, as if there is the least difference' (Forster, 1924, p. 197).

English/Anglo-Indian *rapprochement* occurs sporadically, but cannot be sustained, as in the encounter between Aziz and the nameless subaltern who play polo together on the Maidan – that neat green space created by the Raj for its outdoor entertainment. Goodwill is generated while the equestrians engage with each other on horseback; they part thinking, 'If only they were all like that' (Forster, 1924, p. 57). But they are not, and other spaces for cross-racial intimacy do not exist. Even in the welcoming space of the well-intentioned Fielding's bungalow, reciprocity is short-lived. Fielding's invited guests – Aziz, Mrs Moore, Adela Quested and Godbole – start off discussing why the Indians at the Bridge Party, who had invited the ladies to visit them, never materialise. Anxious to be hospitable, Aziz makes the fatal error of asking the party home to his (one-roomed, fly-ridden) bungalow, and has subsequently to commute the invitation into an expedition to the Marabar Caves. Talk turns to the Hills and Caves. Aziz waxes increasingly loquacious ('flamboyant'), while Godbole's long speech signally fails to explain to the visitors what makes the Caves interesting or significant. Everyone becomes uncomfortable, losing their spontaneity and becoming like stage characters ('A scene from a play, thought Fielding who now saw them from the distance across the garden grouped among the pillars of his beautiful hall' Forster, 1924, p. 76). The chapter closes with Fielding's emotional/ideological focalisation as he considers his guests taking leave: 'Everyone was cross or wretched... Could one have been so petty on a Scottish moor or an Italian alp? Fielding wondered afterwards. There seemed no reserve of tranquillity to draw upon in India. Either none, or else tranquillity swallowed up everything, as it appeared to do for Professor Godbole' (Forster, 1924, p. 77). The chapter ends cryptically, with Godbole's invocation of the god who refuses to come, and the song of the unknown bird.

The next significant containerised space is the Nawab Bahadur's car, which collides with a mysterious creature (goat? buffalo? hyena? human ghost?), sending Adela and Ronny into each other's arms and resulting in Adela's re-instating the engagement she had broken off on the Maidan. But Adela's response here is contradictory. She re-connects with Ronny on the one hand, but on the other registers that now she feels 'labelled', when she 'deprecated labels' (Forster, 1924, p. 91). This oddly revealing little phrase[8] connects with Fielding's thinking: he too wants 'to slink through India unlabelled', to escape categorisation (p. 172). Similarly, long before the Marabar crisis, Adela, resisting the role of colonial wife, announces: 'I won't be bottled up'. She is referring to the practice of sending women and children into the mountains when the hot weather starts; the male administrators choose instead to 'grill in the plains' (Forster, 1924, p. 133). Adela promises Mrs Moore, 'I will fetch you from Simla when it's cool enough. I will unbottle you in fact' (Forster, 1924, p. 135).

Clearly the demoralisation that the Marabar will precipitate has already begun. Adela and Mrs Moore are retreating into themselves: 'Ever since Professor Godbole had sung his queer little song, they had lived more or less inside cocoons' (Forster, 1924, p. 132). Adela's production of psychologically revealing phrases (wanting not to be 'labelled', wanting to be 'unbottled') registers the extent of her repressed anxiety about being squeezed into a compromised and dangerous space. This is repetitively figured in the long train journey to the Marabar. Adela considers 'the Anglo-Indian life she has decided to endure' (Forster, 1924, p. 135), in the confinement of her railway carriage, on the branch-line train slowly winding ('pomper, pomper') through 'dull fields'. About the events – physical or psychic – that take place within the Marabar, enough has already been written. I will limit my observations to pointing out that in chapter 22, while trying to 'think out' the disastrous sequence of events that lead to her collapse and Aziz's arrest, Adela remarks: 'I remember scratching the wall with my finger-nail, to start the usual echo, and then... there was this shadow, or sort of shadow, down the entrance tunnel, *bottling me up*' (Forster, 1924, p. 189). Previously used of the English males who govern India, this phrase is now transferred to Aziz. This is highly significant. Could Adela's reaction to the Marabar catastrophe be a displaced enactment of her repressed rage against European patriarchy whose accidental and inadvertent scapegoat is Aziz?

Just as Adela obsessively thinks about marriage to Ronny Heaslop, and the constrictions of colonial marriage, on the train to the Marabar, so does Mrs Moore, suffering the 'twilight of the double vision' (Forster, 1924, p. 203) while ensconced in the 'swift and comfortable mail-train' returning her to the coast where she will catch her boat home, think about all the places in India that she will never see:

'I have not seen the right places', she thought, as she saw embayed in the platforms of the Victoria Terminus the end of the rails that had carried her over a continent and could never carry her back. She would never visit Asirgarh or the other untouched places; neither Delhi nor Agra nor the Rajputana cities nor Kashmir, nor the obscurer marvels that had sometimes shone through men's speech: the bilingual rock of Girnar, the statue of Shri Belgola, the ruins of Mandu and Hampi, temples of Khajraha, gardens of Shalimar. As she drove through the huge city which the West had built and abandoned with a gesture of despair, she longed to stop, though it was only Bombay, and disentangle the hundred Indias that passed each other in the streets. The feet of the horses moved her on, and presently the boat sailed and thousands of coconut palms appeared all round the anchorage and climbed the hills to wave her farewell. 'So you thought an echo was India: you took the Marabar caves as final?' they laughed. 'What have we in common with them, or they with Asirgarh? Good-bye!' (Forster, 1924, pp. 204–205)

Perhaps the saddest juxtaposition of enclosed space with free space is the burial of Mrs Moore:

Dead she was – committed to the deep while still on the southward track, for the boats from Bombay cannot point towards Europe until Arabia has been rounded; she was further in the tropics than ever achieved while on shore, when the sun touched her for the last time and her body was lowered into yet another India – the Indian Ocean. (Forster, 1924, p. 249)

In a moving sequence (the best imagery he creates in the film is of water) David Lean shows Mrs Moore's burial at sea. As the casket is lowered from the deck into the sea, a voice-over records the words of the Anglican burial service at sea:

> Thou knowest Lord the secrets of our hearts;
> Shut not thy merciful ears to our prayer.
> We therefore commit her body to the deep
> To be turned into corruption,
> Looking for the resurrection of the body.
> And the sea shall give up her dead.
> I heard a voice from heaven saying unto me:
> Blessed are the dead which die in the Lord.

The small casket disappears for ever in the immensity of 'that other India, the Indian Ocean'. Lean's sequence is haunting to the viewer, bringing together the ideas of water as regeneration and destruction. But where Forster's text emphasises geographical and spatial isolation – Mrs Moore's body contained in her coffin and lost in the abyss of the Indian Ocean – Lean's film version of her burial at sea strikingly re-introduces the dimension of the numinous contained in the moving words of the Anglican rite. In the novel, the catastrophic echoes of the Marabar Caves have destroyed Mrs Moore's faith in 'poor, talkative little Christianity', so that her death is recounted in purely secular terms. The film version of her death restores the power and mystery of Christian belief in a way which draws attention to the distance between novelist's and film-maker's perspectives. In the novel, Mrs Moore is given a kind of immortality after her death in the legend which springs up around her name, but it is an immortality imbricated in Indian religion and mythology and entirely removed from Western perspectives. This leads into my final section, where I argue that Forster creates in his depiction of Hindu India the space for expansion that the Raj denies his protagonists.

Coda: Forster's creation of a magic realist space/place in Hindu India

I have argued that the experience of space and place in Forster's novels is of central importance to his protagonists. I have sketched a pattern of constriction or enclosure versus freedom and suggested that this pattern infuses both the short stories and the earlier novels. But where these offer possibilities of escape from restrictive cultures, *Howards End* and *A Passage to India* – Forster's 'modernist' novels – problematise the possibilities of such escape. *A Passage to India* dramatises a situation of radical impasse for the 'liberal humanist' Anglo-Indians Mrs Moore, Adela Quested and Cyril Fielding. David Medalie comments:

> In *A Passage to India*, despite Forster's reputation as the liberal-humanist who spoke for all the century, the implication, albeit couched in wistfulness, is unflinchingly clear: liberal-humanism is no longer *tenable*; there are no longer viable contexts for its articulation. *Howards End* and *A Passage to India* are both about the legacy of loss, its shape and its possibilities. (Medalie, 2002, p. 4)

This is why Benita Parry, who sees the novel as 'at once inheriting and interrogating the discourses of the Raj', calls it 'Forster's epitaph to liberal humanism' (Parry, in Tambling, 1995, pp. 134, 147). But she concedes that the novel 'is a rare instance of a libertarian perspective on another and subordinated culture produced from within an imperialist metropolis' (Parry, in Tambling, 1995, p. 148).

The 'libertarian perspective' referred to by Parry is striking, I would suggest, in Forster's depiction of Hindu India. A chronotope which flickers throughout the novel, alternating with social realism and troubling the reader's consciousness, Hindu India is inaccessible to the Anglo-Indian protagonists and only partly accessible to the Muslim Aziz. It is figured in the depiction of Professor Godbole.[9] Here Forster, whose novel can be seen to prefigure recent postcolonial theory,[10] also prefigures postmodernism in his creation of a magical realist dimension incomprehensible to the Raj and challenging to the reader.[11] Wilson, writing about magic realism in current South American and other postcolonial/postmodernist writing, remarks, 'Magical realism focuses the problem of fictional space. It does this by suggesting a model of how different geometries, inscribing boundaries that fold and refold like quicksilver, can superimpose themselves upon one another' (In Zamora, ed. 1995, p. 210). Forster's apprehension, long before contemporary magic realism, of such 'different geometries', results in his creation of the verbal and conceptual 'muddle' and 'mystery' of the Anglo-Indians' attempt to engage in conversation with Godbole. It is as though the interlocutors in these exchanges are speaking different languages, again a characteristic of magic realism:

> Despite the various critical disagreements over the concept of magic realism, one element which does recur constantly throughout many magic realist texts, and therefore points to a unifying characteristic, is an awareness of the ineluctable *lack* in communication, a condition which prevents the merger of signifier and signified. (Simpkins, in Zamora, ed. 1995, p. 148)

Every conversation in which Godbole participates exemplifies this non-coincidence of (Western) signifier with (Indian) signified. Consider for instance the crucial passage in which Fielding tries to establish Aziz's innocence or guilt:

> [Godbole]: 'I am informed that an evil action was performed in the Marabar Hills, and that a highly esteemed English lady is now seriously ill in consequence. My answer to that is this: that action was performed by Dr. Aziz.' He stopped and sucked in his thin cheeks. 'It was performed by the guide.' He stopped again. 'It was performed by you.' Now he had an air of daring and of coyness. 'It was performed by me'. He looked shyly down the sleeve of his own coat. 'And by my students. It was even performed by the lady herself. When evil occurs, it expresses the whole of the universe. Similarly when good occurs'. 'And similarly when suffering occurs, and so on and so forth, and everything is anything and nothing something' [Fielding] muttered in his irritation, for he needed the solid ground. (Forster, 1924, pp. 174–175)

Another example of the non-coincidence between Western signifiers and Indian signifiers is the apparently trivial incident of the Nawab Bahadur's collision with a mysterious object never identified in the text but claimed by the Nawab himself as a ghost. Zamora remarks: 'Magic realist texts ask us to look beyond the limits of the knowable, and ghosts are often our guides . . . Ghosts are liminal, metamorphic, intermediary: they exist in/between/on modernity's boundaries of physical and spiritual, magical and real, and challenge the lines of demarcation' (Zamora in Zamora ed. 1995, p. 498). Zamora discusses the ways in which magical realist texts, like ghosts, 'subvert the commonsense dichotomies of the daylight consciousness', pointing out that these subversions are 'both ontological and generic' (Zamora, 1995, p. 500).

In *A Passage to India*, Forster the social realist sees no place in colonial India for his liberal-humanist Anglo-Indian characters. Despite their generosity and their difference from the British administrators of the Raj, Mrs Moore, Adela Quested and Cyril Fielding cannot free themselves from the colonial context which defines their identity. By the end of the novel they have returned home. But Forster the magical realist celebrates a Hindu India which neither his characters nor his readers can fully understand. Challenging our preconceptions, ignoring the boundaries of our epistemological categories, Hindu India in the 'Temple' section, which closes the novel, erupts into our consciousness with noise and fireworks and confusion. Nowhere is Forster's depiction of place more powerful. We are forced to suspend the 'commonsense dichotomies' on which our thinking depends, in order to immerse ourselves in the sensorially overwhelming, carnivalesque world-view of Hindu India.

Notes

1. Judith Scherer Herz draws attention both to the diversity and continuity of Forster's oeuvre:

   > Forster was always writing. Indeed, the common notion that somehow his pen dried up after 1924 with the publication of *A Passage to India* could not be more false. The impulse to account, recount, tell, meditate, speculate took form in diary, commonplace book, notebooks, letters, to say nothing of the stories, essays, lectures, reviews, broadcasts and novels. What identifies all the writing as from the same pen is, first, its open-endedness, its unwillingness to dogmatize or reduce; second, its creation of a voice at once vatic and particular; and, third, its powerful narrative impulse (Herz, p. 7).

   Although Herz convincingly argues that the stories and essays are 'closer to the sources of [Forster's] imagination than are the novels' social gestures and graces', I will limit my argument to the novels published in his lifetime. I am interested in the problems of narrative form which Forster has to resolve in the writing of domestic comedy.
2. *The Collected Short Stories* are all about escape from constriction to freedom. As Trilling writes: 'The Pans of Forster's fantastic stories state, in various ways, this eternal lesson. Modern life – it is to be D.H. Lawrence's theme – can kill the masculine power and tenderness; Pan inhabits the woods and fields which men have forsaken' (Trilling, p. 44). Forster's non-Hellenic Wellsian allegory 'The Machine Stops' equally insists that human identity is inexorably

bound to space and place. The protagonist Kuno, wanting to escape from the machine, remarks:

> You know that we have lost the sense of space. We say 'space is annihilated', but we have annihilated not space but the sense thereof. We have lost a part of ourselves. I determined to recover it. 'Near' is a place to which I can get quickly on my feet, not a place to which the train or the air ship will take me quickly. 'Far' is a place to which I cannot get quickly on my feet... Man is the measure. That was my first lesson. Man's feet are the measure for distance, his hands are the measure for ownership, his body is the measure for all that is lovable and desirable and strong ('The Machine Stops', p. 125).

'My Wood' is an essay in *Abinger Harvest*, but it could equally have been a short story. An allegory about the effects of empire, the essay asks 'If you own things, what's their effect on you? What's the effect on me of my wood?' (p. 23). Ambreen Hai remarks:

> Using the spatial allegory of an English wood, the essay also explores how Forster, like the English in India, is tempted to replay the tyrannical role of property-owner, to re-enact the privileges of power and exclusion; how an anti-colonial critique (in his novel) could nevertheless produce a colonizing desire (for his wood) (Hai, p. 317).

3. Forster's anguish over the destruction of the Greenwood sounds clearly in the *Commonplace Book*. Philip Gardner comments on

> Forster's sense of alienation in a twentieth-century landscape increasingly mechanised, built over, and unamenable to being understood by means of the notions of 'Pan' and 'Wessex' which had underlain his early short stories... when writing in 1963 'of fragile Tennysonian Lincolnshire', he remarks that: 'The death of our countryside [which will *never* be renewed] upsets me more than the death of a man or of a generation of men which [will] be replaced in much the same form.' No less moving are his laments expressed between 1928 and 1930 for the 'collapsing countryside' of Surrey, of which there is 'too little... to hide me, even at night, or to go round.'... essentially he remained stranded between past and present, and for much of the Commonplace Book his voice is elegiac, with overtones of bitterness (often self-reproachful) and of an exhausted calm (Philip Gardner, Introduction to the *Commonplace Book*, pp. xvi–xvii.).

4. James Buzard remarks, 'For Forster, the "Baedeker Italy" regulates contact between touristic and Italian life, the latter defined in terms either of local colour or of necessary services for visitors. We recall Baedeker's aim of rendering tourists "as independent as possible of the services of guides and volets-de-place, [of] protect[ing them] against extortion" '(Buzard, 1995, p. 22).

5. For my argument that 'metalanguage or diegesis in *A Passage to India* frequently frames the narrative by retreating from it, so that . . . contradictions . . . are ironically foregrounded', see my 'Arches and Echoes', p. 57.
6. An interesting counter-argument is offered by Elizabeth Outka, who maintains that in *Howards End* characters' attitudes to the past are not merely nostalgic (and therefore reactionary) but potentially transformative: 'Far from a static hold on the past, the new *Howards End* offers the characters both a vital continuity and a chance to remake time's passage to accommodate their present needs' (Outka, p. 345).
7. I am grateful to Linda van der Vijver for drawing my attention to this passage, and to the passage on page 203, in a joint presentation given at the University of Cape Town in September 2004.
8. I discuss this curious 'little phrase' in my 'Arches and Echoes' piece.
9. The extent to which Forster's evocation of Hindu India remains incomprehensible to Western readers is reflected in David Lean's film of *A Passage to India*. Excellent on many aspects of social realism in the British Raj, its depiction of Godbole (played by Alec Guinness) is bathetic, achieving only comedy. The film does not attempt to 'translate' the sequences at Mau contained in 'Temple'.
10. In my recent *Ariel* article, I attempt to investigate some ways in which *A Passage to India* anticipates the work of the postcolonial critic Homi Bhabha, whose *Location of Culture* significantly articulates postcolonial fiction with modernist fiction. I investigate Bhabha's contention that 'critical theory rests . . . on the notion of cultural difference, not cultural diversity' arguing that Forster demonstrates cultural difference throughout *A Passage*, dramatising issues of power in who governs and who is governed.
11. Here Forster's writing in the last novel published during his lifetime circles back to the beginnings of his fiction, the short stories built around myth and magic.

Works cited

Baedeker, K., *Italy from the Alps to Naples* (Leipzig: Karl Baedeker 1904).

Beer, J., *The Achievement of E.M. Forster* (London: Chatto and Windus, 1968).

Buzard, J., 'Forster's Trespasses: Tourism and Cultural Politics', *New Casebooks: E.M. Forster*. Ed. J. Tambling (Houndsmills: Macmillan, 1995) pp. 14–30.

Bradbury, M. (ed.) *Forster: A Collection of Critical Essays* (New Jersey: Prentice-Hall, 1966).

Colmer, J., 'Marriage and Personal Relations in Forster's Fiction', *E.M. Forster: Centenary Revaluations*. Ed. J. S. Herz and R. K. Martin (London and Basingstoke: Macmillan, 1982).

Delany, P., 'Islands of Money: Rentier Culture in *Howards End*', *New Casebooks: E.M. Forster*. Ed. J. Tambling (Houndsmills: Macmillan, 1995), pp. 67–80.

Fincham, G., 'Arches and Echoes: Framing Devices in *A Passage to India*', *Pretexts*, 2: 1 (Winter 1990) 52–67.

———, '*A Passage to India*, Colonial Humanism and Recent Postcolonial Theory: A Response to Lidan Lin', *Ariel* 34: 4 (October 2003) 73–97.

Forster, E. M., *Where Angels Fear to Tread* (Harmondsworth: Penguin, 1905).

————, *The Longest Journey* (London: Edward Arnold, 1907).

————, *A Room with a View* (Harmondsworth: Penguin, 1908).

————, *Howards End* (Harmondsworth: Penguin, 1910).

————, *A Passage to India* (Harmondsworth: Penguin, 1924).

————, *Abinger Harvest* (London: Edward Arnold, 1936).

————, *Collected Short Stories* (Harmondsworth: Penguin, 1947).

————, *Two Cheers for Democracy* (London: Edward Arnold, 1951).

————, *The Commonplace Book* (London: Scolar Press, 1985).

Furbank, N., *E.M. Forster: A Life* (London: Secker and Warburg, 1977).

Hai, A., 'Out in the Woods: E.M. Forster's Spatial Allegories of Property, Sexuality, and Colonialism', *Literature Interpretation Theory*, 14 (2003) 317–335.

Herz, J. S., *The Short Narratives of E.M. Forster* (New York: St. Martin's Press, 1988).

Herz, J. S. and Martin, R. (eds), *E. M. Forster: Centenary Revaluations* (London: Macmillan, 1982).

Kuchta, T., 'Suburbia, Ressentiment, and the End of Empire in *A Passage to India*', *Novel*, 36: 3 (Summer 2003) 307–325.

Littlewood, I., *Sultry Climates: Travel and Sex* (London: John Murray, 2001).

Martin, R., 'Writers' Panel: An Introduction'. (Includes discussion with Eudora Welty)', *E.M. Forster: Centenary Revaluations*. Ed. J. S. Herz and R. Martin (London: Macmillan, 1982), pp. 288–307.

Medalie, D., *E.M. Forster's Modernism* (Houndsmills: Palgrave, 2002).

Outka, E., 'Buying Time: *Howards End* and Commodified Nostalgia', *Novel*, 36: 3 (Summer 2003) 330–350.

Parry, B., 'The Politics of Representation in *A Passage to India*', *New Casebooks: E.M. Forster*. Ed. J. Tambling (Houndsmills: Macmillan, 1995), pp. 133–150.

Simpkins, S., 'Sources of Magic Realism/Supplements to Realism in Contemporary Latin American Literature', *Magic Realism: Theory, History, Community* Ed. L. Zamora and. W. Faris (Durham and London: Duke University Press, 1995), pp. 145–159.

Stoll, R., 'Aphrodite with a Janus Face: Language, Desire, and History in *The Longest Journey*', *New Casebooks: E.M. Forster*. Ed. J. Tambling (Houndsmills: Macmillan, 1995), pp. 30–50.

Tambling, J., *New Casebooks: E.M. Forster* (Houndsmills: Macmillan, 1995).

Trilling, L., *E.M. Forster* (London: The Hogarth Press, 1969).

Wilson, R., 'The Metamorphoses of Fictional Space: Magic Realism', *Magic Realism: Theory, History, Community* (Durham and London: Duke University Press, 1995) pp. 209–233.

Zamora, L., 'Magical Romance/Magical Realism: Ghosts in U.S Latin American Fiction', *Magic Realism: Theory, History, Community* (Durham and London: Duke University Press, 1995) pp. 497–550.

Zamora, L. and Faris, W., *Magic Realism: Theory, History, Community* (Durham and London: Duke University Press, 1995).

4

Travel as Incarceration: Jean Rhys's *After Leaving Mr Mackenzie*

Jeremy Hawthorn

Who you are, where you are

It is impossible to consider a human relationship to space, to the way in which people occupy or traverse a particular geographical area, without taking into account the intersections of geographical, social, cultural and historical space. Our relation to different physical spaces is always mediated through the social, the cultural, and the historical, and for all of these axes the issue of gender is of fundamental importance. This truth is expressed and confirmed more insistently by some writers than it is by others. Few, if any, corroborate it so unremittingly as does Jean Rhys, and in her fiction, 'culture' invariably highlights the issue of gender.

The relationship between gender and place is a complex one. At a simple level, most cultures have or have had spaces that are dedicated to the exclusive use of one gender: harems, 'Ladies Only' compartments on trains, waiting rooms, 'Men only' bars, coal-mines, boxing rings. But this list has a slightly musty air about it. The boxing-ring is now no longer an exclusively male preserve in many places in Europe and North America, and in Britain at any rate the 'Men Only' bar is illegal in public houses. 'Ladies Only' compartments were abolished (at least on British trains) in the 1960s. As for coal-mines, thanks to the action of various governments there are very few of them left in Britain, but there are female coal-miners in others countries, including the United States.

If overt gender segregation – whether in trains, schools or pubs – was largely phased out in Britain by the 1980s, it now appears to be being phased back in, in different forms. A news-item included in the London *Evening Standard* web page of 24 March, 2003, reported that the Park Lane Hilton was to become the first hotel in Britain to open a women-only floor. A 'man-free zone' on the 22nd floor was, it was claimed, to be opened in response to demands from female guests for a safer service. The report noted that women would be able to check in at a private lobby area, that bedroom doors would have more secure locks and bigger spy-holes, and room service would be delivered by a female member of staff. Rates started at £265 a night, £85 more than that on a mixed floor. At these prices, the present-day soul-sisters of the women we meet in the fiction of Jean Rhys will not be making many bookings.

When we discuss the ways in which people occupy spaces, we need to bear in mind the ways in which spaces occupy people. People are defined, constituted, changed, enriched or impoverished by the spaces they live in and move through. Travel may broaden the mind, but it may also change who the owner of the mind is. The title of Terry Eagleton's book *Exiles and Emigrés* (1970) serves as a useful reminder of how central the experience of 'being foreign' is to the modernist revolution. It is by now a critical commonplace that geographical, cultural and national displacement plays a double role in the modernist revolution. On the one hand, it produces experiences that a range of modernist artists – and especially modernist writers – are able to incorporate into their art. On the other hand, these same experiences serve as tokens of a wider, existential alienation in the world of the early twentieth century. However marginal and unrepresentative Jean Rhys's life may have been in some ways, her experience of dislocation, loneliness and abandonment is transformed in her art to represent a much more representative experience of female alienation in the early years of the twentieth century – and subsequently.

Bohemia

In Jean Rhys's *After Leaving Mr Mackenzie*, when Julia Martin travels back from Paris to London to be with her dying mother, her sister Norah is shocked.

> She thought: 'She doesn't even look like a lady now. What can she have been doing with herself?'
> Norah was labelled for all to see. She was labelled 'Middle class, no money.' Hardly enough to keep herself in clean linen. And yet scrupulously, fiercely clean, but with all the daintiness and prettiness perforce cut out. (Rhys, 1971, p. 53)

Travel, life in a foreign space, has changed Julia. Life abroad has relocated her on the scale of class; by crossing a national boundary she has crossed a social boundary. The passage reminds us that talking about gender and class identity is difficult or impossible without also talking about money.

Julia has been leading what we still call a 'Bohemian' life in Paris. 'Bohemia' is a complex territory, one that is defined in relation to physical, economic, social and gendered space – as well as, of course, the domain of art. The metaphorical Bohemia has always had a special relationship with the artist, but this relationship is particularly close during the modernist revolution. According to Jerrold Seigal's *Bohemian Paris: Culture, Politics and the Boundaries of Bourgeois Life, 1830–1930* – a study that just manages to stretch a fingertip to the publication date of *After Leaving Mr Mackenzie* – the terms 'Bohemia', '*la Bohème*' and 'Bohemian' first appeared in their familiar sense in France in the 1830s and 1840s, playing on the common French word for gypsy (*bohémien*) which was coined on the false assumption that the gypsies came from the province of Bohemia (Seigal, 1987, p. 5). According to Seigal:

> Bohemia was not a realm outside bourgeois life but the expression of a conflict that arose at its very heart. Bourgeois progress called for the dissolution of traditional restrictions on personal development; harmony and stability required that some new and different limits be set up in their place. (Seigal, 1987, pp. 10–11)

> One sign that this was the place Bohemia filled was that it drew together the strangely assorted grouping with which we began: artists, the young, shady but inventive characters. All shared – with the gypsies whose name they bore – a marginal existence based on the refusal or inability to take on a stable and limited social identity. All lived simultaneously within ordinary society and outside it. (Seigal, 1987, p. 11)

Seigal's use of words such as 'realm' and 'place' is revealing because it is a usage that does not restrict itself to the geographical, although it does have a clear geographical purchase.

Seigal's study has little to say about women: the 'Bohemians' he discusses are almost exclusively male. But as the existence of Alfred Bunn's and Michael Balfe's 1843 opera *The Bohemian Girl* demonstrates, the idea of female bohemianism exerted a hold on cultural imagination many years prior to Puccini's 1893 opera. (Indeed, the opera was itself loosely based on a tale by Cervantes – 'La Gitanilla'.) Robert Blatchford's 1901 *A Bohemian Girl and McGinnis* offers a diluted version of the cultural fantasy, but confirms that nearly 60 years after Balfe's opera the idea of Bohemia carried with it a sense that women were somehow involved, too. Elizabeth Wilson's *Bohemians: The Glamorous Outcasts* devotes two useful chapters to the women of Bohemia, and Wilson notes that although '[f]rom its earliest days Bohemia had appeared to offer women freedom from the social restrictions of respectable society, and recognition as autonomous individuals in their own right', in practice the freedom and recognition were limited, and 'in the small and enclosed world of literary Paris in the early and mid-nineteenth century misogyny was rampant' (Wilson, 2000, pp. 85, 87).

Like the 'flâneur', the 'Bohemian' of nineteenth- and twentieth-century Paris is, by default, a man, while at the same time the freedom enjoyed by such a man involves a sexual freedom that presupposes the existence of women as sexual objects. However the growth of large cities did also offer women the chance to walk freely, safely and anonymously – by day at any rate. Virginia Woolf's essay 'Street Haunting: A London Adventure', written in 1930, details this process. 'As we step out of the house on a fine evening between four and six, we shed the self our friends know us by and become part of that vast republican army of anonymous trampers, whose society is so agreeable after the solitude of one's own room' (Woolf, 1967, p. 155). Woolf's perception is precise: by leaving the domestic space a woman is able to slough off one self and attain a certain 'republican anonymity'. If we ask 'why *republican?*', one likely answer is that republics have no monarchs – more specifically, no hereditary male rulers. In the same essay Woolf also details the pleasure of returning to one's own room, and this alternation between a sort of democratic community and a privacy-solitude represented by the room is central to a novel such as *Mrs Dalloway* (1925) and to stories such as 'Together and Apart' (1943). However it is hard to read 'one's own room' in an essay by Virginia Woolf without filling in that other phrase that another of her essays has linked so firmly to the idea of a room of one's own: 'and £500 a year'.

Peter Brooker's study *Bohemia in London: The Social Scene of Early Modernism* confirms that if a woman wanted to play a part in 'Bohemia' in the early decades of the twentieth century, then wealth made an enormous difference. Commenting on the spectacular and memorable entry of Nancy Cunard and Iris Tree into the London Café Royal in 1914, Brooker notes that what the young David Garnett was able to observe about Nancy Cunard straight away 'was that there was something remarkable in her simply being there. Unattended women at the Café Royal were either, with some ambiguity, dancers, artists' models, or prostitutes' (Brooker, 2004, p. 103). Moreover, as Brooker adds, of both women, their 'bohemian rebellion was defined, accordingly, precisely by their privileged family background and by the additional fact, not simply that they were women, but young upper-middle-class women born to the new rich in Edwardian society' (Brooker, 2004, p. 104). The binary division is clear: on the one side, dancers, artists' models or prostitutes, on the other side, the rich. It is not hard to determine which side Rhys – who was not only poor but had also worked as a chorus girl after leaving the English school she had travelled from Dominica to attend – belonged to.

Although Brooker is writing about Bohemian London, and Seigal's study neglects the rôle of women, their descriptions of Bohemian life in London and Paris are thought-provoking when applied to the heroines of Rhys's pre-war novels. These women, typically, also live 'a marginal existence based on the refusal or inability to take on a stable and limited social identity'. This choice – between a Bohemian life and 'a stable and limited social identity' – is perfectly illustrated by the lives of Julia Martin and her sister in *After Leaving Mr Mackenzie*.

In the case of the heroines of both *After Leaving Mr Mackenzie* and *Good Morning, Midnight*, this life is lived in Paris – the capital not just of France but also of cultural Bohemia. In her incomplete autobiography *Smile Please*, Rhys describes the attraction of Paris to her youthful self.

> He said, 'Yes, I've overstayed my time here already. I stayed because of you. I'm not asking you to live with me in London. I'm asking you to live with me in Paris.' It came to me in a flash that here it was, what I had been waiting for, for so long. Now I could see escape. (Rhys, 1981, pp. 138–139)

What the Rhys heroine (and perhaps her creator) has to learn is that tunnelling out of one prison may involve tunnelling into another. Moreover, the fact that Rhys's escape follows on from a man's suggestion is also very representative of the subordinate rôle played by (especially poor) women in Bohemia.

Seigal argues that most of the bourgeois inhabitants of Bohemia lived there for only a limited period of time, thereafter returning to the bourgeois life they had forsaken.

There existed a whole class of 'amateur' Bohemians: young bourgeois who turned their backs on respectable society in search of the thrills that came with living the life of chance. Most of them would return to bourgeois life and, warmed by some provincial fireplace, would recount their Bohemian adventures as others told about hunting tigers. Others, however, would be less lucky: rejected by their staid families, some amateur Bohemians might end up in a pauper's grave. (Seigal, 1987, p. 51)

To return, however, required money (one's own or one's family's), and it required that one's family or friends were prepared to welcome back the prodigal. For the 'Bohemian woman', things were not so simple – especially if her background was, like that of Rhys's heroines, impoverished lower middle class. One item of luggage that it was difficult for a poor woman to carry out of Bohemia was respectability – as Norah's shocked response to her sister Julia Martin confirms.

Room of one's own – tomb of one's own

Even if we define 'space' in a narrow, geographical sense, people do not live in a space, but in spaces. Lives involve private and public spaces, movement between closed rooms and open areas, between private enclosures and public open spaces. A private room can be both refuge and prison-cell, both safe haven and solitary confinement. Thanks to Sandra Gilbert and Susan Gubar, Jean Rhys's name is now firmly associated with 'the madwoman in the attic' – the figure of Rochester's mad wife taken by Rhys from Charlotte Brontë's *Jane Eyre* and presented in a new and sympathetic light to readers in her novel *Wide Sargasso Sea*. But the heroine of this novel – Bertha/Antoinette – is only one of a number of women in Rhys's fiction who is trapped in a room away from her native land, confined to a space demarcated by four walls, a floor and a ceiling. This paradoxical combination of movement and imprisonment – the journey involving or ending up with incarceration – occurs again and again in Rhys's fiction.

Rhys knew all about imprisonment in a literal sense. Two of her three husbands spent time in prison, and in 1949 she herself was sentenced to a brief stay in Holloway Women's Prison in London for assault, an experience that she used in her short story 'Let Them Call it Jazz'. Significantly, this story centres on an Afro-Caribbean woman whose imprisonment is essentially the result of cultural misunderstanding; her experience of emigration, deracination and, eventually, imprisonment offers a sort of ghostly foretaste of Rhys's later description of the fate of the first Mrs Rochester. Bertha is actually locked up in her attic room, while many of Rhys's earlier heroines are confined not by the law and the lock, but by lack of money, by emotional deprivation, and by the cultural restrictions that make it hard for a single woman to move at ease in public spaces in the way that men are able to do. And many of them, like their creator, also experience a confinement brought about by excessive and addictive drinking – something else that seems to have gone with the Bohemian territory. Brooker writes about the descent into loneliness and alcoholism of two women who entered London Bohemia in their youth: Nina Hamnet and Iris Barry. Hamnet 'was remembered in the 1930s and post-war years as a pathetic figure, obviously drunk and bemoaning the loss of a new beautiful young man or singing lewd ditties for a drink; a tramp on the cadge' (Brooker, 2004, p. 108). She died in 1956 after falling from her small second-floor flat in Westbourne Terrace, Paddington and impaling herself on railings below (Brooker, 2004, p. 109). If we think of figures such as Fifi in Rhys's early story 'La Grosse Fifi', and Lotus Heath in her late story 'The Lotus' then the similarity to the real-life stories of Hamnet and Barry is hard to miss.

As is made clear in *Wide Sargasso Sea*, the room can be both prison and refuge. Rhys too, oscillated between these opposing views of the private room. On the one hand, in a letter written in 1941, Rhys describes her life as 'solitary confinement' (Wyndham and Melly, 1985, p. 35). But in a letter written in 1954 she tells her daughter: 'We've been in this new room for about two months. I've been busy in my usual way trying to build up my own special retreat from the world, with a few books and pictures, my two glass fish and so on' (Wyndham and Melly, 1985, p. 116). In *After Leaving Mr Mackenzie* Rhys's heroine Julia Martin yearns for the same sort of liberating escape from England that her creator was offered. Julia tells Mr Horsfield about a woman she met in Paris and about a conversation she had with her while sitting smoking and drinking tea.

> I was just going to tell her why I left England. . . . One or two things had happened, and I wanted to get away. Because I was fed up, fed up, fed up.
> 'I wanted to go away with just the same feeling a boy has when he wants to run away to sea – at least, that I imagine a boy has. Only, in my adventure, men were mixed up, because of course they had to be. (Rhys, 1971, pp. 39–40)

Peter Brooker reports that the young Nancy Cunard told George Moore: 'I wanted to run away and be a vagabond' (Brooker, 2004, p. 104). But running away for the rich Nancy Cunard was not the same as for the poor Jean Rhys, or for her poor heroines. Even if what was being run away from was to some extent the same, what was being run away to had to be different. Men 'of course' *have* to be 'mixed up' in Julia Martin's running away, partly perhaps because of emotional dependence but certainly for economic reasons. The boy who runs away to sea abandons social and personal ties – but ends up with new ones, in the all-male community of the ship. *After Leaving Mr Mackenzie* is almost contemporaneous with Virginia Woolf's *A Room of One's Own* (1929), and Woolf's comments about the different situations faced by Shakespeare and his imagined sister in that essay home in on the same sort of distinction that underlies Rhys's account of Julia Martin's dilemma. Both Woolf and Rhys, albeit from rather different social and cultural perspectives, understood that there is no female equivalent to running away to sea – although Rhys's work does contain many positive comments about the all-female community of the nunnery. Later on in *After Leaving Mr Mackenzie*, in London, Julia goes to the cinema and watches a newsreel. The newsreel starts with film of young men running races and collapsing exhausted afterward. 'And then – strange anti-climax – young women ran races and also collapsed exhausted, at which the audience rocked with laughter' (Rhys, 1971, p. 85). The idea of women running – or running away – is literally laughable.

The words 'room' and 'rooms' occur on the second page of *Voyage in the Dark* (1934) and on the initial pages of both *After Leaving Mr Mackenzie* and *Good Morning, Midnight*. For Rhys and for her heroines, the room is the starting point (it is often the finishing point too). The need for £500 a year and a room of one's own is no less pressing for them than it is for Virginia Woolf, and Rhys's pre-war fiction confirms that a room of one's own *without* the £500 a year is closer to incarceration than to liberation or escape. In a perceptive study of *After Leaving Mr Mackenzie*, Coral Ann Howells suggests that this 'is a novel about a woman being locked out from what she desires most'. Howells draws attention to the novel's title, which, she argues, suggests that 'separation is the main thematic motif – separation from others and a more terrifying separation within the subject herself' (Howells, 1991, p. 53). Incarceration can involve both 'restriction to' and 'exclusion from', and for the Rhys heroine it generally means both.

For Howells, *After Leaving Mr Mackenzie* is 'the most forlorn of all Rhys's novels', one that is 'an anxious investigation of the modern-ist condition of exile, from a feminine perspective: how this might be experienced by a woman cast adrift in Paris and London' (How-ells, 1991, p. 53). It is ironic that a desire to do something equivalent to running away to sea ends up with being 'cast adrift'. For How-ells, however, Julia's imprisonment is at least partly *inside* her: her response to Mr Mackenzie's 'male discourse of dominance' is 'a com-bination of hatred and anger which must be imprisoned/unspoken in order for her to survive at all in her dependent condition' (Howells, 1991, p. 56).

The journeys taken by women in Rhys's fiction have a standard format: rapid and considerable geographical movement accompanied by increas-ing enclosure or incarceration: Antoinette/Bertha from Jamaica to the English 'attic'; the heroine of 'Let Them Call it Jazz' from the West Indies to the prison cell in Holloway; Anna Morgan again from the West Indies to a series of theatrical boarding-house 'rooms'; Sasha Jansen from her Bloomsbury bed-sit to a room in Paris. Two of the most powerful examples of the pattern are provided by short stories written, respect-ively, at the start and the close of Rhys's literary career: 'Vienne' (first published in 1927) and 'I Used to Live Here Once' (first published 1976). In both of these stories we witness a striking yoking-together of ostensibly free movement in space with forms of soul-destroying 'solitary confine-ment'. In 'Vienne' the rapid movement from place to place is set against enclosure within the motor-car, an enclosure that matches the closing-in of antagonistic legal, social and cultural forces on the heroine and her husband. In 'I Used to Live Here Once' the unfettered freedom of the narrator to move where she wants to – what one could call her mastery of geographical space – is brutally juxtaposed against her invisibility to others. In a shock ending to what is Rhys's shortest story – it is only a page and a half long – we discover what the speaker is herself portrayed as finding out, that she is a ghost whose presence amounts to no more than a chill in the air to the two children she encounters outside her childhood home. It is impossible to avoid seeing this discovery as representative of a different sort of ghostliness in the life of the 'Rhys heroine' – the effective invisibility of the poor, isolated and no-longer-young woman to the rich and powerful and socially integrated men and women (and children) she meets. If Ralph Ellison wrote about the African-American male as an invisible man, Jean Rhys writes about the poor, ageing, abandoned Bohemian woman as an invisible woman. Ironically, then, the ostensible liberation promised by travel to a new country can involve little more than movement from one room to another, and as Sasha Jansen puts it in *Good Morning, Midnight*, 'All rooms are the same. All rooms have four walls, a door, a window or two, a bed, a chair and perhaps a bidet. A room is a place where you hide from the wolves outside and that's all any room is. Why should I worry about changing my room?' (Rhys, 1969, p. 33).

It is tempting to draw parallels between stories such as 'Vienne' and the genre of the female road-movie that is epitomized by the film *Thelma and Louise* (1991). In both cases we witness rapid movement from place to place, the sloughing off of social and cultural responsibilities, and the simultaneous closing-in of the might of law-enforcement and social conventionality. In the film there are no men in the car with the two runaway women: perhaps this serves as a measure of a degree of cultural change during the years following Rhys's composition of 'Vienne'. If many of Rhys's novels and stories depict the inexorable closing-in of the outer-limits of the heroine's 'room to manoeuvre', Rhys seems to have experienced a similar progressive limitation of the available space in her own life. A parenthetical comment from a diary Rhys kept in the 1940s and reproduced in her unfinished autobiography reads: '(The place I live in is terribly important to me, it always has been, but now it is all I have. The table, the chair, the tree outside, my bed upstairs, it is all I have)' (Rhys, 1981, p. 165).

The first line of *Good Morning, Midnight* is ' "Quite like old times," the room says. "Yes? No?" ' Here we must assume that 'the room' is not just *this* room, but also a generic room, 'the room' which may change its physical appearance and spatial location but which is in important ways 'the same'. If for Virginia Woolf the room is a refuge, a place of retreat, a guarantee of privacy, for Jean Rhys it may start off being this but it rapidly becomes a place of internment. And as long term-prisoners know, being released can be as problematic as being locked up. When, for example, Julia Martin is told that her regular supply of cheques from Mr Mackenzie is to cease, she feels bewildered, and her feelings are compared to those that a prisoner who has resigned herself to solitary confinement might feel when suddenly told one morning that she is to be released (Rhys, 1971, p. 14).

The first page of *After Leaving Mr Mackenzie* repeats the word 'room(s)' four times – with the French *chambre* making a fifth mention. This same first page also presents the reader with a pictorial metaphor of the room in which Julia is confined, with a graphic representation of the landlady's card. The image dominates the reader's experience of the first page of the novel, and it is worth asking why Rhys reproduces the card rather than merely informing the reader of its content. The image confronts the reader with a hard oblong frame, one that encloses and imprisons the text of the card – in contrast to the 'unframed' oil painting that hangs in her room. The card presents a graphic representation of enclosure that is proleptic of the enclosure that awaits Julia in the room, but that is in contrast to the unframed lack of restriction represented by art.

The falsely grand name of the landlady's establishment is 'Hotel St Raphael'. St Raphael is, among other things, the patron saint of blind people, lovers and travellers, and in a metaphorical sense at least Julia is all three of these. It is, furthermore, the name of a French *apéritif*, something that Jean Rhys would doubtless have known all about. The reader is told that Julia's room is 'one-eyed'; it is like a head with no body and with restricted sight.

Later on in the novel, back in London, Julia is taken to Mr Horsfield's room. 'Two walls of the room were covered with books almost from the ceiling to the floor. It was a low-pitched room, and there was only one small window. Nevertheless, it had a pleasant and peaceful, even spacious, appearance' (Rhys, 1971, p. 122). Why is this room so different? Perhaps the books change things. But perhaps, too, being a well-off man rather than a poor woman changes things more.

There is a clear progression in the novel: the room that is initially seen as a refuge, bit by bit turns into a prison.

Julia had come across this hotel six months before – on the fifth of October. She had told the landlady she would want the room for a week or perhaps a fortnight. And she had told herself that it was a very good sort of place to hide in. (Rhys, 1971, p. 8–9)

Julia was not altogether unhappy. Locked in her room – especially when she was locked in her room – she felt safe. She read most of the time. (Rhys, 1971, p. 9)

It was the darkness that got you. It was heavy darkness, greasy and compelling. It made walls round you, and shut you in so that you felt you could not breathe. You wanted to beat at the darkness and shriek to be let out. And after a while you got used to it. Of course. And then you stopped believing that there was anything else anywhere. (Rhys, 1971, p. 62)

The houses opposite had long rows of windows, and it seemed to Julia that at each window a woman sat staring mournfully, like a prisoner, straight into her bedroom. (Rhys, 1971, p. 129)

She told herself that, of course, it was the room which depressed her because it was so narrow, and because it was so horrible not to be able to open the window without having several pairs of eyes glued upon you. She thought: 'We're like mites in a cheese in that damned hotel.' (Rhys, 1971, p. 130)

Julia's sister Norah, after Julia sees her again in London, experiences similar sensations of imprisonment. Looking at herself in the mirror she laughs, but then sees how pale her lips are and is struck by the thought that her life is like death, like being buried alive (Rhys, 1971, p. 75). The idea of the bed-sitting room as tomb containing a live corpse occurs too in *Good Morning, Midnight*: 'Well, that was the end of me, the real end. Two-pound-ten every Tuesday and a room off the Gray's Inn Road. Saved, rescued and with my place to hide in – what more did I want? I crept in and hid. The lid of the coffin shut down with a bang' (Rhys, 1969, p. 37). This image of live burial is picked up later on in *After Leaving Mr Mackenzie* when Julia remembers catching butterflies as a child. The butterfly, once caught, would be put in a tin and its wings would be heard beating against it. But then it would hurt itself, would be no longer of interest, and would be discarded – with inevitable consequence of adult condemnation (Rhys, 1971, pp. 115–116). What is clear is that if Julia as child is the gaoler who discards the pretty things she maims once they are damaged, Julia as adult is the convict, the butterfly whose wings get broken by a gaoler-male. The bleakness of this vision of maltreatment passed along a chain of perpetrators-who-become-victims is chilling.

What human beings do to animals in this novel becomes a metaphor for what they do to one another – and especially for what men do to women. In London, Julia's hopes are high when she meets her sister and she longs for some show of affection or interest from Norah, but her sister just keeps looking at her as if she were 'something out of the zoo' (Rhys, 1971, p. 52).

Art and the demolition of constraints

Paintings are mentioned on three occasions in *After Leaving Mr Mackenzie*. The first mention involves a painting hung up in Julia's room.

The ledge under the mirror was strewn with Julia's toilet things – an untidy assortment of boxes of rouge, powder, and make-up for the eyes. At the farther end of it stood an unframed oil-painting of a half empty bottle of red wine, a knife, and a piece of Gruyère cheese, signed 'J. Grykho, 1923'. (Rhys, 1971, p. 8)

The association between the painted picture and the 'painted' woman is clearly not accidental. Nor is the subject-matter of the painting: alcohol, the cheese that is picked up at the end of the novel in the comment that 'We're like mites in a cheese in that damned hotel', and perhaps the knife representing one possible way out. We learn later that Julia hates the picture, and this may be because it presents her with truths about herself that at this stage of the novel she is unwilling to admit to or to confront. There is, moreover, an interesting comment shortly after this passage that the picture and a red plush sofa in the room are linked in Julia's mind, the picture standing for the idea, the spirit, and the sofa for the act. This association of a painting with a couch or sofa is picked up more powerfully later on in the novel.

However unlike the hotel card reproduced on the first page of the novel the painting is 'unframed'. Art, in the fiction of Jean Rhys, typically manages to burst through social and cultural borders and boundaries, even when (as here) it presents the viewer with a represented 'perversion'. In 'Let Them Call it Jazz', for example, the imprisoned narrator hears a song being sung by a fellow prisoner.

It's a smoky kind of voice, and a bit rough sometimes, as if those old dark walls theyselves are complaining, because they see too much misery – too much. But it don't fall down and die in the courtyard; seems to me it could jump the gates of the jail easy and travel far, and nobody could stop it. I don't hear the words – only the music. (Rhys, 1972, p. 60)

When I'm back in my cell I can't just wait for bed. I walk up and down and think. 'One day I hear that song on trumpets and these walls will fall and rest.' (Rhys, 1972, p. 61)

Alas, after her release a man hears her whistling the tune, sells the song, and gives her five pounds for it.

The third reference to paintings in *After Leaving Mr Mackenzie* occurs when Julia visits the house of a Mr Horsfield.

> When they looked at the pictures he became a different man. Because he loved them he became in their presence modest, hesitating, unsure of his own opinion.
>
> 'Do you like that?'
>
> 'Yes, I like it.'
>
> 'I wish I could get somebody who knows to tell me whether it's any good or not,' he said, talking to himself.
>
> He was anxious because he did not want to love the wrong thing. Fancy wanting to be told what you must love! (Rhys, 1971, p. 83)

Julia's scorn has to be set against her own earlier uncertainty as to whether the painting by 'J. Grykho' is good or not – but she hates rather than loves this painting. She is unwilling to acknowledge her hatred; Mr Horsfield is unwilling to trust his desire to love. The world of Jean Rhys is a world of imprisoned feelings and emotions.

Perhaps the most interesting reference to a painting in this novel comes, however, in-between these two examples. While Julia is reporting her conversation with the woman artist, she describes another painting.

> And all the time I talked I was looking at a rum picture she had on the wall – a reproduction of a picture by a man called Modigliani. Have you ever heard of him? This picture is of a woman lying on a couch, a woman with a lovely, lovely body. Oh, utterly lovely. Anyhow, I thought so. A sort of proud body, like an utterly lovely proud animal. And a face like a mask, a long, dark face, and very big eyes. The eyes were blank, like a mask, but when you had looked at it a bit it was as if you were looking at a real woman, a live woman. (Rhys, 1971, p. 40)

The most recent paperback edition of the novel (New York: Norton, 1999) reproduces Modigliani's 'Reclining Nude, 1917–1918' from the Collection Gianni Mattioli in Milan, and this may well be the painting that Julia comments on, although there are various other Modigliani nudes that it could be. What is striking is that this and a number of other

Modigliani nudes that match Julia's description crop the legs below the knees, and some (like the one chosen for the Norton edition) crop parts of the arms and the model's hair. The result of such pruning is to direct attention on to that which is erotically significant, and thus to reduce the woman to a torso – a limbless sexual object. At the same time there is a powerful counter-effect: the woman is simultaneously pinned down by the lines of the painting's edges, while at the same time she escapes beyond the limits of the picture; she is not contained within the oblong of its surface. If there is a part of her that is the focus of male sexual attention, there is also a part of her that escapes the male gaze, that lives beyond the display directed at men. The paintings attempt to capture, frame and fix their female subjects, like moths pinned in a display cabinet, but at the same time they announce the failure of the attempt as they indicate that there is more to these women than meets the male eye.

The mention of the couch and the eyes in this passage reminds the reader of the sofa and the make-up for the eyes in the earlier passage, but the sense of the woman as a 'proud animal' stands in stark contrast to the imprisoned animals mentioned elsewhere in the text. The mention of the mask also picks up associations from earlier in the text: 'She made herself up elaborately and carefully; yet it was clear that what she was doing had long ceased to be a labour of love and had become partly a mechanical process, partly a substitute for the mask she would have liked to wear' (Rhys, 1971, p. 11).

Julia's 'mechanical process' of making herself up is, later on, extended to her manner of dancing. For Mr Horsfield, 'She seemed to him to be moving stiffly and rather jerkily. It was like watching a clockwork toy that has nearly run down' (Rhys, 1971, p. 107). The woman in the Modigliani painting, then, represents half what Julia is, and half what Julia wants to be and fears to be. The vulnerability makes the mask a wished-for accomplishment or accessory. At the same time, as the woman in the picture is naked and exposed, she is also masked and hidden. We meet her eye, but the reciprocity that normally goes with such a meeting of gazes is denied by the woman's mask-like and impenetrable face.

Mr Horsfield is clearly shocked when Julia, after admitting that she used to pray that her lover would lose all his money so that she could get money to give him, goes on to tell him that she once knew a girl who prayed that the man she loved might go blind (Rhys, 1971, p. 125). At one level this picks up female fantasies of inverting the female–male dependence relationship, crystallized most clearly in

Rochester's blinding in *Jane Eyre*. But it also represents another way of hiding from the male gaze, more total than the solution offered by the mask-like face.

Eyes, however much we try to disguise the fact, tell stories about us: 'He looked rather subdued, till you saw in his eyes that he was not quite subdued yet, after all' (Rhys, 1971, p. 63). Coral Ann Howells claims that by adopting the method of shifting multiple perspectives in this novel, 'Rhys shows the inescapable subjectivity in which all her characters are imprisoned' (Howells, 1991, p. 67). Perhaps. But some subjectivities, like some rooms, are more comfortable than others. According to Elizabeth Wilson, '[m]any different kinds of self-destruction were romanticized in Bohemia, but its allure was also in its eternal hopefulness' (Wilson, 2000, p. 115). There is no romanticizing of the destruction of the self in *After Leaving Mr Mackenzie*, and this destruction is not simply self-destruction. 'Eternal hopefulness' is a little too positive to describe the heroine's resilience, but in spite of its darkness and pessimism the novel does affirm something positive about the right of women to independence and dignity, and to a space of their own.

Works cited

Brooker, P., *Bohemia in London: The Social Scene of Early Modernism* (Houndmills: Palgrave Macmillan, 2004).

Hilton Hotel Creates Man-Free Zone. <http://www.thisislondon.com/news/articles/3975852?source = EveningStandard>, accessed 3/3/2005.

Howells, C. A., *Jean Rhys. Key Women Writers* (Hemel Hempstead: Harvester Wheatsheaf, 1991).

Rhys, J., *Wide Sargasso Sea*. First published, 1966. (Harmondsworth: Penguin, 1968).

———, *Good Morning, Midnight*. First published, 1939. (Harmondsworth: Penguin, 1969).

———, *After Leaving Mr Mackenzie*. First published, 1930. (Harmondsworth: Penguin, 1971).

———, *Tigers are Better Looking*. First published 1968. Includes a selection of stories from The Left Bank (1927). (Harmondsworth: Penguin, 1972).

———, *Sleep it Off Lady*. First published, 1976. (Harmondsworth: Penguin, 1979).

———, *Smile Please: An Unfinished Autobiography*. First published, 1979. (Harmondsworth: Penguin, 1981).

Seigal, J., *Bohemian Paris: Culture, Politics and the Boundaries of Bourgeois Life, 1830–1930*. First published, 1986. (Harmondsworth: Penguin, 1987).

Wilson, E., *Bohemians: The Glamorous Outcasts* (New Brunswick: Rutgers University Press, 2000).

Woolf, V., 'Street Haunting: A London Adventure.' in *Collected Essays* volume 4. (London: Hogarth Press, 1967), pp. 155–166.

Wyndham, F. and Melly, D. (eds), *Jean Rhys: Letters 1931–66*. First published 1984. (Harmondsworth: Penguin, 1985).

5
'Where Am I?': Feminine Space and Time in Virginia Woolf's *The Years*

Merry M. Pawlowski

Things pass, things change . . . And where are we going? (Woolf, 1965, p. 213).

The places we have known do not belong only to the world of space on which we map them for our own convenience. None of them was ever more than a thin slice, held between the contiguous impressions that composed our life at that time; the memory of a particular image is but regret for a particular moment; and houses, roads, avenues are as fugitive, alas, as the years. (Proust, 1981, p. 462)[1]

On February 2, 1933, Virginia Woolf abandoned her project to create a new form for her writing, the 'Essay-novel,' which she had conceived of as a mingling of narrative chapters alternating with explanatory essay. Woolf's experiment to forge two discursive types – fiction and non-fiction, rainbow and granite – into one textual space had, in her mind, failed; but the pressure to continue this work as a narrative embedding of space/time would succeed. For by 1934, Woolf had re-titled *The Pargiters*, the abandoned earlier work, as *Here and Now* (Leaska, 1977, p. xv), a working title which sounds the keynote of the emergent work as a representation of human existence in space and time: *here* in the present, fleeting moment. By September 15, 1935, after trying out a number of provisional names, Woolf had decided on a title: 'And The Years (that name is fixed; dropped like a billiard ball into a pocket)' (Woolf, 1982, p. 342). The new title, whose very plurality implies the passage of time, captured the shape of the book, arranged into chapters each named for the year in which its events occur. Early in the first chapter, '1880,' Woolf would introduce the dominant theme and visual pattern of ceaseless change in time and space: 'Slowly wheeling, like the rays of a searchlight, the days, the weeks, the years passed one after another across the sky' (Woolf, 1965, p. 4).[2]

While each chapter announces its year, time within that year remains fluid, as does space; Woolf consistently resists specificity about day and date, locating the time of each particular year only as a season, while at the same time organizing space as experienced through the motion of time. With the accumulation of years, Woolf constructs a spatial and temporal palimpsest which incessantly modulates an originary English Victorian space/place. The first two chapters represent the Victorian nineteenth century (1880 and 1891), eight chapters are set during the early decades of the twentieth century – the Edwardian and Georgian periods and World War I (1907, 1908, 1910, 1911, 1913, 1914, 1917, and 1918) – and the final chapter, 'The Present Day,' skips 19 years to take as its moment the end of Woolf's writing and the threshold of World War II, 1935.[3]

Working against what Julia Kristeva has called 'Father's time' or linear time, the time of *his*tory (Kristeva, 1986, p. 190), Woolf poses a non-sequential arrangement of years as fault lines, leaving the reader to wonder why these years were chosen and others, in the gaps between, were left out. Part of the reason lies, I believe, in Woolf's decision to resist and even mute the unfolding of history as purely a patriarchal chronicle of external events. Yet another reason is to explore two worlds: the world of sweeping change and global events balanced against life as experienced at the level of the everyday. For to reject history as the material existences of men and women in these years would be to erase the power of *Three Guineas*, Woolf's later companion to *The Years*, and Woolf would never choose to do that.

History and individual existence, then, unfold as series of repeating patterns in the novel suggestive of a feminine, cyclical (time folding back on itself), and circulating (space folding back on itself) conception of space/time, which has little to do with linear time but very much to do with 'imaginary space' (Kristeva, 1986, p. 191). Just as suggestive to me as Kristeva's politically gendered argument is Henri Bergson's more gender-neutral but controversial conception of duration, familiar to Woolf and her Bloomsbury contemporaries. Regardless of whether Woolf read Bergson (she claimed never to have read him), Bergson's ideas were enormously popular and very much a part of any cultural conversation during the first half of the twentieth century.[4] For Bergson, duration is difficult to define as separable from space/time – it is consciousness as *lived* as one state succeeds another without separation from it. As Bergson says, pure duration 'forms both the past and the present states into an organic whole, as happens when we recall the notes of a tune, melting . . . into one another' (Bergson, 2005, p. 100). What is clear is that Bergson distinguishes, as does Kristeva, between two phenomena: (1) successive moments of measured time crossed by the three-dimensional planes of space, and (2) conscious moments which are mobile and enfold both past and present in the unfolding of the ego in a state of endless change (Bergson, 1998, p. 2).

If Woolf never admitted to reading Bergson, she certainly read his contemporary, James Jeans. Her interest in Jeans was largely in his pop-ularizing books on the nature of the universe; in fact, reading Jeans's *The Mysterious Universe* in 1937 inspired her to buy a telescope, through which she saw rather disappointing images. 'We saw the Ring of Saturn last night, like a cardboard collar' (Woolf, 1984, p. 107). Earlier, Woolf had expressed an interest in Jeans's description of the bending back of space, imagining how she might incorporate Jeans's views of space and time in her fiction (Jeans, 1929, pp. 70–71) and writing in her diary, 'You know what Jeans says? Civilisation is the thickness of a postage stamp on the top of Cleopatra's needle; & time to come is the thickness of post-age stamps as high as Mont Blanc' (Woolf, 1982, p. 65).[5] While Woolf's interest in Jeans extends to his theorizing about space as universe, repres-entation of space on the ground and in the air of the Earth's atmosphere had to be her major concern in composing *The Years*.

Space thus conceived was undergoing rapid changes during the years in Woolf's novel. Large, many-storied homes on gas-lit streets inhabited by huge Victorian families and their servants in 1880 were soon to yield to the pressure of the future. Similarly doomed were cobblestone streets where horse-drawn buggies, omnibuses, and hansom cabs in 1891 car-ried traffic to and fro. By the 'Present Day' of the novel, London's theatre district was illuminated by advertisements of pouring beer bottles, streets were lit by electric lighting, the interiors of rooms were lit by pressing of a switch, most homes had telephones and hot running water, and the speed of travel had increased with the advent of motorcars, trains, and 'aeroplanes.' 'Reading' space, Henri Lefebvre suggests, 'implies a process of signification' on an already produced space, which may be decoded (Lefebvre, 1991, p. 17). Yet while such a signifying space may appear to be static, it is in reality ceaselessly changing, as are the codes it provides for reading its meanings. Space, for Michel de Certeau, is 'composed of inter-sections of mobile elements . . . actuated by the ensemble of movements deployed within it' (Certeau, 1988, p. 117). But Bachelard insists that the unconscious must be housed as a form of stability to protect itself from madness. Rather than knowing ourselves in time, he writes, 'all we know is a sequence of fixations in the spaces of the being's stability – a being who does not want to melt away, and who . . . wants time to "suspend" its flight' (Bachelard, 1994, p. 8). 'In its countless alveoli,' Bachelard continues, 'space contains compressed time,' an insight which seems to capture the spirit of Woolf's efforts to stay the motion of time in her fiction.

Even compressed time, though, implies motion, and time as motion through space suggests trajectories, vectors, boundaries, borders, and transgression. Once a political ideology, and the hint of transgression, slips in, of course, space, and time, can be conceived as gendered. Women and men inhabit space, as they inhabit their sexed bodies and socially constructed roles, differently. Space as an arena for the intersection of social relations offers itself to be sectioned, largely, into public and private space and, just as importantly, to be divided along the lines of national and international boundaries (McDowell, 1996, p. 30). 'Space,' argues Linda McDowell, 'is relational and constitutive of social processes' (McDowell, 1996, p. 29). Despite the variety and even apparent conflictedness of these varied perspectives on space/time, *The Years* seems to encompass them all, offering a vision of lived, gendered experience of space/time, in both the particular and global senses, unparalleled in her fiction.

Each of Woolf's years incorporates consciousness as motion, binding present to past through memory, layering multiple sensations and experiences in a symbolic palimpsest which links interior and external reality. My focus in this essay – rather than on the years as linear time, on the exteriority of a family chronicle, or on interior and exterior spaces as static maps – will be the conjunction of space and time through motion to respond to an incessant question about subjectivity posed by the novel: 'Where am I?' Woolf's fictional representation of space/time could not exist without motion and a continual search for location whether real or perceptual. Imaginative aerial flights over London; consciousness of walking in the city/space; awareness of speed through the motion of riding in omnibuses, trains, and automobiles: these all serve to track beings in motion experiencing space/time. Even the act of reading, while not a physical motion, incorporates motion as mental action in grasping the simultaneity of beings in space and time. Indeed, reading the newspaper shrinks distance through its speedy dissemination of events while reading literary classics recreates the simultaneity of time by making the past relevant in the present.

Resisting stasis in the Victorian past

Woolf will resist and supplant stasis and suffocation in the novel, but first she recreates the Victorian parlor in the first chapter as the 'dead' center of life in 1880. Here, at tea time in the center of gathering in Victorian life, the narrator forces us to witness the virtual imprisonment of Victorian women in the private house. Delia and Milly, two grown daughters in the Pargiter household, attempt to maintain an appearance of Victorian custom and decorum, as their mother lies in an upstairs bedroom dying. 'Where am I?' their dying mother calls out in terror as she momentarily rises to consciousness (Woolf, 1965, p. 23). 'Where am I?' Delia echoes later, leaving her mother's room and feeling herself lost on the border between life and death, space/time and non-being (Woolf, 1965, p. 25). Delia inwardly rails against the stifling presence of the angel in the house, her dying mother, and longs to join Charles Stuart Parnell in his fight to free Ireland of imperial rule. Instead, Delia, trapped in private space, looks out of the drawing room window, as street lamps are being lit, to the houses across the street, which mirror her own, and down to the street where a hansom cab stops at a house two doors down. A young man in a top hat alights and Delia's elder sister, Eleanor, warns: ' "Don't be caught looking" ' (p. 19). Delia, returning in memory to 1880 in the midst of her party in the 'Present Day,' the novel's last chapter, exclaims as she remembers life in her family home: ' "Abercorn Terrace! ... It was Hell! ... It was Hell!" ' (Woolf, 1965, p. 417).

Three additional early chapters detail life in the Victorian and Edwardian periods – 1891, 1907, and 1908 – years dominated by deaths and the inevitability of change. The first of the Victorian years, 1880, ends with the funeral of Rose Pargiter, mother to many of the major characters in the novel. In 1891, the world of the novel is riveted by the death of Charles Stuart Parnell, and in 1908, the lives of another branch of the Pargiters are changed dramatically by the untimely deaths of both mother and father, Eugenie and Digby Pargiter.

The year 1910 marks a watershed of change for Woolf both in real relations and in the fictional relations of her characters. 'On or about December, 1910,' Woolf famously wrote, 'human character changed... all human relations have shifted – those between masters and servants, husbands and wives, parents and children. And when human relations change there is at the same time a change in religion, conduct, politics and literature' (Woolf, 1978, pp. 96–97). Woolf had marked, in the view of many, the emergence of modernism as the new shape of life and art.

But 1910 in *The Years* does not take place in December but during an English spring, which heralds more sweeping change to come as Rose Pargiter, the youngest daughter of Abel Pargiter and now at forty a militant suffragette, is on her way to lunch with her cousins Maggie and Sara Pargiter. Rose stands, spatially positioned overlooking the Thames, seeing the pattern of the past in the swirl of the river beneath her. As she turns to the view of the city, she thinks, 'There's *that*, she had said to herself. Indeed it was a splendid view.... There were the Houses of Parliament' (Woolf, 1965, p. 161). Rose leans backward with a queer expression on her face, as though ready to lead an assault on the scene. Her smirk at the sight of the seat of British imperial power might best be explained by its later echo from *Three Guineas* as Woolf's narrating persona stands positioned on this same bridge and proposes to describe the 'crudely coloured photograph' of the public space of London as it appears to women 'who see it from the threshold of the private house, through the shadow of the veil that St. Paul still lays upon our eyes; from the bridge which connects the private house with the world of public life' (Woolf, 1938, p. 34). Rose's assault on public space will have to wait a few years, though, for at the moment she has reached her destination.

The democratic leveling of society announced by Woolf takes shape as Rose enters Maggie and Sara's shabby rented rooms on the south side of the Thames. The only remnants of their more affluent past in their parents' home are a crimson and gold chair and a Venetian looking-glass; they have no servants and Maggie sews her own clothes. Sara tags along with Rose to a meeting where Rose's sister Eleanor sits drawing a recurring pattern, the wheel, the dominant formal and thematic image in the novel; and as the chapter ends, we track Kitty, a cousin to the Pargiter sisters, to the Opera to see *Siegfried* where scenes from the opera barely penetrate her consciousness as she recalls her past and thinks of the king dying. As Kitty hears the hammering of Siegfried's sword in the anvil, Maggie and Sara hear the hammering of their drunken neighbor knocking next door to be let in (Woolf, 1965, p. 190). The nineteenth century dies symbolically both as Wagner's Romantic opera ends and as the chapter ends with the announcement of King Edward VII's death.

Flying over London

Woolf's narrator, though, escapes the stuffy air of the nineteenth century and the Victorian drawing room, flying above towns and cities and sea or swooping down to the pedestrian level to observe, for example, the motion of leaves blown by the wind or the movements of clerks in the shops. This narrator observes the motion of cyclical time, in a Kristevan sense, to connect what Woolf would later describe as the tapping on the walks of everyday life while a universe, in wide sweeps, flows overhead (Woolf, 1965, p. 114). In the prelude to each of the chapter 'years,' the narrator voices a virtual experience of flying, taking in aerial views of London, Oxford, the Channel, and the continent, as well as swooping down to ground level to adopt a pedestrian perspective. In the opening changeable spring of the novel, for example, the narrator appears, like the clouds, to provide an aerial view of terrestrial space from the country fields to London, observing a multitude of shoppers and a stream of horse-drawn vehicles moving like caravans (Woolf, 1965, p. 3). Under the rising, impassive, and indifferent moon, the narrator observes an earthly pattern, the ceaseless passage of time across the sky like 'the rays of a searchlight' (Woolf, 1965, p. 4). Choosing a narrator both outside of and within the wheel of space/time, Woolf constructs a global pattern of ceaseless motion which yields to the pressure of history as she selects for its image the searchlight – not yet invented in 1880, but by 1917, a beacon in time of war.[6]

Flying over the channel

In '1891,' when the aerial narrator blows with the wind across the English Channel to France, a flight of that duration over an extended space was not yet possible.[7] Eleanor's first sight of an airplane reminds her of the day she first learned that an airplane had crossed the Channel. As they stand at the window in the 'Present Day' waiting for a taxi to take them to Delia's party, the capstone event of the novel, Eleanor and her niece Peggy look out at a scene that offers incessant motion as London mapped beneath them (Woolf, 1965, p. 328). Eleanor points to the sky and tells Peggy, 'That's where I saw my first aeroplane...and someone...said: "The world will never be the same again!" ' (Woolf, 1965, p. 329). Eleanor echoes what many English felt after this record flight, that it had shrunk the globe as it increased the speed of motion. England, in effect, was no longer an island, and, in fact, vulnerable to attack as never before.

A cluster of chapters surrounding World War I – 1913, 1914, 1917, and 1918 – circulate around another watershed temporal/spatial moment in *The Years*. In 1913, we learn with Martin Pargiter, Eleanor's brother, as he reads the newspaper, that the Balkan war is over; but, he thinks, more trouble lies ahead (Woolf, 1965, p. 220). Martin does not yet know in January that in June, 1913, the second Balkan War would break out – both wars preparing the way for World War I by escalating tensions among

Serbia, Austria, Bulgaria, and Turkey. The chapter '1914' provides the calm before the storm, taking place during a lovely English spring where Woolf tracks Martin and Sara in the neighborhood of St. Paul's on their way to Hyde Park to meet Maggie. This is a chapter in which, while there is little hint of what looms on the horizon, the characters are aware of the passage of time and clocks strike repeatedly, until the end. The scene shifts from London to Kitty speeding by train and automobile toward her husband's north country estate where she stands at the top of a hill surveying the 'billowing land...singing to itself, a chorus, alone,' experiencing complete happiness: 'Time had ceased' (Woolf, 1965, p. 278). In the words of Bachelard, Woolf has captured in fiction a compression of time in one of the many 'countless alveoli' of space in the novel (Bachelard, 1994, p. 8).

But instead of ceasing, time propels the world toward war. '1917' takes place in wartime on a cold winter's night as a searchlight pierces the sky. Members of the two main branches of the Pargiter family gather in the home of Maggie and her husband, Renny, for a dinner party. A German air raid drives them into the cellar where they hear the sound of guns boom overhead and then fade away. In the silence which follows, even the clocks at Westminster fail to strike until bugles announce the all clear. As Eleanor walks home, she sees a 'broad fan of light, like the sail of a windmill...sweeping slowly across the sky.' 'The raid!' she thinks, 'I'd forgotten the raid!' (Woolf, 1965, pp. 299–300). Life, time, and space, like the rays of the searchlight, continue to move as before.

The end of the war comes in November, 1918, in a very brief chapter which seems almost to announce it as a footnote. Filtered through the consciousness of Crosby, the former Pargiter servant, guns boom and sirens wail as Crosby looks at the sky peevishly. ' "Them guns again," ' she mutters (Woolf, 1965, p. 304). Crosby fails to understand the import of these sounds announcing the end of war until someone standing with her in line at the grocer's shop tells her.

Walking in the city

Dropping from the clouds to the street-level as we double back in time to the nineteenth century, we find that Woolf produces a remarkably detailed London cityscape through which her characters move, intersect, and engage in the construction of social relations. Characters in the novel walk or ride in London in every chapter. Rose, only ten in 1880, ventures out onto her residential street at twilight, galloping, as her imagination sends her to free British soldiers in danger in a foreign land, to the nearby shop to buy herself a box of toy ducks. But Rose has entered the dangerous world of patriarchally identified public space. As she runs past the pillar-box, a man emerges from the shadows under the gas lamp and reaches for her. She rushes past him to the shop, but as she returns home, the man appears again, unbuttoning his clothes under the light from the gas lamp (Woolf, 1965, p. 29). As a female transgressor in public space, Rose has been forced to face her vulnerability and subjected to a visual assault by a sexual predator, which marks her for life.

Eleanor, however, the eldest Pargiter daughter, manages to negotiate public space in performance of charitable work among the poor, an activity that was acceptable for young Victorian women; and by 1891, Eleanor seems to enjoy almost unprecedented freedom of movement through London. '1891' follows Eleanor as she navigates through London, mapping a city where real and imaginary places and streets co-exist. As she rides and walks the city streets, Eleanor appropriates the topographical system, exercising her power of motion. 'Space,' in the words of Michel de Certeau, 'is a practiced place' (Certeau, 1988, p. 117). Indeed, Certeau argues further, '[e]very story is a travel story – a spatial practice' (Certeau, 1988, p. 115).

And, in 1891, Eleanor's story is very much a travel story. Her starting point is her home on the imaginary Abercorn Terrace presumably at the northern edge of Hyde Park, the other end of the park, in fact, from Woolf's own childhood home on the south end at 22, Hyde Park Gate. Eleanor takes off trotting to find she is just in time to catch her horse-drawn omnibus. Relieved from the pressure of rushing on foot, Eleanor can relax as she climbs on top to revel in the ride eastward on the very real Bayswater Road, believing that she will be on time for her meeting. Eleanor is in her element, as the narrator suggests, mobile and free, going to her own work (Woolf, 1965, p. 94).

First she must attend a committee meeting, and Eleanor's destination suggests that she stays on the bus as Bayswater Road turns into Oxford Street and residences give way to shops, alighting near the plate-glass window of a large shop. Despite having caught her bus, however, Eleanor is late for the meeting. The committee meeting over, Eleanor's next destination is Peter Street, another real location south of Oxford Street between Regent Street and Shaftesbury Avenue, just north of Piccadilly Circus. Here Eleanor will walk to meet the contractor on a housing project for the poor to bring him to task for poor workmanship on the buildings, and she is late again. Ending what has already been a very busy and rather confrontational morning, Eleanor swings once more onto the omnibus headed west on the Bayswater Road to loop back home to Abercorn Terrace for lunch, for which she is late. Woolf's reiteration of Eleanor's continual lateness underscores a slower pace of motion in 1891.

After lunch, Eleanor backtracks the morning's route, this time taking a horse-drawn hansom cab down Bayswater Road – a treat that would save her fifteen precious minutes – slowing for a traffic jam at the Marble Arch, continuing onto Oxford Street, turning onto High Holborn, and stopping at Chancery Lane to watch her brother present a case at the Law Courts. Eleanor is only barely conscious of her ride, though, for Woolf presents her negotiation of simultaneously real and imaginary space/time; the entire time she is in the cab, she is reading a letter from her brother Martin. Martin, who writes of having been lost in the jungle, provides an intriguing parallel for Eleanor's journey through the streets of London. The real streets lose their detail as Eleanor experiences the cold and dark of a jungle night with Martin. With only two matches in his pocket to light a fire in the dark, Martin survives a night alone, arising at dawn to climb a tree, find the track, and rejoin his companions. With a sigh of relief, Eleanor re-enters the world as vehicles flow past; she rejoices at being in the center of speed and motion, in the midst of a 'racing' street (Woolf, 1965, p. 112).

Eleanor's journey is capped, though, by her location after she leaves the Law Courts; for she is on foot walking down the Strand past Charing Cross station where, transfixed by the newspaper announcement of Parnell's death, Eleanor stands in Trafalgar Square, looking up at Nelson's Column. 'Suddenly the whole scene froze into immobility....' Eleanor thinks, 'A man was joined to a pillar; a lion was joined to a man; they seemed stilled, connected, as if they would never move again' (Woolf, 1965, p. 113). Eleanor yields to the shock of history impacting her own individual life and stands transfixed in another alveolus of compressed time. She intuits that Nelson symbolically points to Parnell, now frozen and immobilized in time; stasis is death. Eleanor's awareness of the global effect and monumental nature of this death slows her consciousness of the motion of time, but she does not stop moving as she crosses Trafalgar Square, contemplating immortality against triviality. London has turned dark: 'Parnell. He's dead, she said to herself, still conscious of the two worlds; one flowing in wide sweeps overhead, the other tip-tapping circumscribed upon the pavement. But here she was...' (Woolf, 1965, p. 114). Yet where is here? Woolf gives no name to the street or neighborhood, revealing only that Eleanor feels in the aftermath of this world-shattering revelation that the real London has become vicious and obscene.

The persistence of objects

In the 'Present Day,' Eleanor thinks about how technology has changed the pace of life – the speed of aeroplanes and motorcars, the nuisance of the wireless – but she applauds the advent of hot water and electric light, for these represent pleasure and progress to her (Woolf, 1965, p. 330). As she and her niece Peggy ride in a cab to Delia's party, they notice illuminated advertisements in the theater district, and that interior spaces – Sara's rooms, Delia's rented party rooms – are lit by electric lighting. Objects which provide illumination become a major iconic presence in the novel; for example, the gas lamp, rooted in space and a fixture of Victorian nightlife, will yield to the pressure of time and technology with the invention of the incandescent light bulb and the expansion of electric lighting throughout the streets of the world.

Linked irrevocably to the street lamp, not only as contiguous in the space near the Pargiter family home on Abercorn Terrace in 1880 but also as a relay point in Victorian life, is the pillar-box. The pillar-box remains a constant in time, unchanged by technological advances. It serves not only as a relay station for mail to be circulated and for the networks of social and public communication to be sustained, but also as an iconic structure in the later militant struggle for female equality and the vote, a struggle which Woolf introduces directly in the novel but whose relationship to the pillar-box she intriguingly mutes. Suffragettes would make the pillar-box a site of resistance to patriarchal power on November 26, 1912, destroying thousands of pieces of mail by pouring acid, ink, lampblack, and tar into pillar-boxes all over London. Woolf means to bind the future to the present of 1880 at the site of the pillar-box where Rose, the novel's future suffragette, is almost violated by daring to venture outside of that Victorian private space circumscribed as safe for females. However, by capturing Rose's imaginative 'wild' ride as Captain Pargiter, Woolf suggests a deeper interpretation of this scene than one which simply recoils from the scene of perversion, public exposure, and potential sexual assault. Woolf may also wish to call into question the spectre of a future suffragism which, rather than resisting masculine strategies of violence in the name of a cause, embraces them.

For by 1911, we learn that Rose has been arrested for throwing a brick but will escape jail *this* time as Woolf begins to make explicit Rose's participation in suffragist violent activity.[8] By 1914, Rose is not so lucky; she goes to prison for throwing another brick. Emblematic in public space of both public and private communication, the pillar-box survives in Eleanor's memory in the 'Present Day' as she thinks of posting a letter on the evening of her mother's death, but resists pursuing the memory; Eleanor wants only the present (Woolf, 1965, p. 336).

Resisting and yielding to historical time

Woolf resists the specificity of measured time throughout the novel, preferring instead to represent the experience of history at the level of individual consciousness. This witnessing to history tends to occur largely in scenes of reading. Characters read the newspaper, for example, in almost every chapter of the novel. In 1880, Kitty reads *The Times* to her mother and notes several events in passing. Kitty begins to read about Gladstone winning the election; she has already lost her mother's attention. But then she reads another item of interest about an electric light experiment (Woolf, 1965, p. 79). With the faintest suggestion, Woolf deftly indicates, through sweeping change in government and the advent of electric lighting, the threshold on which the world of 1880 stood poised.

With numerous references to events during the intervening years, read in the newspaper or announced on the streets – the death of Parnell, the death of Edward VII, upheaval in the Balkans, news from Ireland, the end of World War I – Woolf sustains a resistance to history as externalized to perceive its effects on consciousness, culminating these references with one to impending war in the 'Present Day.' Eleanor explodes as she looks at the evening paper, seeing there a photograph of a 'fat man gesticulating,' ' "Damned –" Eleanor shot out suddenly, "bully!" She tore the paper across with one sweep of her hand and flung it on the floor' (Woolf, 1965, p. 330). In 1935, the presumed year of the 'Present Day,' England remained passive as Hitler re-armed Germany, developing the Luftwaffe and making his anti-Jewish legislation and persecutory policies increasingly public. However, a 'fat man gesticulating' might even more appropriately refer to Benito Mussolini, who, during the summer of 1935, amassed troops on the Abyssinian border in preparation for a full-scale invasion in October. On August 26, 1935, a *London Daily Mail* reporter interviewed Mussolini in which he threatened war.[9] So the world did not lack for bullies in the summer of 1935.

Civilization and the lessons of the past

Woolf counterpoises scenes of reading the newspaper as contemporary history with scenes of reading literature as lessons from the past. In 1907, Sara reads her cousin Edward's verse translation of *Antigone*. The scene of

Sara's reading merges her consciousness with that of Antigone entombed in her burial cave. Sara thinks of Antigone buried alive, dipping into the play. 'The tomb was a brick mound. There was just room for her to lie straight out...And that's the end....' Sarah yawns, shutting the book and lays herself out between cold sheets, mimicking the burial of Antigone (Woolf, 1965, p. 136). Antigone is a major iconic figure in the novel, suggesting the entombment of women in the Victorian private house and the more far-reaching entombment of society in a Victorian cave. 'In time to come,' Sara, the Antigone figure in the novel, says, 'people will look into the rooms of the Victorian house, hold their noses and say, "Pah! They stink!" ' (Woolf, 1965, p. 189).

In 1911, Eleanor casually opens Dante's *Purgatory*, canto XV, reading: 'For by so many more there are who say "ours"/So much the more of good doth each possess' (Woolf, 1965, p. 212). Dante's words on possessiveness strike a chord that links directly to a major theme which emerges with full force in the 'Present Day': the formation of civilizations, the carving up geographical space into nations, and the disputes over boundaries and ownership, which lead to global warfare. Woolf, on the same date in 1932 when she commented in her diary on James Jeans's theories of time, space, and civilization quoted earlier, wrote in the very next sentence: 'Possessiveness is the devil' (Woolf, 1982, p. 65). In '1914,' Martin repeats Woolf's words, and although Martin is ostensibly speaking of the possessiveness of the woman he is in love with (as Woolf was ostensibly writing about possessive love affairs in her diary), the words spoken in the spring, just before the guns of August, take on more global implications (Woolf, 1965, p. 245).

Eleanor does not imagine those issues in 1911, though, as Dante's archaic Italian fails to capture her consciousness. She watches instead the moths on the ceiling and listens to the owl's liquid call as he flies from tree to tree; 'I'll read it one of these days,' and as she drifts off to sleep, Eleanor thinks, 'Things pass, things change...And where are we going?' (Woolf, 1965, p. 213).

Reading and quoting from literature takes on a heightened presence in the chapter 'Present Day' as if to suggest that it is civilization and culture which may still save the world. Characters read or quote 'fragments' to shore up against their ruins from Shakespeare, Marvell, Maupassant, Conrad, Catullus, and Sophocles. As they wait to leave for Delia's party, North reads lines from Marvell's 'The Garden' to Sara, to the accompaniment of the sounds of Sara's Jewish neighbor bathing in the bathroom which they share. 'Society is all but rude – ,' North reads, 'to this delicious solitude...' (Woolf, 1965, p. 339). Woolf's use of Marvell's poem gestures toward a rejection of the world and society; but escaping society and embracing mental solitude that way, Woolf insists, most presciently leads to madness, underscoring an acknowledgment of the persecution of Jews in 1935, which her text leaves silent.

Woolf's characters continue this underlying meditation on the nature of society and solitude as Peggy, listening to the sounds of the London night, echoes Conrad, and reaching beyond Conrad, William Blake: 'in the heart of darkness, in the depths of night' (Woolf, 1965, p. 389). Peggy is drawn to think, 'On every placard at every street corner was Death; or worse – . . . ; the fall of civilisation; the end of freedom' (Woolf, 1965, p. 388). Her brother, North, makes the allusion to Conrad even more palpable, for he, who has so recently come from Africa, feels that he is in the midst of a jungle, 'in the heart of darkness,' with only broken words and sentences to help break through to the light. And Woolf adds a faint echo of Eliot's Prufrock to North's reverie of trying to break through 'the briar-bush of human bodies, human wills and voices, that bent over him, binding him, blinding him . . . ' (Woolf, 1965, p. 411). Within just a few pages, Woolf returns to the *Antigone*, as Eleanor and Edward consider the relevance of the play to the younger generation. Edward quotes the line in Greek which translates as: 'Tis not my nature to join in hating, but in loving' (Woolf, 1965, p. 414). Antigone has the last word, reinforcing through the dialogue of past and present, newspaper and classic, a feminine and feminist stance toward community and society. Her choice is for love.

Recurring patterns in space/time

The novel, and the 'Present Day,' ends with a symbolic scene at the window. As dawn approaches with the end of Delia's party, Eleanor, along with her brothers and sisters, now the 'older generation,' stands at the window. What she sees binds the present to the past and completes the palimpsestic structure the novel has begun with the scene of Delia and Milly at the window of Abercorn Terrace in 1880 watching a cab stop two doors down. Together the sisters peer from behind the muslin blinds to watch 'a young man in a top-hat get out of the cab. He stretched his hand up to pay the driver . . . ' (Woolf, 1965, pp. 18–19).

Counterpointing Victorian angst in the present day, however, '[Eleanor] was watching a taxi gliding slowly round the square. It stopped in front of a house two doors down . . . A young man had got out; he paid the driver. Then a girl in a tweed travelling suit followed him. He fitted his latch-key to the door. "There,"' Eleanor says as the young man opens the door and the couple stands together on the threshold. ' "There!" she repeated as the door shut with a little thud behind them' (Woolf, 1965, p. 434). The space of 'there' sums the new vision for men and women, which offers the hope of a new equality in the time of the present day. Despite the brutality of the present day and the possibility of 'the fall of civilisation; the end of freedom,' Eleanor, thinks her niece Peggy, 'says the world is better, because two people out of all those millions are "happy" ' (Woolf, 1965, p. 388). Eleanor's 'There' answers the cry 'Where am I?' first voiced by her mother and echoed throughout the novel. As Eleanor's generation yields its space and its time to the next, Woolf's narrator looks up with hope for the future and sees that 'the sky above the houses wore an air of extraordinary beauty, simplicity and peace' (Woolf, 1965, p. 435).

Notes

1. In April, May, and June, 1929, Woolf published a lengthy article in *The Bookman* entitled 'The Phases of Fiction', posthumously published in *Granite and Rainbow: Essays by Virginia Woolf*. In it, she considers a number of novelists, including Marcel Proust. The quotation, taken from *Swann's Way*, captures the spirit of both novelists' engagement with time and space, memory and loss, and suggests a possible source for Woolf's ultimate title for *The Years*.
2. Despite *The Years's* rather obvious invitation to be examined as a fictionalization of human consciousness in contact with space/time, few scholars have done so. See as examples various scholarly approaches to the novel: Gillian Beer, Gloria Fromm, Helen Southworth, Ruth Hoberman, David Bradshaw, the special issue of the *Bulletin of the New York Public Library*, and Sowon Park. See Pamela Caughie for essays responding to Woolf's engagement with new technologies, Susan Squier on Virginia Woolf and the sexual politics of London, and Andrew Thacker's chapter on Woolf's *Mrs Dalloway* and London geographies.
3. Woolf records in her diary on December 29, 1935, that she has 'just put the last words to The Years' (Woolf, 1982, p. 360). Even though the novel would not be published until 1937 and Woolf would continue to revise in 1936, the intellectual content of the novel was finished by the end of 1935, and if the 'Present Day' is meant to exist in any specific year, it is that year.
4. Ann Banfield cites a letter Woolf wrote to Harmon H. Goldstone: 'I may say that I have never read Bergson' (Banfield, 2003, p. 474).
5. Woolf collapses into a sentence what it takes Jeans a paragraph to explain, but she utterly captures his meaning. Jeans sums up as follows: 'Looked at in terms of space, the message of astronomy is at best one of melancholy grandeur and oppressive vastness. Looked at in terms of time, it becomes one of almost endless possibility and hope' (Jeans, 1929, p. 331).
6. General Electric built the first carbon arc searchlight in 1893 and displayed it at the Chicago World's Fair in that year, so the searchlight did not yet exist

in 1880. Searchlights were, of course, in much more widespread use by World Wars I and II when they lit up the night sky against enemy attacks.

7. Louis Bleriot was the first to cross the Channel in 1909, reaching the Dover coast from Calais in just under 40 minutes.

8. In 1911, Woolf's friend Ethel Smyth, upon whom the character of Rose is partly based, joined the suffrage movement and heaved a brick through the Home Secretary's window. She spent two months in Holloway Prison during which she composed the 'March of the Women' for the Women's Service and Political Union.

9. An audiotape of this interview appears on the website *The March Toward War* at: http://xroads.virginia.edu/~MA04/wood/html/ethiopia.htm. For a reading of the figure of Rose and the significance of the pillar-box in suffragism which inspired mine, see Squier (Squier, 1985, pp. 146, 170, 176).

Works cited

Bachelard, G., *The Poetics of Space*. Trans. M. Jolas (Boston: Beacon, 1994).

Banfield, A., 'Time Passes: Virginia Woolf, Post-Impressionism, and Cambridge Time', *Poetics Today*, 24 (Fall 2003) 471–516.

Beer, G., *Virginia Woolf: The Common Ground, Essays by Gillian Beer* (Ann Arbor: University of Michigan Press, 1996).

Bergson, H., *Creative Evolution*, Trans. A. Mitchell, 1911 (New York: Dover Publications, 1998).

———, *Duration and Simultaneity: Bergson and the Einsteinian Universe*. Trans. L. Jacobson (Manchester: Clinamen, 1999).

———, *Time and Free Will*. Trans. F. L. Pogson, 1913 (London: Elibron Classics, 2005).

Bradshaw, D., 'Hyams Place: *The Years*, the Jews and the British Union of Fascists', *Women Writers of the 1930s: Gender, Politics and History*. Ed. M. Joannou (Edinburgh: Edinburgh University Press, 1999), pp. 179–191.

Caughie, P. (ed.) *Virginia Woolf and the Age of Mechanical Reproduction* (New York: Routledge, 1999).

de Certeau, M., *The Practice of Everyday Life*. Trans. S. Rendall (Berkeley: University of California Press, 1988).

Duncan, N. (ed.) *BodySpace: Destabilizing Geographies of Gender and Sexuality* (London: Routledge, 1996).

Fromm, G. G., 'Re-Inscribing *The Years*: Virginia Woolf, Rose Macaulay, and the Critics', *Journal of Modern Literature*, 13 (July 1986) 289–306.

Hoberman, R., 'Aesthetic Taste, Kitsch, and, *The Years*', *Woolf Studies Annual*, 11 (2005) 77–98.

'Italy seizes Ethiopia,' *The March Toward War: The March of Time as Documentary and Propaganda*. Ed. Mary Wood. American Studies Program at the University of Virginia. 17 July 2007. http://xroads.virginia.edu/~MA04/wood/mot/html/ethiopia.htm

Jeans, S. J., *The Universe Around Us* (New York: Macmillan, 1929).

———, *The Mysterious Universe* (New York: Macmillan, 1930).

Kristeva, J., 'Women's Time', *The Kristeva Reader*. Ed. T. Moi (New York: Columbia University Press, 1986), pp. 187–213.

Leaska, M. (ed.) *The Pargiters: The Novel-Essay Portion of 'The Years'* (New York: Harcourt Brace Jovanovich, 1977).

Lefebvre, H., *The Production of Space*. Trans. D. Nicholson-Smith (Malden, MA: Blackwell Publishing, 1991).

McDowell, L., 'Spatializing Feminism: Geographic Perspectives', *BodySpace: Destabilizing Geographies of Gender and Sexuality*. Ed. N. Duncan (London: Routledge, 1996).

Park, S. S., 'Suffrage and Virginia Woolf: "The Mass Behind the Single Voice" ', *The Review of English Studies*, 56 (2005) 119–134.

Proust, M., *Remembrance of Things Past, Volume One: Swann's Way, Within a Budding Grove*. Trans. C. K. S. Moncrieff and T. Kilmartin (New York: Random House, 1981).

Southworth, H., ' "Mixed Virginia": Reconciling the "Stigma of Nationality" and the Sting of Nostalgia in Virginia Woolf's Later Fiction', *Woolf Studies Annual*, 11 (2005) 99–132.

Squier, S. *Virginia Woolf and London: The Sexual Politics of the City* (Chapel Hill: University of North Carolina Press, 1985).

Thacker, A. *Moving Through Modernity: Space and Geography in Modernism* (Manchester: Manchester University Press, 2003).

Virginia Woolf Issue. Bulletin of the New York Public Library, 80 (Winter 1977) 137–301.

Woolf, V., *Three Guineas* (London: Hogarth Press, 1938).

——, 'Phases of Fiction', *Granite and Rainbow: Essays by Virginia Woolf*. Ed. L. Woolf (London: Harcourt Brace Jovanovich, 1958), pp. 93–148.

——, *The Years*, 1937 (New York: Harcourt Brace Jovanovich, 1965).

——, 'Mr. Bennett and Mrs. Brown', *The Captain's Death Bed and Other Essays*. Ed. L. Woolf (New York, London: Harcourt Brace Jovanovich, 1978), pp. 94–119.

——, *The Diary of Virginia Woolf: Volume Four, 1931–1935*. Ed. A. O. Bell (New York: Harcourt Brace Jovanovich, 1982).

——, *The Diary of Virginia Woolf: Volume Five, 1936–1941*. Ed. A. O. Bell (New York: Harcourt Brace Jovanovich, 1984).

6
Imagining the Karoo Landscape: Free Indirect Discourse, the Sublime, and the Consecration of White Poverty

Johan Geertsema

The work of the early twentieth-century South African-born English writer Pauline Smith is noteworthy for a number of reasons. In it we find a somewhat unusual, for English writing in South Africa, focus on Afrikaner characters and, what is more, an empathy with them. Influential figures such as J. M. Coetzee and Nadine Gordimer have therefore, though on different grounds, indicted her œuvre on the grounds that it fulfils a justificatory function for what was the incipient racial discourse of apartheid. Gordimer claims that Smith helped '[create] a justificatory myth of the Afrikaner people' (1976, p. 105), which thus shaped the way they understood themselves as being *of Africa*, as a kind of long-suffering white African tribe. Smith's focus on white suffering turns poverty into a virtue in demonstrating Afrikaner forbearance in the face of adversity. In Smith's stories, Gordimer rhetorically asks (she also mentions the writers Herman Charles Bosman and Athol Fugard), 'are Afrikaners not shown living [as closely] to the earth and natural disasters as any black man?' (1976, p. 106).

Coetzee's more extensive, and more rigorous, analysis focuses on Smith's use of language, specifically free indirect speech, in her attempt to evoke the Afrikaans speech of her characters. Coetzee argues that what he calls 'transfer', defined as 'the rendering of (imagined) foreign speech in an English stylistically marked to remind the reader of the (imagined) foreign original' (1988, p. 117), constitutes a signal (albeit an unusual one) by means of which free indirect speech is presented in Smith's writing. The effect of such transfer, which makes Smith's Afrikaners echo the English of the Authorized Version, is then 'to validate the homegrown Calvinist myth in which the Afrikaner has his type in the Israelite [and is a] member of an elect race (*volk*) set apart from the tribes of the idolatrous' (1988, p. 118). Coetzee continues by observing that the consequences of such mythical identification 'have been far-reaching and serious' in that it served ideologically to justify decades of racial oppression, and thus suggests Smith's complicity with a way of thinking that would eventuate in apartheid (p. 118).

In Gordimer's and Coetzee's critiques we find encapsulated two concerns, which also constitute the dual focus of this chapter: space and language as these relate to white identity in Smith's writing. Where the force of Gordimer's argument is to highlight the degree to which Smith naturalizes the presence in Africa of white Afrikaners, Coetzee pinpoints the degree to which Smith's use of language works towards this end. Taking my cue from them, I investigate the role played by space in the negotiation of white identity in Smith's writing by considering her enigmatic short story 'Desolation' (1930), and I do so by focusing on Smith's language, specifically her use of free indirect discourse (FID).[1]

It might seem unlikely that a story which recounts the journey of a poor white Afrikaner and her grandchild across apparently barren territory – a story which quite literally traces the way its protagonists rootlessly 'drift' (1990, pp. 92, 95) on a dry, desolate landscape, as it were blown this way and that as on a vast sea – would describe experiences of the sublime. Indeed, Coetzee (1988, p. 49) has argued influentially that (South) African landscape in general does not lend itself to the European category of the sublime, which would further complicate an understanding of the story with reference to the sublime. Yet, as I will show, an experience of the sublime is evoked by Smith in the course of negotiating the relation between colonial space and settler identity, though the way the sublime functions here admittedly appears unusual. For whereas the presence of the sublime in colonial contexts has aided, as Spivak shows (26–29), in the process of clearing the land of autochthonous inhabitants, 'Desolation' hardly appears to have the effect of justifying Afrikaner identity or naturalizing Afrikaner presence on the land. Far from it: the story, as I shall show, is marked by a striking ambivalence concerning the place of Afrikaners in Africa. This ambivalence comes to the fore not only in the version of the sublime deployed by Smith in her imagining of space, but is further underscored by her use of FID. Taken together, they render any easy valorization of Afrikaner identity problematic. This then leads to the question as to how the story can, as Gordimer and Coetzee would have it with reference to Smith's larger œuvre, be read as furthering a justificatory myth of the Afrikaner, a process which would, in terms of their arguments, accordingly implicate it as bearing some measure of responsibility for the ideology of apartheid. Though 'Desolation' complicates Gordimer's and Coetzee's discussions of Smith in interesting ways, the story does appear to amount to a justification of white identity, and, I conclude, this may well occur by means of the myth of the 'Volksmoeder'.

*   *   *

Though she had left South Africa with her sister for school in Scotland in 1895 when she was aged 13, and only returned to South Africa subsequently for occasional visits, Pauline Smith is clearly possessed of a 'regional consciousness' that is anchored in the South Africa of her youth. In her work (almost all of which was published in the 1920s) she evokes the Karoo or, more properly, the Little Karoo of her childhood. Indeed, her most significant book, aside from the novel *The Beadle* (1926), is the eponymous collection of short stories, *The Little Karoo* (1925; expanded edition 1930). The Little Karoo region in the south-eastern section of South Africa, though infertile and prone to drought, is dotted with farms and homesteads. It has historically been marked by extremes of great wealth and acute poverty. Rob Nixon's recent *Dreambirds* (1999) gives the reader a good sense of these extremes. Though largely concerned with the Karoo's ostrich elites – farmers known as 'ostrich barons' who made millions during the heyday of the vogue for the bird's feathers and then lost virtually everything with the collapse of this market with the advent of the First World War in 1914 – it also is cognizant of this region's entrenched history of racism and deprivation (see for instance 1999, pp. 210–224).

A good description of the Karoo in the early part of the twentieth century, the time during which Smith's story is set, is provided by Jeffrey Butler's discussion of the Cradock district:

> It is . . . a thirstland suitable for ranching only, especially if there is no irrigation. It lies between the 10″ and 12″ annual rainfall contours, one of a group of Midland districts hard hit by frequent droughts. Furthermore, it suffered after World War I, like the rest of the eastern Cape, from the collapse of ostrich farming, the rapid decline of horse breeding, and then during the depression from the fall in the price of wool, its long-term staple, and lucerne (alfalfa). . . . It is difficult to arrive at the actual process of depopulation and urbanisation, but in addition to drought, the Karoo was undergoing a major change in the extension of fencing which limited casual access to land, and reduced the demand for labour, white as well as black. (1989, pp. 59–60)

The Little Karoo is situated on the threshold of, and anticipates, the even more stark and vast landscape of the Great Karoo, located deeper in the African interior. Dorothy Driver points out that '[with] the exception of "Desolation", which is set in the "grey and desolate region" of the Great Karoo, the stories in *The Little Karoo* are set in one or another farming community in this area, with occasional excursions to the town of Platkops (Oudtshoorn)' (1984, p. 49). The significance of the Karoo from an æsthetico-political perspective is that it constitutes a topos, in the context of 'white writing' in South Africa, for imagining Africa, and has persistently played a key role in negotiating settler identity (as well as the identity of settlers' descendants) in Africa.[2] According to W. J. T. Mitchell, landscapes in some societies, particularly ones with colonial histories (he mentions, among others, New Zealand and Israel), may be said to be 'central to the national imaginary, a part of daily life that imprints public, collective fantasies on places and scenes' (1994, pp. 27–28). The landscape of the Karoo arguably fulfils a similar role in South Africa. But one needs to add the qualification that the focus in this chapter is less on the role the Karoo has played in the construction of some or other putative, yet-to-be-achieved South African national identity, than on its role in the creation of a *white* imaginary.

The relation between space and identity has prompted significant inquiry during recent decades, and the diverse field of 'postcolonial studies' has played an important role in reconceiving that relation. In what has become a classic essay on the role of space as a cultural category, the anthropologists Akhil Gupta and James Ferguson identify a number of challenges for thinking about this concept. Among other things, they question what they call the 'assumed isomorphism of space, place, and culture [and] the implicit mapping of cultures onto places'; instead, they want to 'understand the processes whereby a space achieves a distinctive *identity* as a place' in order to 'reconceptualise fundamentally the politics of community, solidarity, identity, and cultural difference' (1992, pp. 7, 8, 9; their italics). The contemporary forces of globalization, diaspora, and the transnational flows in the wake of colonialism and Empire render any simple identification of culture with space, 'of naturalised links between places and peoples' (1992, p. 12), problematic. Gupta and Ferguson therefore argue that an anthropology 'whose objects are no longer conceived as automatically and naturally anchored in space will need to pay particular attention to the way spaces and places are made, imagined, contested, and enforced' (1992, p. 18).

What this suggests is that there is no 'natural' link between space and identity, nor between culture and identity (i.e., *where* one is cannot fully determine *who* one is). In addition, spaces become places through cultural processes that not only imagine such links but that, moreover, precisely attempt to efface their status as 'cultural' in order to present the relation they establish as 'natural'. If we accept these points, then the process of imagining plays a significant role in the ideological negotiation of the link between culture, space, and identity. And indeed, 'imagination' is a key concept by means of which space, culture, and identity are articulated in Gupta and Ferguson's argument, which suggests that one important task in investigating the processes whereby naturalized identifications with spaces are established would lie in delineating the role of culture itself, including that of literary works, in this process.

Since almost all of Smith's fiction is set in the Karoo, her work therefore also constitutes – in terms of Gupta and Ferguson's argument – an important component of the project of imagining Africa that forms part of the negotiation of an African white identity. Smith's writing is characterized by the representation of what are often highly localized evocations of the landscapes of the Karoo. These spaces – often, though not always, presented as bucolic, idyllic, and otherworldly – are then entered and thus disrupted by outsiders. For instance, in *The Beadle* an Englishman enters the space of Harmonie (the Afrikaans name significantly suggesting the established order as much as an æstheticization of social and physical spaces in this farming community) and disrupts the order of things by seducing the innocent Andrina. In the story 'The Schoolmaster' (from *The Little Karoo*) Jan Boetje is given shelter by the narrator's family and she falls in love with him. Her sense of equilibrium is, however, forever disturbed as Jan goes berserk, stabs, and blinds a pair of donkeys during an outing with the family's children. In each of these cases, which may be taken as paradigmatic for Smith's work in general, the outside world intrudes upon and affects a protected, harmonious, and apparently safe inside world.

In some of Smith's stories, however, such as the story on which I focus in this chapter, this pattern is reversed: here the movement is from the inside to the outside, as the characters trek from a farm-home into the wider world, thus enacting the urbanizing movement of 'poor-whites' in the early decades of the twentieth century. The story traces the misfortunes of the 'poor-white' (1990, pp. 92, 94, 95, 99, 100) Alie van Staden and her orphaned grandson Koos in the desolate landscape of the Karoo. After Koos's father dies of consumption during one of the worst droughts in human memory (1990, p. 93), the owner of the farm on which they have been living as *bijwoners* (tenant farmers) turns them off his land. With no family and nowhere to go, Alie is forced to travel with Koos to the hamlet of Hermansdorp so that she can find work in order to care for the child. The story then describes Alie's and Koos's slow, painful journey through the desert landscape of a region Smith calls 'the Ver-latenheid' (1990, p. 92), explicitly using the translation of this as her title: the Verlatenheid is 'that dreary stretch of the Great Karoo which lies immediately to the north of the Zwartkops Mountains and takes its name from the desolation which nature displays here in the grey volcanic harshness of its kopjes [hills] and the scanty vegetation of its veld. This grey and desolate region was her [Alie's] world'. In Hermansdorp, the store where Alie remembers working many years earlier now no longer exists; Koos is left at an orphanage; and Alie appears to die at the end of the story.

Though, as mentioned before, it is true that the sublime has not been a centrally important aspect of the white writing of landscape in South Africa, its occurrence at certain important historical junctures should not be ignored, and this part of my argument considers both the pos-sibility that an experience of the sublime occurs in 'Desolation' and the political function it might have.[3] The 1920s and 1930s (when Smith was writing the story) was a period during which a series of dislocating events (drought, depression, rapid urbanization, and industrialization) brought white Afrikaners into modernity as they imagined themselves into a nation, a process which gave rise to what would shortly afterwards become apartheid. I here consider the possibility that a per/version of the Kantian sublime plays, in this period, a dual role in this process, helping white Afrikaners come to terms with the otherness of Africa not only by asserting their alleged superiority to it, but also by naturalizing their pos-ition in it through a process of identification with the land. But I then subsequently problematize that analysis by focusing on its ambivalence, and how this is further effected by means of FID.

In Kant's canonical account, the æsthetic confrontation with an object the 'intuition [*Anschauung*]' (2000, p. 128) of which cannot be presented by the imagination in such a way as to correspond adequately to an idea of reason is sublime. The ground for this is that the self experiences not only anxiety and displeasure in the confrontation with the infinite, the enormous, or the powerful, but importantly also pleasure. This pleasure arises in the self since the confrontation with the sublime confirms the superiority of reason over the imagination, as well as over nature. The oscillation of displeasure and pleasure bespeaks, as Lyotard puts it, a

dislocation of the faculties among themselves [which] gives rise to the extreme tension (Kant calls it agitation) that characterizes the pathos of the sublime, as opposed to the calm feeling of beauty. At the edge of the break, infinity, or the absoluteness of the Idea can be revealed in what Kant calls a negative presentation, or even a non-presentation. (1991, p. 98)

And it is this (non-)appearance of the Idea that gives rise to pleasure since it presents to us the fact that 'our imagination in all its boundlessness, and with it nature, [pales] into insignificance beside the ideas of reason if it is supposed to provide a presentation adequate to them' (Kant 2000, p. 140). The faculty of the imagination is inadequate to the task set it by reason, namely matching the intuition apprehended by the subject with a concept or idea of reason: here, infinite or enormous extension or power. The imagination fails to present an image that is adequate to reason's concept of that extension or power. As Lyotard suggests, distinguishing between the beautiful and the sublime, the experience of the sublime involves what he calls *privation*: the sublime leads to a spiritual passion which Burke, in his antecedent account of the sublime, calls terror: 'privation of light, terror of darkness; privation of others, terror of solitude; privation of language, terror of silence; privation of objects, terror of emptiness; privation of life, terror of death' (1991, p. 99). That is, the feeling of the sublime in Lyotard's reading is crucially connected with absence or the threat of absence, with the terror of the imagination as it is overwhelmed by what it cannot grasp or comprehend.

As the two poor-white Afrikaners, Alie and Koos, slowly trek through the desolation of the Verlatenheid, they are confronted with a remarkable scene that quite palpably presents the Karoo landscape as sublime. The mirages they see are a direct consequence of the apparently boundless nature of the landscape that threatens to overwhelm the protagonists. Not coincidentally, in describing the landscape as a 'sea' on which, as pointed out at the start, her protagonists are said to 'drift' (float), Smith uses a synæsthesia to underscore the overwhelming sense of disorientation and vulnerability they experience: 'The country ahead of them now was flat as a calm gray sea, its veld unbroken by any kopje until the long low line of the Hermansdorp hills was reached' (1990, pp. 100–101). It is out of this imaginary sea that 'a strange fantastic world … slipped into being, vanished, and slipped into being again as they gazed upon it' (1990, p. 101). What is more, for these strange phenomena Alie 'had neither explanation nor name', which suggests that they exceed the ability of her imagination to match the intuition of them that she apprehends with a concept or idea of reason, to put it in Kant's vocabulary. The travelling Alie and Koos are overwhelmed by an immense landscape of which they cannot make sense, and that yet, paradoxically, in its 'very mystery' 'brought an added sense of his own personal security' to the boy.

Given the sense of personal security that Koos is said by the narrator to experience, one might argue that he reads the landscape in a way that conforms with Kant's account of the sublime in as far as it strengthens the subject of the sublime and provides a sense of satisfaction. Writing about what he terms the mathematical sublime, Kant considers two stages: 'there is a feeling of the inadequacy of [the spectator's] imagination for presenting the ideas of a whole, in which the imagination reaches its maximum and, in the effort to extend it, sinks back into itself, but is thereby transported into an emotionally moving satisfaction' (2000, p. 136). When confronted with a vast object, the imagination is overwhelmed and fails to present not so much the object as reason's ideational grasp of it – its 'ideas of a whole'. But, paradoxically, this very failure of the imagination is what is pleasurable and comforting about the sublime, in that it serves to confirm the superiority of reason. What we see Koos experiencing is this '[sinking] back into itself' of the imagination.

But the æsthetic of the sublime implies a politics, one which lends itself to settlement. The failure of the imagination has the paradoxical effect of erasing the human from the landscape, but in this erasure an important objective is attained: there is a levelling of difference which tends to deny primordial, autochthonous claims to the land. Since claims by aboriginal inhabitants are thereby invalidated, the process assists the settler in laying claim to the land. Moreover, this argument implies that the position of the settler as settler is erased, that he becomes, or comes to see himself as, native. The sublime work of art offers a dramatization of the founding of a humanizing cultural moment which subjects nature to culture and elevates the latter over the former, something paradoxically achieved by the self's *representation* of nature as overwhelming. This is evidenced, in Kant as in Burke's sublime, by the position of safety in which the subject of the sublime finds himself.[4] The sublime is evidence that nature is no longer overwhelming in itself; presenting nature as overwhelming, for instance in a landscape painting, is the paradoxical proof of the superiority of culture and of the human over nature, and in this way functions as an intimation of freedom from the necessity of nature. Had such presentation, counterfactually, not occurred, this would have implied the actual, as opposed to the presented, superiority of nature over culture. The domination of nature by culture is staged through the presentation by culture of nature's domination over it. Culture paradoxically domesticates nature in empowering it (in presenting it as powerful); the presentation of natural terrain in a sublime landscape æstheticizes it in order to subject it. And this subjection of the wilderness, its domestication as sublime landscape, clears the ground – quite literally – for settlement, for dwelling, for being-at-home, in that it asserts the superiority of the subject of the sublime over the landscape and those who inhabit it. It should therefore come as no surprise that, historically, the sublime has been implicated in the colonial politics of settlement, as a means towards the domestication of the exotic and the other. Seen in this light, the sublime is one particularly powerful way in which the relationship between settler identity and colonized space becomes naturalized, to return to the terms of Gupta and Ferguson's argument that I invoked above.

However, the experience of the sublime in 'Desolation' is ambivalent. The landscape is incongruously described as a 'calm' rather than a 'dark and raging [düstere tobende] sea', which are the qualities Kant (2000, p. 139) thinks might evoke the feeling of the sublime in the mind. What is more, this feeling of the sublime is arguably *not* evoked in the protagonists. Even if it is not entirely missed, it does seem at the very least to be misread by them: despite the added sense of security experienced by the boy, the mirages ultimately leave them, and in particular Alie, bewildered. The reason for this is not hard to find: it may have something to do with Alie's intellectual ability (at the start of the story, she is characterized as 'slow in thought and slow in movement', and is said to evince 'something of the melancholy of the labouring ox' [1990, p. 92]). It may also have something to do with the degree to which she in particular is associated with the landscape (for instance, earlier in the story she is described as a 'great rock in a dry and thirsty land' [1990, p. 96]). The identification of the protagonists with the landscape serves to reduce the distance between them and it: as part of the landscape they cannot read it, because reading requires distance. Thirdly, though Koos feels safe beside his grandmother and this sense of safety is paradoxically reinforced by the mysteriousness of the landscape, nonetheless for Alie and Koos the landscape in the end appears to be anything but sublime, for the danger of perishing is all too real. In both Kant and Burke the sublime presents not actual danger, but danger at an æsthetic remove (see Kant 2000, p. 121; Burke 1998, pp. 86, 94, 163). Since they are in very real danger of being overwhelmed by the landscape, the characters would appear to be in no position to experience it as sublime. In short, the presence of the sublime in 'Desolation' is anything but straightforward, as is evident from the fact that it is not readily apprehended by the characters in the story. The sublime is arguably experienced by Koos only, and then to a limited extent. It would be possible to argue (though I do not have the space to do so here) that rather than the protagonists it is the *reader*, in the comfort of her armchair, who vicariously travels through the Karoo landscape and experiences it as sublime. My point is that the ambiguities attendant upon the sublime and its experience in 'Desolation' should serve to question any reading of the story as a triumphalist narrative of rising Afrikaner national identity that, in any simple way, subjects African others and African spaces to its æstheticizing gaze.

A further complication in understanding the story as (successfully) negotiating the complex relation between space and settler identity, pertains to Smith's deployment of FID.[5] This technique is important in the story since it contributes greatly to the difficulties of identifying and empathizing with the characters, in particular with Alie, the chief protagonist of the story. She is repeatedly described as 'aloof' (1990, pp. 94, 105, 110, 114), and 'patient' (1990, pp. 92, 102, 103, 110), as marked by 'silence' (1990, pp. 94, 95, 98, 105, 108, 112). This aloofness, this patient endurance of suffering, alienates those with whom she comes into contact: Mijnheer Bezedenhout, the farmer who expels her and Koos and who, we are told, could never fathom her thoughts and therefore 'came in the end to hate this old woman, so strong, it seemed to him, in her silence, so powerful in her patience' (1990, p. 94); Jan Nortje's wife, whom they meet during their trek (1990, p. 105); and the two women seated near a wagon whose greeting she does not notice or, perhaps, ignores and who therefore 'watched her curiously, resenting, as Mijnheer Bezedenhout had resented, her aloofness' (1990, p. 114). Now, the way in which Smith incorporates FID results in an interminable dialectic whereby the reader continually slips into and out of the protagonist's consciousness. As Dorrit Cohn has illustrated, FID fluctuates between 'irony and sympathy' (1978, pp. 116–126), and in 'Desolation' too it serves both to encourage readerly identification or sympathy with Alie *and* distancing from, even critique of her.

A good example that will illustrate Smith's procedure and its effects is the following passage, which follows directly on the justification by the farmer of his decision to expel Alie and Koos from his farm:

> To all that Mijnheer had to say Alie listened, as always, in silence. What, indeed, was there for her to answer? Mijnheer spoke of relatives to whom she might turn for help for herself and Stephan's child, but in fact she had none. She was the last of her generation as Stephan

had been the last of his. The poor-white is poor also in physique, and of all her consumptive stock only Stephan's Koos remained. Stephan's wife had died when her son was born, and her people had long since drifted out of sight, she could not say where. The child, therefore had none but herself to stand between him and destitution. All that was to be done for him she herself must do. All that was to be planned for him she herself must plan.

Slowly, while her master spoke, these thoughts passed through her mind. (1990, pp. 95–96)

The passage is explicitly marked as containing Alie's thoughts ('these thoughts passed through her mind'), and while the final sentences ('Stephan's wife . . . must plan') appear to render Alie's thought without explicitly marking it as such, it yet starts off with an extradiegetic narrative voice in the first sentences which describe Alie's response to Mijnheer's words, or, rather, her lack of response. Imperceptibly, as is typical of FID, the narrative voice changes from an external to an internal one, and it is hard to pinpoint the exact moment where this occurs. Does Alie think, rhetorically, 'What, indeed, was there for her to answer?', or is this the narrator's voice? The sentence 'The poor-white is poor also in physique, and of all her consumptive stock only Stephan's Koos remained' seems to present an external voice (the narrator's, though perhaps this might represent Mijnheer Bezedenhout's consciousness), but the next sentence is ambiguously perched between extradiegetic reportage and Alie's own consciousness, as indicated by the final phrase 'she could not say where' which seems to indicate Alie's thought.

The crucial point I want to make here is that the complicated narrative voice in evidence in the story exacerbates (and even occasions) an uneasy ambivalence; indeed, arguably FID might be said to perform Alie's aloofness. The reader, like the various characters whom she disconcerts, cannot penetrate Alie's thought fully, and this inability is formally instantiated in the story by means of the narrator's and thereby the reader's slipping into and out of her consciousness, into and out of identification and sympathy with her. This process therefore serves to underscore the noteworthy forbearance of the protagonist (Alie) in the face of deprivation, a kind of radical passivity that irks most of the other characters and keeps the reader at a distance in complicating any attempt to empathize with her. But her aloofness and its articulation in the technique of FID also powerfully underscore her marginalized status with respect to both the physical spaces of the Karoo and the social spaces out of which she is expelled and into which she attempts to move. For it is precisely Alie's aloofness, as we have seen, that results in her and Koos being expelled from the farm by Bezedenhout, so that it is almost as though Alie's son's death is an excuse for the farmer to get rid of Alie herself: 'And when, in a spell of bitter cold, the bijwoner suddenly died, he [Bezedenhout] thought with relief that now old Alie must go' (1990, p. 95). In other words, the deployment of FID has the effect of articulating for the reader the inability of connecting with Alie in a way that is fully empathetic, or even just understanding. The technique allows for identification with the character but it also strictly limits the amount of such identification, thereby increasing the reader's sense of her as an irreducible enigma.

At this point I want to return to the negotiation of space in 'Desolation'. If we accept Bourdieu's deceptively commonsensical observation that our position not only in physical but also in social space is defined, quite literally, by our taking up a position in it, then we could argue that the ambivalence resulting from FID as well as Smith's version of the sublime suggests the lack of what Bourdieu might term the protagonist's *symbolic capital*. As he puts it, the 'I' understood as a habitus (or 'system of dispositions') 'that practically comprehends physical space and social space ... is comprehended, in a quite different sense, encompassed, inscribed, implicated in that space. It occupies a position there which ... we know is regularly associated with position-takings (opinions, representations, judgements, etc.) on the physical world and the social world' (2000, p. 130). That is, I am taken up into space, and through it into society, in a reciprocal process whereby I 'practically comprehend' space and am in turn 'comprehended' by it: in negotiating space, I grasp that space and thus take my place in it. If, as we saw Gupta and Ferguson argue, it is the case that where I am cannot fully determine who I am, even so who I am is intimately connected with *where* I am, no less in social spaces than in physical ones. As an academic I have a certain social position, and this position translates into certain physical spaces where I find myself: not only offices or classrooms, but also a particular kind of housing. But Bourdieu means not only this; he also means that my position in space (whether physical or social) is to a significant extent informed by the positions which I take in that space – the 'opinions, representations, judgements' and so forth that I espouse. To take positions such as these is to a significant degree dependent on social position, which again relates to physical position. People with social position are people with, in Bourdieu's terms, *social capital*. Conversely, those without social capital do not have the position to propagate their positions and, indeed, often appear inscrutable, other, enigmatic, and aloof. It is in this sense that it would be possible to argue that Alie's aloofness, which is articulated in part in Smith's deployment of FID, signifies her lack of social capital: she is aloof since she does not take positions, and she does not take positions since she lacks the social capital to do so.

In terms of Bourdieu's argument, the absence of social capital is intimately connected with deprivation in the form of physical and social marginality. It follows that the experience of space of those without social capital is marked by privation: 'the stigmatised pariah who, like the Jew in Kafka's time, or, now, the black in the ghetto or the Arab or Turk in the working-class suburbs of European cities, bears the curse of negative social capital' (2000, p. 241). Lack of social capital, lack of recognition, alienation: these are all marked by privative space, by expulsion from society into the wasteland of the ghetto, or indeed into the drought-stricken Karoo or Hermansdorp where no one knows Alie's name.

'Symbolic capital' then involves not only social value but importantly also *presupposes* privation and marginalization. Bourdieu describes it as *illusio*, or 'investment in a social game' (2000, p. 208), which thus 'gives sense' (playing on both senses of the term in French: meaning and direction) in the face of the arbitrariness of all social foundations. In other words, the self who has symbolic capital to invest enjoys in return a meaningful existence, and the life of such a self is justified, or 'consecrated'. But a crucial part of this is that such consecration is, in principle, preceded by privation. The habitus as a system of dispositions – the self disposed in space – is caught up in a dialectic of wretchedness and greatness, terms Bourdieu derives from Pascal. Greatness or grandeur (a term that can be related to the transcendence of the sublime) is a consequence not of wretchedness, but of a knowledge and acknowledgement of it that allow one to overcome it. The sublime would from this perspective be the greatness achieved in the knowledge of wretchedness, a formulation that can be related to Kant's account of the sublime as the overcoming by cultured reason of the realm of necessity that is nature. Moreover, given Lyotard's discussion of the sublime discussed earlier, one might say that logically wretchedness as the absence, the deprivation of grandeur, is a necessary constituent of the sublime. Bourdieu considers the consecration lent by symbolic capital to be mythical and ideological, as is apparent from his discussion of, for instance, investiture (2000, pp. 242–245), and one could argue that the sublime affords an experience of such consecration. Social consecration, given the dialectic of privation and transcendence built into it, implies a moment of privation which is overcome. Consecration may then be understood in terms of the construction of a myth whereby the self can comprehend the physical and social world, which almost per definition involves the sublime: not only privative confrontation with the immense that would annihilate the self but also its overcoming.

Put in concrete terms, Bourdieu's immensely rich discussion of symbolical capital and the consecration which it lends the self, a consecration which precisely offers the self *position* in society, can be related to Alie's position – or non-position – in 'Desolation'. Taking up a position would make sense, quite literally, of the privation that she experiences. As a poor white in the 1920s, as someone with almost no social position at the bottom of the (white) social ladder, Alie is more or less unable to take positions, and thus appears to be aloof, an impression which, as we have seen, is reinforced by means of the deployment of FID in the story. Even though the representation of landscape as sublime has the potential to naturalize the position of settlers in foreign lands, this does not straightforwardly seem to be the case here. Instead, we might say that the moment of the sublime in 'Desolation' has the effect of underscoring the out-of-place position of Alie and Koos in the landscape. Smith's use of FID and of the æsthetic of the sublime leads not so much to valence as to ambivalence.

Yet a consideration of the moment of the sublime discussed above does offer a clue as to how we might read these ambivalences. 'Desolation' can be read as a complex narrative of consecration: a narrative of deprivation and wretchedness, of attempts to overcome adversity that remain ambivalent. As pointed out above, not only is Koos left at an orphanage but Alie apparently dies at the end of the narrative. Yet her death may be read, however ambivalently, as a sacrifice: it is as a result of her long, slow, painful trek across the quasi-sublime, inhospitable African landscape of the Karoo that Alie, worn down and feverish, loses consciousness as 'at last her fingers grew still' (1990, p. 115). But it is also as a result of this very same trek that Koos has found shelter in the orphanage which, significantly, Smith chooses to designate as an 'orphan-*house*' (105, 107, 112, 114; my emphasis). What is more, it surely is significant that Alie is referred to, at a number of central points, including right at the end when she is dying, as 'Ou-ma' (105, 106, 115). This means 'grandmother', but again Smith's apparently eccentric spelling is significant since it renders explicit her designation as an 'old mother'. What is being emphasized here is Alie's motherliness.

If old Alie is an old mother, may she then be understood with reference to the idea of the *Volksmoeder* (literally, people's mother, or mother of the nation)? This stock figure of Afrikaner nationalist discourse, current during exactly the period when Smith was writing, in her acknowledgement of deprivation would mythically transcend it in the greater cause of national identity and serve as inspiration in white Afrikaners' struggle for self-worth (see McClintock 1995, pp. 368–379; Vincent 2000, pp. 64–65; du Toit 2003, pp. 155–160). Alie may then perhaps be argued to embody the mythical process of consecration that lies at the heart of the political discourse of Afrikaner nationalism in that her negotiation of physical as well as social spaces in 'Desolation' involves the sublime transcendence of wretchedness. The ambivalences in 'Desolation' could arguably be accounted for by saying that they form a paradoxical, yet necessary, part of the justificatory myth of Afrikaner nationalism: in tracing the struggle of Alie and Koos to position themselves, a struggle marked by the sublime as much as by the use of FID, 'Desolation' also traces a process of consecration that necessarily passes through wretchedness. It is in this sense that we can understand the story as negotiating the relation between space and white identity, and in which – despite its ambivalence – it works as a means to further a justificatory myth of the Afrikaner.

This returns us to Gordimer and Coetzee. While my analysis broadly supports their conclusions about the role Smith has played in constructing a myth that would come to justify apartheid, my reading of 'Desolation' supplements theirs by suggesting that there is a need to account for the ambivalences and uncertainties in the story, and perhaps in Smith's work more generally. These ambivalences must render straightforward judgments of her problematic and, instead, should lead one to consider the enigmatic character of her work. In the case of 'Desolation', this may be explained with reference to the effects of FID and the sublime. Taken together, they contribute to the creation of a wretchedness – a victimhood – that was to be a prerequisite for the eventual consecration of Afrikaner identity in apartheid. Such mythical perpetuation of sublime victimhood, of course, is not limited to South Africa: it continues to have far-reaching and serious consequences elsewhere in the world, as it works to justify the oppression of others.

Notes

1. Following Jeremy Hawthorn's example, I shall use the term 'free indirect discourse' to emphasize the degree to which this technique can involve the representation of not only speech, but, in particular, also thought. See Hawthorn (1990, pp. 1, 62, n. 2). Thanks to the participants in the Space in Modernist and Postcolonial Fiction workshop for their comments; to the editors for their

incisive feedback; as well as to Jeff Webb and Andrew Leng for numerous very helpful conversations.

2. For an early consideration of this topos, see Stephen Gray's discussion of what he terms the 'Karoo condition' in South African fiction. He specifically refers to Smith (1979, pp. 150–151).

3. In this discussion of the sublime as it might apply to Smith I draw on material that has in different form appeared in 'A "Vast, Unmysterious Landscape": Versions of the Sublime in 1930s South Africa.' *Journal of Postcolonial Writing*, 43.3 (December 2007): 297–309.

4. I use the masculine pronoun here given Kant's, and Burke's, masculinist predispositions. The sublime also needs to be read in terms of the masculinist orientation implicit in it. See Armstrong (1996).

5. Cosser's (1992) is the only major study of which I am aware, other than Coetzee's, that approaches Smith specifically in terms of her deployment of FID. However, his essay focuses on 'The Pain'.

Works cited

Armstrong, M., ' "The Effects of Blackness": Gender, Race, and the Sublime in Aesthetic Theories of Burke and Kant', *The Journal of Aesthetics and Art Criticism*, 54.3 (1996) 213–236.

Bourdieu, P., *Pascalian Meditations*. Trans. R. Nice (Stanford, CA: Stanford University Press, 2000).

Burke, E., *A Philosophical Enquiry into the Origin of Our Ideas of the Sublime and Beautiful*. 1757. Ed. D. Womersley (London: Penguin, 1998).

Butler, J., 'Afrikaner Women and the Creation of Ethnicity', *The Creation of Tribalism in Southern Africa*. Ed. L. Vale (Berkeley, CA: University of California Press, 1989).

Coetzee, J. M., *White Writing: On the Culture of Letters in South Africa* (New Haven: Yale University Press, 1988).

Cohn, D., *Transparent Minds: Narrative Modes for Presenting Consciousness in Fiction* (Princeton, NJ: Princeton University Press, 1978).

Cosser, M., 'Undercurrent Dialogue: Free Indirect Discourse in Pauline Smith's "the Pain" ', *English in Africa*, 19.2 (October 1992) 85–100.

Driver, D., 'Pauline Smith: "A Gentler Music of Her Own" ', *Research in African Literatures*, 15.1 (Spring 1984) 45–71.

Gordimer, N., 'English-Language Literature and Politics in South Africa', *Aspects of South African Literature*. Ed. C. Heywood (London: Heinemann, 1976), pp. 99–120.

Gray, S., *Southern African Literature: An Introduction* (Cape Town: David Philip, 1979).

Gupta, A. and James, F., 'Beyond "Culture": Space, Identity, and the Politics of Difference', *Cultural Anthropology*, 7.1 (February 1992) 6–23.

Hawthorn, J., *Joseph Conrad: Narrative Technique and Ideological Commitment* (London: Edward Arnold, 1990).

Kant, I., *Critique of the Power of Judgment*. 1790. Ed. P. Guyer. Trans. P. Guyer and E. Matthews (Cambridge: Cambridge University Press, 2000).

Lyotard, J. -F., *The Inhuman: Reflections on Time*. Trans. G. Bennington and R. Bowlby (Stanford, CA: Stanford University Press, 1991).

McClintock, A., *Imperial Leather: Race, Gender and Sexuality in the Colonial Context* (New York: Routledge, 1995).

Mitchell, W. J. T. (ed.) *Landscape and Power* (Chicago, IL: Chicago University Press, 1994).

Nixon, R., *Dreambirds: The Natural History of a Fantasy* (London: Doubleday, 1999).

Smith, P., *The Beadle*. 1926 (Cape Town: A. A. Balkema, 1972).

———, *The Little Karoo*. 1930. 2nd edn. Ed. D. Driver (Cape Town: David Philip, 1990).

Spivak, G. C., *A Critique of Postcolonial Reason: Towards a History of the Vanishing Present* (Cambridge: Harvard University Press, 1999).

du Toit, M. 'The Domesticity of Afrikaner Nationalism: Volksmoeders and the ACVV, 1904–1929', *Journal of Southern African Studies*, 29.1 (March 2003) 155–176.

Vincent, L., 'Bread and Honour: White Working Class Women and Afrikaner Nationalism in the 1930s', *Journal of Southern African Studies*, 26.1 (March 2000) 61–78.

7
'Reading' and 'Constructing' Space, Gender and Race: Joseph Conrad's *Lord Jim* and J. M. Coetzee's *Foe*

Attie de Lange

I

John Barth's novel *Giles Goatboy* (1967) starts in a rather unusual and striking way: being 'prefaced' by a so-called 'Publisher's Disclaimer', in which the four 'publishers' – because of the problematic and provocative issues presented in the novel – provide the reasons for their decision to publish such a 'wicked' book, and one publisher and partner in the firm voices his opposition to the publication and announces his resignation from the firm on account of the decision to publish it. I cannot but start this chapter with a rather nervous disclaimer: I am not a would-be male feminist, nor am I trying to 'muscle in' on 'the one cultural and intellectual space' created by female feminist critics as Moi would have it (1991, p. 208). What follows is merely an attempt at responding to the concluding remarks made by Andrew Michael Roberts in the introductory essay of a special edition of *The Conradian* dealing with the topic of Conrad and gender (Spring 1993), in which he argues that [the concept] of gender, distinguishing as it does patterns of social differentiation from biological difference, evokes both the setting up of distinctions and their unsettling. This combination can be especially productive to literary readings, since the processes of fiction seem to be based on the structures of opposition and differentiation and the transformation or dissolution of those structures. If gender in Conrad is a theme which challenges and provokes, it is also one which illuminates. (1993, p. xi)

It is furthermore also an attempt to, in some related way, read *Foe* and its intertextual links with *Lord Jim* as 'a postcolonial countersignature to a

109

modernist text' as indeed Carol Clarkson does elsewhere in this volume with her reading of Coetzee's response to Beckett's *The Unnamable*.

Using Roberts's assumptions above, and Foucault's analysis of hetero-topic spaces in his 1967 lecture *'Des Espaces Autres'* as a starting point, this chapter examines *Lord Jim* (1900) and *Foe* (1986) and argues that – despite the almost hundred years gap between their respective dates of publica-tion – these novels share a number of narrative and thematic traits which provide interesting, nuanced and mutually enriching representations of modernist and postcolonial conceptions of space. At the thematic centre of the intertextual dialogue lies their presentation of various forms of imperialism, colonialism and corruption, manifested through the epi-stemological, ontological and existential problems which both authors explore in their novels. Conrad's presentation of gender and race has stimulated heated debate and sparked off controversy among a number of critics, while Coetzee's work indeed has not been exempt from criti-cism regards these concepts. However, I believe – as indeed Roberts seems to do – that the presentation of gender and race also provides a mean-ingful basis for comparison, as these fictional processes are discernable in both these novels.

A second relevant point of similarity which should be raised at the outset is indicated by Christopher GoGwilt, who, in his influential book *The Invention of the West: Joseph Conrad and the Double-Mapping of Empire* (1995), argues that as a result of

> the failure to consolidate a coherent ideology of the British Empire, the idea of 'the West' emerged to replace and resituate a range of assumptions about race, nation, class and gender. What *Lord Jim* illuminates about this shift is the problematic continuity between nineteenth- and twentieth-century representations of race, nation and culture. (1995, p. 88)

Coetzee's novel, as indeed his whole *oeuvre*, is seen by some critics as a narrative of colonialism and decolonization in which the invocation of the discourses of feminism, postcolonialism and postmodernism is much more obvious, though not less subtle, and offers as incisive a critique as Conrad's work does. Conrad's works indeed invite, and are susceptible to, comments illuminated by postcolonialism and postmodernism from modern critics and readers.

These shared concerns in the novels manifest themselves in the man-ner in which both authors isolate many of their characters in heterotopic spaces, symbolic borderlands or liminal spaces which can be read as sites of struggle, struggle between Western and non-Western cultures, between white and black, between male and female, in which the effects of imperialism, racism and sexism (Dovey, 1988, p. 330) are all foregrounded by the densely woven and intricate interaction between narration, description and theme.

A final, and quintessential point to grasp at the outset, is that long gone are the days in which Bergson's attack on space as 'sterile quantification, the dark side of creativity' (Coroneos, 2002, p. 1) held sway. Space is no longer 'the dead, the fixed, the undialectical, the immobile', and time is not now seen as representing 'richness, fecundity, life, [and] dialectic' (Foucault, 1980, p. 70). Even a superficial glance at Homi Bhabha's essay 'DissemiNation' (1990), with its numerous spatial concepts and phrases such as 'the space of the people', 'colonial space', 'postcolonial space', 'signifying space', 'anterior space', the 'space of liminality', the 'irredeemably plural modern space', etc., should not only convince the reader that space has become a dominant feature in our current way of thinking about the world, but will also possibly confirm that the various conceptualizations of space may lead to confusion and bafflement as the reader tries to 'define' space.

Foucault, in *Des Espaces Autres,* describes his notion of heterotopias within the context of socially produced space when he states that 'We do not live inside a void . . . we live inside a set of relations that delineates sites which are irreducible to one another and absolutely not superimposable on one another' (1986, p. 23). Defining heterotopias, he then describes these as sites 'that have the curious property of being in relation with all the other sites, but in such a way as to suspect, neutralize, or invent the set of relations that they happen to designate, mirror, or reflect' . . . counter-sites involved in 'a sort of simultaneously mythic and real contestation of the space in which we live'.

In order to follow the argument presented in this chapter, it is important to note that 'space' has both a literal and a metaphorical force in both novels under discussion. In some cases the metaphorical force is a natural extension of the literal, but in others they are in opposition to each other, for example Conrad's Jim occupies an imaginative space in fantasy to escape the bounds of his physical space on board ship, or *Foe's* Susan embarks on establishing a textual space in which she can 'recreate' herself.

Linking ideology and narrative practice, the basic assumption of this chapter is that these various discourses are textualized by the interaction between narration, description and theme, and that the feminist and postcolonial paradigms commonly used to read these texts should be

extended to include the wider context of the epistemological and ontological dominants of modernist and postmodernist fiction as posited by
McHale (1987, pp. 9–11). Consequently, this chapter will consist of three
sections: the first will trace the larger contours of Conradian fictional
space. Building on the concepts of 'space', 'entrapment' and 'voice', the
second part will investigate the construction of opposition and differentiation in *Lord Jim*, while the third part will examine the transformation
and deconstruction of these structures through a reading of *Foe*.

II

Conrad's treatment of space is a complex and multifaceted topic not
easily summarized. In very general terms, space in Conrad cannot merely
be regarded as a structural category but must be considered as being an
integral part of the thematic substance of each text. In a certain sense – for
Conrad as for most post-Kantean thinkers, theorists and writers – there
is a dialectic between space as an entity and space as part of an interpretative process. This idea of space as an interpretative process is well
described in May Sinclair's novel *Mary Oliver* (1919), in which Sinclair
suggests that in general, 'Time and Space were forms of thought – ways
of thinking' (1980, p. 227).

Most of Conrad's major characters find themselves – through a combination of volition and destiny – isolated and trapped in strange and
hostile spaces, be they geographical, social, existential or cultural. Wait,
the 'Nigger' of the *Narcissus*, is isolated by his race and his sickness, and
'exiled' to the narrow and claustrophobic confines of his cabin, mir-
roring the crew's isolation by the cosmic forces and their subsequent
confinement on the ship during the storm. Kurtz is enclosed by the
African jungle and finds himself in the void formed in the interface
between 'civilization' and 'barbarism' and the paradoxical inversion of
these forces. The interaction of Marlow and Kurtz with the Africans
leads to a general sense of isolation, an isolation which also results from
what Paul Armstrong calls the 'ambiguous double nature of hermen-
eutic encounters with other cultures' (1994, p. 7). Martin Decoud, in
Nostromo, isolates himself because of his scepticism – he has 'no faith
in anything except the truth of his own sensations' (1991, p. 229); Nostromo is isolated by his vanity and greed; and Charles Gould is alienated
from reality by his belief in the mythical heritage of the mine, while
the shady political anarchists in *The Secret Agent* form small enclaves
in which like-minded political thinkers can undermine the larger and
'unjust' political system.

In most cases this existential isolation is exacerbated by the characters' inability to 'read' the space in which they find themselves. This thematic notion of the indeterminacy of meaning is also simulated on a descriptive and narrative level by the atmospheric obfuscation and visual displacement of spatial boundaries. Space and object merge, foreground and background become indistinguishable. Vision – and by implication interpretation – becomes problematic. This is not only apparent on the thematic level, but also on the descriptive level as this sense of spiritual isolation is invariably accompanied by geographical disjunction: the *Narcissus* is caught in a ferocious storm which throws her off course; Kurtz and Marlow find themselves not in 'civilized' London, but in 'darkest' Africa, while Jim is forced to exchange the 'civilities' of court room conduct for the violent conflict on Patusan. Those with 'material interests' ruthlessly pursue their own ideals, forcing the people of Sulaco to reconstitute their social space, while the political anarchists spread chaos and terror in what seems to be the relatively stable public space in London. Yet at the same time all these novels also present the reader with cameos which confirm that each space that the novel shows is itself riddled with privacies.

Turning to *Lord Jim*, three of the above-mentioned aspects are of importance for the purposes of this chapter: the space in which Jim and Jewel find themselves and the way in which they try to 'read' this space; the implied construction of opposition and differentiation between genders, and, lastly, the effect of this process on the element of race.

In the parts of the novel dealing with the *Patna* episode, Jim is trapped in various kinds of space which incrementally increase his sense of deep isolation: physically, he finds himself alone on duty as look-out in the fore-top, in the dock in the courthouse, or in the succession of ports through which he flees from his past. He is also trapped morally and emotionally by his betrayal of the 'space' of the value system constituted by the brotherhood of the sea, and he finally finds himself enclosed physically in what Mongia calls the 'womb-like enclosure' (1993, p. 7) of Patusan.

Jim's excessive imagination and romanticism, so dominant in the *Patna* section, is the direct result of his continuous 'misreading' of the space or situation in which he finds himself. At the same time each misreading underlines his 'Otherness', adding not only to his isolation but also to the increasingly complex and ambiguous psychological space which he occupies. The reader – along with other 'readers' like Marlow, the French Lieutenant, and Stein – must attempt to reconstruct Jim's 'psychological space(s)' in order to determine the motives for his action or inaction. What makes this an even more challenging task is the fact that even at the start of the novel, before the accident, Jim's fantasizing means that he is, in a sense, in a space of his own, a space that to outsiders is almost impenetrable.

The Patusan section continues this trend and Patusan's geographical isolation can be seen as the culmination of Jim's increasingly claustrophobic experience of space. This part of the novel represents the last leg of Jim's journey and creates yet another 'space' in which Jim finds himself, a new 'sort of reality' (1984, p. 230) which he has to 'read' and traverse; it presents a 'totally new set of conditions for his imaginative faculty to work on' (1984, p. 218). Given Conrad's penchant for irony, it is highly probable that this comment of Marlow's is made ironically; it might suggest that Jim can never accept a space as it is, but must always work to transform it into some imagined alternative. This new space is a multifaceted construct: it is at the same time a geographical, cultural, political, personal and symbolic space which confronts Jim and which he has to 'read', 'interpret' and 'reconstruct'.

Many critics, from Dorothy Van Ghent, in her seminal book *The English Novel: Form and Function*, published in 1953, up to more recent critics such as Darras (1982) and Mongia (1993) have commented on the dominant effect of closure and entrapment and the grave-like quality of Patusan. Van Ghent states that it is only in the 'grave of Patusan' that 'Jim's dream does come true' (1953, p. 243). Darras observes that 'Patusan is a religious tomb, a kind of purgatory where the moral rehabilitation of the hero takes place after his initial confession. Consequently, it is an enchanted place, a mythical enclosure which the chivalric commercial order preserves secretly in order to mend and amend its models' (1982, p. 27), while Mongia sees it as a space which is 'carefully bordered, as space that captures...a space of womb-like enclosure' (1993, pp. 6–7).

The motif of entrapment and enclosure presented so graphically in the novel has a protean nature. In the same way that Jim was trapped by the code of conduct of the sailors during the aftermath of the *Patna* episode, he soon finds his private space, which he has reconstructed so slowly and painfully on Patusan, encroached upon by the expectations of the islanders. Jim is a white man and finds himself in a curious position: at first, he is seen as an intruder, a representative of some imperial force: 'Were the Dutch coming to take the country? Would the white man like to go back down the river? What was the object of coming to such a miserable country?' (1984, p. 252). As time goes by, however, he establishes himself as a brave and courageous man and as an ally of the local people, 'the visible, tangible incarnation of unfailing truth and of unfailing victory' (1984, p. 363), who seemingly cohabits with them in 'their space', but who – the reader knows at this stage in the novel – really finds himself in no-man's land, with both Gentleman Brown and the natives laying claim to his loyalty: Brown, because of Jim's race, and the natives, because of their support and trust. Jim is – as was the case in the *Patna* section of the novel – 'trapped' by the expectations of other people; his personal space is fenced in as it were, by outside expectations. It will be Jim's 'misreading' of these 'boundaries', Brown's deviousness and the people's trust in his invincibility which will ultimately lead to his destruction.

In contrast to his experiences leading up to and following his jump from the *Patna*, Jim is simultaneously 'trapper' and 'trapped' on Patusan. After having penetrated Jewel's private space, he becomes the 'controller' of that space, 'trapping' her in a web of uncertainty and insecurity, in a 'marriage' of unfulfilled promises and failed commitments. Various critics, among them Sullivan, Mongia and Stott, have focused on this aspect of the novel using a feminist or gender paradigm. Sullivan (1981, pp. 59–60), for example, feels that Conrad's landscapes reflect 'internal conflicts and ambivalences' and that the various struggles against the sea, river and jungle 'correspond symbolically to repressed conflicts with the feminine matrix in general'.

Mongia (1993, pp. 1–6) and Stott (1993, pp. 43–44) have interpreted this aspect of the novel in terms of the interaction between colonialism and patriarchal power relations. Mongia suggests that the Patusan section relies on a sub-text of the Gothic with its '[h]elpless women in need of rescue, threatening masculine figures... and the terrors associated with enclosing spaces' (1993, p. 1), adding further that Conrad invests in Jim 'not just the heroic stuff of adventure and romance – virile agency that finds its fulfilment in masculine action – but also the features of the colonized helpless 'feminine'. Jim is as much the figure in white – virginal, helpless, in need of rescue by the master story-teller Marlow – as he is the masculine god who orders the chaos of Patusan' (1993, p. 1).

Stott (1993, pp. 43–44), on the other hand, is less sympathetic towards Jim and reads Conrad's use of the trope of mastery against a late nineteenth-century tradition of characterizing the Orient as essentially feminine and enigmatic. She also argues that Freud's infamous equation of the enigma of woman and the dark continent emerges from this tradition, and presents a survey 'of transracial sexual encounters' with non-European women (1993, p. 43) in Conrad's fiction to substantiate her argument. These women are all depicted as 'spectral brooding presences, alluring and deadly *fleurs du mal*' (1993, p. 43).

Within the context of space sketched earlier, I wish to argue that Jewel's entrapment need not only be seen within a feminist or gender paradigm like that used by Sullivan, Mongia and Stott, but that it should also be seen against the wider context of the epistemological 'dominant' of modernist fiction (McHale, 1987, p. 9), and especially as an integral part of the symbiotic relationship between the epistemological, ontological and existential problems which Conrad tried to work out in his fiction. Seen in this light, this broader perspective acts as a 'leveller' between Jim and Jewel's positions. Consider, for example, the following encounter between Marlow and Jewel:

'What is it he told you?' I [Marlow] insisted.

'Do you think I can tell you? How am I to know? How am I to understand?' she cried at last. There was a stir. I believe she was wringing her hands. 'There is something he can never forget.'

'So much the better for you,' I said gloomily.

'What is it? What is it?' She put an extraordinary force of appeal into her supplicating tone. 'He says he had been afraid. How can I believe this? Am I a mad woman to believe this? You all remember something! You all go back to it. What is it? You tell me! What is this thing? Is it alive? – is it dead? I hate it. It is cruel. Has it got a face and a voice – this calamity? Will he see it – will he hear it? In his sleep perhaps when he cannot see me – and then arise and go. Ah! I shall never forgive him. My mother had forgiven – but I, never! Will it be a sign – a call?' (1984, pp. 314–325)

Jewel's space has been invaded by Jim, an influence 'coming from the outside, as it were, irresistible, incomprehensible – as if brought about by the mysterious conjunctions of the planets' (1984, p. 317). She is trapped as much by 'her own unreasonable and natural fear' of this 'unknown [so] infinitely vast' (1984, p. 309) as by Jim's unwillingness to remove her fear by revealing his secret to her. Despite her sincerity, she is caught in a relationship of subjugation and exploitation, a relationship which is threatened by a force from outside, as well as by Jim's stereotypical 'love-me-and-leave-me' treatment of her.

Some interesting points present themselves here. On the one hand, Jim does not want – nor expects – to love and leave Jewel. And Marlow claims to the privileged reader that Jim's story is *not* another example of the sort that is familiar to them all. But it turns out that Jim does indeed behave as Jewel fears when she claims that white men always abandon native women. For all that he wants to be special, Jim ends up (so far as Jewel is concerned) being stereotypical. And indeed it is the ideological baggage that Jim brings with him from outside that is responsible for his betrayal of Jewel.

The passage quoted above is of major importance, both in the way in which narrative and theme interact to develop the motif of entrapment, and in the way in which it brings into focus the central theme reading. It reminds one very strongly of the compelling passages in *Heart of Darkness* dealing with the white worsted around the young man's neck. Questions are a means of conquering the foreign space surrounding you, a way of gaining knowledge, and understanding. Jewel has been trapped by Jim, kept in the dark about what exactly it is that keeps on haunting him. Yet is it not also ironic that she 'frees' Jim when she saves his life, as she holds the torch that illuminates the darkness where the would-be assassins are hiding? The sense of irony is heightened when one recalls the symbolic and ironic implications of Kurtz's painting in *Heart of Darkness* and its intertextual impact on this scene in *Lord Jim*.

Jewel's natural response to this 'cage' of secrecy is to try and determine its qualities, emphasizing humankind's interpretative need to understand the world which confronts it. Notice the interpretative vigour with which Jewel tries to unmask and conquer the unknown. Systematically, she goes through a repertoire of possibilities: 'Is it alive? – Is it dead? . . . Has it got a face and a voice – this calamity? Will he see it – will he hear it?' Recapping her fears from the attempt to assassinate him, she is desperately trying to 'read' or 'decode' this space in which she has been trapped by using those categories or frames of interpretation which she has applied successfully in the past. Only this time, they do not work; as she gets closer to the 'edge', it becomes quite obvious that this repertoire of categories is not applicable to this new space.

In short, Jewel finds herself entrapped in a space, isolated from her lover and dominated by what can be described as patriarchal and colonizing forces. In contrast to the much-discussed notion of the silence surrounding Kurtz's African mistress in *Heart of Darkness* Jewel does have a 'voice'. It is ironic, however, that her voice does not lead to answers, as she cannot 'read' Jim. Her epistemological quest leads nowhere; she remains entrapped by the enigma that is Jim, by the lack of reason for his leaving, and, as such, is 'silenced' in a way. Jewel's position can be seen as a confirmation of the opposition and differentiation between male and female, and confronts the reader with perspective on the issues of conquest, subjugation and exploitation. And yet, while all this is true, at the same time, Jewel's fear that Jim will turn out to be yet another white man who leaves a 'native' woman turns out to be justified.

However, this should not let us forget Jim's own predicament, trapped and isolated as he is. Jim's 'Otherness' is also foregrounded within the context of 'reading', 'space' and 'entrapment'. It is not only Jim who is isolated by it, but it clearly has an adverse effect on those characters who try to delineate and penetrate without a clear knowledge of the culture to which the 'other' belongs. It further compounds the problem of 'reading' Jim, just as Jim's lack of understanding of the culture of the 'Other' leads him to 'misread' the totemic powers of the ring. The ring is a kind of 'map' that has to be read, a 'sort of credential' (1984, p. 223) which leads him out of his isolation, as '[I]t meant a friend; and it is a good thing to have a friend' (1984, pp. 234–245). The ring is the talisman that would open 'for him the door of fame, love, and success' (1984, p. 415). Jim's belief in the power of the ring makes him misread the full implications of what it means to be a white man among the natives. His interpretation of the ring – namely that it would always safeguard him, just as it allowed him to be received 'into the heart of the community' (1984, p. 258) – extends the theme of misreading to discourse between cultures, to a patronizing appropriation of the cultural goods of the 'Other'. Yet Jim misreads the power of its charm, just as he misinterpreted the events during the *Patna* episode. Only when it is already too late, is Jim able to correct his own 'misreading' of the conventions attached to the ring and its guarantees. It is only after Dain Waris had been killed that

> Jim understood. He had retreated from one world, for a small matter of an impulsive jump, and now the other, the work of his own hands, had fallen in ruins upon his head... Everything was gone, and he who had been once unfaithful to his trust had lost again all men's confidence.... Loneliness was closing on him. (1984, pp. 408–409)

The final irony of Jim's faulty belief in the ring and all its stands for is driven home by his final rejection, when he goes to Doramin, 'ready and unarmed':

> ... the ring which he [Doramin] had dropped on his lap fell and rolled against the foot of the white man, and that poor Jim glanced down at the talisman that had opened for him the door of fame, love, and

success within the wall of the forests fringed with white foam, within
the coast that under the western sun looks like the very stronghold of
the night. (1984, p. 415)

Misreading leads to isolation and, eventually, to death. Just as Jim 'misreads' the ring and what it stands for, so his enigmatic character makes it
impossible for the people of Patusan to 'read' him and what he represents.
Jim's isolation is not merely the result of his stay on the remote island of
Patusan, or his misreadings of the various kinds of space. It is an existential isolation which inevitably results from his racial 'Otherness'. Just
as Wait and Kurtz found themselves isolated because of their race, Jim
is isolated because of his race. One of the greatest ironies in the novel is
found in chapter 27 which describes his success in the attack. Jim finally
gets the chance to be the romantic hero of his dreams. The adoration of
the crowd was 'immense' (1984, p. 271). Yet his racial and psychological
'Otherness' keeps him from becoming one of 'them', poignantly captured by Marlow: 'I can't with mere words convey to you the impression
of his total and utter isolation . . . he was in every sense alone of his kind
there . . .' (1984, p. 272).

III

J. M. Coetzee's fifth novel, *Foe* (1986), presents the reader with a compact
example of the dissolutions or deconstruction of the gender and racial
oppositions posited in *Lord Jim*.

An attempt to 'recolonize' Defoe's *Robinson Crusoe* (1719) by giving it
a female narrative voice, the plot is fairly simple and straightforward.
After a fruitless search for her daughter in South America, Susan Barton
sets off on return to England but is marooned on an island inhabited by
Cruso [*sic*] and his black servant, Friday. After spending some months on
the barren island, she 'rescues' both the desperately ill Cruso and Friday
against their will when an English ship arrives at the island. Cruso dies
at sea, while Susan and Friday return to London, eking out a living by
being meagerly provided for by Mr Foe, the author, to whom Susan has
sold her story.

The first part of the novel describes how Susan Barton finds herself marooned on an isolated island, 'colonized' by the white male,
Cruso, and dominated by him. She narrates a series of episodes which
all contribute to stereotypical constructions of gender. For example,
Susan voluntarily subjects herself to Cruso ('With these words I presented myself to Robinson Cruso, in the days when he still ruled over his

island, and became his second subject, the first being his manservant Friday' (1986, p. 11)). This process of stereotyping is strengthened by scattered comments throughout the novel, and implies that her position of being Cruso's 'second' subject is not merely because she arrived later than Friday, but also implies a sense of hierarchy, despite the fact that Friday is a Negro slave:

> Before setting out to perform his island duties, Cruso gave me his knife and warned me not to venture from his castle; for the apes, he said, would not be wary of a woman as they were of him and Friday. I wondered at this: was a woman, to an ape, a different species from a man? Nevertheless, I prudently obeyed, and stayed at home, and rested. (1986, p. 15)

The construction of gender stereotypes is also extended to Cruso, in the way in which he tries to dominate Susan by refusing to make shoes for her, thereby restricting her movement and 'trapping' her in the enclosed space of the camp. His role in their physical relationship is also described in terms of exploitation and subjugation: 'Cruso did not use me again. On the contrary, he held himself as distant as if nothing had passed between us' (1986, pp. 35–36).

The last important example of this pattern can be found at the end of the first part, when Susan, the desperately ill Cruso and Friday are saved by Captain Smith, who 'tactfully' suggests to Susan that she

> ... call Cruso my husband and declare that we had been shipwrecked together, to make my path easier both on board and when we should come ashore in England. If the story of Bahia and the mutineers got about, he said, it would not be easily understood what kind of woman I was. I laughed when he said this – what kind of woman was I, in truth? – but took his advice, and so was known as Mrs. Cruso to all on board. (1986, p. 42)

The transformation or deconstruction of this process of opposition and differentiation is started by Susan Barton's challenge to the males who dominate her world, and as a result of her so doing, a new oppositional pattern already starts to take shape in the first part of the novel, eventually culminating in the second and third parts. For example, Susan does not wait for Cruso to give her freedom by making her shoes; she makes her own sandals. She has to look after Cruso when he has a fever, and finds herself in a curious position: 'He [Cruso] was a prisoner, and I, despite myself, his gaoler' (1986, p. 43). This pattern is strengthened in the second part by episodes which depict her travelling alone (1986, p. 100), wearing breeches (1986, p. 100), writing her own story (1986, p. 131), taking the dominant role when sleeping with Foe (1986, p. 139), seeing herself as the muse, begetting stories rather than seducing the author (1986, p. 124), and so forth.

Curiously, this process of transformation and deconstruction does not lead to total freedom; like the position in which Jim finds himself, it leaves Susan Barton in a intriguing double-bind, expressed as follows by Rosemary Jolly: 'Yet the novel potential which her sex holds for her creative future is over-written by the predominantly male-determined attributes of her racial identity, namely her inheritance of and admiration for the traditions of writing and colonization' (1994, pp. 61–62).

Phrased in terms of the reading of space, entrapment and voice, the similarities between the processes of opposition and differentiation, transformation and dissolution in the two novels are quite striking. It is perhaps worth adding that just as *Lord Jim* is in some ways a critique of the 'light literature' that corrupts Jim, so too is *Foe* a critique, either of *Robinson Crusoe* or of the ways in which it has been read over three centuries.

Susan is – like Jewel – also caught in an epistemological struggle, trying to 'read' Friday. This struggle continuously resurfaces in the novel, punctuating it with passages asking questions – questions about Friday, about Cruso, about the way in which Cruso keeps Friday captive, about her daughter and so forth. These questions all represent the paradigm which Susan applies in her 'reading' of the space in which she finds herself. Yet very few answers, if any, are forthcoming. It is important to note that on each occasion, the answers are provided only partially or withheld totally, by a male: Cruso, Friday and Foe. As such, she is trapped – like Jewel – by her inability to break free from the control of male forces. Friday, like Jim, remains a 'textual' labyrinth which cannot be read: nobody, apart from Marlow and the reader, knows exactly why Jim keeps moving eastward, as the various interpretations – those of Brierly, Marlow, the French Lieutenant, Jewel, and Stein – indicate. In the same way Friday's origins, feelings, emotions and the reasons for his actions remain enigmatic, unanswered and perhaps even unanswerable. But here even the reader is in the dark.

Susan's position, like that of Jim's, is ambiguous, complex and multi-faceted. On the one hand, she succeeds in usurping Cruso's patriarchal position, stripping him of his position on the island and eventually taking him 'captive' on board the ship bound for England. She is also to 'write' herself out of the entrapped space created by patriarchal society by breaking its taboos and by literally writing her own story. As such Susan Barton can be seen as a force that is able to (at least partially) transform or deconstruct the structures of opposition and differentiation between genders when she insists that 'I am a free woman who asserts her freedom by telling her story according to her own desire' (1986, p. 131).

On the other hand, she remains trapped by these very same forces: just as Cruso kept her trapped by not giving her shoes, so Foe keeps her economically dependent on him. In order for her to write her own story, she has to fight Foe, who tries to 'enslave' her by his attempts to change her narrative according to his point of view, ultimately ending up by sleeping with him. Susan's inversion of sexual roles is given an ironic twist by the captivating effect that Friday's dance has on her: the implicit sexual attraction created by the dance strongly reminds one of an inversion of Gudrun's dance as she taunts the bullocks in D. H. Lawrence's *Women in Love*. Be that as it may, Friday's dance also contributes to this curious position in which Susan finds herself, of being the dominant player (she owns Friday – 'he is mine' (1986, p. 112) as well as the slave: 'Sometimes I believe it is I who have become the slave' (1986, p. 87).

The most striking example of the construction of racial opposition is found in the treatment of Friday. Throughout the novel he is compared to animals that are either controlled by humans or who are afraid of humans. In a complex rewriting of Jameson's concept of 'the prison-house of language', a new language – his music – is found for him as his tongue has been cut out. This 'language' in a way joins him and Susan in a bond, but also keeps her locked out of his world, and thus also a captive. His control over Susan remains almost absolute: she cannot get rid of him – he has become her shadow (1986, p. 115). Whereas Cruso restricted and confined Friday's voice by limiting his understanding of speech, and thereby keeping a hold on him, Susan tries to open up his world by giving him 'writing', a new kind of 'voice'. But Friday's mysterious control over her is underlined by the way in which he deals with her attempts to bring him to the state of speech: 'Somewhere in the deepest recesses of those black pupils was there a spark of mockery?' (1986, p. 146).

There is also a striking inversion regarding the presentation of the characters of colour in these novels. Jewel has a 'voice', but cannot make herself 'heard' and remains powerless; Friday's tongue has been cut out. Through his mere presence, his dancing and music, he asserts an influence, and has a 'voice' far more dominant than even that of Cruso.

It is clear from this brief first reading that the fictional processes identified by Roberts, namely those of opposition and differentiation on the one hand, and those of transformation and dissolution on the other, are not only both present in *Lord Jim* and *Foe*, but that a comparative reading of these novels within the framework of these processes, Foucault's notion of heterotopia and the larger context of space in Conrad, makes for a potentially productive illumination of both these and other related texts, and, indeed, provides a postcolonial 'countersignature' to a modernist text.

Works cited

Armstrong, P. B., 'The Epistemology of Cultural Differences', *Literator*, 15.1 (1994) 1–19.

Bhabha, H., 'DissemiNation: Time, Narrative and the Margins of the Modern Nation', in *Nation and Narration*. Ed. H. K. Bhabha (London: Routledge, 1990).

Coetzee, J. M., *Foe* (Johannesburg: Ravan Press, 1986).

Conrad, J., *Lord Jim*. Ed. J. Batchelor. The World's Classics Series. (Oxford: Oxford University Press, 1984).

——, *Heart of Darkness and Other Tales*. Ed. C. Watts. The World's Classics Series (Oxford: Oxford University Press, 1991).

——, *Nostromo*. Ed. K. Carabine. The World's Classics Series (Oxford: Oxford University Press, 1991).

Coroneos, C., *Space, Conrad and Modernity* (Oxford: Oxford University Press, 2002).

Darras, J., *Joseph Conrad and the West: Signs of Empire*. Trans. A. Luyat and J. Darras (London: Macmillan, 1982).

Dovey, T., *The Novels of J. M. Coetzee* (Johannesburg: A. Donker, 1988).

Foucault, M. 'Questions on Geography'. Trans. C. Gordan *et al.* from the interview in Hérodote, 1 (1976), and published in *Michel Foucault: Power/Knowledge: Selected Interviews and Other Writings 1972–1977*. Ed. C. Gordon (Brighton: Harvester, 1980).

——, 'Of Other Spaces' ('Des Espaces Autres')', *Diacritics*, 16.1 (1986) 22–27.

GoGwilt, C., *The Invention of the West: Joseph Conrad and the Double-Mapping of Europe and Empire* (Stanford: Stanford University Press, 1995).

Jolly, R., 'Voyages in J.M. Coetzee's Novels: Narrative Conquests in *Foe*, Narrative Exploration in *Age of Iron*', *Matutu*, 11 (1994) 61–70.

McHale, B., *Postmodernist Fiction* (London: Routledge, 1987).

Moi, T., 'Feminist Literary Criticism', in *Modern Literary Theory: A Comparative Introduction*. 2nd edn, Ed. A. Jefferson and D. Robey (London: B.T. Batsford, 1991), pp. 204–221.

Mongia, P., ' "Ghosts of the Gothic": Spectral Women and Colonized Spaces in *Lord Jim*', *The Conradian*, 17.2 (1993) 1–16.

Roberts, A. M., 'Introduction', Special Issue of *The Conradian: Conrad and Gender*. *The Conradian*, 17.2 (1993) v–xi.

Sinclair, M., *Mary Oliver: A Life* (London: Virago, 1980).

Stott, R., 'The Woman in Black: Race and Gender in *The Secret Agent'*, *The Conradian*, 17.2 (1993) 39–58.

Sullivan, Z. T., 'Enclosure, Darkness, and the Body: Conrad's Landscape', *The Centennial Review*, 25.1 (1981) 59–79.

Van Ghent, D., *The English Novel: Form and Function* (New York: Harper, 1953).

8
Remains of the Name

Carrol Clarkson

> *When death cuts all other links, there remains still the name.*
> *(J. M. Coetzee, The Master of Petersburg)*

I

In an interview with J. M. Coetzee in 1983, Tony Morphet comments on the setting of *Life & Times of Michael K*: 'The location of the story is very highly specified. Cape Town – Stellenbosch – Prince Albert – somewhere between 1985–1990' (Coetzee and Morphet, 1987, p. 455). A similar observation might be made of later novels such as *Age of Iron* and *Disgrace*, where Coetzee's literary landscapes are evoked with equally striking particularity. The migrations of the fictional characters are meticulously tracked in the recognizable co-ordinates of named towns, roads, and landmarks of South Africa's Cape regions: Salem, Grahamstown, Port Elizabeth, Donkin Square, Guguletu, Buitenkant Street, Schoonder Street, Rondebosch Common, Signal Hill, Touws River, the Outeniqua Mountains and so on. Tony Morphet, in his interview with Coetzee, suggests that the use of familiar place-names brings *Michael K* 'very close to us' (by 'us' he means a South African readership), and Morphet asks whether Coetzee is 'looking for a more direct and immediate conversation with South African readers' (Coetzee and Morphet, 1987, p. 455). It is tempting to assume immediate reference to – and direct conversation about – the real world when a writer makes use of recognizable names.[1] Certainly, for the Coetzee of *Youth*, South African place-names have an almost talismanic quality: sitting in the British Museum, the young John is deeply affected by thoughts of the country of his birth when he reads the South

African place-names in the early travel writings of the likes of Barrow and Burchell:

> It gives him an eerie feeling to sit in London reading about streets – Waalstraat, Buitengracht, Buitencingel – along which he alone, of all the people around him with their heads buried in their books, has walked. But even more than by accounts of old Cape Town is he captivated by stories of ventures into the interior...Zwartberg, Leeuwrivier, Dwyka: it is his country, the country of his heart, that he is reading about. (Coetzee, 2002, p. 137)

But in the 1983 interview with Tony Morphet, Coetzee does not accede to the suggestion of direct and immediate address in his own use of familiar place names in *Life & Times of Michael K:*

> The geography is, I fear, less trustworthy than you imagine – not because I deliberately set about altering the reality of Sea Point or Prince Albert but because I don't have much interest in, or can't seriously engage myself with, the kind of realism that takes pride in copying the 'real' world. (Coetzee and Morphet, 1987, p. 455)

Coetzee's response thus raises a difficult literary-philosophical question: can we readily assume an 'everyday' mode of reference in *fiction's* use of names, especially in its use of recognizable place-names? To formulate the question in this way is to draw attention to the preoccupations of this chapter. Questions about the 'whereabouts' of the characters in Coetzee's fiction oscillate relentlessly between discourses of the topographic and the typographic, and writing about place becomes an interrogation about the place of writing. In Coetzee this interrogation is never simply an inward-looking 'art-for-art's sake.' From *Dusklands* onwards the calling into question of the place of writing has intimately to do with the positioning of a colonial subject, with the testing of the authority of the one who writes, and with representations of landscape that attempt to mark sites of human significance. In Coetzee – and this is the argument of the chapter – the question of names has less to do with the *geography* of the place than it has to do with the *history* of the namers.

I take my conceptual bearings from Coetzee's non-fiction and conclude with a discussion of landscape in the films of contemporary South African artist and film-maker, William Kentridge – whose work also features in Coetzee's essays. My discussion explores the place of writing itself as a site in a literary landscape; thus, by the end of the chapter, the notion of what constitutes a 'literary landscape' in the first place will have been revisited. The chapter reads J. M. Coetzee's use of names in his fiction as a response to Samuel Beckett's *The Unnamable* – that is to say, as a postcolonial countersignature to a modernist text.

II

Here are the opening sentences of Samuel Beckett's *The Unnamable*: 'Where now? Who now? When now? Unquestioning. I, say I' (Beckett, 1979, p. 267). This narrative gesture constitutes at once a challenge to the reader to anchor reference in the world (in a 'where', 'who', and 'when') and an outrageous thwarting of any attempt to do just that, as the deictics 'now' and 'I' mercilessly reel the reader in to the time and place of the discourse itself.[2] This aporetic tension between reference (which is questioned, rather than asserted) and deixis (which, as we shall see, is also deflected) means that the text is never set into narrative motion. The novel enacts what Coetzee identifies as the 'inability to attain the separation of creator and creature, namer and named, with which the act of creating, naming, begins' (Coetzee, 1992, p. 37). Coetzee's juxtaposition, almost a conflation, of naming and creating, reminds me of Heidegger: 'Building and plastic creation ... always happen already, and happen only, in the open region of saying and naming' (Heidegger, 1977, p. 199). But in Beckett, the protagonist-narrator is in a state of suspension before an act of naming-creating, the 'subject of an incapacity to affirm and an inability to be silent' (Coetzee, 1992, pp. 43–44), who suffers from 'the madness of having to speak, and not being able to' (Beckett, 1979, p. 297). Even in the deictic 'I' the Unnamable has no foothold in the narrative, no sure linguistic site from which to speak. The Unnamable is forced to speak 'of things that don't concern me ... that they have crammed me full of to prevent me from saying who I am, where I am' (Beckett, 1979, p. 297). Attempts to assume the subject speaking position of 'I' – to pivot the narrative on a narrating 'I' – are endlessly deferred: 'I seem to speak, it is not I, about me, it is not about me' (Beckett, 1979, p. 267).

It is in the context of Beckett's *The Unnamable* that the opening sentences of J. M. Coetzee's first work of fiction, *Dusklands*, have such extraordinary narrative force: 'My name is Eugene Dawn. I cannot help that. Here goes' (Coetzee, 1998, p. 1). As the inaugural narrative declaration of Coetzee's entire fictional oeuvre, Dawn's announcement is an extravagant affirmation of the naming-creating that will have brought him, and all that follows his assertion, into existence. It is as if Coetzee experiments with the flip side of Beckett's narrative coin: what happens when the protagonist and his world are *inexorably* named? In one of his essays on Beckett, Coetzee draws attention to the conjuring[3] power of nominal declarations: 'make a single sure affirmation, and from it the whole contingent world of bicycles and greatcoats can, with a little patience, a little diligence, be deduced' (Coetzee, 1992, p. 43). This is how the Unnamable baits the reader:

> Equate me, without pity or scruple, with him who exists, somehow, no matter how, no finicking, with him whose story this story had the brief ambition to be. Better, ascribe to me a body. Better still, arrogate to me a mind. Speak of a world of my own, sometimes referred to as the inner, without choking. (Beckett, 1979, p. 359)

I cannot help reading this instruction as an outrageous subtext to the opening sentence of *Disgrace*, where, with declarative and ostensive particularity, the narrative voice presents to us a protagonist with body, mind, and an idiosyncratic psychological state: 'For a man of his age, fifty-two, divorced, he has, to his mind, solved the problem of sex rather well' (Coetzee, 1999a, p. 1).

Yet if the affirmation is sure, it is also surely fictional. An inaugural narrative gesture ostentatiously stakes fictional ground in the instant the possibility of contemplating a self arises. Here is the Unnamable:

> Did I wait somewhere for this place to be ready to receive me? Or did it wait for me to come and people it? By far the better of these hypotheses, from the point of view of usefulness, is the former, and I shall often have occasion to fall back on it. But both are distasteful. I shall say therefore that our beginnings coincide, that this place was made for me, and I for it, at the same instant. And the sounds I do not yet know have not yet made themselves heard. (Beckett, 1979, pp. 271–272)

The coincidence of fictional self and narrative place is unremitting in Beckett:

> what I say, what I shall say, if I can, relates to the place where I am . . . What I say, what I may say, on this subject, the subject of me and my abode, has already been said since, having always been here, I am here still. At last a piece of reasoning that pleases me, and worthy of my situation. (Beckett, 1979, p. 276)

In his essay, 'The First Sentence of Yvonne Burgess' *The Strike*', Coetzee identifies Burgess's opening sentence as being of the type, 'There was once'. The first sentence of *The Strike* reads, 'Finlay closed the book and considered the title appreciatively.' Coetzee comments:

> If we want a gloss on the meaning of 'There was once...' we can go to the Majorcan storyteller's formula 'Era e non era,' which signals that all succeeding assertions...are made in the split was-and-was-not mode of fiction. 'Finlay' and 'the,' pseudo-definitional though they are, are not thereby nonreferential, but their reference is oblique. *They refer not to a man and a book but to the body of discourse that follows*: all assertions succeeding 'Finlay closed the book' are signaled to be in the as-if mode. (Coetzee, 1992, pp. 91–92, my emphasis)

Coetzee's narratives draw attention to vacillations between presumed reference to a recognizable world and reference to their own fictional discourse. This is striking in *In the Heart of the Country*, where the 'as-if' mode is foregrounded to the extent that (as in Beckett) the 'was not' threatens to erode any putative 'was'. Magda speaks of 'the ribbon of [her] meditations, black on white, floating like a mist five feet above the ground' (Coetzee, 1979, p. 64). She reflects:

> Am I, I wonder, a thing among things, a body propelled along a track by sinews and bony levers, or am I a monologue moving through time, approximately five feet above the ground, if the ground does not turn out to be just another word, in which case I am indeed lost? Whatever the case, I am plainly not myself in as clear a way as I might wish. (Coetzee, 1979, p. 62)

If the contingency of the fictional world rests on a 'single sure affirmation', that affirmation itself is not exempt from the very contingencies it instantiates. The narrating 'I' on whom the fiction turns is just as much a consequence of the 'bicycles and greatcoats' as it is the cause. It is thus that the Unnamable can say, whimsically, 'the best is to think about myself as fixed and at the centre of this place, whatever its shape and extent may be' (Beckett, 1979, p. 271). Magda, too, is the arbitrary pivot on whom a fiction turns, even as she herself creates it; little wonder that she should feel that she is not straightforwardly herself. Further, even in

order to question her own ontological status, Magda disrupts complacent assumptions on the part of the reader about an either/or structure
in the pair, real world/fictional world: the 'I' of her utterance seems to
straddle both.

The presumed sequential logic of reference (that is to say, first the
thing, then the name) is inverted in *The Unnamable* – 'I have an ocean
to drink, so there is an ocean then' (Beckett, 1979, p. 288) – and is taken
further in the black humour of *In the Heart of the Country*:

> Why is it left to me to give life not only to myself, minute after surly
> minute, but to everyone else on the farm, and to the farm itself, every
> stick and stone of it? . . . I make it all up in order that it shall make me
> up. I cannot stop now. (Coetzee, 1979, pp. 72–73)

Magda's reflections are certainly an extension of *The Unnamable*'s parting
words, 'you must go on, I can't go on, I'll go on' (Beckett, 1979, p. 382),
and in Coetzee's own terms again,

> It is naïve to think that writing is a simple two-stage process: first you
> decide what you want to say, then you say it. On the contrary . . . you
> write because you do not know what you want to say . . . In fact, it
> sometimes constructs what you want or wanted to say . . . That is the
> sense in which one can say that writing writes us. (Coetzee, 1992,
> p. 18)

III

The 'problem of names', especially as it arises for the writer, is explicitly
addressed in *Dusklands*: 'More significant to me than the marital problem' (says Eugene Dawn), 'is the problem of names'. He claims to be a
'specialist in relations rather than names' and adds:

> It would be a healthy corrective to learn the names of the songbirds
> and also the names of a good selection of plants and insects . . . I hope
> that firm and prolonged intercourse with reality, if I can manage it,
> will have a good effect on my character as well as my health, and
> perhaps even improve my writing. (Coetzee, 1998, p. 36)

The act of creative writing is relentlessly bound up in a question of names –

> I would appreciate a firm grasp of cicadas, Dutch elm blight, and orioles, to mention three names, and the capacity to spin them into long, dense paragraphs which would give the reader a clear sense of the complex natural reality in whose midst I now indubitably am. (Coetzee, 1998, pp. 36–37)

This passage is significant in an important respect: it is a turning point in recognizing that in Coetzee, self-reflexive questions about names and modes of reference in fiction are *part* of a sustained interrogation throughout Coetzee's oeuvre of the supposed sovereignty of a rational self, and of the apartheid legacy of colonialism. Names, for Coetzee, assert a division between namer and named, creator and creature – between 'consciousness and the objects of consciousness' (Coetzee, 1992, p. 37). The success of the name cedes authority to the one who names; but in complex ways it is an authority that is at once necessary, sought after, and contested by Coetzee, the author.

To return to the passage just cited: if 'cicadas', 'orioles', and 'Dutch elm blight' give a clear sense of a 'complex natural reality', the syntactic structures undermine the controlling distance that these names effect: the use of the conditional tense holds Dawn's knowledge of names in suspension, and the deictic 'now' diverts attention away from the world named to the scene of naming. The 'indubitably' is thus rendered ironic, to the extent that 'whose' of 'in whose midst' almost runs the risk of referring to the reader, and 'now' is difficult to be dissociated from the moment of the writing's being-read. The place of writing becomes the focus of attention, and ousts the 'complex natural reality' that the names are meant to call into being in the first place. The passage continues: 'I spend many analytic hours puzzling out the tricks which their authors perform to give to their monologues . . . the air of a real world through the looking-glass. A lexicon of common nouns seems to be a prerequisite. Perhaps I was not born to be a writer' (Coetzee, 1998, p. 37).

In one of the interviews in *Doubling the Point*, David Attwell and Coetzee speak about the intricate relations between modernism, postmodernism, and postcolonialism, where the suggestion arises that the self-reflexiveness of modernism is politically irresponsible. Coetzee responds in an interesting way:

> the general position Lukács takes on what he calls realism as against modernist decadence carries a great deal of power, political and moral,

in South Africa today [ie. 1989–1991]: one's first duty as a writer is to represent social and historical processes; drawing the procedures of representation into question is time-wasting; and so forth. (Coetzee, 1992, p. 202)

One detects a note of impatience in Coetzee's response here; the 'and so forth' puts into question the validity of the assertions that precede it. It is easy to assume that a self-reflexive fictional enterprise and a world of socio-political engagement are mutually exclusive. Yet Coetzee is deeply cognizant of the subtle connections between these two worlds. If the 'problem of names', as Eugene Dawn would have it, calls into question the procedures of representation, it also calls into question the relation between namer and named, the authority of the namer, and the responsive range that the call of a name instantiates.

The notion of contingency has already arisen in this chapter within the context of the status of a narrative hinged on an initial assertion announcing the 'as-if' mode of fiction. Now the contingency of names gains urgency in relation to questions of culture and history. It is in this context that the calling into question of the procedures of representation is part of a profoundly ethical concern with 'social and historical processes'. Cultures within which nominal systems arise are themselves shown to be contingent by the very names that bespeak them.

We see this clearly in *Dusklands*: 'The criteria for a new discovery employed by the gentlemen for Europe were surely parochial. They required that every specimen fill a hole in their European taxonomies' (Coetzee, 1998, p. 116). The name of the grass called *Aristida brevifolia* in Europe, called *Twaa* by the Bushman, and *boesmansgras* by the frontiersman, gives a sense of culturally dependent and therefore relative nominal systems, in which one system does not *naturally* take precedence over another: 'And if we accept such concepts as a Bushman taxonomy and a Bushman discovery, must we not accept the concepts of a frontiersman taxonomy and a frontiersman discovery?' (Coetzee, 1998, p. 116). Once again, the conceptual conjunction of naming and creating, is asserted, but this time, within the context of a moment of colonial 'discovery':

'I do not know this, my people do not know it, but at the same time I know what it is like, it is like *rooigras*, it is a kind of *rooigras*, I will call it *boesmansgras*' – that is the type of the inward moment of discovery. In this way Coetzee rode like a god through a world only partly named, differentiating and bringing it into existence. (Coetzee, 1998, p. 116)

The act of naming is one of *conjuration* – with all the multivalency of that word in force. It is 'a magic spell', an 'incantation', or 'charm' (*OED*) – it brings the world into existence as if by magic,[4] or by a primal act of creation. Yet 'conjuration' also means 'a swearing together; a making of a league by a common oath; a conspiracy ... a solemn charging or calling upon by appeal to something sacred or binding' (*OED*). *All* these meanings have pertinence in the passages cited from *Dusklands*: if the act of naming calls a world into being, it does so insofar as there is a taxonomic pact *amongst those who speak the language*. Even *Twaa* finds place, perhaps, in 'an unspoken botanical order' among the Bushmen (Coetzee, 1998, p. 16), but at the same time, *Twaa* is not 'binding', makes no solemn charge or appeal to those not versed in this 'unspoken botanical order'. Similarly, *Aristida brevifolia* does not have the impact of the 'in common' beyond the cognitive field of a European taxonomy. Thus the conjunctive word-pair, naming-creating, is not one of extravagant or easy optimism about the triumph of a universal language. In the instant of its affirmation, it speaks too, of a cultural contingency.

By now at least this much should be clear: names may be arbitrarily related to their referents, but they are not arbitrarily related to other *names*, slotting as they do, into sophisticated linguistic and taxonomic systems.[5] These taxonomic systems are supervenient upon the cultural context in which they arise, so that the names tell us as much about the *namers*, as they do about their putative referents. That one name should hold, that another fall into disuse, that a name for a particular referent should change in time: all of these nominative drifts track narratives of the contingency and ephemerality of the society of namers, rather than of the referents so named. Names speak of the shifting literary landscapes in which those who hold the authority to name are also revealed.

'When Europeans first arrived in southern Africa' (writes Coetzee in *Giving Offense*),

they called themselves *Christians* and indigenous people *wild* or *heathen*. The dyad *Christian/heathen* later mutated, taking a succession of forms, among them *civilized/primitive, European/native, white/nonwhite*. But in each case, no matter what the nominally opposed terms, there was a constant feature: it was always the Christian (or white or European or civilized person) in whose power it lay to apply the names – the names for himself, the name for the other. (Coetzee, 1996, p. 1)

To view names in this way is to look beyond a simple relation of refer-ent/name, or even a Saussurean signified/signifier. The discussion opens onto questions about the sites of cultural domination, about the para-meters of response drawn up for the one named, and about the field of responsibility that each act of naming instantiates. An intricate eth-ics is thus brought to bear in any event of naming, not least of which is the way in which names draw the limit to the ground of response for the one called. Names calibrate the social settings and the balance of power between namer and named. Coetzee speaks of the 'impot-ence of which being-named is the sign', of the realization that 'naming includes control over deictic distance: it can put the one named at a measured arm's length quite as readily as it can draw the one named affectionately nearer' (Coetzee, 1996, p. 2). But, as Coetzee himself sug-gests, it is whether or not you have the power to apply the names (regardless of whether you are the namer or the one named) that most dramatically affects positionality on the slide-rules of distance and prox-imity, authority, and subjection. Names speak of the *relation* between namer and named, rather than simply of the referent itself. This is why David Lurie is so appalled when he learns the name of the boy who is one of his daughter's rapists: the name is not *other* enough to effect the boy's distance from a Western civilization in which Lurie finds himself so at home: 'His name is Pollux', says Lucy, to which Lurie replies:

> 'Not Mcedisi? Not Nqabayakhe? Nothing unpronounceable, just Pollux?'
> 'P-O-L-L-U-X. And David, can we have some relief from that terrible irony of yours?' (Coetzee, 1999a, p. 200)

In an extreme case, the refusal to name, or to be named in turn, is an attempt to place the other outside of a perceived responsive range.[6] When Lurie sees Pollux spying on Lucy through the bathroom it is *Lurie* – that bastion of European civilized Romanticism – who falls into an 'elemental rage', who strikes Pollux and shouts, '*You swine!* . . . *You filthy swine!*' He thinks, 'So this is what it is like . . . this is what it is like to be a savage!' It is perhaps the realization that a balance of power has shifted, and that 'swine' has no purchase on the young man who is possibly the father of his grandson, that leads Lurie to comment, finally, 'Pollux! What a name!' (Coetzee, 1999a, p. 207). The namer's relation to the other is implicated in the name that he or she is obliged to use, and in this case, Lurie is powerless to *choose* that name.

Being in the position of the one who chooses the names is to be in the position of power; but since names speak of the relation between namer and named, the name for the other is also a way of positioning the self. This throw-back effect of names reminds me of the logic of the middle voice[7], and of Coetzee's linguistico-philosophical understanding of the term, writing: 'in a larger sense', says Coetzee, 'all writing is auto-biography: everything that you write, including criticism and fiction, writes you as you write it' (Coetzee, 1992, p. 17). We use names to refer to something, or to call someone at a place in language, but equally, the names we use give an indication of the place from which we call. That *name–place* is at a complex intersection of social, cultural, and historical routes.

Coetzee speaks of writing that entails 'an awareness, as you put pen to paper, that you are setting in train a certain play of signifiers with their own ghostly history of past interplay' (Coetzee, 1992, p. 63). How does the writer negotiate the effects of this ghostly history? And what part, precisely, do names have to play in this? Perhaps this is the post-colonial response to modernism when it comes to names – whereas a modernist text may question the capacity of names, universally, to refer meaningfully at all, a postcolonial text is likely to chart the particular socio-historic configurations that are brought to bear in each naming event. Differently put: where a modernist writer questions the efficacy of his or her medium in universal terms, the postcolonial writer is interested in that medium's specific historical effects.

IV

To name a landscape is to mark sites of human significance on indifferent ground. In an inversion of the expected sequence – first the landscape, then the name – we can say that a landscape becomes literary (which is to say, it is given written form) precisely *because* it is named. This is the logic of Heidegger's 'The Origin of the Work of Art' – it is the building of the temple that announces the precinct as holy, the ground as native, rather than the other way round (Heidegger, 1977, pp. 167–168). But given the 'ghostly history' of language, any attempt *to signify* the land-scape by name[8] is to signal a human relation to that place at a particular moment in time. Time itself recedes, and the landscape, too, changes, but incrementally, the name carries with it the traces of the human histories that have made that place significant. 'When death cuts all other links', says the Dostoevsky of *The Master of Petersburg*, 'there remains still the name' (Coetzee, 2004, p. 5). It is when the *name* changes that certain histories are elided, and that the place is marked in a different way for future recollection: the name of a place gives an indication of whose past is deemed worthy of recalling as history.[9] This in-built historiography of place-names is not entirely obliterated, even when those names are taken up within a fictional frame.

For artist and film-maker William Kentridge, it is the historiography of names that is lost in visual representations of place – in picturesque painting, for example – and in the sites themselves. Here is William Kentridge on the name, 'Sharpeville':

> *the word Sharpeville* conjures up, both locally, and I would imagine internationally, a whole series of things, the centre of which is the infamous massacre of sixty-nine people outside a police station in the township outside Vereeniging...But at the site itself, there is almost no trace of what happened there. This is natural. It is an area that is still used, an area in which people live and go to work. It is not a museum. There are no bloodstains. The ghosts of the people do not walk the streets. Scenes of battles, great and small, disappear, are absorbed by the terrain, except in those few places where memorials are specifically erected, monuments established, as outposts, as defences against this process of disremembering and absorption. (Kentridge, 1999a, p. 127, my emphasis)

The name itself functions as an outpost against a process of disremembering and absorption, and Kentridge, in his own work, explores, as much as he practises in his techniques, the tensions between memory and forgetting, between monuments and fences on the one hand, and the landscape's process of absorption on the other. Thus Kentridge is interested in depicting 'a landscape that is articulated or *given a meaning by incidents across it*, pieces of civil engineering, the lines of pipes, culverts, fences', what he calls 'the variety of the ephemera of human intervention on the landscape' (Kentridge, 1999b, p. 110, my emphasis). The technique that Kentridge uses in his animated films is one of 'imperfect erasure' (Kentridge, 2001, p. 67) – a charcoal image is drawn, photographed, rubbed out and slightly altered, photographed again, and so on. But the erasures are never absolute, so that traces of the previous image are still visible in the present one. Time passing is projected onto

a spatial, visible plane as palimpsest; the history of the place is refracted through an increasingly complex network of lines: the procession of
layered drawing and gradated fading away gives to the passing of time a
visible spatial depth. When this comes to the depiction of human subjects, we *see* a 'multiplicity of the self passing through time, which would
end up as a single self if the moment was frozen in a photograph, in a
fixed drawing' (Kentridge, 2001, p. 67). One thinks of the dance film that
David Lurie shows to Melanie Isaacs in his flat in Cape Town:

> Two dancers on a bare stage move through their steps. Recorded by
> a stroboscopic camera, their images, ghosts of their movements, fan
> out behind them like wingbeats ... the instant of the present and the
> past of that instant, evanescent, caught in the same space. (Coetzee,
> 1999a, pp. 14–15)[10]

In visual terms, this is the way in which William Kentridge plays up
the 'ghostly history' of the signifier, doing justice to his sense there
can be no 'simple response to a place whose appearance is so different
from its history' (Kentridge, 1999b, p. 110). Kentridge's project, writes
Coetzee, is about the 'unburying' of the past of the South African landscape (Coetzee, 1999b, p. 84). Perceptions of landcape and the resources
of memory are interrelated, and projected onto the synchronicity of a
single visual field.

Now, to return to the novels, it seems to me that Coetzee is also preoccupied with a stroboscopic vision of landscape: temporally different,
yet spatially coincident images of the past and of the present are superimposed, throwing the landscape into historical relief. In the writer's
literary landscapes, the planes of present appearance and historical past
converge *in the name*. Human ephemera are poignantly recorded in the
remains of the name – for future readers. *Dusklands*:

> At one of their halts (August 18) the expedition left behind: the ashes
> of the night fire, combustion complete, a feature of dry climates;
> faeces dotted in mounds over a broad area, herbivore in the open,
> carnivore behind rocks; urine stains with minute traces of copper salts;
> tea leaves; the leg-bones of a springbok; five inches of braided oxhide
> rope; tobacco ash; and a musket ball. The faeces dried in the course
> of the day. Ropes and bones were eaten by a hyena on August 22. A
> storm on November 2 scattered all else. The musket ball was not there
> on August 18, 1933. (Coetzee, 1998, pp. 118–119)

There seems to be no end to the literary *list*, even in the instant that it records a disappearance:

> dead hair and scales . . . crumbs of wax . . . mucus . . . and blood . . . tears and a rheumy paste. rotten teeth, calculus, phlegm, vomit . . . pus, . . . scabs, weeping plasma (Plaatje, a gunpowder burn), sweat, sebum, scales, hair. Nail fragments, interdigital decay. Urine and the minuter kidneystones (Cape water is rich in alkalis). Smegma (circumcision is confined to the Bantu). Faecal matter, blood, pus (Dikkop, poison). Semen (all). These relicts, deposited over Southern Africa in two swathes, soon disappeared under sun, wind, rain, and the attentions of the insect kingdom, though their atomic constituents are still of course among us. *Scripta manent.* (Coetzee, 1998, p. 119)

What these elaborate lists enact is that *the name itself* is the 'relict', the 'surviving trace', that which is 'left by death' (*OED*). The writing remains: *scripta manent*, which reminds me again of Beckett, and of the indelible trace of reference in any use of language: 'If I could speak and yet say nothing, really nothing? . . . But it seems impossible to speak and yet say nothing. You think you have succeeded, but you always overlook something, a little yes, a little no, enough to exterminate a regiment of dragoons' (Beckett, 1979, p. 277).' Molloy can say, 'What I'd like now is to speak of the things that are left' (Beckett, 1979, p. 9), but the writing itself is the thing that is left, and, through it, an historical past breaks in on the surface 'now' of each utterance. The literary landscape of *Disgrace* constitutes a striking instance of the palimpsestic interplay between what Thomas Hardy would call 'the transitory in Earth's long order' (Hardy, 1978, p. 117) and the relicts of the name. Immediately evident in the novel is the legacy, but also the evanescence of a colonial social geo-graphy in a newly post-apartheid Cape. There are several examples of this: David Lurie's reference to the Eastern Cape as 'Old Kaffraria', for instance (Coetzee, 1999a, p. 122), or his reflections on his daughter, Lucy, who farms in the Eastern Cape on what used to be the frontier between colonial settlers and the indigenous Xhosa people. 'A frontier farmer of the new breed. In the old days cattle and maize. Today dogs and daffodils' (Coetzee, 1999a, p. 62). The following comment of Lurie's on the shifting urban landscape of Cape Town leads me back to the passages I cited earlier from *Giving Offense*:

> He has been away less than three months, yet in that time the shanty settlements have crossed the highway and spread east of the airport.

The stream of cars has to slow down while a child with a stick herds a stray cow off the road. Inexorably, he thinks, the country is coming to the city. Soon there will be cattle again on Rondebosch Common; soon history will have come full circle. (Coetzee, 1999a, p. 175)

Lurie's choice of the term, 'shanty settlement', is what interests me here. He does not say 'squatter camp' or 'informal settlement' – both of which would have been in common use at the time of writing *Disgrace*: both terms insist on the transitoriness of these settlements. But neither are the shanty towns referred to by name, and the terms 'settler' and 'settlement', in South Africa, constitute a chiasmatic intersection of seemingly contradictory associations: if on the one hand, a settler is presumably here to stay, a settler is also a new-comer, a colonizer, an outsider, one whose home is elsewhere, and therefore, one who is expected to leave again. It is the term 'settler' that provides the context for the discussion of names in *Giving Offense*. 'Settlers, in the idiom of white South Africa', writes Coetzee,

> are those Britishers who took up land grants in Kenya and the Rhodesias, people who refused to put down roots in Africa, who sent their children abroad to be educated, and spoke of England as 'Home.' When the Mau Mau got going, the settlers fled. To South Africans, white as well as black, *a settler is a transient, no matter what the dictionary says*. (Coetzee, 1996, p. 1, my emphasis)

Lurie refers to Lucy as 'this sturdy young settler' (Coetzee, 1999a, p. 61), but from Petrus's perspective (according to Lurie), 'Lucy is merely a transient' (Coetzee, 1999a, p. 117). In *Disgrace* the legacy of those settlers is inevitably called up in the names – Grahamstown, Salem, Port Elizabeth, New Brighton Station, the Kenton Road – even as human communities coalesce and dissipate across the terrain.

V

I return to the interview with Tony Morphet where I set out: the physical geography of Coetzee's novels may well be less 'reliable' than we are tempted to assume; the place of writing itself becomes an active site in the signifying landscape. The novel, for Coetzee, 'becomes less a *thing* than a *place* where one goes every day for several hours a day for years on end. What happens in that place has less and less discernible relation to the daily life one lives or the lives people are living around one.' (Coetzee,

1992, p. 205, emphasis Coetzee's). William Kentridge, too, steers us away from the imaginative poverty of trying to map literary landscapes in terms of physical geographic co-ordinates:

> Private maps of familiar places do not correspond to any geographer's projection. Pretoria has always been alien...And of course, with a South African passport, all the land to the north is a huge void, something to be taken on trust from pictures in *National Geographic*. (Kentridge, 1999b, p. 109)

But if the question of a physical geography, in a certain sense, is irrelevant to a literary landscape, the 'ghostly history' of the names, and hence of the namers who signify this landscape, is not. It is thanks to the *imperfect* erasure of these histories, even in a work of fiction, that names have any hold at all. The names that a writer uses are outposts in a landscape that in itself is oblivious to human memories of that place. Names trigger sites of individual memory as the reader traces patterns of significance in the language of literature. It is in this sense that a question of names has less to do with the *geography* of the place than it has to do with the *history* of those who have chosen, who use, and who recognize the names. At the same time, these names are a poignant reminder of the forgetting, the transience, or the fears they are created as bastions against.

Notes

1. In this paper I use the word 'name' in the broadest sense – the proper and common nouns that name a landscape and the selves and others who people it. My discussion begins and ends with a consideration of Coetzee's use of place-names.
2. Of course, I am taking the cue from Emile Benveniste here: '*I* refers to the act of individual discourse in which it is pronounced and by this it designates the speaker' (Benveniste, 1971, p. 226) and 'there is no other criterion...by which to indicate 'the time at which one *is*' except to take it as 'the time at which one is *speaking*.' This is the eternally 'present' moment...Linguistic time is *self-referential*' (Benveniste, 1971, p. 227).
3. I use the word in two senses – 'effecting by magic' and 'swearing together.' More of this later.
4. Dostoevsky's utterance of the deceased Pavel's name in *The Master of Petersburg* has connotations of a charm or a spell: 'Silently he forms his lips over his son's name, three times, four times. He is trying to cast a spell' (Coetzee, 2004, p. 5) '*Pavel!* He whispers over and over, using the word as a charm' (Coetzee, 2004, p. 60). Another meaning in the *OED* is pertinent here: 'The effecting of something supernatural by a spell or by the invocation of a sacred

name.' In *The Master of Petersburg* the incantation of Pavel's name is explicitly linked to the myth of Orpheus (Coetzee, 2004, p. 5).
5. This holds true of proper names of persons – where surnames, especially, but also given names hold place within a genealogy and/or other taxonomic patterns. To call someone by name is to call that person at a place in language. A nickname, an alias, a *nom de plume* – all of these, in different ways, bring about shifts in the linguistic site of response, in the responsive field, of the one named. See chapter 4 of my doctoral thesis.
6. Charles Dickens was aware of this, as we see in his outrageous article of 1853, 'The Noble Savage': 'I have not the least belief in the Noble Savage. I consider him a prodigious nuisance, and an enormous superstition. His calling rum fire-water, and me a paleface, wholly fail to reconcile me to him. *I don't care what he calls me.* I call him a savage, and I call a savage something highly desirable to be civilised off the face of the earth' (Dickens, 1853, p. 337, my emphasis). See my doctoral thesis (pp. 169–173). For an extended discussion about the distinction between notions of the 'irresponsible' and the 'non-responsible' (which arises in relation to Dickens) see my chapter, 'The Time of Address,' 2007, pp. 229–240.
7. This is a topic that requires a paper of its own.
8. I use 'signify' in both senses: to refer to the landscape by name, but also, to invest the landscape with significance by naming it.
9. Place-name changes in South Africa, especially since the first democratic elections in 1994, constitute a striking case. The most infamous example is surely Sophiatown, renamed Triomf in 1955, at the time of the forced removal of residents classified as non-white, to make way for poor white Afrikaners. Triomf was renamed Sophiatown in 2005. See Beavon's *Johannesburg: The Making and Shaping of the City*, 2004.
10. Thank you to Kjetil Enstad for reminding me about this passage.

Works cited

Beavon, K., *Johannesburg: The Making and Shaping of the City* (Pretoria: University of South Africa Press, 2004).
Beckett, S., *The Beckett Trilogy: Molloy, Malone Dies, the Unnamable* (London: Picador, 1979).
Benveniste, E., *Problems in General Linguistics*. Trans. M. E. Meek (Coral Gables, Florida: University of Miami Press, 1971).
Clarkson, C., *Naming and Personal Identity in the Novels of Charles Dickens: A Philosophical Approach*, Doctoral Thesis (University of York, November 1999).
Clarkson, C., 'The Time of Address', *Law and the Politics of Reconciliation*. Ed. S. Veitch (Edinburgh: Ashgate, 2007), pp. 229–240.
Coetzee, J. M., *In the Heart of the Country* (Johannesburg: Ravan Press, 1979).
———, *White Writing: on the Culture of Letters in South Africa* (New Haven and London: Radix, in association with Yale University Press, 1988).
———, *Doubling the Point: Essays and Interviews*. Ed. D. Attwell (Cambridge, Mass. and London: Harvard University Press, 1992).
———, *Giving Offense* (London and Chicago: University of Chicago Press, 1996).
———, *Dusklands* (London: Vintage, 1998).

————, *Disgrace* (London: Secker and Warburg, 1999a).

————, 'History of the Main Complaint', *William Kentridge* (New York: Phaidon, 1999b) pp. 82–93.

————, *Youth* (London: Secker and Warburg, 2002).

————, *The Master of Petersburg* (London: Vintage, 2004).

Coetzee J. M. and T. Morphet, 'Two Interviews with J. M. Coetzee, 1983 and 1987', *Triquarterly*. Special Issue: *from South Africa* (Spring/Summer 1987) 454–464.

Dickens, C., 'The Noble Savage', *Household Words*, No.168 (Saturday, June 11, 1853) 337–339.

Hardy, T., 'At Castle Boterel', *The New Wessex Selection of Thomas Hardy's Poetry* Ed. J. Wain and E. Wain (London: Macmillan, 1978), p. 117.

Heidegger, M., 'The Origin of the Work of Art', *Martin Heidegger: Basic Writings* Ed. D. F. Krell (HarperCollins: New York, 1977), pp. 139–212.

Kentridge, W., 'Felix in Exile: Geography of Memory', *William Kentridge* (New York: Phaidon, 1999a) pp. 122–127.

————, 'Landscape in a State of Siege', *William Kentridge* (New York: Phaidon, 1999b), pp. 108–111.

————, 'Interview with Dan Cameron', *William Kentridge* (Chicago: New Museum of Contemporary Art in association with Harry N. Abrams, 2001), pp. 67–74.

9
Houses, Cellars and Caves in Selected Novels from Latin America and South Africa

Marita Wenzel

Contextualization

The historical reality of colonization and the diaspora[1] has resulted in cultural fragmentation, displacement and exile which, at present, is further exacerbated by globalization and a lack of belonging. As a result of this experience of rootlessness and alienation, traditional perceptions of identity as a static concept have been superseded by the postmodernist conceptualization of identity as a process of interaction with various geographical, social and cultural contexts over a period of time. DeToro defines the dynamic quality of identity formation by stating that

> new alignments made across borders, types, nations, and essences are rapidly coming into view, and it is those new alignments that now provoke and challenge the fundamentally static notion of identity that has been the core of cultural thought during the era of imperialism. (1995, p. 39)

Consequently, perceptions of 'space' and 'place' and their influence on the formation of identity have become moot points of discussion and prominent themes in critical and theoretical debates on postcoloniality over the last decade.[2] However, prior to these contemporary debates, philosophers such as Heidegger (1975)[3] and Bachelard (1969) had already contributed valuable insights towards an understanding of the individual's perception of his or her existence in space.

Their ideas have been further developed and expanded by critics such as Crang (1998) and Schick (1999) to focus on the cultural and social implications of space and place. Within this context, postcolonial novels[4] have played a major role in creating symbolic or narrative spaces that enable the colonized to come to terms with their past and to attempt to reconstruct a semblance of identity and cultural context.

This chapter focuses on the significance of 'space' and the concept of defined space or 'place' as definitive points of orientation in the representation of history as a cultural space and in the formation of identity as a result of the human being's interaction with his or her environment. History is represented as the intersection of a specific time and 'place' that produces unique cultural products and structures such as buildings and houses (clearly illustrated in the titles of the Latin American novels included in the present discussion). It is argued that houses and their respective subdivisions of personal and shared space(s) reflect cultural and historical periods and value systems. Their positioning in relation to the outside world identifies them as points of orientation and symbols of cultural identity. When Schick (1999, p. 8) refers to houses as metaphors, he implies that 'places have significances that transcend their physical/geographical characteristics, and these significances mediate our relations with our environment'.

Many Latin American and South African novels reflect these issues in different ways, since they share colonial legacies of political oppression, cultural hegemony and social discrimination. A form of social critique expressed in the novels mentioned below concerns the re-writing of history with particular attention to the inclusion of voices from peripheral communities and women, who were previously omitted from official documentation or 'history'. Inclusion in re-written historical documents is therefore an important aspect of identity conceptualization in postcolonial novels. In this sense, houses as symbols of origin and their association with history and identity feature quite prominently in the following novels: Isabel Allende's *The House of the Spirits*, José Donoso's *A House in the Country* and Rosario Ferré's *The House on the Lagoon* from Latin America; and André Brink's novels *Imaginings of Sand* and *The Rights of Desire* from South Africa. In particular, rooms of hidden regions described in these novels relate to suppressed family histories.

Perceptions of space and place

The respective meanings attributed to the concepts 'space', 'place' and 'home' in this chapter are mainly based on Heidegger's definition of the terms in his thought-provoking essay entitled 'Building Dwelling Thinking' (1975).[5] Heidegger's (1975, p. 150) perception of the human being as an integral part of a 'fourfold' entity together with earth, sky and the divinities, emphasizes the interaction between the individual and his or her environment. Within this context, Heidegger perceives 'place' as a specific category of 'space' expressed in terms of a structure or house that constitutes a point of orientation. The positioning of an object or person as a central point of orientation in the apprehension of spatial experience is illustrated in terms of a bridge: 'the bridge does not first come to a location to stand in it; rather, a location comes into existence only by virtue of the bridge', and he concludes that 'only things that are locations in this manner allow for spaces' (Heidegger, 1975, p. 154). In particular, Heidegger (1975, p. 146) claims that houses do not become defined spaces or structures until inhabited; they only assume the connotation of 'homes' when dwelt in by people, as 'dwelling and building are related as end and means'. A home could be described as a personal dwelling 'space'. In this sense, *space* will then be used to designate the internal structure or house that, by implication, relates to the external space or context called into being or defined by a building or landmark.

Bachelard describes space in terms of individual experience that differentiates between internal and external spaces in his *Poetics of Space* (1969). In relation to the external world, the house forms the point of orientation or 'place'. Furthermore, Bachelard adds another dimension of space which he calls 'intimate space' that relates to the realm of the imagination, or memory, and the construction of literary space. Both Heidegger and Bachelard therefore perceive houses as points of orientation or places, while homes (in the sense of 'dwellings' or personal spaces) function as significant and relevant spaces or spheres of influence in personal and public life.

From a cultural, geographical stance, Crang (1998, p. 102) also views the individual's position as point of orientation in the perception of space, emphasizing his or her interaction with external space or context. Crang (1998, p. 110) expands on previous interpretations of place by attributing additional functions to his use of the term 'context' as: the organization of experience that includes bodily situation (direction), perceptual space (what we look at/observe), existential space (social meaning) and cognitive space (how we abstractly model spatial relationships).

Heidegger and Bachelard's interpretations of space provide us with frameworks of reference within which humans function. While Heidegger focuses on human beings in interaction with the universe, Bachelard identifies different spatial dimensions of human awareness as personal (internal), public (external) and intimate spaces. This background proves invaluable in the analysis of space in the novels concerned, which all address contemporary perceptions and representations of history, culture and identity.

Houses as homes or lived spaces or places

The combination of dwelling and belonging is usually associated with the concept of home and identity, but as several critics point out (Hummon, 1989, p. 220; Douglas, 1991, pp. 289 and 294; and Stea, 1995, p. 184), home does not necessarily indicate a specific place or house and people attribute different connotations to the idea of home. Schick (1999, p. 5) reminds us that physical landmarks or structures (in the conventional sense of the word 'place') have become subsumed by abstract perceptions because '*places* are not "objective" realities but exist only through particular human spatial experiences'. Schick (1999, p. 24) also perceives a definite correspondence between lived space and identity as do Carter *et al.* (1993, p. vii) and especially Hummon (1989, p. 208), who refers to houses as 'nonverbal signs for defining and communicating identity in modern society'. Morley and Robins (1993, p. 7) add an additional dimension by claiming that 'home' evokes a feeling of nostalgia and memory of the past, of roots and origins. Diana Brydon (1991, p. 199) identifies both a social and a moral side to a home when she claims that apart from 'community and family relations', the home also implies 'accepting responsibility and learning to choose within a world determined by the contingencies of values'. Appiah conceives of 'home' from a cosmopolitan perspective, which is inclusive and yet exclusive at the same time:

> the cosmopolitan patriot can entertain the possibility of a world in which everyone is a rooted cosmopolitan, attached to a home of her own, with its own cultural particularities, but taking pleasure from the presence of other, different, places that are home to other, different, people. (1991, p. 12)

To summarize, the most significant associations of 'home' relate to social relationships and networks, to the idea of a place as a refuge, and to the sense of continuity gained from its existence. Hummon (1989, p. 209) explains how the interpersonal dynamics in a home create emotional ties which aid us to 'identify ourselves' as well as connect '*with* others or significant objects, forging a sense of belonging and attachment'. Therefore the association with people – whether the quality of the personal relationships in a home is congenial or inhibiting – takes precedence over place; that is, a house could act either as a refuge or a prison, depending on the inhabitants. All these ideas signify home as a defined 'space' that shapes identity; but they also underscore the role of society, the existence of emotional and social ties as well as values, in the creation of a home.

Bachelard relates our memories to the images of houses:

> Not only our memories, but the things we have forgotten are 'housed'. Our soul is an abode. And by remembering 'houses' and 'rooms', we learn to 'abide' within ourselves. Now everything becomes clear, the house images move in both directions: they are in us as much as we are in them . . . (1969, p. xxxiii)

Memories of houses as an 'inhabited space' or a home could therefore be associated with identity (Bachelard, 1969, pp. 5–9). Dreams, memories and aspirations form a composite picture of the past which inhabitants transfer to a new house to create 'illusions of stability' (Bachelard, 1969, p. 17). Crang expands on this perception by referring to landscape as a cultural palimpsest (revealing and incorporating traces of previous cultures) or a text. He explains that

> landscapes may be read as texts illustrating the beliefs of the people. The shaping of the landscape is seen as expressing social ideologies that are then perpetuated and supported through the landscape. (1998, p. 27)

The concept of a cultural text is also replicated in the intimate or literary space of the novel as it reflects the perceptions of a specific period in history that has been reviewed in many postcolonial novels.

Bachelard's (1969, p. 37) attention to the arrangement of rooms or living spaces in a house and its relationship to the outside world, which he describes as 'the dynamic dialectics of the house and the universe', is very useful for this discussion. He points out the significance of attics and subterranean rooms such as cellars and caves when he argues that the verticality of the house harbours a specific significance in terms of the imagination:

> Verticality is ensured by the polarity of cellar and attic, the marks of which are so deep that, in a way, they open up two very different

perspectives for a phenomenology of the imagination. Indeed, it is possible, almost without commentary, to oppose the rationality of the roof to the irrationality of the cellar. (Bachelard, 1969, pp. 17–18)

He explains that the clear outline of the roof and the definite pattern of rafters in the attic are conducive to rational thinking, but that the cellar is 'first and foremost the *dark entity* of the house, the one that partakes of subterranean forces' (Bachelard, 1969, p. 18). Cellars, that could also represent the unconscious, as Jung's research in this respect has indicated (Bachelard, 1969, p. 18), feature prominently in the novels discussed below, but the main concern in this chapter lies with the dialectic between houses as cultural structures and their representation in literature.

Especially in European-style houses, the cellar room was often used to store old or useless objects and books or remnants of furniture not intended for the public gaze or consumption. In a figurative sense, these divisions or subterranean rooms would then be associated with the past and be perceived as repositories of individual histories that harbour memories of particular societies and cultures. However, in literary representation, they seem to constitute part of a collective unconscious of a nation or society in a specific place and time. As Douglas (1991, p. 289, 294) points out, a house or home 'also has some structure in time; and because it is for people who are living in that time and space, it has aesthetic and moral dimensions'.

Since the inception of novels, houses are portrayed to have played an important role in shaping and reflecting the lives of their inhabitants. For instance, several nineteenth-century novels, such as Emily Brontë's *Wuthering Heights* and Charles Dickens's *Bleak House*, portray houses as metaphors of the characters' lives in the novels. In particular, Satis House in *Great Expectations* reflects the decay and stultification of Miss Havisham's life, while Wemmick's castle in the same novel serves as an illustration of his social isolation. The importance of the past as a foundation for the future, and the implications of a precarious or flawed foundation are graphically illustrated in *The Fall of the House of Usher* by Edgar Allan Poe.

As products of human experience that only acquire meaning from particular contexts (Davis, 1987, p. 24), novels are loaded with ideological baggage that aids people to 'adapt to the fragmentation and isolation of the modern world' (Davis, 1987, p. 12). Davis (1987, p. 64) points out how perceptions of space and place have changed from the colonial period that emphasized the ownership of property 'as controlled space or location' (whether at home or abroad) to the postcolonial period that paid more attention to the moral and aesthetic justifications of ownership (Davis, 1987, p. 100). Rapoport (1989, p. xix) and Lawrence (1989, p. 92) remark that houses act as links between people and their settings, when they emphasize the social distinctions between traditional and modern communities: while the former regarded houses as shelters and meeting places, the latter erected houses as status symbols and objects of personal pride and affluence – very evident in Allende's *The House of the Spirits* and Ferré's *The House on the Lagoon* that will be discussed below.

Davis (1987, p. 55, 57) points out that it is 'through the intersection of the literary imagination and the social mythology' that the geographical, fictitious and renamed spaces in literature attain symbolic significance (Davis, 1987, p. 57). Henry James's (1968) comparison of the structure of a novel to the structure of a house, represents an important point of departure for an exploration of spatial constructs and their relationship to identity formation in literature. To James, the identity of Isabel Archer is central to the structure of *The Portrait of a Lady*; and it also determines the contours and dimensions of her environment. James's (1968, p. 58) description of innumerable windows in the 'house of fiction' can be interpreted as different views or glimpses of life beyond the limitations of the structure of the building (into the world of the imagination), but it could also indicate the boundaries of perceived freedom. His comment (James, 1968, p. 58) that 'they are but windows at the best, mere holes in a dead wall, disconnected, perched aloft; they are not hinged doors opening straight upon life' also highlights the difference between art and life. Isabel Archer is given the freedom to choose and yet she misconstrues the signs. She is a free spirit who is 'not confined by the conditions, not engaged in the tangle, to which we look for much of the impress that constitutes an identity ... ' (James, 1968, p. 59). The Italian palazzo that Isabel inhabits after her marriage is a house that lacks the warmth of personal relationships, an empty shell that cannot be defined as a home.

Houses, stories and women

Schick (1999, p. 12) unerringly focuses on the social aspect of narrative when he states that it not only 'provides individuals with roadmaps to the societal landscape' but also determines their behaviour and defines their identities. Schick (1999, p. 21) argues that 'perceptions of the self are not simple truths unproblematically reflecting a material reality, but discursive constructions in which societal views, norms, and assumptions are (as it were) made flesh'. In this regard, narrative provides some meas-ure of stabilization for perceptions of identity construction, because stories and myths give human experience meaning and coherence; they enable an individual to determine his place in the world (Schick, 1999, p. 21). In addition, the 'other' stands in a dialectical relation to the self and forms a necessary component in the determination of identity as he/she acts as a type of antithesis of the self, because 'no human experi-ence can be viewed independently of the system of signification within which it is lived' (Schick, 1999, p. 19). This idea of comparison is also implemented in this chapter.

The fact that time and place determine the interpretation of his-tory prompts González Echevarría to perceive Latin American literature as an archive in which each reading 'corrects the others, and each is unrepeatable insofar as it is a distinct act caught in the reader's own temporality' (1990, p. 26). In a similar way, the South African post-colonial novels represented by Brink in this chapter also attempt to re-vision South African history within the present context. Like the Latin American novels, Brink's novels also seem to strive for a new interpret-ation and a new text 'which is endowed with specific power to bear the truth at a given moment in history, owing to a given set of socio-economic circumstances' (González Echevarría, 1990, p. 39). This idea seems to correlate with Crang's (1998, p. 27) perception of a palimpsest of texts.

The depiction of women's lives and their experiences in the novels are highlighted to expose injustices from the past in various forms of oppression and slavery. Within the Latin American context, Allende and Ferré both use male and female narrators to create a more representative history and to emphasize stereotypical perceptions of male and female relations, while Donoso focuses on appearances, hypocrisy and family relationships – or lack of relationships. In contrast, Brink reverts to the construction of female lineage to show the development of a political consciousness in the women characters in *Imaginings of Sand*. He uses an introspective approach in the *Rights of Desire* where the reader experi-ences how both the author and the narrator become gradually aware of their prejudiced perceptions of women in the past. The main difference in approach between the Latin American and the South African novels lies in the choice of narrators. As a male writer, Brink seems to empathize with his male narrator, Ruben, who attempts to analyze his former pre-conceptions about women, while Allende and Ferré use dual narrators (male and female) that seem to render a more convincing representation of events.

The houses in the novels do not merely depict lifestyles and cultural atmosphere, but also illustrate the significance of the different internal or inhabited spaces of houses or 'homes'. These houses appear sombre and secretive; they consist of labyrinthine dimensions, contain brooding silences, and store deep and dangerous secrets that often emerge in the form of haunting spirits, skeletons of slaves from the past. Although they reveal fascinating stories of their inhabitants, they also harbour evidence of a past that is locked away from the public gaze: stories of exploitation, slavery, the abuse and neglect of women and children. Consequently, the various spaces – chambers, caves and cellars – assume a significance and a life of their own by reviving or re-enacting personal (life)stories. These are 'memories' that need to be excavated and exposed, to be exorcised by personal confrontation or public exposure through the acts of writing and telling of stories, because in the final instance, as Carter *et al.* (1993, p. x) correctly observe, it is necessary to acknowledge 'the brutal reality of events' that spark the need for such stories.

Allende's *The House of the Spirits* and Brink's *Imaginings of Sand* focus on a type of meta-history of women by suggesting that the writing and telling of stories is a way of re-writing history. The stories told by the grandmothers Clara and Christina to their granddaughters Alba and Kristien respectively are intended to provide an inclusive version of the history of the women in their families. The grandmothers attempt to create awareness and nurture a sense of historical and political conscious-ness in their granddaughters, in order to furnish their granddaughters with a sense of identity. A similar process is followed in *The House on the Lagoon* by Ferré when the narrator, Isabel Mendizabal, attempts to write the family history of her husband, Quintin, but he intervenes with his own comments (in italics) because he believes that she is fabricating a different history.

An interesting correlation between the different houses and their inhabitants emerges if one were to assume that the houses serve as status symbols of male affluence, while the ornate facades of the respect-ive houses reflect the female tendency to embellish, just like the often incredible and grotesque memories and stories recounted by the female characters in these novels. The fictitious houses could therefore be perceived as a fusion of male economic success and female artistic expression.

In the *House of the Spirits*, Clara, the grandmother, evinces and asserts her position as a woman and individual against the high-handed beha-viour of her family and her chauvinist spouse, Esteban Trueba. By choice she remains mute for several years of her life (Allende, 1990, p. 12), only expressing herself in writing through her diaries to record stories told to her as a girl by her uncle Marcos (Allende, 1990, p. 20) and her mother Nívea (Allende, 1990, p. 99). Clara entrusts this legacy to her granddaughter Alba to interpret and record. However, Alba aspires to a more comprehensive version of history by incorporating her grandfather's stories and memories as well.

Esteban Trueba built a luxurious house, designed by a French architect, for Clara when they were married. In this space she would be able to give her strong will and artistic inclinations full reign. Esteban intended the house to serve as a monument to his status and affluence in life and therefore dictated that it should take after the fashion of 'the new palaces of North America and Europe' and have none of the conventional structures favoured in his country (Allende, 1990, p. 114). His house should be the only one 'with German stained-glass windows, moldings carved in Austria, faucets of English bronze, Italian marble floors, and special locks ordered from catalogues from the United States, which arrived with the wrong instructions and no keys' (Allende, 1990, p. 114). It is ironical that, as a result of his wife Clara's wilful inspirations, the house finally attains similar convolutions and extraordinary proportions as the house on the farm Sinai described by Brink in his novel *Imaginings of Sand*. Under Clara's guidance, the

> solemn, cubic, dense, pompous house, which sat like a hat amid its green and geometric surroundings, would end up full of protuberances and incrustations, of twisted staircases that led to empty spaces, of turrets, of small windows that could not be opened, doors hanging in midair, crooked hallways, and portholes that linked the living quarters so that people could communicate during the siesta. (Allende, 1990, p. 115)

Clara who transforms the mansion 'into an enchanted labyrinth' (Allende, 1990, p. 115) fulfils a similar task to that performed by Kristien's grandmother. Both grandmothers want their granddaughters to record the past, especially the history of their female ancestors so that they can learn from them. Consequently, the architecture of the houses displays the incongruous and quaint personalities of their inhabitants.

In the South African context, Brink's *Imaginings of Sand* and *The Rights of Desire* depict cellars as places and spaces with suppressed personal memories that need to be 'aired'. In *Imaginings of Sand*, he describes the ostrich farm belonging to Kristien's grandmother and her family. The house built on the farm 'originally came from a mail-order catalogue'

(Brink, 1997, p. 6), and it is described as 'an improbable castle in the desert' (Brink, 1997, p. 5). Kristien remembers the house with fascination when as a child she and her cousins explored:

> the maze of archways and branching corridors, magnificent marble or teak staircases and unexpected other, dingier, flights of steps leading to dead-ends or upstairs doors opening on the void; attics and rooms and closets and cubicles with no obvious or imaginable purpose... (Brink, 1997, p. 7)

It was a 'place where anything or everything was possible, might happen, did happen' (Brink, 1997, p. 9). But Kristien, the narrator, claims that the basement was her favourite place. It was an exact replication of the ground floor and seemed 'like a subconscious mind, a memory of the house above... a space frequented by the spirits of the dead' (Brink, 1997, p. 8). Consequently, as the novel develops, the reader becomes acquainted with the various uses for the basement and the 'stories' interred there. Kristien's great-grandmother, Rachel, spent lonely hours painting there, locked away from society after she was raped by a servant, and Kristien herself shelters a coloured man, Bonthuys, there from the wrath of her narrow-minded brother-in-law, Casper. The significance of Rachel's paintings in the basement lies in the fact that, despite subsequent layers of paint, they stubbornly refuse to be effaced; they are therefore symptomatic of the irrepressible nature of historical realities, the skeletons in the cupboard of history. Thus the stories told by the grandmothers acquire permanence in the same way as does history; in fact, they become history.

Women, patriarchy, servitude and slavery

All the writers discussed here use caves and cellars to indicate the hidden histories that characterize the houses in their novels. Although Donoso and Ferré place their emphases on different aspects in the composition of their respective novels, both delve into the Pandora's box of appearances and reality of dual lives. Whereas Donoso addresses power relations between master and servant, and parents and children, and criticizes the corrupting influences of wealth and social status on individuals and societies, Ferré bases her investigation on gender relations and social hypocrisy – as does Brink in *The Rights of Desire*.

Donoso's *The House in the Country* illustrates the gradual degeneration and decay of a rich family which, as a result of the greed and cruelty of its members, falls victim to the servants and the underpaid labourers who work in the tunnels of their goldmine. The title of the novel already implies that the house is a type of 'country seat or summer residence' of the Ventura family. Marulanda, their country house, is also the source of their wealth which originates from gold mined on their ground. The house is situated in parkland emulating classical designs with leafy bowers and marble nymphs 'banishing any trace that might compromise it with the indigenous' (Donoso, 1985, p. 34).

Signs of corruption and precarious relationships built on false values are prevalent in the family, which consists of the seven Venturas, their spouses and thirty-three children. The relationships are riddled with spite, hatred, suspicion and petty preoccupations. To crown everything, a spirit of overindulgence and complacency characterizes most of the adults, who regard their children as nuisances to be ignored or as playthings to be summoned at will. Otherwise the children are left to be raised and disposed of at the discretion of the servants. Due to the laxity of the adults, the servants have become all-powerful in the household which literally belongs to them for about 9 months of the year.

Despite the evident signs of insurrection among the servants, mine labourers and their own children, the older Venturas stubbornly and blindly refuse to accept that their easy lifestyle is threatened, and actually undertake a picnic that leaves their children unprotected and unarmed in the care of the vindictive servants who virtually rule the vast house. Consequently, the superficial relationships and power play of the 'house' of Ventura – the 'families' and their servants – threaten to destroy it from within. However, nature also poses a threat from without. We are told that the grass plains are busy invading and swamping the gardens of the house that have been so carefully demarcated from the outside world by a railing fashioned like spears. To compound this threat, one of the children is systematically removing this barrier and thus exposing the Venturas to a possible invasion by cannibals. The house also appears to be built on hollow foundations as it is situated on a number of caves – created by mining endeavours – which provide accommodation to servants and labourers who live under terrible conditions. Just like the servants and slaves, the caves hold various secrets that the family conveniently forgets:

> in the cavernous foul-smelling cellars beneath the house, where the lowliest servants heaped their lives, quarrels and intrigues simmered, vendettas and denunciations, threats to reveal shameful secrets or to call in debts not necessarily in coin . . . . (Donoso, 1985, p. 25)

As a Puerto Rican, Ferré is very much aware of her hybrid status as woman and citizen, because the island is a protectorate of the United States (Hintz, 1997, p. 357). That is one of the reasons why she wrote *The House on the Lagoon* in English. However, she is also aware of the patriarchal shackles that still fetter women in Latin American society. Like Donoso, Ferré makes use of irony to underline the duality of the characters' lives and perceptions of reality. As Hintz (1997, p. 359) remarks, her 'writing style showcases the ironic play on words and the use of the double with its associated "double meaning"'.

The focal point of the novel is the lagoon or the swamp, which harbours many secrets and has been a silent witness (and accomplice) to Buenaventura Mendizabal's rise to fame and fortune. His prosperity is marked by a series of houses erected on the banks of the lagoon while his sexual transgressions with slaves are punctuated by suspect blue-eyed offspring that his daughter-in-law notices in the servants' quarters and later on the island (Ferré, 1996, p. 213). Buenaventura arrives in Puerto Rico without a penny and manages to gain a foothold in the town, initially by selling water from the spring but later on by branching out into more unsavoury occupations such as smuggling and supporting German submarines during the war. His first house is a wooden shack, which is soon discarded for the former keeper-of-the-spring's house. He moves into the keeper's house when the latter is discovered dead, due to 'a mysterious blow to the head' (Ferré, 1996, p. 11). The reader assumes that Mendizabal might have had a hand in this death, but no one seems to care. This action sets the trend for Mendizabal's shady deals which ensure an affluence that is further fortified by his marriage to Rebecca, whose grandfather donates some of his ships to Mendizabal. Symbolically, the spring becomes the central point in the first house on the lagoon which is built to reflect the taste and affluence of the inhabitants: a tribute to Rebecca's artistic tastes and Buenaventura's exaggerated pride. The front entrance was to be 'a magnificent mosaic rainbow... the ceilings were to be twice as high' as those of the famous architect Wright's houses and 'the edge of the gabled roofs would be decorated with a glittering mosaic of olive boughs' (Ferré, 1996, p. 48). In a fit of rage, Mendizabal razes the first house to the ground because he is infuriated by his wife Rebecca's artistic interests and her friendship with the architect Pavel. The first mansion is replaced by 'a Spanish Revival mansion with granite turrets, bare brick floors, and a forbidding granite stairway with a banister made of iron spears' (Ferré, 1996, p. 67). The second house is a complete contrast from the first in that the entrance hall is decorated with a lamp converted from a 'spiked wooden wheel that had been used to torture the Moors during the Spanish Conquest' (Ferré, 1996, p. 67). This second house then reflects Mendizabal's vindictive character when he reverts back to type by treating his womenfolk in the same brutal manner that his forefathers treated their women.

The structure of *The House on the Lagoon* echoes the external and internal structure of the second house(s). It is divided into the upper and nether regions for the servants. In the cellar rooms, Petra the housekeeper, reigns supreme. From the common room for the servants

> A door had been cut into the dirt wall... It led to a dark tunnel into which twenty cells opened. The cells had earthen floors and no windows; they were ventilated by grilles embedded into the top of each end wall... the storage rooms had been turned into servant's quarters. (Ferré, 1996, p. 236)

In the same fashion as Donoso, Ferré continues the imagery of caves and cavernous rooms below the house that, in *The House on the Lagoon*, harbour the pagan and alien Vodoo rites of their servants headed by Petra. The main narrator, Isabel, attempts to write the history of her husband's family, but her accounts and Quintín's accounts of the Mendizabal family saga are juxtaposed (Hintz, 1997, p. 362). The main irony lies in the confusion between fact and fiction. Quintín's insistence on historical accuracy does not alter or affect the message of Isabel's fictional version, because he fails to realize that she has created an alternative version, a re-written history of the Mendizabals (Hintz, 1997, p. 362), in recognition of other voices. Ironically, Quintín's reaction and his attempt to take control of Isabel's story, is reminiscent of the control his father used to exert over his mother, a chauvinist habit that Isabel strongly resents.

In *The Rights of Desire*, Brink attempts a retrospective assessment of his own personal role as a male aggressor in gender issues through the role of his narrator and protagonist, Ruben, who seems to serve as his double. Ruben lives alone in an austere old house in Cape Town which is purported to be haunted:

> The house is haunted. Which is why it was so cheap, long ago – almost forty years ago; thirty-eight years and four months ago – when we first bought it. Ghosts were not yet fashionable. Two fixtures came with the house. The ghost of Antje of Bengal. And the housekeeper, Magrieta Daniels. (Brink, 2000, p. 1)

Antje of Bengal was a slave and 'the poor victim of her violent lover and master in the early Dutch days of the Cape' (Brink, 2000, p. 1). Apart from Antje's spirit that is supposed to haunt the house, Magrieta, his house-keeper, is Ruben's only form of companionship. However, memories of the more recent past, such as that of his broken marriage to Riana, haunt Ruben who refers to it as 'the intricate treachery of memory' that keeps him awake at night (Brink, 2000, p. 1).

When Ruben unwillingly takes in a boarder, Tessa, he is attracted to her but she resists his sexual advances and remains adamant that she prefers his friendship. After a few futile attempts, he accepts her decision and finally realizes that 'his right to desire' also invokes 'the right of the other to refuse' him (Brink, 2000, p. 154). He reviews his previous relationships with women and realizes that he has always treated women either as sexual or work objects – an attitude no different from the treatment of slaves, and in particular, women slaves, who had to accede to their masters' 'droit de seigneur' behaviour towards them. This causes the reader and Ruben to draw an uncomfortable correlation between the contemporary women in his life and the lives of slaves in the past. Consequently, he realizes that he shares a history with the maid Magrieta: 'private and public, hers and mine, Riana's, our children's, the country's' (Brink, 2000, p. 285), and by implication, with the unfortunate Antje of Bengal who haunts his house. He finally grasps the implication of his responsibility in the reconstruction of history, when he realizes that his attitude towards Magrieta and Tessa represents his attitude towards all women, as either objects of labour or desire. He recognizes Magrieta as 'the vital if unlikely representative of Antje of Bengal in the flesh, the keeper of my fate' (Brink, 2000, p. 285).

Ruben's insight also allows him to see Antje's ghost for the first time whereas previously he had to rely on Magrieta and Tessa's testimonies about its 'existence'. When he searches for a lost ring under the floor-boards of his study, he finally also discovers and disinters her skeleton. His new insight lends him the patience and sensitivity to painstakingly restore and re-member the scattered remains of Antje of Bengal's skeleton:

> I left her, for the moment, just as I'd found her. Except for restoring, very carefully and gently, as best I could, the small bones of the severed hand, and returning the skull to the top of the vertebrae of the neck, where it belonged. (Brink, 2000, p. 281)

Conclusion

All the characters and families in the novels discussed here harbour dark secrets from the past in their bosoms. This 'otherness' of memories is part of their make-up and emerges despite efforts to repress it. The protagonists live double lives, trying to reconcile their past with their present. Within this context, the role of women and slaves is foregrounded and emphasized. Thus both the South African and Latin American novels display a preoccupation with history, with the recovery of personal and social histories and stories from the past. It is this recovery and re-vision that González Echevarría (1990, p. 14) perceives as a characteristic of the contemporary novel to transform 'history into an originary myth in order to see itself as other'.

It is the novel's intervention in history, its focus on personal history intertwined with 'national' history that defines culture. As Couldry (2000, p. 45) correctly points out, 'to study culture on the scale of wider cultural formations' (such as historical documentation), without including individual experience, would be to deny 'crucial insights into what culture is'. In fact, personal memories and stories counteract fixed perceptions of historical documentation, thereby creating a space for new versions of past realities that qualify as hybrid perceptions of identity. This comparison does not imply that differences do not exist between the regions or countries discussed, nor is it an attempt to essentialize or universalize. Rather it indicates that these texts share similar patterns of human experience.

Notes

1. Ashcroft *et al.* (1998, pp. 68–69) define diaspora as 'the voluntary or forcible movement of peoples from their homelands into new regions'.
2. For instance, the Poetics and Linguistics Association (PALA) conference on 'boundaries' in Istanbul, 2003 and the European Association of Commonwealth Literature and Language Studies (EACLALS) conference on 'sharing places' in Malta, 2005.
3. This edition was compiled from the proceedings of Vorträge und Aufzätze (Pfullingen: Neske, 1954).
4. Although the term 'postcolonial' has elicited controversial reactions and various definitions (Appiah, 1991; Bahri, 1995; Michel, 1995) I shall use the term here to designate the fiction, in particular novels, emanating from various countries previously subjected to hegemonic practices. Such novels all share counter-discursive strategies.
5. First presented as a lecture entitled 'Man and Space' in a colloquium that he delivered on 5 August 1951 in Darmstadt, the essay on space was then printed in the Proceedings of the colloquium (1952) and subsequently published

as 'Bauen Wohnen Denken' in Vorträge und Aufzätze (Pfullingen: Neske, 1954). The references were taken from the collection cited above, which was published in 1975 (p. xxiv).

Works cited

Allende, I., *The House of the Spirits*. Translated from the Spanish by Magda Bogin (London: Black Swan, 1990).

Appiah, K. A., 'Is the Post- in Postmodernism the Post- in Postcolonial?' *Critical Inquiry*, 17: 2 (1991) 336–357.

Ashcroft, B., Griffiths, G. and Tiffin, H. (eds), *Key Concepts in Post-Colonial Studies* (London: Routledge, 1998).

Bachelard, G., *The Poetics of Space*. Translated from the French by Maria Jolas (Boston: Beacon Press, 1969).

Bahri, D., 'Once More with Feeling: What is Postcolonialism?' *Ariel: A Review of International English Literature*, 26: 1 (1995) 51–82.

Brink, A., *Imaginings of Sand* (London: Minerva, 1997).

Brink, A., *The Rights of Desire* (London: Secker and Warburg, 2000).

Brydon, D., 'Contracts with the World: Redefining Home, Identity and Community in Aidoo, Brodber, Garner and Rule,' in *The Commonwealth Novel Since 1960*. Ed. B. King (London: Macmillan, 1991), pp. 198–215.

Carter, E., Donald, J. and Squires, J. (eds), 'Introduction,' in *Space and Place: Theories of Identity and Location* (London: Lawrence and Wishart, 1993), pp. vii–xv.

Couldry, N., *Inside Culture: Re-Imagining the Method of Cultural Studies* (London: SAGE, 2000).

Crang, M., *Cultural Geography* (London: Routledge, 1998).

Davis, L. J., *Resisting Novels: Ideology and Fiction* (New York: Methuen, 1987).

DeToro, F., 'From Where to Speak? Latin American Postmodern/Postcolonial Positionalities', *World Literature Today*, 69: 1 (1995) 35–40.

Donoso, J., *A House in the Country* (Harmondsworth: Penguin, 1985).

Douglas, M., 'The Idea of a Home: A Kind of Space', *Social Research*, 58: 1 (1991) 287–307.

Ferré, R., *The House on the Lagoon* (New York: Plume, 1996).

González Echevarría, R., *Myth and Archive: A Theory of Latin American Narrative* (Cambridge: Cambridge University Press, 1990).

Heidegger, M., *Poetry, Language and Thought*. Translated by Albert Hofstadter (New York: Harper Colophon Books, 1975).

Hintz, S., 'Freedom to be Heard, Freedom to be Chosen: Rosario Ferré and the Postmodern Canon', *Monographic Review/Revista Monográfica*, 13 (1997) 355–363.

Hummon, D., 'House, Home, and Identity in Contemporary American Culture', in *Housing, Culture, and Design: A Comparative Perspective*. Ed. S. M. Low and E. Chambers (Philadelphia: University of Pennsylvania Press, 1989), pp. 207–228.

James, H., 'The House of Fiction', in *The Theory of the Novel*. Ed. P. Stevick (London: Collier-Macmillan, 1968), pp. 58–65.

Lawrence, R. J., 'Translating Anthropological Concepts into Architectural Practice', in *Housing, Culture, and Design: A Comparative Perspective*. Ed. S. M. Low and E. Chambers (Philadelphia: University of Pennsylvania Press, 1989), pp. 89–106.

Mda, Z., *Ways of Dying* (Cape Town: Oxford University Press, 1995).

Michel, M., 'Positioning the Subject: Locating Postcolonial Studies', *Ariel: A Review of International English Literature*, 26: 1 (1995), 83–99.

Morley, D. and Robins, K., 'No Place like *Heimat*: Images of Home (Land) in European Culture', in *Space and Place: Theories of Identity and Location*. Ed. E. Carter, J. Donald and J. Squires (London: Lawrence and Wishart, 1993), pp. 3–31.

Rapoport, A., 'Foreword', In *Housing, Culture, and Design: A Comparative Perspective*. Ed. S. M. Low and E. Chambers (Philadelphia: University of Pennsylvania Press, 1989), pp. xi–xxi.

Schick, I. C., *The Erotic Margin: Sexuality and Spatiality in Alteritist Discourse* (London: Verso, 1999).

Stea, D., 'House and Home: Identity, Dichotomy, or Dialectic? (With Special Reference to Mexico)', in *The Home: Words, Interpretations, Meanings and Environments*. Ed. D. N. Benjamin and D. Stea (Brookfield, Vt.: Avebury, 1995), pp. 181–201.

10
Transformation of Ordinary Places into Imaginative Space in Zakes Mda's Writing

Ina Gräbe

Introduction

This chapter investigates Zakes Mda's versatile use of space in depicting rural and urban localities. These reflect either the hardship of social inequality or the turmoil brought about by political intolerance in contemporary South African society, in the period from the 1990s to the present. I will scrutinize Mda's uncanny ability to transform places reflecting a seemingly bleak existence into an imaginary space of artistic creativity. In the three novels to be discussed, this refiguring of otherwise ordinary or dreary places is achieved in different ways: *Ways of Dying* (1995) creatively transforms deadly places into liveable places; *The Heart of Redness* (2000) uncovers the magic inherent in rural localities, while *The Madonna of Excelsior* (2002) effects an artist's reading of the landscape through its paintings of specific scenes.

Now widely acknowledged as one of South Africa's leading novelists, Zakes Mda, born in 1948, originally became known as a published playwright in the mid-1970s. He was then living as an exile in Lesotho, an independent state on the eastern border of South Africa, so it is hardly surprising that he deliberately focused on exposing the inequalities of the apartheid regime in his plays, thereby intentionally subjecting his writing to a political goal. As Bell and Jacobs note, it was inevitable that the struggle for freedom and democracy would predominate in his earlier writing before the change of government in South Africa. His writing before 1994 was conditioned by 'the binarism of the apartheid/antiapartheid discourse' and by major political events such as the unbanning of Nelson Mandela in 1990 and the first democratic election held in the country in 1994 which 'fundamentally altered this meta-discourse'(Bell and Jacobs, forthcoming).[1] Whereas the plays were overtly political in scope and intent, sensitizing a wider audience to the inequalities of an unjust regime and simultaneously urging South Africans to become part of the struggle against apartheid, the novels by contrast deal with issues of a seemingly less urgent and more mundane character, depicting the lives of 'ordinary' people in their engagement with everyday issues. This would seem to echo the prominent writer and critic, Njabulo Ndebele, who in 1991 appealed to writers to turn their attention to those issues which had been neglected during the latter decades of the apartheid regime. He urged them instead to start writing about issues dealing with the everyday existence of 'ordinary' people. While this holds true, to some extent, for the Mda novels which have been appearing regularly since 1995,[2] they still deal with political or politicized issues. More importantly, they show how 'ordinary' people, in coming to terms with life under the new postapartheid era, counter adversity by transforming 'ordinary' places into special and sought-after sites.

Turning to Mda's exploration of space, it is worth noting that he focuses mainly, though not exclusively, on black experience in his depiction of current South African conditions and the varied responses of different communities to the changing environment. The contextualization of current realities in terms of historical events, social circumstances or political ideology provides one with a sophisticated, if often ironic, reading of the different responses to specific environments that may be encountered within the broader South African community. This means that the main stories, in the present of the novels, are put into perspective by providing a broader sociopolitical context. This depends either on a rewriting of remote history (of the period before and during colonization in *The Heart of Redness*) or on a new perspective of the more recent past (the white government in general and the apartheid regime in particular in both *Ways of Dying* and *The Madonna of Excelsior*).

Although Mda is no longer committed, as he was in his earlier writing, to advocating the specific cause of protest against the unjust policies of the apartheid regime, he remains critical of undesirable policies and conditions under a new political dispensation. To address such issues, he switched to 'storywriting' as a preferred writing strategy, claiming that '...my main mission is to tell a story, rather than to propagate a political message'.[3] Such storytelling incorporates facts. This factual basis makes Mda's explicit or implied criticism more credible as he addresses the inadequacies of the new political leadership to confront the problems which ordinary South Africans have to contend with on a daily basis. For example, the stories recontextualized in *Ways of Dying* were lifted from reports on violent deaths in the townships which appeared in a South African newspaper, while the character Camagu in *The Heart of Redness* reflects Mda's own experience of failing to secure viable employment in the 'new' South Africa on his return to the country after a prolonged period of voluntary exile. Finally, the events disclosed in *The Madonna of Excelsior* originate from Mda's scrutiny of court records of an actual instance of miscegenation brought against eminent members of the white community of a provincial town during the heyday of the apartheid regime.

In view of the fact that the 'present' of his stories reflects South Africa in a transitional phase and under a new political dispensation, Mda may perhaps best be viewed as a postapartheid novelist.[4] While the stories of how and why men, women and children were being killed in *Ways of Dying* can be compared with the testimonies of the victims of violence presented at the hearings of South Africa's *Truth and Reconciliation Commission* chaired by Archbishop Desmond Tutu at the time,[5] the reader of *The Heart of Redness* and *The Madonna of Excelsior* similarly becomes familiarized with life as experienced under the new political dispensation. What makes Mda's portrayal of rural and urban localities remarkable is the fact that space becomes a significant indicator of meaning in that it is intricately interwoven with both the depiction of characters and the exploration of social and political realities in his writing.

I

The title of his first novel, *Ways of Dying* (1995), sets the social and political scene during the turbulent years of political transition on the eve of the first democratic elections ever held in South Africa on 27 April 1994. The constant presence of death in the violence-infested space of black townships and squatter camps provides a factual backdrop to the social and political upheaval prevalent during this period of change and insecurity in the country.

Following Anita Desai's observations on the importance of 'spirit of place or "feng sui"' (cf. Olinder, 1984, p. 101) in her writing, one may define Mda's exploration of space in his novels as a sustained attempt to penetrate to the deeper meaning of place. In the process the reader progresses from mere looking at a landscape to looking at it with real understanding and vision:

A writer who wishes to capture the spirit of place requires not the power of observation so much as a burning intensity of vision. If his vision has such intensity, his gaze will become powerful as the magnifying glass that is held between the sun and a sheet of paper, compressing and generating enough heat to burn a ring through the paper. (Desai in Olinder, 1984, p. 109)

Given the grim elaboration of different 'ways of dying' in the above-mentioned essays on Zakes Mda (Bell and Jacobs, forthcoming), one would expect the immediate environment to have captured the spirit, if not the presence, of death in the places defined by violence and death. Mda certainly captures the spirit of the various localities referred to in the course of the novel by deliberately exploring their deadly characteristics on the one hand, and by showing, on the other, how artistic creativity may be used as a strategy of intervention in transforming such places into (imaginative) space. This means that despite the fact that the ingrained violence of the politicized urban space depicted in the novel constitutes the very fabric of his tale, Mda surprisingly advocates the need for acquiring an aptitude for living, or, more precisely, loving. This is demonstrated, for example, by the protagonists' capacity to find happiness in the reconstruction of Noria's new shack.

Throughout the text, *stories* of killings (violent or otherwise) and, indeed, *actual* killings inform the numerous accounts of Toloki visiting sites of violence and death. In fact, so common is death during these terrible and terrifying times that it ironically provides a means of survival for some characters. The main protagonist, Toloki,[6] devises for himself the role of 'Professional Mourner' and thus becomes dependent on funerals for his livelihood. In his exploitation of death Toloki pursues his 'vocation' with dignity, passion and sincerity, showing empathy with the bereaved family, while sitting on the mound that will later be used to fill the grave and producing the studied moaning sounds he deems fit for the occasion. As far as his use of space is concerned, Toloki divides his time between a corner of a room at the dockyard and a mound at some graveside or other where he is constantly and directly confronted with the reality of death – in other words, he is living, so to speak, 'in the presence of death'. However, despite the fact that he seems to be trapped in places literally 'smelling' of wretched poverty, or, worse, reeking of death, Mda enables his protagonist, Toloki, to transform such places into liveable and even enviable space.

By exploiting the device of the Nurse's role at funerals, Mda is able to introduce the reader in the course of the novel to different forms of violent death caused by various means and suffered at the hands of different parties for any number of reasons.

As an example of the community's familiarity with places associated with illness, violence and death, such as hospitals, morgues and grave-yards in the main city,[7] Mda lets the sister of a man who went missing and who died a 'mysterious death' (Mda, 1995, p. 12) preside as the Nurse at her brother's funeral. Thus, in using the device of the Nurse's role at funerals, Mda is able to assume responsibility by 'hiding' in the omniscient communal role of the plural narrative voice, thereby getting access to all deadly locations explored in the novels. So, for example, the chilling inhospitality and hostility of the mortuary as a space assigned to the dead is forcibly underscored by the account of how the Nurse was first led to a corridor with naked corpses lying on the floor, then to a room with naked bodies more recently killed and eventually to a very cold room where the bodies of unidentified people were stored at freezing temperatures.

However, it is important to note that deadly environments, sadly, are not restricted to places usually associated with illness (hospitals), death (morgues) or violence (hostels). This becomes evident, for example, when at the funeral of a five-year-old the Nurse laments a little girl's presumed killing by a random police bullet while she was innocently playing with mudpies in the yard of a township house.

The combined strategies of *telling* (the Nurse's account of the circum-stances of any particular death) and *acting* (Toloki's turning of mourning into spectacle as complementary accompaniment to the Nurse's role) distinguish Mda's fictional representation of death from the kind of stat-istics to be found in police records or daily newspapers or television news. However, there is one particular death so horrific as almost to defy description. This is indicated by the opening words of the novel, ascribed to the Nurse at the funeral of Vutha the Second, Noria's five-year old little boy named after his deceased elder brother, Vutha ('to burn'):

It is not the first time that we bury little children. We bury them every day. But they are killed by the enemy those we are fighting against. This our little brother was killed by those who are fighting to free us! (Mda, 1995, p. 3)

The novel opens with this funeral, strangely conducted on Christmas day, that marks the occasion of Toloki's rediscovery of his childhood friend, Noria, from his 'home town'. Although the reader is prepared by the words of the Nurse to expect that something unusually disturbing must have happened, it is only towards the end of the novel that the true horror is finally revealed of how Vutha the Second was killed by his own playmates at the instigation of the 'Young Tigers', a militant youth faction within the community. The deadly environment of 'home' is foregrounded in the vivid description of Vutha's execution by means of the notorious 'necklace' method because he and his friend were summarily judged to be 'sell-outs' after they had been abducted by inmates of the hostel and bribed with sweets to disclose certain information about a planned ambush. It strikes the reader as all the more horrific because the 'Young Tigers' turned the killings into a public display by calling all the children together and by instructing them to watch and see what would happen to any 'sell-out'. Then, the execution culminated in the final cruelty when they gave Danisa, Vutha's six-year old playmate, and another child burning matches to ignite the petrol in the tyres they had already put around the doomed boys' necks. The two boys tried in vain to run, but were soon pulled down by the weight of the burning tyres, so that the air was filled '[w]ith the stench of burning flesh' (Mda, 1995, p. 177). Mda forcibly drives home the point that death permeated both the ground and air space of 'home', thereby demonstrating how what should have been a place of comfort and safety could be changed into a deadly site with chilling suddenness and finality.

Given such grim events in an environment marked by any number of lethally dangerous places, it is not surprising that to Toloki 'ways of dying' should have become indistinguishable from and interchangeable with 'ways of living' (Mda 1995, p. 89).

Among the numerous locations defined by poverty, violence and death, the dwelling places of the main characters, Toloki and Noria, are singled out for attention. The manner in which Toloki, with Noria's help, is able to transcend adverse conditions by beautifying, for example, the desolate site of Noria's burnt-down shack is truly remarkable given the grim statistics of death itemized in the course of the text. Mda uses two main strategies for enabling Toloki to overcome seemingly inescapable adversities: the first concerns his ability to 'imagine' different places while actually remaining rooted to the same location; the second, shared by Noria, involves his creativity and resourcefulness in transforming artistically an otherwise dreary place into something beautiful resembling, in Toloki's opinion, a work of art.

Before his reunion with Noria, Toloki's fluctuation between the waiting room at the dockyard and various graveyards reflects the extent to which death had become a daily companion to him. By depicting Toloki's turning of a corner of the waiting room into his 'headquarters',

Mda creates an awareness of the different *purposes* to which public space may be put. To the privileged (whether white or black) using the beach and its facilities for recreational purposes, the public showers would be a mere convenience for getting rid of irritating sand before going home; for the likes of Toloki, however, an open shower on the beach presents the *only* affordable means of washing oneself.

However, more important than having access to the most basic of necessities is Toloki's ability to transpose himself to an imagined space. This is illustrated when, through the pages of a pamphlet obtained from 'a pink-robed devotee' (Mda, 1995, p. 19) who had disembarked from a boat two years previously, Toloki is able to conjure up a remote mountain site where he imagines himself belonging to some eastern fraternity of monks. To this end, he even devises meals consisting of Swiss cake and green onions because, in his opinion, it gives him 'an aura of austerity' (Mda, 1995, p. 10).[8]

By further exploiting his imaginative capabilities, Toloki is able to enact his role as professional mourner once he has donned his revered costume for the occasion. Such is his dedication to the business of mourning that he progresses to the point of preferring the fulfilment of a day at a graveside to the utter boredom of mending clothes in the corner of the waiting room at the quayside. In focusing on Toloki's clown-like, dressed-up appearance Mda shows how art, in this instance, theatre and the theatrical, may be used to make the impossible circumstances of violence and squalor bearable. Because an odour of uncleanliness and death clings to his person, Toloki can be recognized (literally smelt) by the people he encounters when walking, riding in a taxi or performing the self-devised rituals of mourning at a graveside. Toloki therefore becomes identifiable in terms of both the space he has made his own (the dockyard and the graveside) and the profession he has chosen. Even Noria asks him nicely to take a shower before visiting her again; when saying good-bye to him at the taxi-rank she remarks: 'Just because your profession involves Death, it doesn't mean that you need to smell like a dead rat' (Mda, 1995, p. 90).

In the squatter camp where a costumed Toloki walks '[a]mong the shacks of cardboard, plastic, pieces of canvas and corrugated iron' (Mda, 1995, p. 42) the cruel heckling of the motley collection of children pursuing him amongst the squalor is indicative of the intertwinement of place and character:

The fact that he has become some kind of spectacle does not bother him. It is his venerable costume, he knows, and he is rather proud. Dirty children follow him. They dance in their tattered clothes and spontaneously compose a song about him, which they sing with derisive gusto. Mangy mongrels follow him, run alongside, sniff at him, and lead the way, while barking all the time. He ignores them all, and walks through a quagmire of dirty water and human ordure that runs through the streets of this informal settlement, as the place is politely called, looking for Noria. (Mda, 1995, p. 42)

The eventual description of how Toloki and Noria go about rebuilding her shack provides Mda with the opportunity of revealing how shacks, made from any type of waste material, define the lives of hopefuls who had flocked to the city in futile attempts to escape the abject poverty of a bleak existence in the rural areas where they had been born and (partially) educated. Toloki's resourcefulness is the driving force which results in the rebuilding of Noria's burnt-down shack at the same stand as the original – a place which notably bears the mark of violent destruction. The rebuilding of the shack from waste material would not in itself have been remarkable, as squatter communities had become notoriously adept at rebuilding bull-dozed shacks during the apartheid regime. However, the joint efforts of Toloki and Noria to transform a place marked by violence and destruction into something beautiful resembling a work of art distinguish their creation from the efforts of squatters in general.[9] After they had decorated the walls with pictures of luxurious interiors taken from the *Home and Garden* magazines so that 'every inch of the walls is covered with bright pictures – a wallpaper of sheer luxury' (Mda, 1995, p. 103), Noria shares in Toloki's ability to escape into some imagined space. In a game of make-believe, Toloki and Noria walk from the bedroom to the kitchen to the lounge, eventually even going for a stroll in the garden. Mda elaborately describes the imagined beauty and luxury of the interior and exterior of the shack, thereby demonstrating clearly how a scene of devastating destruction can be transformed into a truly desirable space.

It should be clear that by foregrounding the transformation of Noria's humble shack into an almost magical place of beauty in this unusual love story, rooted as it is in a shared knowledge of hardship, death and destruction, Mda is able to demonstrate how a formerly deadly place may be turned into something radiating beauty and happiness. When, at the end of their story, the figurines Toloki's father used to create while listening to a much younger Noria singing to him are delivered at the shack, the magic of the place becomes visible even to the onlookers, who imagine 'seeing' the figurines through the boxes, 'shimmering like fool's gold' and clearly affecting the appearance of the shack:

Somehow the shack seems to glow in the light of the moon, as if the plastic colours are fluorescent. Crickets and other insects of the night are attracted by the glow. They contribute their chirps to the general din of the settlement. (Mda, 1995, p. 199)

The positive note marking the end of the novel is all the more remarkable if considered in the context of the pervasiveness of death throughout the entire text; however, it borders on the miraculous if the chilling circumstances of a five-year old boy's execution by his own playmates are taken into account. Without shunning the stark reality of death present everywhere, this artistic recreation of the environment indubitably results in the creative transformation of places of death into liveable and even enviable space.[10]

In his latest novel, *Cion* (2007), which is situated in America rather than the South African locations of his other novels, it becomes apparent that the various 'ways of dying' focused upon in the course of the text essentially define the urban locations singled out for meaningful transformation. When the reader encounters Toloki amongst the quilt makers of Kilvert, a small town in the United States of America, there is a reference to Toloki's mourning practice in South Africa which had reportedly become boringly predictable, so that he had decided to come to America in search of new ways of mourning, because of the *sameness* of death (everybody was dying of illness) and the *fake* explanations given at funerals by the Nurse (AIDS is never acknowledged as the cause of death). Here Mda is critical of conditions in South Africa 13 years after the institution of democratic rule, in a passage worth quoting at some length:

Death continued every day, for death will never let you down. But the thrill of mourning was taken away by the sameness of the deaths I had to mourn on a daily basis. Death was plentiful – certainly more than before – but it lacked the drama of the violent deaths that I used to mourn during the upheavals of the political transition in that country. Now the bulk of the deaths were boringly similar. They were deaths of lies. We heard there was the feared AIDS pandemic stalking the homesteads. Yet no one died of it. Or of anything related to it. Instead young men and women in their prime died of diseases that never used to kill anyone before – diseases such as TB and pneumonia that used to be cured with ease not so long ago. At the funerals I mourned the dreaded four letters were never mentioned, only TB and pneumonia and diarrhea. People died of silence. Of shame. Of denial.

And this conspiracy resulted in a stigma that stuck like pubic lice on both the living and the dead. (Mda, 1995, p. 3)

II

While the rural settings provide the context for the description and transformation of urban places in *Ways of Dying*, the focus in *The Heart of Redness* is on the yearning for a fulfilling rural way of life, true to the traditions and customs of the Xhosa people, as opposed to the emptiness and dissatisfaction characterizing life in a metropolis such as Johannesburg or New York. The main story deals with Camagu, an educated man who returns to South Africa to vote in the 1994 elections after working in the United States of America for 30 years. Unable to find suitable work and thoroughly disillusioned with the new government, he is on the point of returning to America when he is enthralled by the beautiful singing of a young woman at the wake of an unknown man:

Her voice remains hauntingly fresh. It is a freshness that cries to be echoed by the green hills, towering cliffs and deep gullies of a folktale dreamland, instead of being wasted on a dead man in a tattered tent on top of a twenty-storey building in Hillbrow, Johannesburg. (Mda, 2000, p. 27)

The artistic performance as part of a wake differs as an expression of mourning from Toloki's impressive array of sounds encountered in *Ways of Dying* in that the emphasis is on alluring singing rather than on dramatic spectacle. So strong is the contrast between a dismal urban location on the one hand and the envisioned idyllic landscape, induced by the singing, on the other, that Camagu, instead of returning to the USA, follows the young woman to a small Eastern Cape village; and it is here, in Qolorha-by-Sea, that the former political exile, Camagu, is re-introduced to the culture of the Xhosa people, metaphorically defined as 'redness' in the novel. In the course of his chief protagonist's initiation, Mda explores at length the relevance of identification with a particular place for the rediscovery of a lost identity. Towards the end of the novel Camagu reflects 'on what this place has done for him. It has rendered him unrecognizable to himself' (Mda, 2000, p. 263).

The focus is directed towards a picturesque setting being exploited as a tourist attraction because of the proximity of Nongqawuse's Valley, made famous (or infamous, depending on the point of view) by the ancient prophecy which commanded the Xhosa people to slaughter their livestock and to destroy their crops, while waiting for the dead ancestors to rise and deliver them from their enemies. The Xhosa people obediently responded to the dictates of the prophecy and their actions caused widespread starvation which inevitably resulted in what may be termed the 'mass suicide' of the Xhosa people in the nineteenth century.

As these historical events resonate in the present of the novel, Mda continuously switches from present to past and vice versa in an interesting interaction with and rewriting of this major event in the history of the amaXhosa. In the process of dealing with ancient history, Mda refocalizes the events through 'post-colonial', more precisely 'post-apartheid', rather than 'colonial eyes'.[11]

Camagu's initiation in the traditions of the amaXhosa involves both an appreciation of the inherent beauty of the landscape and an understanding and acceptance of the intrinsic 'magic' of the historically significant site and its continued spiritual significance in 'modern' times for an 'educated' person such as himself. His expectation of a picturesque landscape is made graphic when, on arrival, he perceives the village of Qolorha-by-Sea as a colourful canvas, where the blue of the skies and the distant hills and the green of the meadows, valleys and tall grass result in '[s]plashes of lush colour' (Mda, 2000, p. 61). At a later stage, while taking a walk along the beach, he is dazzled by the colours of the rocks, '[t]he yellows, the browns, the greens and the reds that have turned the rocks into works of abstract art' (Mda, 2000, pp. 118–119). As opposed to *Ways of Dying*, then, where 'beauty' has to be created artificially in order to transform otherwise dreary urban localities, the ingrained beauty of the small village of Qolorha-by-sea ensures its status as 'painting'.

This natural beauty contrasts with the potential exploitation of the place as a tourist attraction requiring major development and the inevitable destruction of the landscape. In this regard Camagu's transition from modern educated man to supporter of the culture of 'redness' is brought about by his preference for Qukezwa, the uneducated daughter of Zim, rather than Xoliswa, the schoolmistress daughter of Bhonco. The novel seems to imply that by choosing 'redness' over 'development' Camagu has succeeded in detecting the potentially destructive elements inherent in self-enrichment schemes under the guise of so-called black empowerment. He opts, instead, for a collective enterprise from which the whole community can benefit.

Nongqawuse's valley is not only a real site with seemingly unlimited tourist potential in the present of the novel, but also a magical place where some of the present-day characters claim to be in touch with the prophecies of Nongqawuse and, through communication with their ancestors, with the events that took place 150 years ago. This is notably illustrated in the scene where Camagu experiences the magic of the site when joining Qukezwa in a moonlight bareback ride on Gxagxa, the much beloved horse belonging to her father. It is on this occasion that Qukezwa displays, in addition to her skill of talking with her father in bird-like whistles, her talent for singing in split tones. Through this singing she illustrates her ability to communicate with beasts and landscape by transcending human language:

> She bursts into a song and plays her umrhubhe musical instrument. She whistles and sings all at the same time. Many voices come from her mouth. Deep sounds that echo like the night. Sounds that have the heaviness of a steamy summer night. Flaming sounds that crackle like a veld fire. Light sounds that float like flakes of snow on top of the Amathole Mountains. Hollow sounds like laughing mountains. Coming out all at once. As if a whole choir lives in her mouth. (Mda, 2000, p. 175)

The intertwinement of art (singing, painting) and landscape is found throughout the text whenever Camagu 'sees' Qolorha-by-Sea through the eyes of the likes of Zim and his daughter Qukezwa, who wish to preserve their heritage as particularly embodied in the valley and pool of Nongqawuse. That Camagu eventually learns to appreciate the 'magic' inherent in a particular location of historical and spiritual relevance to the amaXhosa underscores Mda's belief in the professed mystery inseparable from and induced by the African landscape:

> Here in Africa there is magic happening all the time. There are many belief systems and in fact a lot of the things that the Western world refers to as superstition. For me such things actually happen and I portray them as such in my writings. (Naidoo, 1997, p. 250)

Camagu's transition from an educated Westernized man to an individual belonging to tradition involves an initiation into the 'wonders' of Qolorha-by-Sea; he becomes familiar with ways of communication which transcend human language. In this formerly exiled protagonist, who paradoxically holds a doctorate in communication, the transition becomes complete once he comes to understand and accept an aspect of African culture which celebrates the African landscape by means of songs and the ability to 'communicate' with animals.[12]

III

In *The Madonna of Excelsior* Mda continues the strategy of providing an alternative account of hitherto authorized versions of events shaping the history of South Africa's people. Rather than the rewriting and recontextualizing of the remote history of the Nongqawuse prophecy and its disastrous consequences for the amaXhosa during the nineteenth century which *The Heart of Redness* relates, Mda in *The Madonna of Excelsior* focuses on a more 'local' and fairly recent event. It invokes a case against some farmers from Excelsior, a small town in the Orange Free State, who are accused of transgressing the Immorality Act of 1971. Using the narrative strategy of 'localizing' history by focusing on a specific place, a seemingly insignificant small town, Mda eventually achieves a wider perspective. He not only tells the story of the town's current and former inhabitants, but also offers an informed reading of the manner in which different races sharing the same geographical space have left their imprint on the South African landscape.

While the relevance of art for the representation of space is apparent in both *Ways of Dying* (Noria's rebuilt shack is compared to 'a work of art') and *The Heart of Redness* (the scenery is described in terms of a canvas and compared to abstract art), it is centrally in *The Madonna of Excelsior* that art is explicitly invoked throughout the text as a means of telescoping the landscape. Mda starts every chapter with a small reproduction of a different painting of the Free State landscape by the famous painter Father Frans Claerhout, and then re-inscribes this painting in his story. He thus indicates that the reader has to comprehend not only a verbal representation of the landscape, but also a verbal translation of an existent visual representation of the landscape and its people. The notion of ekphrasis, in the sense of 'the verbal representation of visual representation', or the 'narrativization of a work of visual art' as defined by Carmen Concilio in her study entitled 'Reading history through the landscape' (Concilio, 1998, p. 119) becomes pertinent in a consideration of Mda's deliberate framing of the narrative by the Claerhout paintings. Johan Jacobs accurately diagnoses this narrative strategy as follows:

> The iconic narrative world is translated into a verbal one, and the verbal one re-translated again into an iconic one, as Mda creates an African literary expressionism, which he combines in this novel with documentary realism to produce his most remarkably hybridised text to date. (in Bell and Jacobs, forthcoming)

Mda organizes a causal reference to time, followed by a relatively 'neutral' description of the landscape, followed by a description of a Claerhout painting of the same landscape in the opening paragraphs of the text. This ordering suggests the manner in which a particular location will serve both as 'objective', descriptive background to, and as determining factor of, the destiny of people inhabiting the particular stretch of Free State 'platteland'. Let us consider, here, the introductory paragraphs of the text:

> All these things flow from the sins of our mothers. The land that lies flat on its back for kilometre after relentless kilometre. The black roads that run across it in different directions, slicing through one-street platteland towns. The cosmos flowers that form a guard of honour for the lone motorist. White, pink and purple petals. The sunflower fields that stretch as far as the eye can see. The land that is awash with yellowness. And the brownness of the qokwa grass.
>
> Colour explodes. Green, yellow, red and blue. Sleepy-eyed women are walking among sunflowers. Naked women are chasing white doves among sunflowers. True atonement of rhythm and line. A boy is riding a donkey backwards among sunflowers. The ground is red. The sky is blue. The boy is red. The faces of the women are blue. Women are harvesting wheat. Or they are cutting the qokwa grass that grows near the fields along the road, and is used for thatching houses. Big-breasted figures tower over the reapers, their ghostly faces showing only displeasure. People without feet and toes – all of them.
>
> These things leap at us in broad strokes. Just as they leapt at Popi twenty-five years ago. (Mda, 2002, p. 1)

The first sentence seems to both predict and interpret the major event of the text – a punishable and 'sinful' sexual relationship between (a number of) white men and black women and girls. According to the official account, the notorious 1971 case focused on the scandal involving nineteen white citizens of Excelsior who had been charged with transgressing apartheid's Immorality Act, which prohibited sex between black and white. By contrast, the fictional corrective draws attention to the injustice suffered by powerless black women and young girls subjected to the indignity of selling their bodies or forced to succumb in silence to abusive relationships.

The second sentence of the first paragraph sets the tone for Mda's strategy of representing his historical corrective in terms of a representation of the particular landscape in which a number of small towns on the Free State platteland are situated. The proximity of 'mother' and 'land' in the first two sentences of the text suggests an underlying comparison whereby the land is not only personified but used to suggest abuse of the 'mothers' in the implied comparison 'the mothers are like the land that lies flat on its back for kilometre after relentless kilometre'. Still, the overall meaning is positive, since the cosmos flowers 'form a guard of honour for the lone motorist' in a painting celebrating an abundance of colour: 'The sunflower fields that stretch as far as the eye can see. The land that is awash with yellowness. And the brownness of the qokwa grass' (Mda, 2002, p. 1).

In the next paragraph, the reader is given the verbal translation of the visual representation of the landscape. The close relationship between human figure and landscape, indeed the identification of 'boy' and 'land', is suggested by the fact that they both are assigned the colour red in the painting. Similarly, the colour blue links the women and the sky. And it is by means of this visual representation of the landscape that the protagonist Popi is introduced, showing that art, in this case Father Claerhout's paintings, transcend time. The same painting could affect both the current observer – the narratorial voice represented in typical Mda fashion in the plural as ('us') – and the historical fictional protagonist Popi.

Personification of the landscape in Father Claerhout's paintings, in which the painter is perceived by Mda as the one who had tamed 'the open skies, the vastness and the loneliness of the Free State' (Mda, 2002, p. 2), subsequently achieves an almost magical identification of the actual and 'painted' people who inhabit the real and painted landscapes respectively. The omniscient narratorial voice describes the effect of the paintings on the five-year-old Popi as follows: 'Yet his very elongated people overwhelmed her with joy. She saw herself jumping down from her mother's back and walking into the canvas, joining the distorted people in their daily chores. They filled her with excitement in their ordinariness' (Mda, 2002, p. 2).

This switching between real and painted landscape permeates the entire text. Sometimes the transition is so subtle that the reader is surprised by the transference from real to painted landscape and vice versa.

The idea of fruitfulness, in a bonding of nature and painted people on the canvas, is continued in the verbal translation of the painting of

Madonnas with 'voluptuous thighs', wide open and 'ready to receive drops of rain' (Mda, 2002, p. 11) or kneeling with 'buttocks opening up to the sky. Ready to receive drops of rain' (ibid.). The same idyllic colourful landscape, 'deep in the sunflower field', is also the site of Niki's shame when she is forced, as a girl of only eighteen, to endure the sexual encounter with Johannes Smit. The rape is described in terms of a landscape where 'Yellowness ran amok' and 'dripped down with her screams' (Mda, 2002, p. 16). When, after some years of marriage, Niki becomes a willing partner, partly to take revenge on her employer's wife who had shamed her, this is described from her former rapist's perspective as a 'gathering of the partakers of stolen delicacies', and mention is again made of the yellow sunflower fields to which Niki and Stefanus Cronjé would regularly retreat.

While the setting of this and similar transgressions remains the Free State platteland, it is a changed platteland harbouring a devil running amok by 'Grabbing upstanding volk by their genitalia and dragging them along a path strewn with the body parts of black women' (Mda, 2002, p. 89).

Occasionally the narratorial voice resorts to social commentary by drawing the reader's attention to discrepancies between the painter's representation of characters and the historical corrective the narrative is trying to achieve. This corrective account tells the story of the injustice suffered by black women arrested and temporarily imprisoned for having contravened the Immorality Act.

The reader is informed by the narratorial voice that while Niki and her friends were being prosecuted, Farther Claerhout resorted to painting nuns instead of madonnas nursing babies:

[n]uns in flowing blue habits. Nuns in a procession. Their child-like brown faces peeping through head-veils that flow almost to the ground. Hiding their feet. Five nuns that only live in the continuing present. Their world has nothing to do with the outside world of miscegenation. Yet each of them is carrying a baby. Babies with slanting eyes. Babies that look grey at first glance, but have the colours of the rainbow if you look hard enough [.] Babies wrapped in blue shawls. Only their round heads are showing. (Mda, 2002, pp. 94–95)

In the second part of the novel Popi and her brother Viliki become political activists with disastrous consequences which eventually lead to their betrayal at the hands of Viliki's so-called brothers. However, after this lengthy interlude, Popi and her mother find peace when they are re-absorbed into the landscape:

And then the bees began to swarm. They buzzed away from one of the hives in a black ball around the queen. And then they formed a big black cloud. We saw Niki and Popi walking under the cloud, following the bees. Or were the bees following them? We did not know. We just saw the women and the bees all moving in the same direction. Until they disappeared into a cluster of bluegum trees a distance away.

We knew that the bees had succeeded in filling the gaping hole in Popi's heart. Popi, who had been ruled by anger, had finally been calmed by the bees. The bees had finally completed the healing work that had been begun by the creations of the trinity.

Yet the trinity never knew all these things. His work was to paint the subjects, and not to poke his nose into their lives beyond the canvas. From the sins of our mothers all these things flow.(Mda, 2002, pp. 267–268)

Space, visually and verbally transformed into a specific landscape, is optimally exploited in Mda's text to focus on actual events, thereby contributing to a re-imagining of a more representative history.

Mda's exploration of space in the three texts under discussion demonstrates his uncanny ability to transform otherwise ordinary places into significant indicators of meaning. By exploiting art (singing, painting, dramatic spectacle) in his depiction of the relationship between man and space, he continues to surprise the reader with original recontextualizations of socio-political conditions in the postapartheid South African landscape.

Notes

1. In their 'introduction' in *Ways of Writing: Critical Essays on Zakes Mda*, D. Bell and J. U. Jacobs provide an extensive overview of Mda's literary career to date. I am grateful to Johan Jacobs for making available to me an electronic pre-publication copy of the manuscript for research purposes. Henceforth references to this publication will be indicated as Bell and Jacobs (forthcoming 2008).
2. See *Ways of Dying* (1995), *The Heart of Redness* (2000), *The Madonna of Excelsior* (2002), *The Whale Caller* (2005) and *Cion* (2007).
3. See his remarks on the influence of an African storytelling tradition in an interview with Benjamin Austen (quoted in Bell and Jacobs, forthcoming 2008).

4. To my knowledge no one has to date attempted a theorization of postapartheid literature comprising works produced by both black and white South African authors. Such a study would have to take into account literature published in the metropolitan languages (Afrikaans and English), as well as in any of the nine indigenous languages spoken in South Africa. Given the linguistic constraints, any study of black writing (as a counterpart to J. M. Coetzee's 'white writing' (Coetzee 1988)) is mostly restricted to black authors writing in English. With regard to Zakes Mda, see Bell and Jacobs (forthcoming 2008).

5. I have compared Mda's depiction of the many faces of death, as told by the Nurse at funerals, with the stories told by victims of violence according to the recordings of testimonies heard at the TRC-hearings in a paper read at the XVth ICLA Congress, held at Leiden, The Netherlands in August 1997. (See Gräbe 2000). The present chapter is an extended version of a paper first read at the joint AUETSA-SAACLALS-SAVAL Conference held at the University of Cape Town in July 2005 (Unpublished).

6. It is worth noting that van Wyk (1997, p. 88) explains Toloki's name as a Xhosa derivation of the Afrikaans 'tolk', meaning 'interpreter'.

7. Van Wyk (1997, p. 84) makes the important point that the harbour city remains nameless, thereby invoking an allegorical image of all South African cities in the late apartheid era. Courau and Murray (in Bell and Jacobs) argue that Mda engages fictionally with the city as postmodern space; and they consider Toloki's interaction with and utilization of the physical objects at his disposal within the urban landscape as an 'act of territorialisation'.

8. Judging from Desai's (1984, p. 105) description of the atmosphere of a small town at the foot of the Himalayan mountains, and especially the spectacular view from the top leaving the spectator with a sense of solitude, Toloki's vivid imagination actually brought him very close to a real site.

9. I would agree with Wenzel's analysis of the notion of 'home' in the novel, arguing that '[T]oloki, freed by the boundless realm of the imagination, is able to transcend the barriers and boundaries imposed by apartheid and abject poverty, by creating and "living" his dream of the ideal "home"' (Wenzel, 2003, p. 320).

10. For an opposite reading see Mazibuko (in Bell and Jacobs) who finds that 'Mda's pessimism about the urban space permeates his narrative with its thematic over-reliance on the power of the spiritual and creative, which is insufficiently grounded in material realities. Perhaps magic is the only way to survive the urban spaces'.

11. In her analysis of the intertextual play between Mda's *The Heart of Redness* and Conrad's *Heart of Darkness* Gail Fincham (in Bell and Jacobs) discusses the contrasting depiction of the African landscape in the two novels; whereas Mda's text is 'saturated with colour', Conrad's text 'generates' black, white and grey only.

12. See Gräbe (2004) for an exploration of the transcendence of, inter alia, technology as a sophisticated means of communication in *The Heart of Redness*. Warnes (in Bell and Jacobs) provides an elaborate discussion of magic realism in Zakes Mda's writings.

Works cited

Bell, D. and Jacobs, J. U. (eds), *Ways of Writing: Critical Essays on Zakes Mda* (Durban: KwaZula Natal University Press, forthcoming 2008).

Coetzee, J. M., *White Writing: The Culture of Letters in South Africa* (New Haven: Yale University Press, 1988).

Concilio, C. 'Reading History through the Landscape: Ekphrasis in the Fiction of Michael Ondaatje and Romesh Genesekera', in *Saval Conference Papers: A Sense of Space* (Johannesburg: Wits University Press, 1998).

Courau, R. and Sally-Ann, M. 'Of Funeral Rites and Community Memory: Ways of Living in *Ways of Dying* ', in Bell and Jacobs (Forthcoming 2008).

Desai, A. ' "FENG SUI" or Spirit of Place', in *A Sense of Place: Essays in Post-Colonial Literatures*. Ed. B. Olinder (Göteborg: English Department, University of Gothenburg, 1984).

Fincham, G. 'Community and Agency in *The Heart of Redness* and Joseph Conrad's 'Heart of Darkness', in Bell and Jacobs (Forthcoming 2008).

Gräbe, I., 'Telling the "Truth": Collective Memory of South Africa's Apartheid Heritage in Oral Testimony and Fictional Narrative', in *The Conscience of Human Kind: Literature and Traumatic Experience* . Eds E. Ibsch, D. Fokkema and J. Von der Thusen (Amsterdam and Atlanta: Rodopi, 2000), pp. 249–263.

———, 'Theory and Technology in Contemporary South African Writing: From Self-Conscious Exploration to Contextual Appropriation', in *Cybernetic Ghosts: Literature in the Age of Theory and Technology*. Ed. D. M. Figueira (Brigham Young University: ICLA, 2004), pp. 203–212.

Jacobs, J. U., 'Towards a South African Expressionism: *The Madonna of Excelsior*', in Bell and Jacobs (Forthcoming 2008).

Mazibuko, N., 'Love and Wayward Women in *Ways of Dying*', in Bell and Jacobs (Forthcoming 2008).

Mda, Z., *Ways of Dying* (Cape Town: Oxford University Press, 1995).

———, *The Heart of Redness* (Cape Town: Oxford University Press, 2000).

———, *The Madonna of Excelsior* (Cape Town: Oxford University Press, 2002).

———, *The Whale Caller* (Johannesburg: Penguin Books, 2005).

———, *Cion* (Johannesburg: Penguin Books, 2007).

Naidoo, V., 'Interview with Zakes Mda', *Alternation* , 4: 1 (1997) 247–261.

Ndebele, N. S., *Rediscovery of the Ordinary: Essays on South African Literature and Culture* (Johannesburg: Congress of South African Writers, 1991[1984]).

Smit, J. A., Van Wyk, J. and Wade, J.-P., *Rethinking South African Literary History* (Durban: Creda Press, 1994).

Van Wyk, J. 'Catastrophe and Beauty: *Ways of Dying* , Zakes Mda's Novel of the Transition', *Literator* , 18: 3 (November 1997).

Warnes, C. 'Chronicles of Belief and Unbelief: Zakes Mda and the Question of Magical Realism in South African Literature', in Bell and Jacobs (Forthcoming 2008).

Wenzel, M. 'Appropriating Space and Transcending Boundaries in *The Africa House* by Christina Lamb and *Ways of Dying* by Zakes Mda', *Journal of Literary Studies* , 19: 3/4 (December 2003).

11
No-Man's Land: Nuruddin Farah's *Links* and the Space of Postcolonial Alienation

Harry Garuba

The novel of the cultural nationalist period of modern African literature was often heavily invested in the rural. Also sometimes referred to as the rediscovery phase of African literature, the novels of this period usually focused on the lives of characters inhabiting a 'pure' rural space, undistorted by the alienations of colonialism and modernity. In this body of writing, the rural was seen as the social space in which the African subject lived in organic harmony, integrated into a functioning social order and at one with the rhythms of nature. This, the reasoning went, was the state of pre-colonial African societies. For the writers of this period therefore, the rural represented the space of unsullied 'Africanness', where the authentic essence of Africa could still be found. Colonialism was seen as the disruptive force that severed the link between the African self, the social order and the natural world. By introducing a new order of things that destabilized the continuity of tradition, colonialism in effect introduced a regime of alienation on the people. In the literature, this alienation was not only portrayed as epistemological, in the sense of the ways people understand and orient themselves to the world, but also spatialized, in terms of the division between the rural and the urban. The idea of colonial alienation is fairly commonplace in African literature and the 'city' was depicted as the space of its location, the site of its unfolding. This is perhaps the most common depiction of alienation, and, in this regard, African elaborations of the sources of colonial alienation do not differ from descriptions of alienation in the West, often seen as consequent upon the mechanization and bureaucratization of life in modern industrial and post-industrial societies.

But what I shall be calling 'postcolonial alienation' in this chapter differs significantly from colonial alienation and derives from a different historical trajectory. If the earlier narrative presented colonial alienation as a consequence of the breakdown of the mores and norms that sustained rural life in the migration to the city, the notion of postcolonial alienation that I propose to examine in this chapter is a reversal of this earlier narrative. The version of postcolonial alienation that I have in mind here is the alienation that results from the *wholesale transference of these rural norms into the space of the city*. Where the loss of these norms in the city had been portrayed as the root of alienation, what does their retention in the time of postcoloniality portend? The questions that I seek to examine therefore are: what happens when the norms that sustained and guaranteed the functioning of a specific social order in its rural environment are transferred to the new space of the city and the city becomes spatially demarcated along the lines of rural habitation? Do they function as instruments of order and harmony in their new location? Does this transference reverse the psychic and social dislocation of colonial alienation or does it create a new kind of alienation because of the disjuncture between social space and subjectivity? What does this new configuration of space and subjectivity mean for the rationalization of social relations and for legibility which, supposedly, are key to understanding the dynamics of the city? And what does this mean for use of public space in the city? I explore these questions against the inherited background of colonialist discourse and African literature of the nationalist period foregrounding their dichotomization and spatialization of African subjectivity between the rural and the urban. I use a recent novel by the Somali author Nuruddin Farah as a case study of the new figuration of postcolonial alienation.

In examining these issues, I rely on the conceptual grounding of two definitive ideas of the modern and of the metropolis: the notion of rationalization and the concept of legibility. First, I take it for granted that the notion of rationalization is central to conceptions of the city, at least in the West. As Achille Mbembe describes it in 'The Aesthetics of Superfluity': 'the Western imagination defines the metropolis as the general form assumed by the rationalization of relations of production (the increasing prevalence of the commodity system) and the rationalization of the social sphere (human relations) that follows it' (373). The rationalization of human relations means the movement away from bonds of blood to other forms of association dependent to a large degree on the autonomy of the individual subject, freedom of choice and a terrain of social exchange mediated by more impersonal instruments. Edward Said describes this as the shift away from 'filiation' to 'affiliation.'[1]

Second, I use the concept of legibility the way James Scott develops it in his book *Seeing Like a State*. According to Scott, legibility is the driving force of the modern state; its paradigms and practices arise from the quest to order society and nature in ways that make them 'legible'. Modernist planning sets outs out to make society and the world available for surveillance and monitoring by an omniscient eye rather like the example of Jeremy Bentham's panopticon which Foucault deploys in his works. As Scott puts it, 'Legibility implies a viewer whose place is central and whose glance is synoptic' (79). The Enlightenment vision evident in this way of looking at the world is summed up by Descartes' view of the difference between the planned and unplanned city:

> These ancient cities that were once *straggling* villages and have become in the course of time great cities are commonly quite *poorly laid out* compared to those *well-ordered towns that an engineer lays out on a vacant plane* as it suits his fancy. And although, upon considering one-by-one the buildings in the former class of towns, one finds as much art or more than one finds in the latter class of towns, still, upon seeing how the buildings are arranged – *here a large one, there a small one* – and how *they make the streets crooked and uneven*, one will say that *it is chance more than the will of some men using their reason that has arranged them thus.* (Descartes, 6; quoted in Scott, 55)

This vision of geometrical order, of straight lines that eliminate unevenness, an order imposed by reason, is very much embedded in the rationalizing character and the conceptual paradigm of the modern and of the city.

However, these accounts of the modern metropolis, I suggest, often rest on the premise of modernist order, of rationalization and legibility; they do not sufficiently take into account or problematize what I refer to as questions of 'primordial legibility' such as what we see enacted in Farah's novel. The reverse side of this modernist legibility is not opacity or invisibility as labelled in the literature; rather, it is, I would argue, a form of 'non-rationalized' legibility which follows the pattern of older forms of social and spatial imagining based on relations of blood.

In my examination of Farah's *Links* therefore I bring up these questions and highlight the ways in which paying attention to them may help us in re-thinking our conventional notions of the city, modernist rationalization and conceptions of the public and of public space. In doing this, I attempt to assess the extent to which the novel seeks to subvert, reverse or reinforce the logic of the epistemological division between the rural and the urban inherited from colonialist mapping of space.

Spatializing subjects and subjectivity

In Africa, the contrastive construction of the rural and the urban, the one as the home of tradition and the other as the locus of modernity, was rooted in the binarist logic of colonialism. This logic plays itself out in what Okwui Enwezor *et al.* refer to in their 'Introduction' to the book *Under Siege: Four African Cities – Freetown, Johannesburg, Kinshasa, Lagos* as 'the hard-nosed colonial formal distinctions that established an epistemological division between urban and rural, tradition and modernity, formal and informal, village and city, authentic and inauthentic, chaotic and orderly' (13). The 'epistemological division' that the editors speak of here was the underlying premise that informed the work of African novelists who sought to capture and represent the cultural essence of pre-colonial Africa. Their objective – in setting their novels within the space of the rural – was to get to the heart of the traditional and the authentic, to show (or showcase?) its functionality and orderliness and to express the logic and rationality of its practices and systems of belief and the beauty of its forms of expression. In doing this, they implied that the source of chaos and disorder was the alienation fostered by colonialism, and this was most in evidence in the cities where the social codes that sustain rural life invariably broke down under the pressures of modernity, modernization and the heterogeneity of urban populations.

This binary framework of spatial imagining was also, to a large extent, predicated on notions of the different forms of sociality available in each of these spaces. The rural was regarded as a domain that was characterized by social and cultural homogeneity – a homogeneity anchored in relations of blood and 'natural' forms of kinship – and a collective identity, expressed in shared rituals, customs and values. Apart from the bonds of ancestry, language and culture which provided points of communal and collective identification, social cohesion and continuity were also ensured by modes of social reproduction within the community in which these shared norms are ritually passed on from one generation to the other. As shown again and again in the writing of nationalist orientation from Camara Laye's *L'Enfant Noir* or Chinua Achebe's *Things Fall Apart* to Nelson Mandela's *Long Walk to Freedom*, the rural is the space of a cultural and spiritual wholeness and harmony founded on a homogeneity of people and values. In contrast to this, the heterogeneous populations of cities ensure that no such singular, collective identity is possible and other forms of sociality beyond those based on the bonds of blood and shared cultural beliefs and practices have to be cultivated. Within this spatialized conception of subjectivity and community, the city – the kingdom of heterogeneity – was seen as the primary site of alienation.

It is necessary to note that contrasting descriptions of rural and urban identities and subjectivities and the notion of urban alienation are not unique to these discourses. In fact, the ideas can be said to derive from Western conceptions of the country and the city that have a long genealogy. However, what may have been distinctive of the African or colonial case in general was that these distinctions became part of a state-driven process, a political order underwritten by a host of administrative instruments. According to Mahmood Mamdani, the politicization of this 'epistemological division' was realized in the form of the colonial state in Africa:

The African colonial experience came to be crystallized in the nature of the state forged through the encounter. Organized differently in rural areas from urban ones, that state was Janus-faced, bifurcated. It contained a duality; two forms of power under a single hegemonic authority. Urban power spoke the language of civil society and civil rights, rural power of community and culture. Civil power claimed to protect rights, customary power pledged to enforce tradition. The former was organized on the principle of differentiation to check the concentration of power, the latter around the principle of fusion to ensure a unitary authority. (18)

In the same manner that two structures of political governance were put in place, two processes of subject formation and normalization were set in motion – the one producing citizens and the other producing subjects of traditions and culture. John Comaroff summarizes these processes in this manner:

Unlike the European polities...colonies were never places of even tenuously imagined homogeneity. For the most part, their adminis-tration was vested in states without hyphe-nation: in states without nations. Here lay the ideological contrast between metropolitan and colonial governance. One depended for its existence on the cultural work of manufacturing sameness, of engineering a horizontal sense of

fraternity (Anderson, 1983); ... The other, despite its rhetoric of uni-
versalizing modernity, was concerned with the practical management,
often the production, of difference. (114)

Comaroff deals with the many ways in which this difference was produced by compiling copious documentation on the life-ways of various
'tribes' and creating ethnological fixities and bounded geographies of
the habitations of these tribes. 'Native' cultural practices and categories
were thus codified, objectified, primordialized and dehistoricized; and,
in the process, 'the state naturalized [these categories] elevating them
into hegemonic forms of naming and knowing' (117).

The deliberate manufacturing of Otherness in this manner is perhaps
the most enduring legacy of colonialism in Africa because it fashioned
the language for making rights claims that simultaneously looked in two
directions: the first by an appeal to Western liberal conceptions of the
individual and of citizenship and the second appealing to the essences
of culture and tradition and the hegemony of the group. The opposing
conceptions were – supposedly – located within the urban and the rural
respectively.

Although this 'epistemological division' was the product of a colonial
delusion of mastery over the space and subjects of its territory and was
never, in reality, as neat as the categories claim, the important point of
note is that it was re-created by the literature of cultural nationalism and
deployed with an auto-ethnographic passion that turned it into a truism
of colonialist and nationalist discourses on the question of modernity
and the African subject. It is for this reason rather than the accuracy
of its representation of the facts that I wish to retain this spatial characterization in making the argument of this chapter. For, it is against
the background of this proposition, affirmed again and again in African
literature, that the village is – or was, until colonization – the space of
unalienated being that I explore the central question and the related
paradoxes that are the objects of focus in this chapter. To elaborate a little
more on the questions: What happens when this rural ethos and ethic
are manifested in the spatial reconfiguration of the city into enclaves
defined by bonds of filiation that resist the movement of bodies across
their boundaries? In short, does the spatial ruralization[2] of the city, so to
speak, result in the same solidarity and normality that it ensured in its
rural base? What does such refusal of rationalized social relations within
the physical space of the city inhabited by different groups mean for the
management of difference constructed, in this instance, primarily along
lines of clan identity? And, finally, what does this do to the very notion

of public space as a defining characteristic of the city? If the city is carved up between different clan families, as Nuruddin Farah calls them in his novels, what happens in the unclaimed spaces that have not been taken over by one or the other of these clans? Being no-man's land, or more appropriately no-clan's land, what ethos and ethic rule in these places?

Nuruddin Farah's *Links* is a novel that thematizes this very question of the ruralization of the city. Set in the Somali capital of Mogadiscio, *Links* focuses on Jeebleh, an exile who returns to Mogadiscio after 20 years, and finds the beloved city of his youth remapped along lines of blood and based on the Somali clan system. The novel takes us through his struggle to affirm links of a more rationalized sort beyond customary notions of birth and beginnings. In the Mogadiscio he returns to, clan identities and their attendant subjectivities have been re-created in the spatial geography of the city. Jeebleh and his friends attempt to resist this denial of the freedom to imagine other forms of sociality beyond bonds of blood; they seek a new social and geographical imagination that can sustain a new moral community. The novel, in the final analysis, can be read as a narrative of this struggle.

Writing postcolonial alienation

Nuruddin Farah has always been concerned with issues of space and subjectivity, collective representation and individual identity. In an earlier novel, *Maps*, Farah examines the relationship between nation, space and subjectivity. Set in the period of the war between Somalia and Ethiopia, the novel explores the nationalist quest to create a single nation for all ethnic Somali by annexing the Ogaden region into a greater Somalia. This war is depicted not simply as a territorial dispute but, more fundamentally, it is portrayed as a contest over the very nature of Somaliness in relation to subjects, bodies and space. As Hilaal explains to Askar, the protagonist of the novel: 'The Somali in the Ogaden, the Somali in Kenya, both, because they lack what makes the self strong and whole, are *unperson*' (175). Hilaal proposes a relationship of identity between subject, identity and space; a Somali outside of the geographical, political entity known as Somalia is an *unperson*. This view of the subject and political space is what Farah questions in *Maps*.[3] In *Secrets*, a later novel set in the last days of the dictatorship before Somalia imploded and warlords carved up the country into territories controlled by different clan armies and militia, Farah turns to the question of clan identity at the heart of the Somali social system. Farah interrogates the biological, primordial basis on which clan identity is affirmed. In a patriarchal society in which clan lineage is traced through the fathers, the novel exposes the fabricated, constructed nature of fatherhood in this society. Kalaman, the protagonist of this novel, is the child of a gang rape and his uncertain biological origins contrast sharply with his solid social insertion within a family and a clan. The most closely kept secret of a patriarchal social order, the novel suggests, is the instability of the most basic claim of its authorizing discourse. Using this kind of kinship as the basis of a political order is even more problematic for the protagonist. He says:

> Forming a political allegiance with people just because their *begats* are identical to one's own – judging from the way in which clan-based militia groupings were arming themselves – is as foolish as trusting one's blood brother. Only the unwise trust those close to them, a brother, a sister, or an in-law. Ask anyone in power, ask a king, and he will advise you to mistrust your kin. (77)

But it is precisely this kind of social and political order of allegiance that reigns in the Mogadiscio of *Links* with the city divided between Strongman North and Strongman South and the spaces in between known, in the novel's often repeated term, as 'no-man's-land' or 'no-man's-territory'. It is to this city, overtaken by the rural ethos and ethic of filiation, that Jeebleh returns after over two decades of exile in the United States of America. It is a city where blood lineage determines physical residence, the social space of possible association and of possible political loyalty. In language almost identical to that used in the earlier novels, Af-Laawe says that 'those of us who think of ourselves as progressive argue not only that the clan is a sham, but that *you cannot organize civil society around it*' (139; emphasis added). And earlier on, Jeebleh speaks of his 'unease at the thought of privileging blood over ideology' (127).

The binary oppositions drawn between 'clan' and 'civil society' and 'blood' and 'ideology' in these utterances clearly follow a pattern of contrasts in the novel which show where the main character's (and indeed the author's) sympathies lie. The contrast between the city dwellers and the rural folk is highlighted again by Af-Laawe:

> Some of us are of a 'we' generation, others a 'me' generation. *You mix the two modes of being, and things get awkward, unmanageable.* I belong to the me generation, whereas my clan elders belong to the we generation. A man with a me mindset and a family of four – a wife and two children – celebrates the idea of me. It is not so when it comes to our clansmen who visit from the hinterland, and who celebrate a

'we.' They believe in the clan, and they know no better – many of them have never been to school or out of the country. I am included in their self-serving 'we.' This leads to chaos. (139; emphasis added)

It is taken for granted that those with the 'we' mindset come from the country or the hinterland (and have never travelled out or gone to school) or are from the ranks of the aged, in contrast to the 'me' people who are educated and belong in a nuclear family. (I will return later to the significance of the language of pronouns in the novel.) This is, of course, the normative model of the rural and the urban and, in the novel, Jeebleh often seems to spot this difference or deviation from the city norm in dialects, accents, dress codes and the uncouth manners of certain characters. The difference between the rural and the urban is seen not simply to be affirmed in the obvious terms of geography, but it is described as 'two modes of being' mapped into speech – 'the hard-to-follow dialect' (21) – and subjectivity. Even time is evoked to bolster this understanding when the Major accuses Jeebleh: 'He thinks our reliance on blood kinship is backward and primitive.... that he belongs to the twenty-first century, while we belong to the thirteenth.'[4] (30) In Farah's novel therefore the epistemological divide is firmly in place and its authority depends upon the spatial separation of the rural and urban. But when you 'mix them' the result, as Af-Laawe says, is chaos. It would appear that Farah summons the ubiquitous trope of alienation deployed in colonialist and nationalist writing only to give it a postcolonial perspective markedly different from its uses in the antecedent discourses.

Another trope of nationalist discourse that *Links* foregrounds is that of exile and homecoming. Exile and return, it must be mentioned, are common tropes that African literature shares with modernist writing. In its African version, exile may be depicted as literal (in terms of physical space) or metaphorical (in terms of cultural deracination). Homecoming is thus the restoration of home in both literal and metaphoric terms. Farah once again invokes this trope in unusual ways. Living in the heart of the metropolis of New York, Jeebleh is almost knocked down by a Somali taxi driver, obviously new to the city and driving illegally. (He is not overwhelmed with a nostalgia and longing for home. On the contrary, it is as if the violence of 'home' stalks him to New York – a clear indication that 'home' will not be all hearth and harmony.) This brush with death at the hands of a fellow Somali convinces him to return 'home' to 'Mogadiscio, the city of death, [hoping] he might disorient death' (5). The reason he gives himself for going back over the protestations of his wife and daughter is that he is returning to pay his respects to his mother who has been dead and buried for several years. Since he had not been able to go home at the time of her death, this will be his opportunity to do so. Here the conventional feeling of loss and nostalgia, the longing for home, that narratives of colonial alienation foreground is displaced. Going home is simply a duty one needs to perform.

But the city he returns to is not the home he used to know: there is no state authority; no functioning banks; the national university is now defunct and everywhere he encounters dysfunctionality. His memories of the Mogadiscio of old are the conventional pictures of order and peace, unfettered mobility, commodities and consumption.

> Jeebleh's Mogadiscio was orderly, clean, peaceable, a city with integrity and a life of its own, a lovely metropolis with beaches, cafes, restaurants, late-night movies. It may have been poor, but at least there was dignity to that poverty, and no one was in any hurry to plunder or destroy what they couldn't have. (35)

In contrast, in the new city, as Af-Laawe tells him, 'people stay in the territories to which their clan families have ancestral claims, where they feel comfortable and can move about unhindered, unafraid' (12). For someone who feels no clan loyalty himself, this represents the very death of the city. Home is where death is.

To describe this, the author draws once again upon a grammar of contrasts which ends up creating a signifying system of binary oppositions in which everything is fixed in an axis of normal versus abnormal. To take two immediate examples, normative descriptions of the metropolis emphasize mobility and heterogeneity as central to the city and city life. This sense of mobility and heterogeneity is invoked again and again in descriptions of the old Mogadiscio as different from the new. Jeebleh, for instance, remembers the time of his youth 'when the city was so peaceful he could take a stroll at any hour of the day or night . . . go to the Gezira nightclub and then walk home at three in the morning' (14). As if to underscore the heterogeneity of the city, he recalls, on more than one occasion, the waves of invaders who have come to the peninsula: 'The Arabs, and after them the Persians, and after the Persians the Portuguese, and after the Portuguese the French, the British, and the Italians, and later the Russians, and most recently the Americans' (124; see also 14–15). This list of foreign invaders is recalled almost as a eulogy to the city's 'openness' to outsiders in contrast to the hermetic insularity of the regime of the clan that now rules over it. In a telling linguistic collocation, soon after speaking of the Arabs who 'pushed their commerce . . . along with their Islamic faith', he asks the question: 'Would Mogadiscio ever know peace? Would the city's inhabitants enjoy this commodity ever again' (15). The description of peace as a commodity to be enjoyed resonates with the conventional idea of the city as the site of consumption. There is also more than the hint of a suggestion that invaders come and go but some of the peoples and the commodities they bring remain: the Yemenis who seem to have taken up permanent residence in the city, the Yemeni coffee, the Russian AK-47s, the American jeans and T-shirts and so on.

In contrast to this mobility and heterogeneity, the new city actively prevents mobility: Gunmen shadow the protagonist wherever he goes, either as protectors or assassins; a restaurant is hidden away from public view and is signified by a hole in the wall that can be read only by the knowing few; the streets and the beaches are deserted and a walk in the street or a stroll to and on the beach is laden with unseen dangers. However, in terms of openness to the world and consumption this story is slightly different. There is still an openness to the global in the sense that part of the financing of the militias comes from clan members resident abroad. Smuggling syndicates do brisk business in cars stolen from Europe and brought in through the Middle East; mobile phones are easily available and, in spite of the conflict, mobile phone companies make a killing by ensuring that you can speak to anyone in any part of the world. Though mobility is highly restricted, and heterogeneous mixing appears prohibited, commodities seem to fare better, moving, as it were, without restriction, subject only to the forces of finance and the market.

Public spaces, the sites where the heterogeneity of city life is conventionally best enacted, are patrolled by gangs of militias loyal to one warlord or the other where only those of identical clan loyalty can feel safe. Where such spaces do not fall under the authority of a warlord, they become a no-man's-land where one ventures only at his or her own risk. Falling under no one's clan authority, they become places of random violence and sudden death. The novel begins with one such incident of violence at the airport where a gang of armed youth take bets on picking a target at random and taking a potshot at it. On this occasion, one of them shoots and kills the ten-year old son of a woman who was about to board a plane. The youths celebrate with high-fives and congratulate the marksman on his skill while the crowd cowers. In places such as this where the authority of the clan warlord does not reach, death is a game kids play. So danger and death stalk the airport, the beach, the hotel, the streets – in short, any space remotely associated with the coming together of a heterogeneous public. As the example of the restaurant to which Af-Laawe takes Jeebleh shows, in this city 'legibility' is the product of a non-rationalized local knowledge, lodged in the body by way of family and clan. And when, on arrival, Jeebleh chooses to check into a hotel to avoid clan complications, the elders of the clan seek him out as surely as blood will find its own.

It is possible to argue that the death of the city is only the result of the war and the warlords and the militia that have balkanized it. But this will only be a half-truth because Farah's primary concern in this novel is with the nature of this spatial division along lines of clan identity. As we have seen from the other novels mentioned earlier, it is clear that the relationship between the subject as citizen and the subject as subjected to primordial forms of identification construed and constructed as identical with specific spatial and political coordinates is an abiding concern of Farah's work. In *Links* those not inserted into this compact of clan and space become 'unpersons' and are physically treated as such by the armed militias that police space and identity and metaphorically, by the narrator who names them in accordance with body parts.

We may recall that Hilaal in *Maps* refers to Somalis not resident in Somalia as 'unpersons' because they lack what makes a person whole. In *Links*, the metaphor of wholeness seems to determine the narrator's approach to descriptions of setting and event and the naming of characters. This may be, perhaps, because everything is focalized through the eyes of Jeebleh, the main character, whose view of the world is unremittingly Manichean. But as the narrative perspective, on the whole, does not demand of us, the readers, any circumspection with respect to Jeebleh's views, I suspect that he may well be the author's mouthpiece, particularly in his attitudes and comments with regard to the clan system and to spatiality. The narrator extends this attitude of 'unpersons' to all of the characters he does not like. As soon as we encounter those characters, they are transformed into metonyms that emphasize parts of their bodies. The list of the appellations he gives them are numerous: Af-Laawe (meaning No Mouth),[5] OneArm, Bucktooth, FourEyes, EatShit, etc. By doing this, the narrator invokes a discourse of the abnormal and unwhole. So pervasive and rigid does this become that it offers a ready-made schema for reading the characters. In this mode, character is biologized and social life naturalized; people are instantly transformed into metonyms and nature becomes an index of the social world.

This transformation of real life into metaphor through metonymic appellation passes over to the animal world, to nature, and seems to hover over everything else:

there were no shrubs, and the grass and cacti were dry. The cows...chewed away at discarded shoes for which the goats had no stomach. The dogs looked rabid and were so skinny you could see their protruding ribs....vultures, marabous, and the odd crow were having a go at the pickings. (133)

Death, decay, absence, lack: there is a deliberate touch of the eschatological in these descriptions. The focus on the use of pronouns also constitutes part of the displacement and reduction that is a primary concern of the author. The collective 'we' of the clan that ensures that everyone is part of the group and plays by the rules is a continual source of unease and discomfort to the narrator. Very early in the novel, Af-Laawe's use of the pronoun alerts him to the specificity of its Somali meaning as different from its more neutral usage:

> Jeebleh took note of Af-Laawe's use of 'we,' but was unable to determine if it was a gesture of amiability or whether someone else was involved in the arrangements being made for him. Was this 'we' inclusive, in the sense that Af-Laawe was hinting that the two of them belonged to the same clan? Or did Af-Laawe's 'we' take other people into account, others known to be from the same blood community as Jeebleh? (12)

So pervasive is the use and questioning of pronominal usage that in the first (South African) edition of the novel,[6] the pronoun 'we' is the very last word in the novel. For the narrator and author, making the word stand ominously alone – preceded by the conjunction 'And' – as a sentence and a paragraph all on its own and as the last word of the novel, is apparently not enough to signify its import; there is also an exclamation mark after it. The narrator continually draws our attention to the use of this pronoun in this society as a mark of clan collectivity and its exclusion of those who do not belong. It is the struggle against this hegemony of the clan that the narrator conducts by drawing attention to the power of the pronoun at every turn.

In the language of insistent pronominal denomination deployed in the novel, the use of metonymic characterization and the description of settings that emphasize the abnormal or the deformed, it may be argued that the narrator and author seem – in these instances – to partake of the reductive logic of the clan system that they want to depict. Therefore, it is quite easy to forget in the midst of these unalleviated reductive rhetorical strategies that the objective is to draw attention to and deconstruct the bigotry of the system and the ridiculousness of its policing of space. It is for this reason that it is important to bear in mind the alternative publics he endorses by looking at the role of the Refuge and of the miracle child Raasta and her companion, Makka, as representations of the desired moral order of choice, heterogeneity and respect for difference in the novel.

The Refuge is the house of refuge that Bile has established to take in all the children who are fleeing the war, have been orphaned or abandoned. The orphaned, the homeless, the starving and others are welcomed at the Refuge, irrespective of clan. Here they are provided with food, shelter and a home where they can grow up as normal children in an environment of peace in the midst of a war-ravaged country. It is, for Bile, also a kind of experiment in bringing children from different clans together to share the same physical space and to eat in the traditional communal manner. Bile explains it to Jeebleh in this manner:

> We've resorted to the traditional method of eating together daily from the same *mayida*... in the belief that we create a camaraderie and we all trust one another. Some might consider hogwash the idea that those who look one another in the eye as they eat together are bound closely to one another. But our experiment bears it out – anyone meaning to do harm to a fellow sharer of the *mayida* will not dare look him, or anyone else, in the eye. Around here... many people prefer staying away to coming and sharing the *mayida* when there is bad blood. And when they share the *mayida* there can be no bad blood. (157–158)

Bile's experiment in creating a new kind of public is clear from this quotation, and the constant invocation of the word *mayida* underscores Bile's desperation to have his experiment succeed. Although the project is obviously future-oriented in that his faith is placed in the children, the need to anchor it on a traditional practice from the past is an index of this desperate desire.

The symbolic importance of children is carried into the character of Raasta, the miracle child, who in her body signifies this imagined public. The openness of public spaces denied by the clan militias is affirmed in her person as when, just a few days old, 'it was discovered that she drew people to herself. They came in their hundreds.... They felt safe in her vicinity' (53). We are also told that 'by the time she was three she could speak, read, and write three languages. At five and a half, her mastery of a few more tongues was exemplary' (54). In her ability to draw people together her body becomes the site around which the conventional heterogeneity of city life can be performed. And, in her mastery of

numerous languages, her tongue becomes important as the abode of linguistic diversity. She is thus a threat to the order of things. It is only to be
expected that she will be kidnapped before she spreads the contagion of
tolerance and diversity. The quest to rescue her becomes not only a mission to free a kidnapped child but also the quest to bring about a new
social order. Within this symbolic scheme, her disabled friend Makka
comes to represent the arrested development of the country and the city
and the potential locked away in its inarticulacy.

Conclusion: metropoetics and a context for postcolonial alienation

Surveying the vast literature on cities from various parts of the world,
Patricia Yaeger in an introductory essay to a recent *PMLA* special edition
on cities sketches an outline of a metropoetics for the analysis of city
literature:

> I want to propose a new practicum for looking at city literature, includ-
> ing (1) the fact of overurbanization, (2) the predicament of decaying or
> absent infrastructures, (3) the unevenness of shelter (which along with
> food, energy, health care, and water make up the mythos and ethos of
> the nurturing city), and (4) the importance of inventing counterpub-
> lics or communal alternatives to the official, bureaucratized polis. My
> goal is to produce a brief taxonomy or metropoetics that will enable
> us to rethink the urban imaginary in the light of contemporary urban
> crises. (13)

Yaeger's metropoetics is important in trying to devise a system, a set
of grids, so to speak, for studying literature on the city. In its admirably
simple taxonomy, it condenses and categorizes to an adequate degree the
major themes that animate contemporary discourses of the city. It is in
fact possible to locate each of her themes – to varying degrees – in Farah's
novel. Still, it is worth noting that all the topoi she evokes here are underwritten by the premise of the modern. Trying to fit my concern in this
essay into this system, I find that my argument does not fit neatly into
any of her categories. It comes closest to her fourth class which focuses
on 'inventing counterpublics and communal alternatives to the official
bureaucratized polis', but the fit is tenuous because this category depends
upon assuming that the normative model of the modern polis is a highly
rationalized space. But as several commentators have observed, this does

not accord with the reality of many postcolonial cities. And, paradoxically, the alternative, 'counterpublic' (if one can call this a counterpublic)
that *Links* proposes is exactly the conventional, rationalized public of
modernity. Indeed, the preoccupation of the novel is the undesirability
of 'counterpublics and communal alternatives to the official bureaucratized polis', especially those based on blood and biological origins. Sophie
Watson warns that 'there is a danger in urban studies, all too prevalent,
that analyses of American (first), British (next) and other European cities are deployed to describe cities in other parts of the globe, notably
Africa, Asia and Latin America, in ways that are utterly inappropriate
and even pernicious' (3). Though, to be fair, Yaeger does not do this, her
conceptual grid is implicated in this assumption of modern, Western
normativity.

Herein then lies the difference between the postcolonial alienation
that I speak of and conventional descriptions of alienation in the city
as evidenced in the alienation of Simmel's urban subject or Kafka's
characters or the hollow men or walking dead of T. S. Eliot's poetry.
This kind of postcolonial alienation is not grounded on the model of
the rationalized, bureaucratized polis from which the subject is alienated by its overbureaucratization or overmechanization or its surfeit of
sensory stimuli. Rather it is grounded on the model of the 'epistemological division' between the city and the village in which space and
subjectivity are naturalized and primordialized in particular ways. Farah's
Links provides a good textual illustration of the workings of this kind
of alienation; and the solution he proposes to it lies not in inventing communal alternatives and counterpublics but in re-affirming the
conventional secular public of modernity and the importance of its con-
solidation in the space of the city. This, needless to say, is a startling
reversal of the mainstream narratives of alienation and the city that
we find specifically in African literature and literature on the city in
general.

Notes

1. For a discussion of these terms, see Edward Said, *The World, the Text, and the
   Critic.*
2. In an earlier draft of this essay, I had used the term 'villagization'. I am grateful to Fiona Moolla who drew my attention to the fact that this term was
   inappropriate since – to use her own words – ' "true", "noble", "patrician"
   Somali identity from which clan primarily derives is proudly *nomadic* and
   would thumb its nose at settled "village" life.'

3. For a more detailed examination of this, see Harry Garuba, 'Mapping the Land/Body/Subject: Colonial and Postcolonial Geographies in African Narrative.'
4. For a fuller discussion of the use of time as an othering device, see Johannes Fabian, *Time and the other.*
5. The name – one of the many by which this character is known – evokes Dante's *Inferno.* As the novel explains: 'Af-Laawe – meaning "the one with no mouth" – was also an assumed name, which, to a Dante scholar, might allude to the *Inferno*' (23). The references to and resonances of Dante in the novel are numerous and significant. Among them are the status of exile shared between Dante and Farah, the civil war, etc. For a more detailed list of the similarities between both authors and texts, see Fiona Moolla.
6. *Links* was first published in Cape Town, South Africa, in 2003 by Kwela Books but a revised edition was later published in the United Kingdom in 2005 by Gerald Duckworth & Co. Ltd. All page references in this essay are to the Duckworth edition.

Works cited

Comaroff, J., 'Governmentality, Materiality, Legality, Modernity – On the Colonial State in Africa,' in *African Modernities: Entangled Meanings in Current Debate.* Ed. J.-G. Deutsch, P. Probst and H. Schmidt (Portsmouth, NH, Oxford, UK: Heinemann and James Currey, 2002).

Davis, M., *City of Quartz* (New York: Vintage, 1992).

———, *Planet of Slums* (London and New York: Verso, 2006).

Descartes, R., *Discourse on Method.* Trans. D. A. Cress (Indianapolis: Hackett, 1980).

Farah, N., *Maps* (New York: Penguin, 1986).

———, *Secrets* (Cape Town: David Philip, 1998).

———, *Links* (Cape Town: Kwela Books, 2003).

———, *Links* (London: Gerald Duckworth & Co. Ltd, 2005).

Garuba, H., 'Mapping the Land/Body/Subject: Colonial and Postcolonial Geographies in African Narrative,' *Alternation*, 9.1 (2002) 87–116.

Lehan, R., *The City in Literature: An Intellectual and Cultural History* (Berkeley, Los Angeles, London: University of California Press, 1998).

Mamdani, M., *Citizen and Subject: Contemporary Africa and the Legacy of Late Colonialism* (Kampala, Cape Town, London: Fountain Publishers, David Philip Publishers, James Currey Ltd, 1996).

Mbembe, A., 'Aesthetics of Superfluity,' *Public Culture,* 16: 2 (2004) 373–405.

Moolla, F., ' "Worldliness" to "Worldlessness": Unquestioned Individualism in Nuruddin Farah's *Links.*' Paper presented at the AUETSA conference, Durban, South Africa, 2007.

Okwui, E., C. Basualdo, U. M. Bauer, S. Ghez, S. Makaraj, M. Nash and O. Zaya (eds) *Under Siege: Four African Cities – Freetown, Johannesburg, Kinshasa, Lagos* (Documenta 11_Platform4. Germany: Hatje Cantz Publisher, 2002).

Said, E., *The World, the Text, and the Critic* (London: Faber, 1984).

Scott, J. C., *Seeing Like a State: How Certain Schemes to Improve the Human Condition Have Failed* (New Haven and London: Yale University Press, 1998).

Soja, E. W., *Thirdspace: Journeys to Los Angeles and other Real-and-Imagined Places* (Oxford: Blackwell, 1996).

Watson, S., *City Publics: The (Dis)Enchantments of Urban Encounters* (London: Routledge, 2006).

Yaeger, P., 'Introduction: Dreaming of Infrastructure,' *PMLA,* 122.1 (Special Issue on Cities. January 2007) 9–26.

12
Changing Spaces: Salman Rushdie's Mapping of Post-Colonial Territories

Frederik Tygstrup

Salman Rushdie is a writer of an expanding world. The settings of his novels – whether in India, England, Pakistan, USA, Kashmir, or South America – are all deeply implicated in the predicaments of intensified global exchange. Most of Rushdie's characters are migrants who follow the tides of their contemporary social processes and find themselves caught up in between different social and cultural settings, between the roots and the ramifications of different historical genealogies. The histories of their lives take place in spaces undergoing processes of radical change, just as their lives are changing the spaces in which they unfold.

In recent decades, the question of the extent to which such changing spaces can be mapped has become the object of intense debate among geographers, cultural analysts, anthropologists, and social scientists. It has grown increasingly obvious that various historical phenomena usually summarized under the heading of 'globalization' – including post-colonial nation-building, rapidly growing rates of migration, developing technologies of media, ubiquitous implementation of capitalist market economies, and new modes of warfare in the guise of global policing and terrorism – conspicuously defy the notions of space and the spatial intuitions inherited from the era of industrialism and colonialism. In a situation of increasing connectedness, in which the spatial setting of social and individual action, self-reflection, and experience is further mediated by network structures (dispersed ethnic communities, financial markets, the diffusion of media communication) rather than localized in self-contained regions (nation states, production sites, local communities), the actual human spaces of action and experience are becoming still less dependent on the dimension of propinquity, and concomitantly still more dependent on the dimensions of imagination, mediation, and complex relational patterns. To map such spaces, the vocabulary of physical mapping and the traditional neat distinction between objective (physical) space and subjective (phenomenological) space become increasingly inadequate. Rather, what we need is a cartography that can render how the material, the discursive, and the individual experiential qualities of human space merge in the production of specific spatial structures.

The changing spaces of our contemporary world, then, demand mapping techniques that can supplement the basic processes of registration and plotting with a more sophisticated reading-practice that engages with these complex spatial configurations and spells out the relational mechanisms upon which they rest. Literature here plays a seminal role as an appropriate medium to grasp the multifarious and richly stratified spatial structures issuing from late twentieth- and early twenty-first-century life forms. The propensity for spatial arrangements in modernist fiction – as in the radical experiments establishing new patterns of spatial perception and representation in the fiction of Proust, Musil, Joyce, and Kafka – in fact develops a rich formal repertoire of techniques for the rendering of space, one that is adopted and further developed in contemporary fiction. Salman Rushdie is among those novelists who have most intransigently pursued the literary examination of our present spaces, often defying our sense of normality and reality by insisting on accepting the full consequences of the way in which spaces are changing around us, something which we might intellectually acknowledge albeit without being able to actually imagine what it entails. This chapter will attempt to conceptualize some salient features of Salman Rushdie's mapping of the 'visible but unseen' spaces of contemporary reality. His description of spatial realities ranges from physical things and structures via cultural practices and understandings to imaginary and experiential ways of inhabiting a social and cultural space. The first part of the chapter will introduce the notion of territoriality as a concept of space that may more helpfully identify the contemporary changes pertaining to our spatial practices than the ideas of space handed down to us by traditional philosophy. Against this backdrop, the chapter's second part will sketch how territorial order, deterritorializing tendencies, and reterritorializing practices are represented in Rushdie's latest novel, *Shalimar the Clown*.

Territorial spaces

The notion of territoriality offers an alternative to the way in which we usually distinguish, in keeping with the modern philosophical tradition from Kant to Husserl, between objective space and subjective space.

According to this distinction, we can consider either 'space' as the external framing of events, to be described positively in terms of things and their relational positions, or the individual experience of these surroundings: the perspective from which they are perceived, the specific quality of bodily presence amongst them, the moods and feelings attached to being in a specific location, and so on. Territoriality, on the other hand, defined in terms of the discipline of zoology, deals with spaces that are indiscriminately objective and subjective at the same time: spaces that objectively lay out the conditions of habitability for an individual or a species, and spaces formed and reproduced through the life forms inhabiting them. Whereas this conceptual re-orientation will not alter dramatically the underlying analytical understanding of space as a system of effective relations formalized by Kant, it will offer a number of new interpretative approaches that will enable us to grasp the complexity of spatial relational systems. These approaches can be reduced to four: (1) the reciprocity of life forms and spaces, (2) the interplay of spatial relations and power relations, (3) the historicity of space, and (4) the spatial nature of subjectivity.

The basic idea underlying the correlation of spaces and life forms is that a full notion of space cannot be attained solely by measuring it as a static framework: spaces are brought into being, and assume a fluid historical identity, as a result of specific spatial practices. The system of relations underpinning a specific spatial reality is made and sustained by agents who create relational networks – or insert themselves strategically into existing networks – in order to fulfil some action: as the bird does by its song, by building nests, by its patterns of movement, or as the gang does in quite similar ways when inhabiting the corner of a parking lot. Space here, again, is not just the frame containing certain practices, but the result of these practices. When bodies or other agents establish functional relations with what is around them, using the capacities they carry within them, spatial structures emerge. Prompted by these life forms, these spatial structures provide the framework within which they can maintain themselves.

A fundamental conceptual outline of this bi-directional functional mechanism was proposed by Heidegger in § 24 of *Being and Time*. For Heidegger, the idea of space follows from the primitive experience of distance (hyphenated as *Ent-fernung*): something is set at a distance from you which can be apprehended but not reached immediately; you are separated from it, and the obstacle thus encountered is the first index of the phenomenon of space. Approaching this 'something', you recognize the barrier represented by the initial distance and you act in order to master it. Elaborating on his characteristically literal use of everyday words as philosophical concepts, Heidegger goes on to consider space not as noun but as verb: to space (*räumen*). When you act to overcome the distance experienced, you submit to it while at the same time becoming engaged in a spatial structure: this double meaning is conjured up in another hyphenated construct: *Ein-räumen*. Through this twofold movement of submission and spatial agency, you then eventually encounter what was first separated from you by distance: you do with it whatever you wanted when first apprehending it. By this token you inaugurate a specific spatial structure, a place in space – *Be-gegnung* is Heidegger's term here.

This admittedly somehow idiosyncratic – and indeed very Heideggerian – analysis has the significant merit of taking as its point of departure that original and insurmountable entanglement of human and non-human elements which coalesce in the inauguration of a territorial structure. The territory takes shape, neither as a human construct nor as a natural ground, but as an *ecology* where these two elements blend together to produce a life form with specific spatial characteristics. The merit of Heidegger's approach to the question of space is the functional stance it implies. The system of reciprocal relations that make up an individual space is understood as the result of the functional relations forged by a life form. In agreement with Deleuze and Guattari we could see this as a necessary complementarity between the territorial form of a community and the assemblages of human and non-human agents upon which it rests (Deleuze and Guattari, 1980, p. 412). A bold example of this complementarity would be the traditional analysis of the pre-modern rural life form, where an assemblage of human bodies, animal bodies, patches of soil, and the technology of the plough inaugurates the peasant life form and territorializes land by transforming it into fields. These fields are in turn laid out for individual and collective purposes, distributed around villages, associated with rituals and structures of feeling, and so on. Rural territorialization emerges with the assemblages of rural production and the life forms they entail, and it withers away when other social assemblages take over. This happens when, for example, farmland is enclosed for the domestication of sheep, and rural life forms are literally deterritorialized, giving way to a new industrial territorialization in which steam-engine based factories and the settling of urban space by mass communities come together in a different assemblage. Analyses of life forms and of territorial structures thus converge in an understanding of the functional assemblages that underpin these life forms and that produce the corresponding territorial structures.

This point highlights the second feature involved in the interpretation of territorial structures: the seminal role of power relations in spatial relations. The notion of power has two different aspects here. On the one hand, there is the quite straightforward sense of domination, the power to expropriate agricultural land, to keep populations confined to certain areas and excluded from others, the power of sovereignty and command over the bodies of others; but, on the other hand, the power relations that are relevant to a consideration of territorial forms are not restricted to this aspect of hegemony and authority. The specific life forms and their associated assemblages also imply a power that enables individual agents to act, think, and perceive in distinctive ways. Participation in a life form *empowers* the individual agent: the peasant is empowered by the plough; the broker is empowered by the stock exchange information hubs. The space of a life form implies a horizon of possible imaginations, a range of possible actions, and ideas of what is close at hand and what is distant, which relations between here and elsewhere are feasible and which are not. Such spatial coordinates enable societies and individuals to fulfil very different actions, to think in singular ways, and to situate their lives and unfold their aspirations in characteristically individual ways.

The introduction of the notion of power here underscores what might otherwise tend to be marginalized in the fundamental phenomenological analysis of the territorial experience, namely historicity – the third term involved in understanding territoriality. The crucial insight here of course is that you rarely, if ever, operate on neutral ground, as you would in breaking virgin land, or building a hut in a forest. When experiencing space, when crossing a territorial perimeter, you are most likely to be on someone else's ground. And any individual or collective agency will find this ground already stratified, implicated in power relations resulting from others' use of this space. Time is inscribed in space through the agencies that territorialize it; therefore the experience of space and the appropriation of space will inevitably have to come about as a negotiation with one's predecessors over how this space was used and was made to be used. The historicity of space is expressed through the stratifications that give it its individual form: the ways it is built, the ways it is conceived of and conceptualized, the ways it is experienced. So space is, then, as Kant maintains, a transcendental form that precedes and determines any individual intuition. But it is so in a historical way; at different times and in different locations what is transcendentally given as the condition of any intuition are not the same stratifications. The historicity of space unfolds as transformations of what has been handed down – that is, as an interplay between decaying and emerging forms. The building of territories deterritorializes ancient territorial edifices (material edifices, discursive edifices, experiential edifices), and new practices reterritorialize the ground on which they operate.

The close relationship between space and subjectivity – the fourth and last point mentioned above – follows from the previous points. When space is not considered merely as an objective framework surrounding the historical being of life forms, but as intimately entangled with them – with the relational networks that uphold these forms, with the structures of power that delimit them and empower them, and with the historical processes of their evolution and transformation – subjectivity is precisely the point at which this entanglement is performed. Therefore, the contents we address by means of the notions of subjectivity and of space will invariably cross and intersect. Maurice Merleau-Ponty has noted that 'space is existential because existence is spatial' (Merleau-Ponty, 1945, p. 339), that is, space should be understood in terms of its human use: the human would be unimaginable without its incarnation in space. This observation applies to the strictly existential understanding of the subject as well as the social understanding of subjectivity in a more extended sense; here again, space is social because society is spatial. This cross-circuit linking up our understanding of the subjective and the spatial in a perpetual mutual reference takes us back to the idea of an ecological interaction, rather than a confrontation between their different forms. Any subject, whether considered in existential or in social terms, is a territorial subject. And every territory is formed around the work of agents and the relations among agents, who are again endowed with the qualities of subjects through their territorial belonging.

I now proceed to show how space is represented as territories – how spatial practices, intuitions of space, and experience of space as spatial experience are unfolded as territorial phenomena – in a novel that is extremely attentive to the spatial predicament of social and individual existence: Rushdie's *Shalimar the Clown*. The focus will be on the ecologies that characterize the different territorial locations: the assemblies of human and non-human actors, and the social and material networks and functions in which they go together. Through these networks and functions, the specific character of some problematic but extremely interesting contemporary spaces appears.

Spaces of belonging and becoming in *Shalimar the Clown*

Sedentary characters are rare in the novels of Salman Rushdie; mostly, his characters are migrants in a shrinking, and still more elaborately, inter-connected world. This world in turn privileges otherwise improbable encounters of world-views, habits, and cultures, and engenders highly significant tensions and juxtapositions. Migration, as one of the most conspicuous characteristics of the re-making of the world order in the twentieth century, is the backdrop of Rushdie's fictions. Uprooting old and establishing new settlements, the processes of deterritorialization and reterritorialization are inscribed in his depiction of the characters of real people in different configurations of these changing relations.

Changing spaces are a necessary outcome of migration and migrat-ory characters. Whereas the immediate territory of a human life form still has as its core a space of propinquity, it is no longer embedded in a set of expanding perimeters such as the district, the town, the region, the country, and so on, but is rather related to different circuits. Arjun Appadurai's notion of global 'scapes' seems appropriate here: the ethnoscapes, mediascapes, technoscapes, financescapes, and ideoscapes (Appadurai, 1996, p. 33) through which any individual location is linked up directly to a number of quite heterogeneous networks and contextu-alized in an altogether new way. Such structures have underlain many of the spatial changes of the late twentieth century, and they have gained momentum in the twenty-first century. *Shalimar the Clown* traces some of the ways in which this situation came about in the course of the second half of the twentieth century by situating a small handful of characters at different hotspots of contemporary history and charting how the spaces to which they are affiliated change. The novel explores how this change affects their movements and how in turn their movements change the spaces they traverse.

In the context of Rushdie's oeuvre, *Shalimar the Clown* stands out by way of its simplicity. First of all, it is tightly plotted as a crime story, investigating the pre-history of a murder committed in its opening pages. Also, perhaps because of its plot-based scaffolding, the novel is less dependant on style than is often the case in Rushdie, where stylistic elab-oration and imaginative unfolding of oneiric events mediate the drive of the fiction. This relative simplicity in turn also seems to facilitate a very direct involvement with historical and political matters: in this case the destiny of Kashmir, devastatingly trapped between Indian occupa-tion forces on the one side and Pakistani fundamentalist warlords on the other. Many reviewers have seen this novel as a loving obituary for

the beauties of Kashmir, in terms of both its natural scenery and its traditions and culture. Others have seen only the novelist's fierce repudiation
of the increasing power of Muslim influence in the region.

The scene of the crime is Los Angeles in the early 1990s: a renowned
octogenarian diplomat is stabbed to death by his Kashmiri driver
Shalimar in front of his daughter's apartment building where he is planning to see her shortly after her 24th birthday. The novel tells the
stories of the four characters involved: the ambassador Max Ophuls,
his daughter India Ophuls, her mother Boonyi, who was a dancer in a
Kashmiri village band, and Boonyi's husband, Shalimar the clown. This
constellation already reveals the melodramatic nature of the plot: during
his service as American Ambassador to India, Max Ophuls has seduced
the beautiful dancer; she has borne his child who has subsequently been
brought back to America; and the stabbing, thus, is the revenge of the
cuckolded husband after 25 years. The crime scene brings together a
handful of people who are in different ways out of place, and since there
is really no hidden mystery to solve behind the crime, simple as it is –
although the author contrives to hold back some clues for the benefit of
the reader who needs a bit of suspense – the novel instead narrates the
individual paths that lead the characters to this fatal encounter. These
paths in turn outline the maps of global migration, deterritorialization,
and reterritorialization that emerge in the second half of the twentieth
century, through the destinies, strategies, and spatial practices of four
exemplary characters.

Max Ophuls is a man with multiple talents. Born into a wealthy Jewish
family of book-printers in Strasbourg, he is educated in the 1930s in
Paris, where he subsequently rejects a promising career in law, dislik-
ing Parisian self-sufficiency, and returns to his native city to work for
the family business and, occasionally, as a painter and art dealer. When
France is occupied he joins the resistance, where he makes himself useful as printer and forger of documents. On the announcement of the
impending deportation of the Alsatian Jews, he arranges for himself and
his parents to escape to the south, which the aging and somewhat senile
couple stubbornly refuse. On the planned night of the escape he comes
back and finds the house ransacked and demolished, his parents depor-
ted. They have been subjected, he later learns, to medical experiments
by the Nazis. He eventually escapes by flying, in a prototype Bugatti
airplane, into the neutral zone of France, where he is hailed as a resistance fighter. After a subsequent series of actions with the resistance,
he is sent to England to assist General de Gaulle in the planning of the

post-war European economy, an encounter that involved mutual dislike and suspicion. At the age of 35, he leaves Europe for the United States with his British wife, herself another acclaimed resistance fighter, on his appointment to a professorship in economics. His subsequent career carries him from research on development of economies into diplomacy, to the post of Ambassador to India. He resides in India until he is forced to resign owing to an adulterous affair – one of many, to be sure, but this one gets public attention – after which he serves from the mid-1960s through the 1980s as ambassador *sans portefeuille* and *de facto* head of the American anti-terror campaign. This involves unofficial negotiations and arms deals, the routine making and unmaking of third-world dictators.

In geopolitical terms, Alsace is not an arbitrary starting-point for this destiny. As a repeatedly contested borderland between Germany and France, it has throughout history been claimed – and indeed ruled – by both sides. Strasbourg is quintessentially European, but without the standard European nationalist arrogance, which is what Ophuls-the-Alsatian dislikes about France. This European *cum* cosmopolitan background, which is once more underscored through his Ashkenazi affiliation, displays both a kind of superiority towards a Europe of different, competing nationalisms and an extreme vulnerability. When the border between Germany and France once again passes over the Rhine with the Nazi occupation, it is not only a part of France that is put under siege; it is also this piece of European culture that is subdued. There is thus a certain tragic consistency in Ophuls the elders' refusal to flee. The Second World War is not merely a matter of German versus French national sovereignty, it is – far more ominously – a deterritorialization of their sense of a ubiquitous European culture.

Max Ophuls is a product of this deterritorialization, one which comes about as a sequel to the ancient European negotiation of national borders, and as a suspension of the cultural notion of Europe imposed by Fascist mass movements. Unlike his parents, however, Max is reterritorialized; the belonging of which he is deprived is replaced by a becoming. In a trivial sense this is achieved not only by his becoming American like so many before and after him, but also, in a more radical way, by his going global. He is reterritorialized on the global circuits of post-war politics, economy, and warfare – not accidentally, however, with an American passport. His reterritorialization drifts with the powers-that-be, leaving behind the ancient Europe for the new global stratification of world affairs. He moves from one map to another: from Alsace where the habits of an ancient European bourgeoisie developed in the borderland between rivalling European national ambitions, to the immaterial networks of intelligence summits, corporate headquarters, and government offices, where the future of the global geopolitical divides is negotiated. Ophuls does not settle, but remains on the move; and although he ends up owning a house in Los Angeles, his preferred dwelling is the hotel. Peculiarly, though, it seems to be precisely this incessant circulation between 'non-places' (to take up the term coined by Marc Augé) that in turn permits Max Ophuls to stick to and to cultivate his personal preference for the long-dead life forms of the ancient European bourgeoisie, such as his silk suits, his personal valet, his chauffeur-driven British cars, his elaborate manner with words, and his overt distaste for television and the cultural industry. This anachronistic life form is difficult to imagine re-enacted today in a home territory like that of his parents in pre-war Strasbourg. But Ophuls's life form seems to work: his lifestyle embodies ancient Europe reterritorialized on the orbits of global scapes, in vivid contradistinction to the belated European attempts to reclaim these life forms on their native ground. Ophuls's divorced wife is an example of such a failed attempt; after her repatriation to England she has to realize – without ever fully really realizing it though – that even Mayfair doesn't work that way any more. Her existential territory rapidly becomes a neurotically claustrophobic space, from which her adopted daughter will soon feel obliged to escape.

Ophuls's history originates from the thorough and devastating deterritorialization of old Europe through fascism and warfare, and it stands out as a rare example of a felicitous reterritorialization facilitated by the opening vistas of globalization. Here, his existential, social, and material territories seem to converge in a powerful model of a post-bourgeois prince of the late twentieth century.

Deterritorialization may end up in reterritorialization; or it might not. It also might happen to terminate in a lasting confinement to places where existential strategies of reterritorialization do not connect with empowering social and material opportunities. This is the case for Ophuls's wife on her return to England, as it is the case for Boonyi the dancer, the mother of his only child. The history of Boonyi's youth and her home in the Kashmiri village of Pachigam is a beautifully written sketch of an idyllic environment that no longer exists, and a masterful demonstration of how different ominous powers emerge on the horizon and threaten to disrupt an ancient and highly refined life form. Pachigam is a peasant community, and a village of actors. The inhabitants perform a show based on ancient myths and religious tales, mostly based on Hindu tradition, but eventually also drawing on Muslim sources; the show comprises a complex amalgam of telling, acting, music, singing, and dancing, and it celebrates festive events in the valley. Life in the village is comfortable; the climate and the soil are rich; and gastronomy is an integral part of life – the village competes with the neighbouring village, cooking thirty-six and forty-eight course meals for community celebrations. Scarcity is never an issue to divert attention from devising new and elaborate plays or dishes, practising ancient artistic techniques, or telling tales. Adolescent Boonyi, renowned for her extraordinary beauty and sensuousness, is featured as the central female dancer in the band, and Shalimar is the clown and the acrobat who can walk the highest tightropes, can literally walk on air. Their marriage, bringing together the village's two first families, is the last unequivocal happy event of the village, a sumptuous feast luxuriously adding everything his Muslim family expects to what her Hindu family finds appropriate.

The Pachigam idyll stands out as a perfect blend of natural, social, and existential modes of territorial belonging, a micro-climate of well-being hidden away in the depth of a valley matured by a history of prosperity and high culture over generations, and the home of a proud and beautiful people. The sentimental strain in this image stems not only from a perfection that occasionally verges on the kitschy, but also foreshadows a destruction the text reveals to be inevitable. Deterritorialization here again, as in the case of Max Ophuls's native Strasbourg, derives from geopolitical change, as the conflict between India and Pakistan crystallizes on the question of Kashmir. Intruding in the territorial ecology, there is on the one hand the Indian military presence, personified by General Kachhwaha, a philosophically minded officer whose reflection and action combine British ideals of strategic audaciousness (and brutality) with a pedagogic ideal of civilizing the charming but irresponsible Kashmiri peasants, and on the other hand the 'iron mullahs' who show up here and there, eager to reform local habits according to religious standards and to foster resistance to the Indian invasion.

The apprehension of the imminent uprooting of a comfortingly familiar life form troubles the adolescent Boonyi. She feels that married life in the traditional village style cannot be the final script for her life story, knowing that when a way out appears, she will take it. And such a way out presents itself when the band performs at a party for the distinguished American ambassador visiting the region. She runs off, then, to become the ambassador's mistress and is put up conveniently in a flat in Delhi with no other obligations (and no other prospects) than to be there for an occasional *tête-à-tête*. In her idle hours she develops a new habit of voracity – a kind of perverted development of her natural sensuality – and grows absurdly obese, as if to fill out the entire constricted space of her new life by her immobilized and expanding body. This change of course soon collides with her role as mistress. After having delivered the baby she has made sure to conceive as a kind of revenge on the ambassador, she is sent back to Pachigam, having had to trade-in the child to the ambassador's wife. For Boonyi, though, there is no coming back; after having mourned her desertion, the villagers have buried her *in absentia* and cannot celebrate her return. She is offered a hut on the outskirts of the village in which she can live on as a barely recognized phantom, constricted in a social limbo, feared and avoided by the living. It is an existence very much like that in the apartment in Delhi, only no longer waiting for a lover to pass by, but for the return of her former husband, who has sworn to kill both her and the man who seduced and abducted her.

Boonyi's *déroute* begins as a wilful deterritorialization, an escape from the territorial order in which the course of her life seems predetermined in every way. But this deterritorialization then subsequently offers no possibility of reterritorialization. There is no space for developing what she brought with her when she broke up with the ambassador, and she ends up imprisoned. In this respect, her destiny parallels that of the ambassador's wife who breaks from Ophuls's world. Both end up in places, in territorial structures, that radically disempower them.

Shalimar the clown, like Max Ophuls, and unlike both his and Ophuls's wives, manages this passage from deterritorialization to reterritorialization in a quite different manner. When the prospect of revenge enters his life, he rapidly loses interest in theatre, tightrope walking, and clowning; but as revenge is not at hand for immediate action, his awakening leads him on to political action against the forces invading Kashmir, reminiscent of representatives of foreign powers who turn up in villages and seduce its women. He leaves Pachigam to be away for the next 15 years, most of them spent on the itineraries of the region's ever changing constellations of warriors and patriots, first with the Kashmiri Liberation Movement, and subsequently, as it gradually ceases to exist, with increasingly well-organized Muslim organizations in whose service he eventually becomes a highly appreciated assassin and agent of special missions. He finds a new territory in the network of training camps, hideaways, trafficking routes, and unregistered vessels that grows and expands to become an unprecedented actor in the state of world affairs during this period. This new territory is becoming still more attractive to the region's young men as the infrastructure of traditional life forms deteriorates, while at the same time the numerous attempts at militarizing the region (for varying and diverging reasons, and with or without the sanction of the UN) provide this emerging territory with plenty of resources, empowering its inhabitants to engage in still more efficient acts of warfare.

Shalimar's reterritorialization and new path of becoming thus perfectly match those of Ophuls. They both experience how the spaces of their primordial belonging are unsettled through large geopolitical manoeuvres, and they both give in to the process of deterritorialization in order to re-connect and re-configure their spatial coordinates, to re-emerge as agents in a new spatial arrangement that allows them to claim agency in a new territory. To be sure, there is a certain pedagogical strain in Rushdie's demonstration of the making of a terrorist and of an occidental forger of the new world, as they eventually meet in a melodramatic *ménage à trois*. Yet although the narrative convenience of this arrangement may appear almost too felicitous, it nonetheless gives Rushdie the opportunity to make two important points: on the one hand that these two parallel processes of global reterritorializations are two sides of the same coin, inextricably interdependent in the process of what we call 'globalization', and on the other hand that this is not a mere 'political' question of convictions and strategies, but a question of how the human spaces of dwelling and becoming are inscribed in a historical process of changing modes of territorialization.

When considering the spatial practices of the *dramatis personae* in Rushdie's *Shalimar the Clown* and the mapping of territories they suggest, we have on the one hand those – the female characters – whose uprooting terminate in constricted spaces where they are trapped and disempowered, where the plasticity of existential territorialization is arrested. On the other hand, we have the male characters who are in fact able to reterritorialize themselves in a changing global distribution of space and seize opportunities of agency and becoming. When eventually their conflict comes to actual confrontation – once Shalimar has fulfilled his vow to kill Boonyi and then comes to Ophuls in Los Angeles – they have reached the ages of 45 and 80. Their life-stories have figured a new world map divided between suffocating territories of stasis and belligerent territories of latent global warfare.

India Ophuls, born Kashmira Noman, the improbable offspring of the encounter between the ambassador and the dancer, is in every sense the heiress to this conflict. Having grown up with her stepmother in London, she is intimately familiar with the untimely and inauthentic life form of the European upper middle class. Her childhood and adolescence are one long, extended protest against this class through sociopath behaviour, drugs, and sexual delinquency. At a particularly critical moment, her otherwise absent father shows up and takes her to a clinic in Switzerland for detoxification and, after that, to his house in Los Angeles. India's reterritorialization comes about as a withdrawal, a somatic reclusion in her self – curled up in chairs, receding into rooms – to the smallest possible territory from which a mastery of bodily and mental reactions to the surroundings can be built. And she very much sticks to this zero territorial behaviour as she gradually starts studying, moves to an apartment of her own, and ventures into a career of documentary film-maker, dealing with people and the world around her as through a hygienic glass pane, cultivating her body in innumerable different posh studios and her work through lonesome rumination.

Los Angeles seems somehow to be the ideal setting for this monadic territoriality. Here India is surrounded by people living like her: people for whom an effective life-world is either behind them – the widows, *rentiers*, and dog-walkers of her block – or ahead of them – the beauties and generic talents attracted to the city of images and manufactured dreams. And outside, off-circuit from the sun-lit habitats of those cultivating dreams of the past or the future, there is a war going on, with riots, killings, and fires: a territory to be policed. It is an image of the world, uprooted in a state of war, sporadically dispersed with enclosed, individual territories of self-cultivation. When Shalimar the clown turns up and in addition turns out to be the assassin of both her mother and her father, this itself launches shock waves at India's fragile – although determinate – project of self-making. And while he is detained in different Los Angeles penitentiaries for endless trials and appeal cases, she ventures into the histories of her parents, visiting her mother's Kashmiri village (eventually eradicated as a result of routine unitary precautions) and revisiting her father's dossier of glorious and less glorious achievements, establishing a genealogy of her present territorial perimeter.

Such a genealogical endeavour does not, to be sure, bring about radical changes in the territorial construction of her existence, nor does it provide alternatives to the disconnected micro-territoriality of contemporary LA life. But it does nonetheless suggest a different way of dealing with the general map proposed by the novel, that is, the contemporary prevalence of two models of territoriality: the constricted territory with no prospects of transformation and becoming, and the perilous territory of global networks of warfare and power. At first sight, India's space is most akin to the former, an isolated spot of private self-cultivation surrounded by a disorderly and tensely stratified battleground. But hers is a privileged isolation when compared to her mother's – she is not kept at distance from the world by a border, but herself maintains a distance from it. When the space of her life nevertheless seems to mediate between the two spaces of fixation and of circulation exemplarily mapped by the itineraries of her parents, it is because she is in fact reclaiming both of them. Her territory embraces both centripetality and connectivity. It is centripetal to the extent that she insistently reterritorializes every single experience onto a small and controlled bodily mediated field of her own, wanting to ground, as it were, every intellectual and phenomenological impulse she receives in an acute bodily presence. And it is connective to the extent that she is capable of entering into exchange with the global territorial networks around her. Having assessed her father's history and assisted at the trial against Shalimar (and at a final, dramatic shoot-out with him), she has localized her own territory according to the coordinates of the networks they represent.

In this sense, India occupies a privileged position vis-à-vis the other characters of the novel, because she is not exclusively predetermined to follow one of the two prevailing territorial modes. To be sure, she does not represent any consistent model for an alternative existential territorialization of her own. Rather, her privilege consists in two features. First, she is in fact in a position from where she can gauge and overlook the different territorial strategies unfolding around her; she is – not unlike the author – able to map these territories. This is precisely what she does as a documentary film-maker: one of her projects is to map the contemporary settlings along the routes once tracked by the pilgrims as they first territorialized the Californian landscape; another is to map her grandparents' universe in pre-war Strasbourg. Because of this reflective stance, she is potentially in a position that enables her to manoeuvre within her – and our – contemporary landscapes of highly complex territorial structures. The mapping of territories, then, not only of the immediate objective and subjective spaces of human lives, but also of the spatial structures pertaining to specific life forms and their associated historical lineages, balances of powers, and modes of subjective becoming, stands out as an appropriate tool for a strategic insertion of individual, existential territories into the spatial frameworks surrounding them. Literature, to be sure, is but one medium among others involved in such mappings. As an artistic agency of mapping, however, it contributes significantly to the rendering of an image of space, because of the wide array of territorial relations it embraces, and the narrative grounding of these relations in tangible renditions of human life forms. In this sense, literary maps remind us why we need maps in the first place: because they are indispensable equipments for living.

Works cited

Appadurai, A., *Modernity at Large* (Minneapolis: University of Minnesota Press, 1996).

Augé, M., *Non-lieux: Introduction à une anthropologie de la surmodernité* (Paris: Seuil, 1992).

Deleuze, G. and Guattari, F., *Mille Plateaux. Capitalisme et schizophrénie II* (Paris: Minuit, 1980).

Heidegger, M., *Sein und Zeit* (Tübingen: Max Niemeyer Verlag, 1979).

Merleau-Ponty, M., *Phénoménologie de la perception* (Paris: Gallimard, 1945).

Rushdie, S., *Shalimar the Clown* (London: Jonathan Cape, 2005).

Index

In this index the introduction is not indexed. Notes are indicated by n. in italics, e.g. *Arbinger Harvest*, 55(*n.2*) Works are indicated in italics.